To Flore

THE SCREENWRITER

AMANDA REYNOLDS

Love Amanda x

B

Boldwood

First published in Great Britain in 2023 by Boldwood Books Ltd.

Cover Design by Head Design Ltd.

Cover Photography: Shutterstock

A CIP catalogue record for this book is available from the British Library.

Paperback ISBN 978-1-83751-368-0

Large Print ISBN 978-1-83751-369-7

Hardback ISBN 978-1-83751-366-6

Ebook ISBN 978-1-83751-370-3

Kindle ISBN 978-1-83751-371-0

Audio CD ISBN 978-1-83751-362-8

MP3 CD ISBN 978-1-83751-363-5

Digital audio download ISBN 978-1-83751-367-3

Boldwood Books Ltd
23 Bowerdean Street
London SW6 3TN
www.boldwoodbooks.com

For Scout, my faithful writing companion.

PROLOGUE

BLYTHE – 2ND JULY 2023

It's the smoke I see first, just shy of the boundary wall, no more than a curling wisp at the end of our long, sloped lawn. Then the flicker of a flame which swells and beats hard against the sunset. The urge to go towards it building even as I resist, massaging my temples and praying for this damn headache to lift, or the pills to kick in.

I'd come up here an hour ago, to the tallest point in the house, as I often do after supper. The panoramic view always a balm to my soul, particularly when my husband is in one of his moods. Which is pretty much all the time. It's unbelievable Dom and I have withstood three decades together despite never being on firm ground. All these years of fighting for survival, our relationship's longevity no indicator of its solidity, fracture lines opening up daily, then papered over.

'What's the secret to such a long and happy marriage?' I was recently asked in a magazine interview. Not that I am above speaking to the British press, far from it, but I am rarely asked. It was for one of those 'glossies' that specialise in celebrity news. The request on account of mine and Dom's impending 'big' wedding anniversary, or so my agent, James, said. 'It'll be all style, no substance,' he'd quipped, as if that were a selling point. I'd looked forward to it, but it was not a pleasant experience. The dour photographer taking fewer than ten shots despite the stylist's extended efforts with hair and make-up.

'You have a gorgeous home,' the young journo prompted, crossing her tanned legs as she surveyed our Hampstead residence. 'The Towers it's called? Although there is only one tower?'

'Yes, that's right. A sixty foot folly of sorts,' I replied. 'And just one tower, despite the name, which we inherited when we bought this place.'

'So, thirty years of marriage!' she'd gushed. 'What is your secret, Blythe?'

'There is no great secret,' I'd told her. 'Only tenacity. Much like show business. You just keep turning up; with hope, if not expectation.'

She clearly hadn't liked my response as she didn't quote it. Just a rather nasty line about Dom's 'reclusiveness' and my 'former fame'. Although I'd explained that Dom and I are working on a comeback. A starring role for me penned by my brilliant if reclusive screenwriting husband, who'd refused to be interviewed, or pose for a joint photo. 'Something daring,' I'd told her, teasing Dom's script, although she hadn't asked. 'And potentially game-changing, for us both.' An idea so audacious, so close to the bone, that at times it spins my head. Which is another reason why I'm up here, trying to make sense of Dom's reluctance to press on with the script, his change of heart expressed via a thrown plate that I ducked to miss.

Is he right? Am I mad to think we can crack our lives open, allow opinion to crawl over us and still get away with the impunity of dramatic licence? Pretend, not only to each other, but the entire world, that we are something other than we truly are? Our truth hidden in plain sight.

The flames lick higher. The smoke a trail now, stretching beyond the garden wall. A sign to the world that we are in trouble. And yet it had felt so different these past months. So good again. Ever since Dom started writing about me. His muse.

I'd forgotten how it felt to wake up with purpose, spend the day in a flurry of excitement then fall into bed filled with exhilaration and pleasurable exhaustion. A much-needed reminder of when Dom and I were first together, in the sprawling gated house on Mulholland Drive. Hollywood spread out below us in the smog, yet perennially glittering as we made our plans for a life filled with love and passion and joint creative endeavour. Our ambition matching one another's.

Recapturing those hazy heat-filled days and star-spangled nights of thirty years before has been an utter joy. A reminder of when we were invincible in the way only the young and in love can ever hope to be. Dom's elation at a good writing day, then his moroseness after a bad one, taken in my stride. The screenwriter and his actress wife. We know the muse is capricious, his talent to be nurtured. Whatever happened, it was going to be OK. We were in it together. The great Blythe and Dom Hopper. Back in the game! Or so I'd thought.

But tonight, Dom was unreachable, telling me I'm crazy – can't I see how dangerous this all is? We have to stop. *It* has to stop. Dom was drunk, a permanent state for him, but much worse than usual. He'd been drinking all day, and he was the melancholic kind of drunk which means he was nasty. Accusing me of all sorts, then the threats. That we're done, in every sense. He doesn't mean it. He never does. But there was something in his vitriol that scared me. Something new. A desperation and jeopardy that jolted and jarred.

So I retreated. As far from him as I could get without leaving the house. Up to the glass room at the top of the eponymous tower. My private space where I write, and think and *be*. To allow the heat of the day, and our emotions, to dissipate as the sun sets. We've weathered worse. So much worse. Tomorrow is a fresh start. Every day wipes clean the last. That's one of the few things my mother said that has stayed with me.

Curls of dark smoke rise up, catching in the trees that line the wall behind. The flames dipping to expose, for a second, my husband's face. And what I see in it terrifies me: a call to arms in his sly smile.

I run. Down the spiral staircase from the viewing tower, along the landing, past our bedroom and then down again, to the hallway, the same expansive space that took our breath away when we first stepped inside The Towers almost twenty years ago and spied that red carpet running up the grand staircase. An omen? Or a portent? It had seemed unfathomable that we might live somewhere other than Hollywood – the land of dreams – but this palatial but neglected slice of London took our broken hearts and our smashed dreams and made space for them. Our departure from LA a bitter taste even as we smiled at the thought of living here. In this imposing property with its majestic views, where Dom and I envisaged a future. A place we could rebuild what we'd lost. Hollywood scrubbed out and left five thousand miles and an ocean away. But of course it came with us. Our mistakes cast through us, dividing us. Darkening shadows in corners we never looked into except in the most private of moments.

Barefoot, I tear along the corridor to the newer part of the house. The extension we added to a property that was already enormous for two people. The white walls lined with photos that smile at me, macabre as I fly by. Happier times, that's what I've always told myself, the lie taunting me now more than ever. History catching up with me after all these years of running from it. A rewind of the last three decades mocking me. But memories are precious, especially when they are all you have. That's what my husband told me. When we cared enough to believe one another's lies. When our shared story was all that mattered. Our version of the truth enough for us both.

The kitchen is a mess: shards of smashed glass and plate on the Moroccan tile floor, a stain on the Farrow and Ball where I ducked that flying plate. Only a matter of two, three years since this place was redecorated, all in the name of keeping up appearances. Dom's whisky tumbler is empty on the table, his favourite cut-glass decanter in a million pieces on the floor. A splinter embedding in my bare foot so I yelp in pain. I limp to the flip-flops I cast off by the glass doors after an earlier dip in the pool, the terrifying scale of the bonfire hastening my efforts. I press a palm to the glass to steady myself. The bonfire has bloomed. The flames, even way across the lawn, overwhelming. And I can no longer see Dom through them.

The door keys, usually hanging in the lock, are gone. I bang on the glass over and over, call Dom's name, look for him through the flames. Relief as I spot him again. But he's too far away to tell his expression. My terror reflected back at me in the glass. Eyes wide. Fist thumping.

I need to get to him.

The spare keys are kept in the messy drawer, half the contents emptied onto the floor as I rummage through, and still no sign of the patio key. Then a glint of dark metal at the back of the kitchen drawer draws my eye.

The gun.

So casually stuffed in, along with batteries and a coil of string, a spaghetti server and roll of tape. I can only recall the pistol being brought out once, at a drunken garden party, laughter with friends at our tale of smuggling it back from the US – different times – and keeping it hidden, and loaded. Back when we still had friends to laugh with. A collective scream ending that laughter as a cracking sound tore through the summer sky. Dom had run out into the garden and fired the gun in the air. A murder of crows squawking and flapping from the trees. A group gasp as a limp feathered mass landed soft and still on the grass, black-blue eye accusatory, even in death. Then a cheer.

I run back to the door, squeeze the trigger and aim at the lock, ringing ears and the patio door swinging on its hinges my reward. I've always been a good shot.

Sweat pouring, adrenalin fuelled, I sprint towards the flames.

Dom's dark hair is all I can make out through the choking smoke and intense heat. 'What the hell are you doing, Dom?' Fear replaced by frustration as it's painfully clear to me what he's using to fuel the flames. 'Please tell me you have backed up the latest copies of our scripts?'

'Nope,' he replies, so calmly I don't believe him at first until I see the molten mass of metal at the epicentre of the pyre. His laptop. 'I've destroyed everything.'

'Why, Dom? Why would you do this?'

'Because this was a crazy idea from the start and someone has to make it stop.'

'Oh, for fuck's sake, Dom, stop being so dramatic. This is just cold feet.'

He shakes his head, throws in a bunch of other pages, laughs in that patronising way of his, then looks up. 'I don't want to be a part of this, Blythe. It's sick. I just want it all to go away.'

'And you think this will achieve that?'

He shakes his head again, but it's not an answer, just a dismissal. Or an admission of defeat. *Coward!*

I skirt the flames, reach out to him. 'Come inside, Dom, we can talk. I've still got my notes, and more ideas.'

'No!' He withdraws, recoiling from my touch. 'Just let it go, Blythe. Please.'

'Dom, listen, I understand your... reservations. But trust me, this will be our greatest success.'

'Ours?' he asks, bile in his voice. 'Or yours, Blythe?'

'A fresh start, my love. For us both.'

His face, creased and worn but still so handsome, reddened and soot-smutted by the fire, twists with hate. 'It's over, Blythe. All of it. Game's up. Game over, in fact.'

'I don't understand, why are you dead against this all of a sudden?'

He reaches in his pocket, pulls out a scrunched piece of paper, a compliment slip, then tosses it on the ground between us. I step forward, skirting the fire, grab it, the logo all too familiar as is the handwriting scrawled beneath it.

Not one for me, James.

'You sent the scripts to our agent, without telling me?'

'Just a treatment, and he hates it!' Dom tells me, feeding the flames with more pages of script and notes. 'Hates everything about it. Told me to back away from it, back away from writing altogether, in fact.'

'No, you're wrong, he wouldn't say that.'

'He's dropped me, Blythe. Your precious agent has dropped me, and he's right to. This is toxic. Fucked up. It's wrong!'

'You've been rejected before, Dom; we both have,' I tell him, screwing up the vile compliment slip note and throwing it into the inferno before I step back, my eyelashes fizzing. 'Rejection is part of the process. We'll do what's needed to make it work. As always. Find new representation. There's always a way if you want it enough.'

'Like you did back in Hollywood, my love?' he sneers.

'What's that supposed to mean?'

He stares at me, mouth distorted with revulsion. The same mouth that's kissed me thousands of times.

'I know what you're prepared to do to get what you want, Blythe. How far you'll go, and I'm out!'

He's walking away, the pool glimmering ahead of him as the sun sets over it. A perfect backdrop. The final few frames in a great love story.

'Dom, please.' I stop him, grab his hand. 'We can work this out. Between us. Talk it over, make it work, like we always do.'

'No, we can't.' He shrugs me off. 'I can't live with this, with you, for a day longer, let alone the rest of my days. It's poison, Blythe. You're poison!'

'You don't mean that. Not after everything we've been through together.'

'Jeez, Blythe, do you hear yourself? This isn't a fucking movie script, it's us, real life with all the disgusting bits!'

A dog barks and the flames catch the final shrivelled pages Dom threw in and crisp them, hissing their approval. In the distance, I hear the sound of children playing on the Heath, or maybe that's wishful thinking, the sun dipping into the water, turning it to gold as he walks towards it. I feel for the gun, tucked in the back of my waistband, reassuring.

'Say it then!' I call after him, and he stops. 'To my face, this time, Dom. Say exactly what you mean. I want to hear you say what you think I did to get what I wanted!'

He turns, slowly, profile caught against the sunset one last time, and then he accuses me of the worst thing imaginable. And he believes it. Every word of it. And even before the gun is raised, we both know there's no way back from this. Not now, not ever.

A MONTH LATER – AUGUST – MARNIE

1

'Do you believe in ghosts?' I ask the distinguished man seated to my right, who looks so important the host asked me my name twice before she showed me to his table. As if my tattoos and short hair somehow preclude our being suitable lunch companions. My best dress and heels were clearly not enough to impress, despite the discomfort I've endured on this, the hottest day of the year so far. All in the name of looking like the professional young screenwriter I am for this much anticipated lunch with my agent, Harry.

'Sorry, Marnie, my darling,' Harry replies, distracted as always, his jaunty moustache twitching. 'Ghosts, you say? Of course I do! And you're one of the very best there is, when you apply yourself, that is.'

Harry has misinterpreted my meaning, but seeing as he has endowed a rare professional compliment upon me, I shall allow the misconception to remain uncorrected. Besides, we are in the midst of ordering lunch; the hovering waiter, a handsome young man with a strong jaw but nervous demeanour and smattering of red-raw acne, noting down Harry's request for the Caesar salad as if he were officiating his last will and testament. Each syllable greeted with solemn nods and sage, 'Mmmm, wise choice, sir' comments. Harry often engenders such reverence. His linen suit and silk tie are Brideshead meets Groucho Club. His handsome face referred to widely as 'striking'. His blue eyes 'dazzling'.

'With grilled chicken, but no anchovies; I'm allergic,' Harry instructs. Then, in a perfectly audible aside to me, 'I'm not allergic as such, darling, but they sneak them in if you say it's a preference.'

This is one of many mortifying remarks Harry has bestowed in the almost ten years he's represented my writing career. He has a relaxed relationship with how others see him. Years of handling creative people and tricky situations immunising him to the usual filters, as if his behaviour is recalibrated and justified by theirs, which is relatively speaking much worse – at least if his stories of Soho Farmhouse debauchery are to be believed. Harry's approach is self-proclaimed 'old school'. A mature man in his early fifties who's been around the block enough times to claim he cannot and will not appease. But as far as allergies go, in my experience, you only have to hint at an intolerance and you're scanning a folder containing multiple colour-coded spreadsheets and fending off kitchen staff explaining how the chef may have touched a sesame seed in the last twenty-eight days. It's not something to be messed with.

Harry snaps the menu shut, startling me and the waiter. 'And you, Marnie? Steak and a large red as per usual?'

'I'll have the chicken Caesar salad too,' I tell the waiter, handing my menu back in what feels like an overly grateful, possibly patronising manner. 'And a glass of tap water, please, with ice.'

Harry eyes me with dazzling blue suspicion. 'We will require a bottle of chilled Veuve and two champagne glasses,' he corrects, one eyebrow raised at my half-hearted protests. 'And make sure the glasses are clean this time. Quick-sharp!'

The waiter shifts from fast walk to run at the bellowing command, making Harry chuckle.

Harry's not a bad man, but he is dismissive. It's a unilateral policy. He's the same with everyone. He's also a ridiculously charming man, which means he gets away with far too much, although not generally with me. I'm impervious to his allure. On account of my ageism, at least according to Harry, who finds it irritating in the extreme that I don't fall at his feet. Although there was that one occasion back last summer when the bright lights of Hollywood and a few too many cocktails, plus the convenient closeness of a hotel bed... but no, he's old enough to be my—

'Marnie, are you with us?' Harry is grinning at me, straight white teeth matching his handmade shirt. He's undeniably visually appealing. A bit of the George Clooney about him with his grey hair and rogue but winning smile. I wrote him into my script. An homage to his flamboyant approach to life. A cameo version in episode five, which would have most likely ended up on a metaphorical cutting room floor had the television series actually been made, but he liked that I'd included him. It appealed to his uncontained ego. It's immaterial now, but there, I did it. I'm that much of a suck-up.

'Yes, sorry, I'm here, Harry.'

'Good, I was beginning to wonder if you'd sent a place marker whilst the real Ms Wilde is passed out under an avalanche of cheap Merlot?'

'I'm not that bad, Harry, but yes, I am trying to be healthier.'

'You do know I'm paying, Miss Tap Water and Salad?' Harry asks, accepting a top up of his water glass from a woman who has the figure and face of a young Scarlett Johansson. Is that her whole job, to circle with a jug? Not so bad, if so. I bet she's an actress, earning minimum wage between roles.

'Yes, I do know it's on you, and thanks, Harry. Much appreciated.'

He always pays, it's his thing. Any attempt by me to split the bill would be waved away as if it were an insult. Not that I'm about to offer. I can't afford grand gestures and anyway, our relationship is set in stone. We are imbalanced but we both understand the dynamic. It has its compromises, but I'm grateful for his generosity.

'I really am on a detox kind of thing,' I explain. Although it's about as accurate as his fish allergy. 'Although... if we're celebrating something?'

'Detox? As in, one glass not two?' Harry smirks, avoiding my clumsy attempt to move on to the 'exciting news' he'd trailed as the reason for lunch. 'Oh, don't look like that, Marnie. Relax a little, enjoy my marvellous company. It's been ages.'

It has. And not by choice, at least not mine. Although I'm in no mood for Harry's boyish ebullience. I'm nursing a hangover, and I didn't even drink that much last night. Cheap plonk, that's the trouble. As Harry suspected, annoyingly. The champagne will sort it out. The hangover, I mean. My latest relationship – the trigger for said drinking – is beyond repair, despite the late-night texts to my ex who was/is, on LA time.

'Need to be somewhere?' Harry asks, as I check my phone, again. Still no response from my ex, Jake. 'Or is this your endlessly complicated love life?'

'No, I'm all yours,' I reply, tucking my phone in my bag. 'I mean... not in that way. For lunch. That's all. And work! You said there was something to discuss?'

'Yes...' Harry replies, smiling as I blush. 'But allow me a moment to recover from that brutal rejection.'

I arrange my face into what I hope is an approximation of casual but professional interest. It's all part of the dance with Harry. Never show weakness, or worse, desperation, much like most relationships. I'm not much good at playing the game, as evidenced by the desperate texts last night and subsequent hopeful checking of my phone, but Harry is clearly going to make me wait to discuss the matter at hand, waving at a glamorous passer-by who blows him an air kiss after he mouths at her, 'Call me soon, darling! We need to talk!'

I break into a bread roll and slather the soft innards with the pat of salt-encrusted butter which has been artfully sculpted into a quenelle and displayed on a slice of slate.

I'm still chewing as Harry returns his attention to me. 'I can see the detox is going well, darling.'

'I'll work it off later at the gym,' I reply, sucking my stomach back from the edge of the tablecloth. 'This butter is amazing!'

My curvy figure is a gift from my mother, or so I assume. I certainly don't look like Dad, who's all skin and bone and still over six foot in his socks, even with a stoop. Dad and Harry are those lucky souls who can get away with eating whatever they like without gaining an ounce. Although my claims about the gym are exaggerated. The fitness suite in the basement of my London riverside apartment building has seen me twice in the almost ten months I've lived there. The exorbitant rent justified at the time of signing by the 'freebie' gym membership and an inflated sense of my future earnings potential. Plus that little voice in my head demanding to know why the hell shouldn't I rent a trendy wharfside apartment in a glass building with a private gym and a view of the Thames? I was, after all, on the brink of leaving behind ghostwriting for a career as a screenwriter, the pilot of my scripted series green lit and two days from cameras rolling. How deluded I was, in so many ways. I had no idea Hollywood dreams could be crushed to grit, even right up until the last moment. I'll never come to terms with this industry. The way it serves up hope in the form of signed contracts, stellar casting, enough smoke to blow anyone's arse up themselves and then snatches it from right under your nose at the eleventh and a half hour. Two fingers stuck up to your protests as if you were being unreasonable as you haul yourself off the floor of your frankly ludicrously expensive and yet tiny apartment, that is currently so hot you can barely sleep now you can no longer afford to run the air con. I take a deep breath, then ask, as nonchalantly as the residual desperation allows. 'So, any updates from LA?' Patience is running as thin as funds.

'No, not as such,' Harry replies, brushing non-existent crumbs from his lap.

'Not as such?'

'I really do think you need to forget about the screenwriting side of things for now, Marnie,' he says, the mask of geniality slipping. 'Concentrate on the ghosting. It's a much more reliable income. And on that note—'

'I very much hoped screenwriting *was* the day job,' I interject, although I sense the uselessness of my appeal, even as the words spill out. I pull in my pout and sit up straighter. I'd promised myself I wouldn't do this. Have some pride, Marnie Wilde. Manifest and you shall receive. But I'd said the same thing about the late-night texting to my ex, and look how that ended up. The photo of my right nipple was a low point, even by my standards, and still no fucking response from Jake. Bastard. I'm not dating any more writers. They are definitely higher maintenance. And they never message! Mind you, it's been over seven months since we split, but he was so gorgeous, and talented, and those eyes—

'Marnie? Put your phone away!'

'Sorry.' I shove the phone in my dress pocket. 'I was under the impression the project was only on hold. That's the last I heard.'

'I know you thought that, you've told me, often, but as we both know, the production is definitely no longer proceeding.'

'Do we both know that?'

'Given the nature of the accusations against the male lead, Marnie, which are—'

'Absolutely nothing to do with any of the other cast members, or me!'

Harry ignores my protests and nods at the waiter to open the fizz he's carried over with some pomp, and now nurses at the side of the table, label displayed; the acned jaw dropped as I'd argued my case.

'What I still cannot fathom,' I persist, allowing a filled glass of champagne to find its way to my lips, 'is why everyone's hard work should go to waste, just because one utter prick turns out to be an arsehole of the first degree?'

'That's somewhat of an understatement,' Harry chides, inspecting his coupe glass before he takes a sip. 'The arsehole in question is now facing multiple allegations of the most serious nature and quite possibly a court case.'

I swallow the bubbles and inhale deeply, which calms me a little, but Harry's dismissive attitude is not helping. He is now waving to another woman, whom I recognise as a top screenwriting agent, one I currently wish were mine. I'd imagine the feeling is mutual. For Harry. Not her. She has no idea who I am. My presence discounted as he continues to wave wildly.

I'd loved Harry last summer when every call or email had been good news. Drinks with potential show runners and Zooms with cast members who'd seemed delightful in every way, even the arsehole lead. Not a hint of anything unsavoury. Option contracts and fees were agreed for generous terms, the big payout due to be triggered the moment principal filming began. I'd been in demand. Emails every day from Hollywood. To me, the architect of a 'ground-breaking' project, a hybrid of podcast and drama set to soaring music and fast-paced dialogue intercut with social media live streams. Harry and I were flown out to LA for a few wild days of meetings and partying and exorbitantly priced salads, and then months more Zooms at home to finesse the full eight-episode script. The official announcement in the trade press elicited a flurry of good wishes from people I'd never thought would notice me, let alone take the time to check in. My big break. No more ghost-writing dull memoirs for demanding 'authors' – air quotes intended – puffed up by their fleeting fame and resultant self-importance. I would be credited, on IMDb no less, and as a screen-writer. The dream. The anonymity of ghosting a thing of the past. This was it. I'd finally done something I could be proud of. My name was literally all over it. I rented my glass box of an apartment and sat in it tapping away as if I was the next Shonda Rhimes. I was also in a committed and healthy relationship with Jake, a fellow writer who loved and supported my success. All good. It had to go wrong. And boy did it go wrong.

The explosion that blew apart my world also came via social media. The arsehole exposed by multiple allegations, each one more damning than the last. Trial by public shaming and of course the tabloids. And if that wasn't enough, Jake deserted me only a few weeks later. Two days before Christmas, in fact. I like to think the two cataclysmic events were unrelated, but honestly, who knows? Clearly the universe hates me. But everyone loves a winner and no one wants to be associated with a sad loser.

'The accusations against our lead actor are multiple and serious, darling,' Harry reminds me, as if the details might have slipped my mind in the last, God, it must be almost nine months. 'They cannot be swept under the carpet. They have to be properly investigated. We are living and working in a post *#MeToo* industry, thank God!'

'Yes, of course... thank God!' I echo, feeling less than the appropriate level of solidarity for the sisterhood. The patriarchy, on the other hand, can go fuck itself, including my ex. 'But let's not give up on that script as yet, eh, Harry?' I chide. 'It's too good to lose, you know that, right?'

His shrug sends me to the bottom of my champagne glass, despite my best intentions. I have a right to feel hard done by, even if I daren't show any self-pity in front of my agent. His indiscreet stories of clients he's phased out for exhibiting exactly that response, an unsubtle warning I have not forgotten. But I cannot let go as easily as he has. Not when I was so close. My golden ticket in my hand and ready to wave at the gatekeepers until the arsehole's cache of dick pics and up-skirting snaps derailed everything. There must be a plan B? Nothing as final as this has ever been said before, not to my knowledge. Although the vacuum of information has been difficult in the extreme. Emails ignored, calls not returned. *Ghosted.* But there is always a way back, isn't there? Recasting? A fresh direction, new production company? I've presented these options in as many ways as I can over the last few months, but it seems to no avail. The option contract ties us in to the production company for the foreseeable and they have gone deathly quiet; and no one else would want the script now it's tainted goods. Fuck political correctness. Fuck it all.

I slurp my topped-up fizz after Harry pours. I literally have champagne problems. But it's worse than the loss of a dream. I'm broke, completely flat broke. Although, hope floods my veins along with the pleasant hit of alcohol. Or maybe it's not hope. Something more akin to anxiety at the thought of what's really up for discussion today. A hidden agenda, as yet undisclosed, although I assume Harry is aware of an initial discussion that's taken place for a new ghostwriting project, and that's why he suggested lunch and steered me back to ghosting as a preferred option, for now.

Our salads are placed before us in enormous white bowls, the dominance of greenery studded only meanly with a few tweezered slices of charred chicken and slivers of shaved parmesan. It seems I have been denied anchovies too, presumably in case one should leap across the table towards Harry's bowl, like a salmon swimming upstream.

'So, we move along,' Harry says, my stomach knotting as he pushes a forkful of leaves onto the tines of the shiny tableware. 'And before you tell me again, Marnie,' he dabs a starched napkin at the corners of his lips, 'I know a return to ghostwriting is not what you'd hoped for, but hear me out.' He picks up his glass and clears his throat with a slug of the amber bubbles, dabbing again. 'This project has got a lot going for it, darling. And totally on-brand for you. A real step up, if you behave this time!'

I fight the urge to bite back, chewing instead, the cheesy dressing spicy with a kick of garlic whilst the chicken is dry and claggy in my throat. Despite myself, I cannot relinquish the possibility of that screenwriting credit so easily. A wad of emotion resistant as I try to swallow. 'So, you definitely don't think—?'

Harry shakes his head. 'No, I don't. But anyway, onwards... It's a high profile, tell-all memoir,' he explains, somewhat needlessly as I'm already knee-deep in research and fully invested in the backstory of the once mega-famous actress in question. Not that he knows that I'm one step ahead, or why. Knowledge is power, as they say, and this transcends the usual familiarity between us. This is personal.

'Could be a big deal, Marnie, in every sense,' Harry adds, upselling. Always a red flag.

'Another ghostwriting job, that's the only reason I'm here?' The smart of disappointment won't let go. It's ridiculous. I want this ghosting job. And I need it, for many reasons, prosaic and profound.

'Not just *another* ghosting job, Marnie. This is a massive jump from the kind of celeb you're used to writing for.' He catches my expression, a glint in his eye. 'Oh come on, darling, you must be a teensy bit excited? Priscilla said you seemed keen when you chatted?'

Priscilla is a non-fiction editor for pretty much the largest publisher of memoirs on the planet, and one of Harry's 'dearest friends'. A fact I shouldn't have overlooked when I extracted a promise that our chat the other day was, 'just between us for now'. She specialises in the money-spinning biographies of reality stars, entitled pricks that they are, which is also something of a forte of mine – or at least it was until things started to look up with my screenwriting career. I began the script as a side project, but it's also saved my sanity. The crap I've had to deal with when I've ghosted... and the demands. But I have gained a reputation for churning out half-decent shelf-fillers, and largely without too much drama. That was until a slight hiccough on the last memoir Priscilla and I worked on together, over a year ago now. Her willingness to consider me for this job was therefore somewhat surprising. Although, in fairness, I didn't get a great vibe off her, more reluctant resignation. And she couldn't wait to end the call. As if her hand were forced and she'd been going through the motions. But she's a funny one, Priscilla; blows hot and cold, as Dad would say.

'This really is a plum project, my darling,' Harry tells me, upselling again. There's something toxic about this memoir. I can sniff it a mile off. 'And in your circumstances,' he adds, 'let's not dismiss it out of hand.'

'My *circumstances*?'

Harry grimaces in what I hope is a show of sympathy. I regret sharing with him my perilous financial situation, but I thought it might incentivise him into pursuing the stalled TV series. 'Oh, don't look at me like that, Marnie. Beggars really cannot afford to be—'

'I'm not quite at that stage yet!' I drop my fork into my disappointing salad and hold up my glass, which Harry refills. 'I can wait for something else, if needs be.' A blatant lie.

'You know how these things work, Marnie. You need to increase your profile, get a bestseller under your belt, then who knows where it might lead. This could be the ghosting project to launch you in a whole new space, including the screenwriting. The subject of the memoir has won a bloody Oscar; you do know that?'

'So you're saying Blythe Hopper wants me as her ghost?'

Harry glances about, as if the mere mention of her name were in contravention of the ghostwriters' code of conduct, which in a sense it is, but the cavernous restaurant is raucous with activity; there's no chance of being overheard.

'As I understand it, Marnie, our actress has been extremely picky in the past about her choice of collaborator, so let's not count chickens quite yet, but yes, Ms Hopper is considering you as her ghost.'

Harry has a knack of making me want something, then snatching it away again, rug pulled just as I feel the comforting presence of carpet beneath my feet. 'But Priscilla gave me the impression that Blythe had—'

Harry winces again, perhaps at my use of Blythe's name, or maybe the chewy chicken I'm picking from my teeth.

'My understanding is that Priscilla is presenting her with a shortlist, from which she must accept her ghost or the deal is off,' Harry replies, swallowing. 'Your name is on the list, that's all I know.'

'Is she likely to choose me, do you think?'

'We can but hope!'

'And if not?'

A tight smile crosses his lips before he wipes his mouth again then drops the napkin over his half-finished salad. 'Oh come on, sweetie. You know something always comes up, eventually.'

I force a smile, although my disappointment is not for the reason Harry thinks. I don't want another ghosting job; I want *this* one. 'I do want the job, if it's offered. To be clear.'

'Yes, and I'm extremely hopeful but, Marnie, if you do get the gig, you need to be on tip-top behaviour. No lateness, and definitely no shenanigans.'

'Shenana-what?' I splutter, mid-sip.

'You know what I mean! And word is she's already rejected every other name on the list at least twice. So I think you'll be the last resort, or the memoir's canned.'

'Now I feel really special.'

Harry laughs. 'Marnie, Marnie, Marnie... Look, let's draw a line under the past and face a brighter future. I mean, unlike Blythe,' he whispers her name. 'We are not selling our Hampstead mansion for seventeen mil, which is quite honestly a snip.' He laughs again, then more solemnly adds, 'But in all seriousness, our actress has had to let all her staff go and her former manager is now chief cook and bottle washer. Terribly sad.'

'Yes, awful,' I reply, sarcasm dripping. 'But surely given her *situation*, a memoir's not exactly top of her list of priorities, even if she is a bit broke?'

'Her lawyer is a whizz at pulling off the seemingly impossible, so I've heard, but at a pretty price.' Harry rubs his thumb over his raised fingers. He sits back, sips his water and picks his teeth too, an act which is overdue, a stem of rocket lodged in the upper set, front and centre.

'But she's confessed to murder!' I reply, Harry shushing me. 'Surely no lawyer, however expensive, can fight that?'

'He's got her a stay of execution, as it were, out on bail whilst the CPS decide if it's a murder charge or not. And as far as the memoir goes, she's an actress, darling. Whatever kind of diva-ish objections she's raised about the previous ghosts, we all know how these types love attention. She's been trying to stage a big comeback for years. I imagine she wants to use the tell-all memoir to raise her profile as well as pay her legal team to keep her out of prison for as long as poss. Which is why you, my darling, are the perfect choice.'

'I am?' My glass is empty again as I reach for it. Harry does the honours. 'How so?'

'Because you are, when you apply yourself, a bloody good ghost,' he tells me, sloshing champagne expertly into our glasses. 'Just whoosh in, work your magic, then whoosh out again.' He inverts the emptied bottle in the ice bucket. 'Anyway, you'll love it! A few days of living the dream in her massive house. And you know her husband was a screenwriter back in the day? You'll fit right in.'

'Her dead husband.' I half drain my glass and avoid Harry's acquisitive gaze, head swimming as Harry regales me with details of the victim, Dominic Hopper.

'Rather a legend,' he says, shaking his head. 'But for all the wrong...'

I put my glass down and nod, feeling the room receding from me, Harry's booming voice too. It's a warning sign. One I'm familiar with.

'Marnie? Are you OK, Marnie? You're not going to... Marnie!'

'I'm fine, Harry. Stop staring at me. Just, you know... hungover.' I pick up my water glass and drain it, then the champagne, feeling better.

He laughs, relief spreading across his taut features. 'Thank fuck for that! You know I'm not great with medical stuff... Anyway, let's get another bottle, shall we? If you're up to it, that is?'

'Yes, course. Like I said, just a hangover.'

'In that case, three glass rule. You'll be right as rain soon.'

Harry signals to the waiter and orders a second bottle.

'So, we're celebrating already?' I ask, raising my empty glass as we wait.

'It's not a done deal quite yet, but like I said, I have a very good feeling, darling, and you know I'm always right about these things.'

I resist the temptation to point out that our last deal went very much tits-up despite Harry's endless 'good feelings', whilst he is already sharing his thoughts on the potential size of my fee, pound signs in his eyes (another of Dad's phrases) as he carelessly drops the possibility of a six-figure sum, once the memoir is delivered.

'Six figures, seriously?' I raise an eyebrow, but the thought of Dad is a dampener on the celebration, guilt surfacing as it so often does when I think of him. Not that I have anything in particular to fixate on today, just my general failing to be a daughter he can be proud of. No regular income, no regular partner.

But like Blythe Hopper, I do need an injection of funds, and fast. And Dad would have no objection to that. Although that's not the primary driver for me, not this time. Not that I'm not about to share the very personal reason I'm drawn to Blythe's story. Not with Harry. And certainly not with Dad. It would sound ridiculous. I mean, how do I even begin to explain that a ghost of a very different kind haunts me? An email from a dead man urging me on to take this job, in the Hoppers' mansion in Hampstead.

* * *

I leave lunch woozy and ever so slightly nauseous, the champagne chugging around my digestive system and landing heavily in the base of my stomach where it douses the garlicky salad, curdling the mayo in the heat.

I shove on the designer sunglasses I bought in LA and stagger home through the grilled grime of a London August afternoon, frustrated by the slowness of the tourists, and angered when I can't find a taxi. Not that I can afford one, but the stupid heels make me footsore and the sunglasses are so scratched I can barely see through them. And I still feel light-headed, despite my assurances to Harry there'd be no repeat of my 'medical stuff'.

I reach my building with an increasingly heavy heart, the reality of my impending homelessness something I can no longer afford to ignore, confirmation of that waiting for me as I collect the post from my lock box in reception. The concierge waves at me as he always does, oblivious to my panic as I head for the lift, the dreaded letter clutched in a sweaty hand.

I ride up to the tenth floor, the view that greets me as I go into my studio apartment and then step out onto my tiny balcony, plucking at heart strings I thought were broken beyond repair. The river is of course especially glorious on this hottest of August days as I face eviction. I can't give all this up without a fight. It's been lonely since Jake, but it is still my home. Although I can't get anywhere near the edge of the balcony, not even with a bottle of champagne inside me and the longing of potential loss sharpening my desire to enjoy the view whilst I still can. The view someone else's to enjoy soon, or, as I do, step back from, heart hammering.

I go back inside and spread the letter out on my desk. A final ten-day notice of vacation, or the management company will begin eviction proceedings. The rent is two months' overdue and my credit cards are completely maxed out, my overdraft stretched to breaking point too. Which makes it even more imperative I secure this ghosting job. The suggested fee would clear my debts and fund another year besides. I could take that year to write another script. Maybe even make a return trip to LA, remind everyone I'm still here, still relevant. It's all about confidence, and the appearance of success. *Emperor's New Clothes* in the form of 'buzz'. And Harry's right, Blythe's name does carry weight. Who knows where the completed memoir could lead? A screen biopic would be timely and God knows her story is a gift. The meteoric rise to fame in the nineties complete with an Oscar win, then freefalling into obscurity via a dreadful guest appearance in a 'continuing drama', and now her recent notoriety as a cold-blooded killer. It has it all and I need this gig, for many reasons, but of course, there's always a downside. That gnawing fear of the past. A past I can't seem to let go of.

A familiar image returns. Greyscale, and yet fast moving. More a feeling than a recollection. I'm freefalling, although I resist it, recalling instead something Mum told me before she disappeared. The words paraphrased now. I was only four when she left, but the gist was that I should go for my dreams, take the risk, scare myself. Do whatever it takes. Always.

I open my laptop and using my most persuasive prose beg for a month's grace on the back rent, explaining that I've just signed a contract for a huge sum which will more than cover what I owe. A slight bend of the facts, but Harry intimated it's as good as mine. We clinked glasses for God's sake! And he has a good feeling.

I squeeze my eyes tight and hit send. It's a big ask when I'm already in arrears and they could so easily rent this place five times over, and probably for more than twice as much, but I offered to pay extra. Trouble is, it's a landlord's market.

The river is bustling with life as I peer over the balcony. Tables outside the bars, and restaurants filling up. I consider going for a drink myself, but finances dictate otherwise so I settle for a can of G&T and sit on one of the two plastic chairs I pushed as far from the edge as the narrow balcony allows. We were going to read the papers, Jake and me. Or at least, that was what I envisaged when I moved in. Sunday mornings with the broadsheets and a coffee, just as he liked it, an evening walk along the river. Or was that an invented narrative he'd never shared, let alone bought into.

The ping of an incoming email recalls me to my desk. It's a

miracle! I have my month. One month in which I need to secure and nail the ghosting job and thereby save my home.

My stomach lurches, the salad dressing not to blame this time. There's a lot more at stake than a studio apartment with the smallest balcony in the world and a giddying view. I close my eyes and step out, hands grasping the banister. When I open them, the ground sweeps up from ten floors down, pinpricks of people rushing at me. I step back. Frightened by the possibility presented. Head light. A vague memory stirring and bright, for a second. I scratch at it, but it's gone. Maybe next time.

It's dark by the time another email arrives. From Harry this time, copying me in on Priscilla's to him, which is unwise as she's used phrases like, *unreliable*, *risky choice*, and *last chance, but if we must*. It's hardly fair. I've always delivered on time and without mishap, bar that one slip-up. Anyway, all water under the bridge it would seem, as Priscilla is saying the deal is done.

I read the email, twice, the cans of G&T blurring the twelve-point font.

Blythe is amenable to my name. The game is on. I'm a ghost again.

2

I've never met a murderer before, not to my knowledge, but I guess they must walk amongst us. A bank robber brushing our shoulder in a shop and apologising, or a knife carrier holding a door which we thank them for, exchanging smiles. They probably look like good people, maybe nicer than those who are dealing with private battles who don't smile or make eye contact or thank us for stepping aside or letting them join a queue of traffic. The good ones are those we tut at, or mumble about, thinking them a bad person when they've just been given a cancer diagnosis or broken up with the love of their life. The real bad guys, or girls, are most likely utterly charming, at least on first glance.

The closest I've come to known contact with a hardened criminal was an armed robber I ghosted years back. He'd held two women at gunpoint for three hours and then shot his own foot off as the police barged into the small branch of HSBC in Cheltenham. Lenny was a charming man, with a decent if unsurprising tale of a dysfunctional childhood and the inevitable descent into crime, but appearances of course, can be entirely deceptive. His limp proved his downfall as he tripped and fell down a flight of prison stairs before the memoir was completed. And I never visited him inside. Emails and calls my preferred methods of communication.

It's therefore with some trepidation that two days after my lunch with Harry, I find myself contemplating an actual encounter with a gun-wielding murderer, one whose aim was truer than Lenny's.

Overnight bag in hand and blinking into the bright sunlight, I emerge from Hampstead tube station and fill my lungs with London's polluted summer afternoon air, pulling in those diesel particles and the scent of sourdough and artisanal coffee. A moment to gather my thoughts. This project has been moving way too fast, the usual preliminary meeting to ensure a good fit between the ghosted 'author' and their writer waived in favour of expediting the memoir as quickly as possible. I do understand Priscilla's fears about Blythe potentially backing out. And there's also an impending murder charge to factor in, a ticking clock – despite Harry's optimism that freedom is available at the price of a top lawyer, Blythe's defence is, according to Priscilla, crumbling – but it would have been nice to at least break the ice before moving in. But, as Priscilla pointed out in one of her succinct emails:

> The bail conditions are stringent, Marnie, so it makes sense for you to stay there. Work hard and fast, OK? It's good you have full access, make the most of it. Px

The obvious desperation to get on with the memoir before it's too late hasn't helped my nerves – in fact, quite the reverse. I'd banked on that chemistry meeting with Blythe to suss her out as much as she would no doubt be sussing me out too. Not even a quick Zoom. The great Blythe Hopper, permanently indisposed. Which is, I guess, understandable. Although I'd only asked for five minutes. But no. That was not going to happen. Instead I am to move in. Sight unseen. Living with a murderer, 24/7, for the duration of the interviews, which I hope will take a few days at most.

'Just be grateful the gig is yours, my darling,' Harry advised late last night as I downed another, even cheaper bottle of red whilst I tried and failed to pack a bag for an indeterminate stay.

It was almost midnight by the time he'd returned my call. I'd stalked his Twitter to discern his whereabouts, the sound of London's late-night traffic confirming the evening at an awards ceremony for one of his more illustrious writers, was drawing to a close. Harry sounded pissed, in more ways than one. He was alone in the black cab (he never takes an Uber, or walks) which was good. I can't stand the writer he'd been honouring. Every one of her Insta posts are of her stupid face, grinning from behind her book or with her dog! Does she have no friends? Mind you, I'm a fine one to talk. I haven't spent time with anyone but Harry in weeks.

'Not going back on the deal are you, Marnie?' Harry had asked, surprising me with his directness. 'She's an actress, what's so surprising about her dictating terms and being elusive?'

He was testing the water of course, not expecting me to renege at such a late stage, but there was a sombre note to his tone which, if I hadn't had more pressing concerns, would have rattled me more than it did. I'd felt justified in expressing a few qualms, not only about interviewing a murderer who is under house arrest, but staying with her. And Harry then added more fuel to my bonfire of anxiety.

'I'm sure the fact the gun has never been located is—'

'What the actual fuck, Harry? The murder weapon, you mean?'

'It's probably just conspiracists winding up one another on the dark web. You know, the ones who say you shouldn't drink water or eat frogs.'

Harry was drunker than I'd thought. There seemed little point quizzing him further, but I couldn't leave it there. The alarming revelation Blythe might still be in possession of a gun had not occurred to me. Surely the police would have found and impounded the murder weapon?

'Harry, I need you be one hundred per cent positive the gun is no longer at The Towers.' I'd been looking at my empty bag, still prevaricating about what to pack, London's lights blurring tears that had sprung without warning. 'I'm too young to take a bullet, Harry. I'm not even thirty! Not until next January!'

'Oh don't be so dramatic!' Harry had chided, his dismissiveness actually quite helpful. 'Priscilla and I wouldn't send you to live at The Towers if we thought you were in danger now, would we?'

In a heartbeat they would. 'Do you know Blythe, Harry? Have you met her?'

'A few times over the years, at this and that, and I promise, she's a sweetie. I'm sure Priscilla would say the same. You'll get on like a house on fire. And it's a beautiful house. You'll have a ball.'

'A sweetie who recently shot her husband straight between the eyes.'

'That's a one off.'

'Well, let's hope so,' I'd said, sensing Harry wrapping up, the sounds of the cab ride replaced with echoing footsteps as his ubiquitous laced brogues made their way up the marble steps to his mansion block apartment. It's quite beautiful, and stuffed with books. He inherited it, jammy bastard. Right beside Harrods, where he shops.

'Night, Marnie. Talk tomorrow, and don't worry.'

'Don't worry about what?'

It was academic by then anyway; I'd signed the contract and he'd ended the call. I fell into a drunken sleep and woke at midday, rushing to finish my packing and make my way here.

* * *

The scratched sunglasses slide down my shiny nose as I jostle into the Hampstead High Street traffic, attempting an ambitious cross at an unfamiliar junction. I flip a finger as I jog to the other side, shouldering my heavy bag. I'm a Londoner, of ten years standing; I have earned the right. And I am feeling confident in my summer dress, tattoos on show, hair cut short and spiked up. I have no doubts I can do this job. If anything, the interviews and penning those opening chapters for Priscilla are the part of the process I'm most comfortable with, flexing the muscle memory of a skill I have honed over almost a decade of ghosting. Skating the thin ice of truth whilst mindful of creating a good story. Crafting books that will not only read well, but *sell*. An account the celebrity 'author' will happily get behind and promote the hell out of which is at least half the battle. The celebs don't have to write the book, or in some cases even read it, but they have to like it enough to show up for the publicity. I'm good at building the necessary rapport, and that's what I will focus on. Everything else is a bonus. And for once in my twenty-nine years, I'm actually on time, possibly even a bit early!

It's just a few nights with Blythe, in what is, according to Rightmove, the premiere house bordering Hampstead Heath. I like a challenge, and I love a brush with fame. Real fame, that is. Even notoriety has its allure. And Blythe is a proper star. Or was.

I head down the steep incline towards the Heath, the dull thud of reality creeping in to slow my pace as I follow the bobbing arrow on my phone. Because this isn't only about writing a bestselling memoir of a Hollywood star. If only it were. This is intensely personal and that places me in a precarious, even dangerous, position. Because I am bringing a secret that is very bad news for my host. Something she won't want me to know, let alone discuss. Not that I *know* anything, not yet, but I'm here to find out what she knows, or suspects, about the contents of that email sent to me by her dead husband.

The intersection where Google Maps tells me I'll find Blythe's home is ahead of me now, the house not visible, but close, waiting. Like a portent of doom. Not least because, aside from Blythe and her officious business manager, Ludo, who has brokered all the arrangements, the only two people in the world who know where I am are Harry and Priscilla. And they couldn't give two hoots about me other than as a ghostwriter about to pen a potential money-spinner.

I could vanish off the face of the earth and I'm not at all certain either of them would rush to come looking for me. And even if they do, it might already be too late.

But Harry's right, I'm being dramatic. A tendency of mine. This is a well-paid job and there's no reason for anyone, especially Blythe, to suspect my motives or wish me harm. As long as it stays that way, I'll be fine.

3

The Towers lies at the apex of two impressive roads. One lined with desirable residences and the other – where I am, Hampstead Heath behind me – clogged with crawling traffic. I sweat in my too-tight dress, hoping someone will let me across the road soon, as that ridiculously tall tower looks down on me.

The house name suggests two or more towers, but that's a misnomer. For there is only one. Something I have learnt from the estate agent's online sales brochure, along with the fact its construction, just over a century ago, is in the 'Gothic Italianate' style. The main house and tower were built at the same time, whilst a modern kitchen extension was added by the Hoppers more recently. The property is surrounded on all sides by extensive grounds and bounded by high brick walls, the tops of fruit trees just visible as I sprint across the road and approach along the quieter residential side.

I press my nose to the sliver of air between the ridiculously high gates, glimpsing coronets, chimney stacks and of course that dominating tower, three storeys high and boasting a panoramic view of many miles, at least according to the sales blurb. The view behind the gates is less impressive, my pressed eye surveying what looks like a service entrance comprising a collection of wheelie bins and the back of what could be a garage. There must be a buzzer somewhere amongst the overgrown ivy and brambles, but I can't immediately see one, the disrepair reminding me of Harry's comments about Blythe's lack of funds. Clearly hard times chez The Towers.

With no obvious means of rousing anyone, my conviction to get this show on the road rapidly wilts. London is in the grip of a heatwave and I'm miraculously running early, which means I have time for a quick drink. Just to steady my nerves.

* * *

The nearest bar is a cute thatched inn located at the base of a stepped alley and only a five-minute detour, an establishment of over four hundred years according to the weathered sign above the door, which even a short-arse like me has to duck to pass through. The place is deserted. The guilt of being a daytime drinker, sadly amplified by my solitude.

Dad has rarely spoken of my mother since she left us, but there have been hints that his errant wife was a heavy drinker, his disproportionate disapproval of my teenage binges on account of that, I assume.

I'll just have one, then get back to those gates and find a way to make my presence known this time. Celebs are always running late. Harry and Priscilla's dire warnings about being on my best behaviour silenced as I pick up the tempting cocktail menu.

'I can mix anything you like,' the young man behind the bar suggests. The comment tossed over a square shoulder. You've got to love London. A back-street pub hiding a trendy mixologist sporting a flirty smile on a quiet Thursday afternoon.

'You a cocktail lover?' he asks.

'How could you tell?' I ask, smiling back.

He grins. 'Haven't seen you in here before.'

'No,' I reply, concerned at both the cheesy line and giving away too much.

The headlines about Blythe have been loud, but the secrecy of ghosting can all feel a bit precious. I mean, outside of publishing, literally no one even thinks about whether the words came from the celeb or some unnamed writer. But a non-disclosure has been signed. The main gist of which is that if any press-leaks about Blythe's memoir occur ahead of a formal announcement, I will be the number one suspect. Thus risking not only a possible infraction of Blythe's bail conditions – Harry was foggy on the legal ramifications but it's thought Blythe talking to anyone, let alone moving them in, would be a definite no-no – but also the forfeit of my negotiated fee. And most likely the end of my ghosting career. Not to mention scuppering the more personal quest that's brought me here.

'Ah, super-enigmatic,' the attractive bartender replies, his grey-green eyes reminding me of my ex, Jake, who, like the bartender has a sleeve of tattoos, which I love.

'I'd recommend an amaretto sour,' he suggests. 'That's my favourite.'

'Sounds great.'

'Take a seat and I'll bring it over.'

I choose the window nook, a predilection for the romance of such cosy reading spaces, the cushions lining the seat eclectic and musty, the books classics. I reach for a copy of *Jane Eyre*, caught by the similarity of the house on the cover to The Towers, Blythe's Gothic home pressing down hard on me from its vantage point on the hill as I look out. I'll just about be on time if I down this drink and be on my way. All good.

* * *

'Yeah, I'd have remembered you if you were a regular,' the bartender says, adding a dangerously sexy smile as he sets my cocktail down in front of me an agonising ten minutes later. This was meant to be a quick pit stop, not an afternoon drinking/flirting session, although...

He lingers, still smiling. His teeth are crooked, but they are pure white. He's probably a student, earning a bit of extra cash. English or psychology, or maybe he's a linguist, in his second or third year. The tongue piercing is fascinating as he adds, 'I love your tatts, what are they all?'

'Random stuff,' I reply, burying my blushes as he holds my right arm and comments on the serpent and the heart, stroking them and asking why I chose them, then sighing when the door opens and new customers walk in. 'We close soon, but if you fancy staying just let me know. We can compare ink.'

I nod, but there's no way I can stay. I'm now officially running late. Why do I do this? Self-sabotage or masochism? I was being polite, waiting patiently as he took ages mixing my drink, but my reluctance to leave now is more about what lies ahead of me than what's on offer here, my nerves mitigated only a little as I work my way down my first drink of the day.

It tastes great. Sour with lemons, three I'm informed when the creator catches my eye from the bar. I offer a thumbs up, super-cool twenty-nine-year-old that I am.

The sweet but tart taste reminds me of the lemon sherbets Mum always had in her handbag. Sticky in a white paper bag. I'd pester her for one and sometimes be indulged. I stole the lot once and rubbed the skin off the roof of my mouth as I read *Jane Eyre* for the first time, terrifying myself when I was maybe nine or ten? But I'm getting mixed up. Mum was long gone by then so they must have been Dad's sweets. I suck deep on the straw and taste the syrupy layer of marzipan from the Amaretto. Like the thick yellow almond paste Mum draped over a Christmas cake, the cuttings passed to pre-school me, and tooth-achingly sweet. All my memories of her are sugar-glazed and unreliable. All except one.

'You OK?' the bartender calls over and I am recalled to the room, nodding too enthusiastically so my head swims.

The egg white topping of the cocktail is marbled in the same way Mum feathered an iced Bakewell tart, her speciality. I dip a fingertip in the floating pattern and taste the sour and sweet again. My memories are almost a quarter of a century old, a scrapbook collection. I am standing on the kitchen stool whilst Mum pulled a toothpick through the dark lines of chocolate icing she'd piped across the pure white puddle of ground sugar. The feathered grid like a magic trick to a small child. Then I am floating in the air, her hands around my waist, both of us laughing. A child's-eye view of someone I wonder ever existed as she recedes ever further into the past. There are no photos at Dad's other than a hidden away wedding snap, and strictly no discussions about her. She vanished from our lives when I was too young to remember her properly, only a handful of recollections in the deck. A shuffled card pulled out at random and perused, afraid they might fade if I don't turn them in my mind's eye and inspect them often. I don't even ask Dad to fill in the gaps any more, having to trust my own remembrances which despite careful and ongoing curation have aged to dream-like quality, all fuzzy around the edges. 'She left us, Marnie,' Dad would say whenever I asked. 'Why do you waste your time worrying about her when she abandoned you?'

But how can I not wonder when she was my mother and she vanished? She's literally a part of me. In my DNA.

I take a photo of the cocktail and post it on my Insta account, leaving off any location reference, but hinting at my good fortune with the caption,

So excited to start a new project!

It's taking a slight liberty with the terms of my contract, but I haven't officially reported for duty yet and neither have I given away anything, other than a tease. Mainly for the benefit of Jake. Not that he will be in the least bit bothered. He's well and truly moved on. A writer on a weekly TV show in the US and with a new partner who is tanned and tall and everything I'm not. She's described in her biog as an actress-slash-model. I hate the slash the most. It's so greedy. And disingenuous. Pick one thing or I don't believe you, *bitch*.

My change in circumstance when the scripted series I wrote was suddenly pulled, coincided with an upturn in Jake's screen-writing career which provided him with a convenient excuse to cut ties. We'd talked about moving to LA together for months before that, or at least I had raised it as a possibility. I'm not sure he ever replied. And he's ignoring me again now, despite the odd message over the past few weeks which gave me hope. Not even a smiley face emoji on Insta, but I guess it's early in LA and he's probably worn out by the actress-slash-model. She looks hard work.

The cute bartender fades in comparison to Jake. Jake is a man, not a man-child. With a cool job in Hollywood, not a cash-in-hand zero hours student job.

I gaze out the window at a cobbled street filled with terraced houses decorated with window boxes.

There's no doubt Hampstead is its own little world. From the upscale clothes shops on the high street to the bookstore where a royal memoir was displayed. Even the charity shop I passed on my way here had designer offerings, a fantastic pair of Dr Marten boots calling to me which are currently stuffed in a second-hand carrier bag under the table. I slip off my comfy, slightly frumpy sandals and pull the boots on, crossing my legs so the bartender will notice. The drink has slipped down nicely. Time less of a concern as the alcohol eases my thoughts.

'Another?' he calls over.

'Sure, why not!' I reply without thinking. Classic Marnie.

A few more punters come and go, the bartender getting up from beside me each time, the hand he'd placed on my thigh only mildly missed. I sip my second cocktail and type up a few notes about the area on my laptop to assuage my conscience about the time. I really should make a move but it wasn't a hard three o'clock, was it? And everyone knows the bigger the star, the longer they make you wait.

'You want another?' The bartender picks up my empty glass and tilts his head. 'Third one is always the tipping point!' He grins, clearly more on offer than the drink.

I hold up my glass and smile. 'Go on then!'

4

The sun is blinding as I emerge from the pub an hour later, the lip of the exit finding the toe of my new boots and sending me tumbling knees-first onto the cobbles. The pain in my skinned knees is the least of my concerns as I check round to see if I've been observed. The door behind me is empty, the street thankfully the same. I brush myself down and hoist my overnight bag onto my shoulder, an ominous rattle coming from inside. If my laptop is broken, I may as well give up and go home now. Except having a home is very much dependant on me not giving up on this well-paid job.

Jeez, what is wrong with me? I don't understand what I'm trying to sabotage other than my own future. But it's the past that's holding me back, as always. Fascination and fear finally urging me on, despite Karma's swift retribution for that second and third drink, my knees oozing blood as I stagger towards the steps that lead back up the way I came. I reach the top and take a breather. Using an old tissue I find in my dress pocket to dab at the wounds, the fibres sticking to the congealing cuts on both knees, blood running down my right calf even as I attempt to staunch the flow.

I'm beside a deserted school yard, the play area empty. Summer holidays.

The cottages that face the school are painted in different pastel shades, as twee as the jigsaw puzzles Dad always has on the go in his Brighton flat. He's seventy-eight now, forty-nine when I was born. Which isn't exactly old, but life has aged him beyond that. And by life, I mean me, and I guess my mother too, in absentia. She was curvy and short, younger than Dad who is all long limbs and angles. They looked odd side-by side in the wedding photo tucked in Dad's sock drawer. Mum looking so young! The only one of her I've ever seen. I was clearly the archetypal accident. Unplanned and unwanted.

Katherine. That was Mum's name. And aside from the photo, that's about all I know. It's as if she vanished off the face of the earth twenty-five years ago, leaving no mark except on those she left behind.

I tuck the tissue away and shoulder my bag. The alcohol is making me melancholy, and my childhood was in many ways entirely blessed. I was loved, even if that was implied rather than said. Raised by a man I always thought of as an embarrassment which is a terrible thing to admit, but true. Taunts in the playground about him being an older father and the fact I'm motherless, which of course I'm not. Everyone has one. Somewhere. I just don't know where. But I have been given renewed hope on that front. By a dead man of all people. An email from Dominic Hopper, Blythe's late husband, spurring me on in my never-ending search for Katherine Wilde.

I turn the corner, The Towers across the road again, a pang of doubt swelling. I know in my heart, gut, my pounding head, no good will come of this, which I guess is why I've been delaying this moment. The last person who challenged Blythe Hopper ended up with a bullet through their brain. But I have to stop thinking that way, my propensity to spiralling thoughts not helpful.

I need to know why Dom sent me that email. I need to know what he knew about me, and my mother. The trail ended a month ago on the night Blythe shot and killed him at their Hampstead mansion. Which is why this is the place to start. I just wish I wasn't looking such a state. Marnie the fuck up, yet again. Except I'm not. I'm good at my job, a good ghost; it's just the rest of it I'm shit at and I think I always will be until I make sense of my abandonment.

I double-check my phone for the emailed instructions from Blythe's business manager, the grandly named Ludo Villander, heart-sinking at the specified instruction that I should arrive 'promptly' at three to have time to meet Blythe and get settled in before 'supper' in the kitchen at six. *Fuck.* It *was* a hard three, but I'm here now, and frankly three hours for a quick hello before supper – who calls dinner supper these days, anyway?! – is way over the top. Although I should probably have read Ludo's instructions more thoroughly. I get the impression Villander is one of life's sticklers and my propensity to skim has tripped me up, again. His emails were getting on my nerves, to be honest. I've never had much patience for mansplaining.

I drop my bag by the tall gates. The weight of it was killing me, but there's also a strong and recognisable smell coming from within I can no longer ignore. I open the long zip and the powerful scent of my favourite perfume hits my nostrils. It's my last bottle. A present from Jake after unsubtle hints from me. The blue glass bottle is broken into two neat parts, the contents decanted over everything except, thank goodness, my laptop which is in a separate zipped compartment. The loss of the perfume, however, is a genuine tragedy. I shouldn't have packed it, but I wanted something of Jake here with me, for luck. God knows why, but that's the last of him. Gone.

I leave my bag in a tangle of brambles beside the gates to walk a little lighter as I navigate the circumference of the property's boundary, looking for an alternative entrance, or some other way to make my presence known. I've no contact number. Although I'm certain a sniffer dog could follow my trail as I wipe my perfumed hands down my dress, my phone buzzing in my pocket.

'Harry?'

'Marnie, what the fuck is going on? Blythe's manager has been in touch and said you're a no show. It's gone four!'

'Well I'm here now,' I tell him, turning round and walking towards the gates again.

'Where are you, *exactly*? And if it's propping up a bar somewhere, I swear, Marnie—'

'Harry, please, just trust me. This is important to me too.' I hold a palm up and push on the gate, no movement in it whatsoever, a van driving past and beeping loudly.

'Marnie, where are you? Is that Soho?'

'No! I told you, I'm here. At the house.' I retrieve my bag, shouldering it. 'Trying to find a way in.'

'Outside the gates?'

'Yes, by the gates, as I just said.'

'OK, I'm sending an email to Blythe's manager. Stay put and hopefully Ludo will meet you there. Never met him, but he seems thorough... there, sent!'

'Thanks. I'll wait here. Bye.'

'Marnie, listen, before you go—'

'Harry, please, trust me. I need this job. I'm not going to mess up this time.'

'No, not just that. I want to say something... You're a good ghost, my darling, but you *have* to focus. Be professional. Priscilla hasn't forgotten what happened last time, but she's giving you another chance... because of all the bad luck you've had with the screenwriting, I suppose. Can't think why else. I want you to make this a success, you deserve it.'

I appreciate the acknowledgement, finally, that it has been completely shit to lose a series I'd poured my hopes and dreams into, not to mention the financial loss, but surely it is time to forget my previous ghosting project. One where lines became, admittedly, a little blurred. It was unprofessional of me, sure, but entirely consensual on both sides and not my fault we got caught by the paps as we fell out the club, lips locked. I wasn't the one with a psycho wife. It was just before I met Jake. So I was single at the time. And I've done the wife a favour, really.

'Thanks. Ouch!' A bramble has attached itself to my bare arm, beads of blood bubbling from the inked heart.

'Marnie? You OK?'

'Yeah, I'm fine.' I lick the wound, alcohol weighting my limbs as I lean against the gates, phone pressed to my ear. 'You know me, Harry, accident prone.'

'Marnie, listen, you take care of yourself, OK?'

I have the sudden urge to cry, his kindness threatening to tip me over the edge. 'Yeah, whatever.'

'Seriously, Marnie, if you need to get out of there, just go.'

'Get out? What does that—' But he's gone.

I take deep, sobering breaths, Harry's words staying with me. It's very unlike him to show any concern. Maybe I should cut my losses and go back to the pub, order another cocktail and take up the offer of a 'wild' night out with the bartender. But what would I do tomorrow when I wake up hungover in a student let? I'll be thirty next January. Far too old for cheap drinks in the union bar and unwashed sheets. I have an apartment to cling on to, a career to revive, a dead man's trail to follow. Without this job, and the payday it offers, I'll have to face the inevitable and move back in with Dad. To jigsaw puzzles, and *Well, never mind, love, at least you tried to make a go of the writing lark.*

I adjust my bag and then turn on my heel. There are too many signs to ignore. Locked gates, grazed knees, the bramble attacking me. This was a terrible idea.

I'm ten paces down the road when I hear the whirr of an electric gate opening and a small, officious-looking man dressed entirely in black emerges, calling after me. 'Ms Wilde, is that you at last?'

5

There is a rational explanation for most things, the truth invariably far more dull than one might have hoped, but it's also the case that fact is often stranger than fiction, which is one of the many reasons I enjoy writing a blend of the two. It feels disingenuous to represent an absolute truth with no space for interpretation or alternate opinion. I've always felt my job as a writer, regardless of the project, was to open the discussion, not close it. It's the maybes that provoke thought, which is ironic as my search for answers in my personal life has defined me. So when I received that email from Dominic Hopper, two days *after* his murder, which was by then widely reported, I worked my way through the options to try to explain away the seemingly inexplicable. An email sent by a dead man. How could that possibly be?

My first thought – or rather hope – was maybe Dominic Hopper isn't dead. An elaborate hoax to allow him to escape to a new life? Escape from what, I don't know. An unhappy marriage? Debts? Failure? Blythe? Himself? The list is as extensive as the speculation online. Mostly centred around the state of the Hoppers' almost thirty-year marriage. Unnamed friends quoted as 'deeply concerned' by drunken poolside parties at the couple's luxurious home where explosive arguments were witnessed and 'horseplay' was commonplace, including 'a bird shot down from a tree' on one notable occasion.

Troubling, especially since Harry mentioned the murder weapon has not been recovered, but if you dig deeper, these incidents were years ago, decades even. The Hoppers were virtual recluses. Which is a worry too.

And I don't believe Dom's alive, not really. His bagged body was stretchered out these same gates that have opened behind me, Ludo Villander calling my name again.

I walk towards him, the gates juddering as they come to a stop, allowing barely a wide enough gap for a person to squeeze through, let alone a car. The courtyard behind is giving off an unbearable stink, the smell coming from the overflowing wheelie bins lined up on the right-hand side. A ripeness to the odour.

'Hi, you must be Ludo?' I stick out my hand. 'I'm Marnie.'

Ludo Villander's displeased expression confirms my preconceptions. Short and slight, with slicked back and unnaturally dark hair, he is wearing a black polo top, skinny black jeans and loafers – Gucci loafers if I'm not very much mistaken. It's a strong look and instantly recognisable from the photos of Blythe as she left the police station in the aftermath of the shooting, Ludo shielding his client from the relentless glare of the photographers. I hadn't matched the image with the author of the fussy emails, but it's definitely the same man.

Blythe's business manager's tight-lipped, narrowed eyed gaze is unblinking as he eyes me as if I am an unwelcome intruder, although he'd called after me.

He pointedly checks his watch, a large, gold monstrosity which hangs loose on his thin wrist. 'You are seventy-seven minutes late,' he says, dropping his gaze to my bloodied knees, which are exposed between the hem of my short dress and the chunky boots. 'Have you been in a fight?'

'No! I tripped over.'

'Is that what detained you?'

'No, there was an issue with the train.'

'The underground is running on time; I checked.'

'Did you?'

He leads the way across the courtyard and up a flight of concrete steps, a bag of rubbish abandoned halfway up which he tosses down, narrowly missing me.

'Thanks for making all the arrangements for my stay,' I call up, trying to atone for a bad start.

'Personally, I think it's a terrible idea.'

'Oh! You do?'

He doesn't respond, ascending the steps with a swiftness I cannot replicate, my overnight bag smacking my ribs so I stumble back and almost lose my footing a couple of times before I reach the top.

A shingle drive pocked with thistles and tufts of rye grass greets me, the enormous house partially obscured by tall trees that line the sweep of gravel which leads to a porch guarded by two stone dogs. Ludo regards me from between them with undisguised disdain and a deal of suspicion – no offer of help with my bag extended. He doesn't want me here. But Ludo is staff; it's Blythe I need to impress. Her story I am employed to write. I don't love his attitude but it's immaterial. Although, I could do without his negativity. Especially as I've come across the same opinion of ghosting, albeit in veiled forms, many a time.

Ludo clearly doesn't get it and I've no inclination to explain. You can't fully understand the relationship of a ghost to the named 'author' until you've been a ghost yourself. It's *their* story, not mine. I am the means by which the narrative reaches the hands of readers. A conduit as much as the keyboard, or the pen, or the editor, or the proofreader. A collaboration where one person, quite rightly, takes centre stage, but it is a village who gets them there, ghost included. Teasing out the truths and making them sing. It's their story.

Or maybe he has more fundamental concerns. Which begs the question, what is he anxious about his client revealing?

Or maybe he just doesn't like the look of me. Which is a distinct possibility. I've hardly given the best first impression. I'll dazzle him later. When I'm more presentable and showing my skills as an interviewer. For now, I'm struggling to keep up. Ludo walks fast for a small man.

The path – for it's more that than a drive now, the weeds taking over – slopes away behind me, running down to the front boundary wall, beyond which is the busy road I crossed from the Heath. It's such a prime location. Only a short commute into central London and yet the overgrown drive clearly hasn't been used by any vehicles in a long while, large tufts of wild grass peppering it right up to where it meets a half moon of gravel in front of the house.

I pause, taking in the full splendour of The Towers. A home of mansion-like proportions that's so ornate, so enormous, it's hard to absorb it all in one gulp. Multiple eaves and coronets spiking upwards and that crazy-tall tower clinging to the right-hand side, a limpet of monolithic proportions. The kind of haunted house that inhabited my fevered, childish nightmares. Populated by locked rooms at the top of tall towers containing mad relatives. Except this isn't the benign, tamped down, illustrated version of my childhood. This place is sinister, even in glorious sunshine, every brick, every mullioned window, telling a story. I hate to think what it will evoke in my fertile imagination come nightfall. I resist the urge to make an excuse and bolt, focusing instead on the reasons I'm here. The most compelling one being a crazy plan to follow a dead man's quest. Echoes of Dominic surely left in the fabric of the building, and imprinted on his wife of almost thirty years? The woman who knew him best. And also shot him dead. But now, my only hope of finding the truth.

'Ms Wilde?' Ludo is still standing between the two imposing stone dogs who guard the front porch. They reach his shoulders, making him look like an angry boy. 'Are you ever coming in?'

And with that, he slips inside.

I shake my feet to repel the gravel that's dug into the heavy tread of my recently purchased boots, the stones staying put whilst the right boot comes free and lands ahead of me. I knew they were a size too large when I bought them, but they were only twenty-quid and I love them. What I don't love is the way they've shaved layers off my sweaty feet. Thank goodness for the soft sandals tucked in my bag. I drop my holdall on the drive and rummage through, and that's when it comes to me.

Shit! I must have left them under the pub table. Kicked off as I changed into the boots to flirt with the bartender. Double shit!

I limp towards the lost boot and slide my blistered heel back in, folding my neck back and shielding my eyes with a straight palm. The tower has a room at the top, glass-walled and with a 360-degree view apparently, my vertigo kicking in even at the thought of being up there. It's used by the current owners as a 'meditation room', visions of a modern day Mrs Rochester in the lotus position dispelling some of the foreboding the vertiginous tower induced, but I sincerely hope Blythe doesn't expect me to go up there with her. I am about to grab my bag and follow Ludo inside when I see movement, maybe, up in the tower. Someone at the glass, looking down.

'I believe you can see for thirty miles, maybe more,' Ludo observes, making me jump as he emerges from the entrance porch.

'You haven't been up there?' I ask, the shadow gone.

'No,' he replies, standing beside me. 'That's Blythe's space, always has been.'

'Her husband didn't use it?'

'No, he preferred not to.'

'It's a beautiful house,' I gush, eliciting the first hint of a thaw in Ludo's icy demeanour.

'The house belonged to a comedian when it was built in the thirties,' he explains. 'And then a musician of some renown.' Ludo's voice is full of pride. 'It's had quite a few celebrity owners since, but it was about to fall into the hands of a property developer when the Hoppers stepped in back in 2005 after they moved back from LA. The developer would have most likely divided it into studio apartments or something equally awful.'

'Yes, awful,' I reply, feeling protective of my beautiful studio flat, but I know what he means. It would be a shame if this place was converted. 'Is that when you first met Blythe, 2005?'

He checks his watch again. 'Shall we go in, Ms Wilde?'

'Yes, great, is Blythe available for a quick hello now I'm here?'

'She *was*,' he says, his mood frosty again. 'But now, sadly not. Shall we?'

The scent of stately homes inside The Towers transports me back to endless visits to National Trust properties with Dad, his Sunday-afternoon activity of choice. I lift my phone to capture every detail of what is a cavernous and impressive foyer, but am stopped in my tracks by Ludo's echoing shout.

'No photos! As per the contract you signed, Ms Wilde; I think the terms were made abundantly clear.'

'Sorry, and do call me Marnie,' I tell him, pocketing my phone.

'Yes, whoever chose *that* name for you?' he asks, pausing to wait for me to catch up, the Gucci loafers already halfway across the expanse of marble flooring.

The rudeness of his questions startles me. 'I believe my mother did, and I happen to like it. Who chose yours?'

Ludo looks suitably winded, but my attention is divided by the distractions of my surroundings.

The entrance hall is the full width of the house, a sweeping staircase straight head and carpeted in a vibrant crimson runner, gold stair rods keeping the red carpet in place. The epitome of Hollywood glamour.

'Wow!' I say, spinning round to take in the vast windows either side of the front door which are draped with emerald-green velvet swags and the double-height ornate ceiling. It's like stepping back in time. To the nineties. When Blythe was at the height of her fame, the excesses of that decade reflected in the polished side tables and enormous chandeliers. The poignancy of hanging on to the past giving me goosebumps.

'The house has been extended and renovated over the years the Hoppers have lived here,' Ludo tells me, that same hubris in his voice as before, as if he were the owner. 'This is the only room left entirely untouched.'

'It's beautiful.'

I walk slowly, taking it all in. Not only the old-fashioned décor, but the decision I've made to come here. Following in the footsteps of a dead man, which is maybe more to blame for the goosebumps than the step back in time.

Dad would have undoubtedly tried very hard to dissuade me from coming here, had I told him even a fraction of the truth. But Dad being Dad, he did pick up on 'something not being quite right' when I called to explain I'd be out of touch for a few days. I explained how I couldn't say who the memoir is for, but a big name, so he is definitely not to worry. I suppose that last comment is a red flag to any parent, but Dad's pretty level-headed. My ability to catastrophise, I can only assume, another gift from my flighty mother.

Although Dad did have some questions, reasonable ones too. Like, why I wouldn't be permanently attached to my phone as always? I quoted my favourite line, the same one I always use in these circumstances: 'I could tell you, Dad, but then I'd have to kill you.' I imagine him throwing his eyes up to the ceiling, a hand too, wedding band still in place a quarter of a century after the day we watched Mum leave, his voice a little shakier as he'd then said, 'I'll never understand what you do, Marnie, so don't try to explain it to me. It's another world.'.

He's not wrong, about the explaining or the strangeness of what I do, but I've promised I'll be in touch when I'm done. And that I'll visit soon.

'I have to be available 24/7, Dad. You know what these slebs are like.'

'Not really,' he'd said.

It's helpful with Dad that he has no point of reference, but he totally gets that a contract signed must be honoured. It's the creed by which he's lived his whole life, my school holidays often spent sitting in the reception area of his office with a book and a packed lunch, watching the warring couples arrive and wondering if one of them might have changed their mind before my father, respected divorce lawyer, was ready to see them. I'd imagined them exchanging a small smile, then linking hands, the woman lifted up and carried out, happy ever after. Which of course, never happened. Not even close. Some did walk out. Just not together.

'Impressive, isn't it?' Ludo prompts as he follows my appreciative gaze. 'The staircase was modelled on *Sunset Boulevard*. Have you seen it? It's something of a classic.'

'Yes, one of my dad's favourite films.'

The stairs are empty, but I can imagine Blythe descending them

Norma Desmond style, silk kaftan and turban in place, a winning smile for the camera, ready for her close-up. I can only hope the comparisons begin and end there. Although the body in the pool is another unfortunate similarity, the bullet between Dom's eyes sending him reeling backwards into a final plunge, if the social media sources I follow are to be believed.

The sweat on my back turns cold, a shiver running through me. I could do with a shower. Maybe a lie down before I meet Blythe. My head is like cotton wool. Never a good sign.

'Can I go to my room now, Ludo, freshen up?'

I look up to the first-floor landing, curious to find out which suite will be mine. Although all the guest suites were gorgeous in the online brochure. There's even a sales video. No hammered in *For Sale* sign outside The Towers, though. Far too tacky for a property of this value.

Ludo appears nonplussed, or maybe he didn't hear me, walking instead towards the far side of the hallway where there's a narrow entrance to what looks like a connecting corridor.

'Ms Wilde?' he calls back. 'If you don't mind following me this way now?'

We walk single-file down the white-walled passage where an impressive collection of framed photos forms a gallery of younger versions of Blythe, circa early nineties, a smile for us from each captured moment. Blythe had the classic Hollywood look down to a tee – a sleek, shoulder-length, precision-cut blonde bob, high cheekbones, and a tiny cinched waist. Tons of jewellery – more was definitely more – and where visible, white stilettos. The pleasingly symmetrical facial features are familiar from every poster and publicity shot I've viewed over the last few days and weeks of researching her and Dominic Hopper obsessively.

'An amazing collection of photos,' I call after Ludo who is ahead again.

Movie directors, fellow actors, even royalty accompany Blythe's now familiar film-star smile. Premieres and glitzy parties, poolside cocktails raised to the camera. A kiss on the cheek from a former president. A scarf wound elegantly around Blythe's silken hair as she poses in front of what looks like a temple, then another with arms wound around the waist of a woman who sits astride a motorbike, Blythe riding pillion.

'Who's this?' I ask Ludo, who doubles back, somewhat reluctantly.

'That was Blythe's stunt double. Shall we move along now?'

I study the woman in front of Blythe on the motorbike. The resemblance between the two women on closer inspection, not good. The double less attractive but more spirited, her smile wild and she's wearing a terrible blonde wig. 'What's her name, the stunt?'

'She was called Josie,' Ludo replies.

I linger a moment longer, less interested in the guided tour than the photo. There's something about it that's off, but I can't put my finger on it. Maybe the smiles?

The sleek, dark figure of Ludo disappears through a door at the end of the corridor. I should catch up, but I can't tear myself away, another image catching my eye. One of Blythe and Dominic this time, faces pressed together, a cake covered in candles held between them, a sparkling pool behind. Taken at their house in LA, I guess. It looks glitzy, the cake iced with two words:

Happy Anniversary!

'I'm here, Dominic,' I tell him, in a whisper so light it's mainly breath. 'Now what do I do?'

Dominic Hopper stares back at me. Enigmatic. His secrets taken with him to the grave. He has deep-set eyes, and there's something familiar and comforting in them – or is that wishful thinking? I have most likely manifested those positive attributes, needing someone on my side, even from beyond the grave. Blythe sure as hell won't be. Not if she finds out why I'm really here. And Ludo is chilly to the point of rudeness.

As I slowly move on, Blythe's undeniably beautiful face watches me from every angle. Fragments of the brief spell of fame she enjoyed sandwiched behind glass, although it feels like something more tangible is prickling the back of my bare neck, an involuntary shudder as I sense her presence, close by. I turn around, the corridor empty, but the feeling remains.

I dither, the bag digging into my shoulder. There's no sign of Ludo ahead. I'm alone. Now or never to double back and see who was there.

The fall of my boots echoes across the marble of the hallway, the red carpet rising above me, the gold banister ornate as I take a few steps up. Then another flash of movement. Gone even as I see it. Blonde hair leaning over the banister, maybe? Or is that a throwback to the photos I've been studying, my mind playing tricks on me? I blink hard, wiping sweat from my eyes and try to get a purchase on what was up there. Maybe nothing. I can't even see the landing unless I climb up further. But the feeling of surveillance remains. I was being observed, I'm sure of it.

Another of Mum's phrases echoes in my head, although seen through the prism of adulthood, it was wholly inappropriate to direct it at such a young and impressionable child. And she said it often. Well, often enough for me to remember.

Someone walk over your grave, Marnie-moo?

This place creeps me out, but I've always had a vivid imagination. No doubt fuelled by my mother's early influence. Monsters lurking under the bed, ghosts of the past returning to haunt me. But I swear I saw someone. And I'm sure they saw me.

6

I retreat and run along the photo-lined corridor after Ludo, emerging into a modern kitchen diner at the back of the house. A large and light room overlooking the garden. Cream cabinets line the walls and there's a long, scrubbed oak table by the sliding glass doors, which appear to be broken. One side swinging unnaturally outwards, pivoting in the wrong direction. Ludo holds it open and frowns at my 'tardiness' as he calls it, directing me through.

'Please take care!' he tells me, more concerned about the door than me it seems, tutting as I squeeze out with my bulky holdall. 'And don't wander off again without me,' he says, following me outside. 'As advised in my correspondence, there are strict rules attached to your stay. I'd be grateful if you'd adhere to them at all times.'

'Rules?' I ask, but he's ahead again, marching across the expanse of a long, sloping back lawn.

I struggle to keep up, especially with my heavy bag, which I'd have left in the hall if I'd known I was getting the full tour. The enormous, oval-shaped back lawn is a verdant shade of green, which is also a surprise given the drought the whole country is experiencing. Glimpses of bright gold up ahead catch my eye, the dappling sunlight bouncing off a clear surface, the house retreating at our backs. I crane to see the pool, but a low wall denies me the rectangle of water. Unfurled parasols also cluttering the view.

'Ms Wilde! This way please?'

Ludo has turned in the exact opposite direction to me, the path he's now following headed towards a large, wooden structure that looks like a summerhouse, the glass-fronted outbuilding wedged into the curve of the gravel path, thereby blocking a space that must have once been the vehicular point of exit from The Towers. I can't see how cars can now either enter or leave the house with that giant shed blocking the side access. The parking area within the small courtyard by the gates was empty of cars, but it still doesn't make sense for visitors or deliveries. How odd.

'Ms Wilde?' Ludo beckons to me with a scoop of a short arm. 'Quickly!'

The summerhouse is fronted by a veranda made of planks of wood the same pine-yellow colour as the building itself. The decking furnished with a rattan-effect corner sofa and matching low table. Faded cushions and a rusted parasol complete the shabby ensemble. It's pleasant enough, but I don't really see why Ludo has brought me out here.

'This, Ms Wilde, is *The Writing Annexe*,' Ludo announces, producing an ornate key on a hideous rabbit's foot fob. 'I think you'll find it a comfortable workspace.'

'Oh, right!'

He unlocks a glass door in the glass frontage and waits for me to go in, lurking outside as I drop my bag on the planked floor, a cloud of dust disturbed and evoking an overwhelming odour of pine and neglect.

'Sorry, I did clean up a bit this morning,' he says, 'but it's been locked up ever since Dom... well, a few weeks now.'

'So this was Dom's office, before he...?'

My question hangs in the trapped air along with the dust motes as Ludo peers inside, the wall of glass intensifying the trapped heat. The scent of wood and the past is cloying. It reminds me of a vivarium I had in my bedroom as a teen, two fire salamander lizards desiccated by adolescent neglect.

'Dom would write out here, yes. But as I say, I have cleaned since his... leaving.'

The interior is entirely clad in the same sickly shade of yellow pine – floor, ceiling, three walls. There's also a further room I can't see fully through a partially open door at the far end. A desk stands straight ahead of me, a swivel chair pushed up to it, and an empty bookcase against the left-hand wall. To my right a compact kitchenette. Ludo, still lurking outside on the veranda, suggests I open the internal door fully which, when I do, hits the end of a metal framed bed. The realisation of what that means, hitting me too.

'You expect me to sleep in here?'

'I've left clean bedding,' he says, poking his head further inside, a slim leg lifted behind him to counterbalance the angle of his lean. 'I hope that's acceptable?'

The windowless, airless bedroom which just about accommodates the bed – a double, at least – is compact. A pile of bedding dumped on top of the thin mattress.

'I thought The Writing Annexe would be perfect for you,' Ludo says as I meet him back at the door, his lips stretched into an approximation of a smile. 'Seeing as you're a fellow writer. Dominic spent a lot of time out here.'

Evidently. The presence of a bed begging a question about the Hoppers' marriage I half form and then reject, as another more pressing concern has taken over.

'Is there a bathroom?'

'Oh yes,' Ludo says, a lift in his tone to express his enthusiasm as he explains that what I'd assumed was a built-in wardrobe behind the bed is in fact, a tiny en suite. 'Toilet and shower,' he advises, calling to me from outside. 'All mod cons.'

I assume it's the smell that keeps Ludo at the door. The stench of mould and drains is overpowering. A single towel hangs on a hook behind the door. It's grey. Once white. Maybe.

'You not coming in?' I call back. Although I don't blame him. This place is rank.

No response.

'So Dom spent nights out here?' I ask, then correcting the familiarity. 'Dominic, I mean.'

'He did,' Ludo calls back. 'When he was in full flow. But I have cleared it of his possessions. I think you'll be comfortable enough.'

'There's no sink,' I say, still looking for one in the tiny en suite.

'Ah, but there is.' Ludo points to the kitchenette as I return.

Next to a two-ring hob are two flannels, which sit folded on the edge of the small sink as well as a washing up cloth.

'Multipurpose,' I reply, inhaling deeply. 'Perfect.'

'Indeed, Ms Wilde. Indeed,' Ludo allows himself a self-satisfied smile. 'If it doesn't suit, I can escort you back to the gates?'

'No, no, I'm sure I'll be fine,' I tell him, looking around the small office-cum-kitchen. 'It's only short-term.'

'Exactly!'

The lack of soft furnishings or any embellishment reminds me of Dad's aversion to cushions or ornaments, though the annexe's sparseness could be ascribed to Ludo's recent clear out. The only concession to personalisation is a framed photo of a rather louche looking Ernest Hemingway hung above the desk.

'I left that on purpose,' Ludo explains. 'As you're a writer. Although, I haven't been able to find anything you've written.'

'I'm a ghost, Ludo. There and then gone, like a thief in the night.'

Ludo nods, although I note the swallow, his Adam's apple pulsing. 'Well, I'll leave you to it, Ms Wilde.' He turns to go, then spins back. 'Oh, I almost forgot!'

Ludo instructs me to open the desk's deep drawer and remove a heavy ring binder which I drop from a height onto the scratched leather blotter, another cloud of dust disturbed. Ernest looks down as if I've also troubled his creative process, the black and white image of him at his typewriter not much of a comfort. I'd imagine Ernest would be every modern woman's worst nightmare.

'Everything you need to know about your stay is in there, Ms Wilde,' Ludo says, tapping the outside air as if he were tapping the cover on which is a handwritten label:

THE RULES – READ CAREFULLY!!!

'I have been very thorough,' Ludo continues, 'and therefore expect no transgression from my instructions, but in the unlikely event anything isn't clear, do let me know and I can clarify.'

'Wow, that's...' I inspect the folder, opening the cover and flicking through the typed contents, the thirty or more pages pressed into plastic wallets. 'A lot of reading material.'

'It's pretty comprehensive,' Ludo says with no trace of irony.

'Can you maybe give me the gist, Ludo?' I ask, leaving the folder on the desk. 'I'm not big on instructions.'

'Read it from cover to cover!' Ludo instructs, turning again to leave.

'Will there be a test?' I ask, grinning at Ernest. I need an ally and if it has to be him then I'll embrace his hard-drinking, brilliant writer attributes and set aside the bull fighting and possible misogyny. 'Multiple choice, at least, Ludo?'

'No,' Ludo replies, with not a trace of amusement. 'It's important, Ms Wilde. Take the time you have before supper to read and digest. If you want to last more than five minutes in our company, that is.'

'And whose choice was it I stay out here rather than in the house?' I ask, leaning against the door to stop it swinging shut. 'Yours or Blythe's?'

'It's best all round, Ms Wilde. Blythe isn't herself, not since... She needs her space to grieve. I hope you understand?'

'Of course, sorry.' I step back from the door and away from my attempts at sassiness, holding on to the handle as the breeze tries to slam it shut. 'Dominic was a Hemingway fan?' I ask, gesturing to the photo.

'I guess,' Ludo says. Then he points to the folder to attract my dwindling attention. 'All of it, Ms Wilde. Before you meet Blythe at supper.'

'Oh, sure, no chance I can grab her before that? Just for a quick hello?'

'See you at six, Ms Wilde. And FYI...' He glances at my bloodied knees. 'I'd use the time to freshen up, as you put it. Blythe is very much a fan of making an effort.'

The glass door swings shut as I let it go, the rabbit's foot rattling in the fob.

I sling my bag onto the bed and toe the front door open again as I watch Ludo's progress back to the house. He has a funny little walk: pigeon-toed and remarkably fast. He reminds me of a penguin, the way his arms scissor out as he strides.

I kick off my boots and step out onto the veranda, then sink my bare feet into the long grass beyond, the cool and damp of the lush lawn refreshing as my toes curl and stretch. The garden is huge but unkempt, the grass in need of a good cut, the borders overgrown but clearly once magnificent, shards of pink and white and orange and red between the choking weeds.

I can smell the pool too, curiosity getting the better of me despite Ludo's sternness about reading the rules, one eye on the house as I walk over, glances to the kitchen door I assume Ludo must have disappeared through. Although, there's no sign of him.

The scent of chlorine takes me straight back to Saturday mornings at the leisure centre with Dad – *if we're going to live by the sea, Marnie, you need to be a strong swimmer* – memories of him prising my arms from around his neck as he taught me how to tread water, and the way to time breaths between strokes, as clear as if I was five or six again. Dad was stern, his warnings full of parental care, although I often felt an implication that I was a burden to him.

Maybe I've overlayed my insecurities onto a sensible choice. A single, working parent taking the necessary precautions to protect his only child. And I *am* a strong swimmer. Which is a good thing, Dad also instilling in me a healthy respect for water.

The surface of the pool glistens with splinters of bright, afternoon sunlight, glittering between the cream canopy of two unfurled parasols, the light so dazzling I close my eyes for a second. An image of Dominic Hopper's body floating face down, blood like red ink emanating from his head wound, filling the dark void. I open my eyes, forcing the image away. I don't want to think of him like that. I don't even know for sure that that's what happened, rumour and speculation all I have to go on. And if he did end up in the water then he was likely dead before he hit the surface.

Was that a better way to die? A burst of pain then nothing. It feels preferable to the burn of lungs screaming for air whilst slowly filling with water. I've always thought drowning must be a terrible way to go. And although I never met Dominic Hopper, and now I never will, I don't like to think of him suffering.

It's impossible not to feel closer to him now I'm here, staying in his writing annexe. Closer than when I first read that email he sent me two days after his death. I'd wondered at its sudden arrival, and then him, and his death, going over every syllable, the words burned into my memory so I can see them even as I am blinded by the sun reflected off the water. The font, the spacing, the sign off, clear as day.

Dear Marnie,

I believe we have a connection in common: your mother, Katherine Wilde. I am searching for her and if you are too, we need to talk.

My wife, Blythe Hopper, a name surely familiar to you, is not aware of my plans, and it's imperative, for your safety and mine, this ignorance should prevail, at least for now.

Please use this email address as our only means of communication and speak of this with no one.

More soon.

Dominic Hopper, Screenwriter.

7

Ever since that email arrived from Dom a month ago, and two days *after* his death, I've been obsessed by the man who sent it, my preoccupation only intensifying now I'm here, seated at his desk, no less, and soon to meet his wife. The woman who confessed to murdering him.

Ludo advised me to smarten myself up before supper, but since my wander towards the pool, I have passed the rest of the time in a total panic at the lack of a reliable Wi-Fi connection. All my nerves channelled into that one frustration. I even tried to find Ludo to check the password in his folder of rules is correct, the buffering on my laptop screen maddening, but the kitchen was empty and the photos of Blythe in the corridor freaked me out. So I came back here and watched the spinning wheel on screen. This is Hampstead, London! Surely there's some 4G, even if 5G hasn't quite made it past the high street. But no, it's a black hole, apparently.

Having said that, the signal had briefly flared on my phone as I approached the house, those blessed bars reappearing, albeit fleetingly. But in the annexe it's intermittent at best as I go over my research on my laptop and refresh my thoughts prior to meeting Blythe, although it's her husband who fascinates me.

Dom – a man whose story had not troubled me one iota before his untimely death – now my obsession. His Wikipedia entry short and not so sweet.

> Dominic Hopper was best known as the long-term husband of Oscar-winning actress, Blythe Hopper. His screenplay for *The Man* (1992) failed to achieve either the predicted award recognition, or box-office success, despite receiving critical acclaim. He was killed on the second of July 2023 by a single gunshot wound. His wife, Blythe, has confessed to his murder. He died instantaneously at their Hampstead home.

Notwithstanding the shortage of information, the life and death of Dominic Hopper could be my specialist subject. Which reminds me of when Dad asked me what I'd choose if I were a *Mastermind* contestant. It was a bleak Sunday night. School looming for me and work for him. Neither of us looking forward to our week. Although my thoughts did not extend beyond my own reluctance. The selfishness of youth.

'Maybe Sugababes?' I'd replied, whilst painting my nails a lurid shade of green.

It's funny how some things stick and others don't. The photos I've found online of Dom's first wife, for instance. Wendy Hopper. Her innocent and adoring smile at Dom's side especially poignant given the fact she died so young and in such tragic circumstances. My notes on her kept in another saved folder I open up to review.

Wendy and Dom met at Cambridge. Both scholars, they married young, their first son born two months later. So I'm guessing maybe that's why? Wendy gave Dom two more sons before the family moved to LA in the late eighties, presumably for

Dom to pursue his screenwriting ambitions. Wendy, a primary school teacher, was a mousy-looking woman with dark hair and a curvy figure who looked uncomfortable in the few photos I've found of the couple at Hollywood events, clinging on to her husband's arm as if she knew he was a flight risk, the smile doting but also nervous. Particularly the one of the two of them at the premier for Dom's only big success: *The Man*.

After Wendy's tragic death in April 1993, the boys were taken back to the UK by their maternal grandparents, and, as far as I can tell, have had little if any contact with their father since. At least, that's according to the press reports in the wake of Dom's death, the negative media commentary mainly aimed at Blythe, who is painted very much as the woman who not only killed her husband, but stole him away from his loving family three decades before.

Dom is hardly presented in a beneficent manner either. An adulterer who severed all family ties to be with his mistress, Blythe, he is only saved from the worst of the criticism by the fact he was eventually murdered by the woman he abandoned his family for. Almost as if he deserved to die.

Which is in some ways not as shocking as it might sound, given the heart-breaking way Wendy Hopper lost her life at the tragically young age of only thirty. By accidental drowning. Her body washed up on the stretch of beach beneath the family's home in Monterey.

The boys, fortunately, were staying with a friend the night Wendy died. As was their father. Dom in LA working on a new screenplay with some big-shot producer friend of his, according to reports at the time. He was, I suspect, with Blythe. The overlap in their relationship alluded to multiple times.

An inquest blamed Wendy's 'fragile mental state', the protestations from her 'broken-hearted' parents who had travelled from the UK to appear as witnesses for their only child, ultimately discounted. A single photo of Dom leaving the courthouse, with

Blythe, was used a lot. It was insensitive of them both, in my opinion, and that of the press.

Maybe that was why Dom allowed Wendy's parents to take the boys back to the UK? The price he paid for being with Blythe. Although, you'd have thought Sean, Jack and Callum, by then aged just eight, six and four, would have wanted to be with their father and he with them, or at least in the same country? Instead, they were raised by their maternal grandparents, now deceased, and have not followed their father into any of the creative industries. An accountant, a banker and a personal trainer, they are normal people, shunning publicity, and haven't been available for comment since their estranged father's death. There was too much bad blood, their mother's death and Dom's hasty marriage to Blythe earning a large question mark from the boys, as well as the wider public.

My tentative attempts to contact Dom's sons have been ignored. No surprise there, but I'd have loved to talk to them. Can't imagine there's any love lost. Dom was hardly dad of the year, the newlyweds cosy in their Hollywood hills' home and already socialising on an epic scale barely weeks after Wendy's death. Married within three months.

I check the wobbly fridge, just a bottle of fizzy water in there, the SodaStream left on the counter for refills. I pour a full glass of bubbly water and return to my laptop at Dom's desk and the tawdry tales of 'wild parties' at the Mulholland Drive house which often made the papers, even in the UK. Mainly on account of Blythe's and Dom's British roots and of course, Blythe's star status once she was cast in her Academy Award winning role, her career soon eclipsing Dom's, only to burn bright and fizzle out too soon, for reasons I intend to dig into in my interviews with her.

The Mulholland Drive house was glitzy but not extravagant, at least as far as I can tell from the photos I've found of it. But it was certainly party-central by all accounts and also the scene of another tragic death – that of a young actress, Florence Saint John, in May 1993, just a month after Wendy Hopper's death, in fact. I hadn't connected those facts before. Flo was the exquisitely beautiful and talented star of *The Man*, Dom's big break as a screenwriter, filmed only a year before her death.

She was found 'unresponsive' in a guest bedroom after an all-night party at the Hoppers' that had 'angered neighbours'. More details, all these years later, are hard to track down, but Flo's death seems to be an all too familiar tale of Hollywood excess. 'Too Much Too Young' one headline proclaimed. Poor Flo, she was only twenty-two. And an incredibly talented actress by all accounts.

My notes on Dom's recent death are also scant, the media coverage careful to keep to the facts, an embargo on reporting until the CPS decide what charge to bring against Blythe. I have little legal knowledge, despite my dad being a solicitor, but it must be a no-brainer? She killed him. And she has admitted to that. As I say, I'm no expert, but surely Blythe will be charged with murder, and soon?

Harry suggested her expensive lawyers are putting together a workable defence, but it's hard to imagine what that might be? A loophole found, a workaround presented that bamboozles the jury? But this isn't a speeding fine, it's self-confessed, point-blank murder.

The trouble is, much as I've tried to tell myself the night of the shooting was a one-off, a moment of high passion not to be repeated, there's always the darker side of the web to trawl for an alternative narrative. From the outlandish to the frankly ridiculous, every theory of what transpired between man and wife on that hot July night is out there.

There have even been possible sightings of Dom. In the wild, buying a can of Diet Coke of all things, or on a flight to LA.

I'd love it to be true. The thought of Dom by a pool, writing away, and then emailing me, two days after his escape, far more attractive than the reality of his body being stretchered out through the gates I just walked in through. But there have been no further emails, despite my many responses to that first one. His death a reality I must accept.

There's another popular theory out there about his death. That Dom, tortured with guilt about Wendy and the boys, begged Blythe to end his misery with a shot between the eyes. An act of mercy. But it's been thirty years since Wendy's drowning. Why now? Unless there was a trigger that brought it all back? A recrimination or revelation that made it imperative Blythe fire the gun? Because she did. She's said so.

Too many theories, but few facts.

My head is spinning as I look up from my laptop, Ernest looking down at me. I grip the edge of the desk and hold on. Squeezing fingers tight. It's always in these moments, when I might tip into the darkness, that I see my mother's face. Feel her breath on my cheek. The void waiting to take me down. I force myself back from the brink.

It's less than half an hour until supper; I should shower and change, dress my wounded knees and do something with my short but unruly hair. My limbs are stiff from my earlier fall. I slowly get up from Dom's desk and contemplate 'making an effort' as Ludo so delightfully put it, recalling then his hefty folder of rules.

I take the plastic binder outside on the veranda for a quick read before my shower, but I'm soon distracted by movement over by the pool. Or at least, I think it was.

I put the folder down, stepping off the veranda and then taking a detour off the path to head across the lawn towards the water. My scraped knees burn as I walk. I must look like the kid who fell off her bike and I kind of feel like her too. But a closer inspection of the pool area is definitely required. I glance towards the house to check for Ludo, although there's nothing in the folder about not wandering the grounds, at least not as far as I've read in my quick skim-through. The tower looms high above, casting a long shadow across the grass. I can't see anyone up there, but the sun is in my eyes and the tower is so crazy-tall, anyone could be watching me.

Another flutter of movement by the pool urges me on. The pool area is sunk into a dip, the blue surface of the water dancing with a thousand diamonds as I approach. Palms in pots beside it. A slice of Hollywood glamour in central London and yes, there's someone under the farthest parasol. A glimpse of tanned legs and cherry-tipped toes.

'Stop! Halt there! At once! Ms Wilde.' Ludo is running towards me from the house, arms flapping wildly. 'That's strictly off-limits! Halt, Ms Wilde. Halt!'

His frantic calls are ludicrous enough for me to smile in disbelief, his raspy voice raised at least an octave. I lift my hands in mock-surrender and duck my head in supplication, acting an exaggerated deference before returning my attention to the pool, just in time to witness a figure rising gracefully from the lounger.

Our film star is wearing a white one-piece swimsuit, cut high at the legs and low at the bust. Her legs are slim and bronzed, her shoulders square, clavicle pronounced. Every inch of exposed flesh glistens, her once-famous face obscured by the brim of an enormous straw hat and oversized dark sunglasses which are encrusted on the arms with a bejewelled logo, recognisably Chanel.

I should say something by way of a greeting, but I have no idea what. Blythe is so utterly impressive, perfectly backlit by the pool, the sun, and the blue sky, it feels wrong to break the spell. It's as if I'm watching her on screen, very much as I have been for many hours of late.

A smile, wide and welcoming stretches Blythe's glossed lips

across straight white teeth. It should be an encouragement, but it's very much not. For impressive as she is, I find her entirely chilling.

Maybe it's her stillness. Her expression behind the glasses, hard to read; her perfectly timed smile appealing and yet there's a detachment to it, as if she is performing this moment rather than living it. It reminds me of the smile in the photo with her stunt double, something disingenuous about that one too. The temperature drops until I have to resist a shiver, a cloud passing over the sun. Can Blythe really be so self-involved as to act out this first encounter? Surely there's a reality to this moment even an Oscar-winning actress cannot deny? She and I must be honest with one another. We need to earn mutual trust to get a decent story written. Some of it even needs to be the unvarnished truth.

'Ms Wilde,' she says, removing her sunglasses. 'So pleased we can finally meet.'

8

The fleeting moment in Blythe's company is interrupted by Ludo's arrival, still comical in his panicked trot across the lawn and stumble towards me, despite Blythe's overbearing presence. He then executes a neat extradition procedure as he shepherds me back across the grass with a degree of force.

I shrug him off. Blythe gone when I glance back. 'What is your problem, Ludo?'

'The first and perhaps most important rule in that folder, Ms Wilde,' Ludo tells me, breathless as he jabs a finger towards the abandoned folder of rules, 'is that you do not approach Blythe without invitation. *Express* invitation. Do you understand?'

He gasps for lost breath, hands on hips as we square up just shy of the veranda. His unflattering shade of black hair, surely dyed, reminds me of a Lego model, the taut pale skin like the terrible waxworks in the knock-off Madam Tussauds on the seafront, near Dad's flat. I stifle the urge to laugh. He's ludicrous.

'You find me amusing, Ms Wilde?'

'No, not particularly. I find you rude.'

My laptop is open on the desk inside. My research on the Hoppers left open. The glass door concealing nothing. Ludo is further from the desk than me, but there's a risk he might see it as he leaves. Although, I'm only doing my job.

'Ms Wilde? Are you listening?'

'Yes, sorry.'

'Good, because this is yet another infraction so I need you to understand that—'

'No, I don't understand, Ludo. Not at all. I've been invited here to work with Blythe on a memoir. Or that's what I thought. What exactly is the issue with me approaching my author to say I'm here and looking forward to getting started?'

'Did you not read the rules, Ms Wilde?' Ludo repeats, broken-record style. 'Page three, in particular, but the summary at the back covers the same.'

'Yes, I read them, well some of them, but I didn't sign up for them, Ludo. Not all of them, anyway.' Rules, especially the nonsensical kind, have always been problematic to me. 'I just don't get why I was invited to stay, if I'm to be treated like an inconvenience?'

'This is not about you, Ms Wilde. It's about Blythe Hopper and it's my job to protect her and her image.'

'From what? Me?'

Ludo looks over at the pool. 'She has a lot to contend with right now. The pool is her calm space. She will seek you out, not the other way around.'

It's a strange observation about the pool, considering that was where Dom is thought to have ended up after Blythe shot him. A dog walker spotted a plume of smoke from a bonfire, then heard raised voices followed by the single gunshot and a loud splash.

'Blythe didn't seem to mind me saying hello.'

'Well, Blythe is of course, always gracious,' Ludo concedes.

There's no sign of the white-suited bather as I rise up onto my toes and look over again, although she could be back on the lounger, out of sight, or maybe in the water?

The same water Dom's bloodied body floated in.

'What's the point of me being here if I can't talk to her?' I repeat, tiring of the circular conversation.

'This is Blythe's home, Ms Wilde,' Ludo reminds me. 'You are an invited guest, here to work, yes, but you must allow her some space. She's grieving, as I've said. And facing some grave concerns about her future. She deserves her privacy.'

'Of course, I do understand that, Ludo. But I don't appreciate being made to feel like a prisoner here too.' I gesture to the writing annexe behind me. 'This is not what I expected.'

'You find our hospitality lacking?' Ludo asks, his lips pressed so tight they're bloodless, a straight line of censure. 'Perhaps we should call it quits and abandon this folly before it's begun?'

'Is that what Blythe wants, or just you? You've suggested it twice since I arrived.'

There's a long pause before Ludo ends the stand-off. 'Please, keep a respectful distance in future.'

'A respectful distance? What does that mean?'

'You are at liberty to walk the path up to the house before supper each evening. Ask me if you need anything else. I can run through the folder with you if you'd like?'

'So you want me to stay in there all day until Blythe wants to see me?' Ludo shrugs. 'Fine, but it's like an oven in there, a fan of some sort would be good. We all need one of those.'

Ludo doesn't laugh at my attempt at a joke, not even a smile. The funny walk as he retreats amuses me at least, until he turns back and shouts, 'Ten minutes until supper, and please, do make an effort!'

* * *

At five-past-six, changed into my favourite outfit – a smiley face T-shirt tucked into the waistband of a knee-length floral skirt, and the flip-flops I'd thankfully packed as a back-up to the lost sandals – I lock the annexe door and head towards the house. The awful rabbit's foot fob stowed in the skirt's handy hip pocket, a fresh notebook tucked under my elbow, pen inside, as I watch my phone like a hawk, hoping for those bars of signal.

I applied a dab of eye make-up using my hand mirror as a final thought after the dribble of a shower, but I wiped off the unwise choice of pink lipstick. I need to hang on to a sense of who I am if I'm to make it out of here in one piece, and that is not bright-pink lipstick. I don't normally wear any make-up at all but I suppose it's an attempt at false amour, or maybe because Blythe, even by the pool, was impeccably presented. I have the feeling that despite that glossy smile, or because of it, Blythe's formidable reputation will make her a force to be reckoned with, and that means standing my ground to win her trust. Marnie Wilde, ghostwriter extraordinaire: without the badly applied lipstick, but still plenty of attitude.

There's the hint of a breeze now, the fabric of my skirt swishing around my exposed knees so the grazes chafe as I walk the path to the house, phone in hand.

Stepping off the gravel to cut the corner via the lawn, in another pleasing defiance of Ludo's ludicrous rules, I pause and inspect the grazes, dabbing at the right one with a licked finger. It's looking a bit weepy, but I can't worry about that now, the satisfying ping of notifications drawing my attention back to my phone. I delete the spam and check on socials, making the most of the returned signal. Jake is having, as always, a truly fabulous LA day, his smile erupting and triggering something painful in my chest that threatens tears. But I do feel a little better for the connection to the outside world and also at the prospect of starting the work I'm contracted to do. The memoir will be a good focus and I've always been able to compartmentalise professional and personal. Well... mostly.

I tuck my phone away in my skirt as I near the patio door and quickly check my appearance in the glass, noting the lock has been sheared off. A break in, maybe?

My skirt is looking good at least. A patchwork of fabrics, it was made by my mother, or so I have deduced from the hand stitching and lack of labels. Dad remained tight-lipped when I found the bag of clothes in the back of his wardrobe. I was twelve and although I fancied myself on the cusp of womanhood, I still enjoyed playing dress-up in Mum's handmade items. I'm not sure why he kept her stuff all those years, and the collection had soon gone after he found me literally walking in her shoes, but I smuggled the skirt into my room and stuffed it behind the wardrobe. It was far too pretty for the dustbin. No way I was giving it up. It's one of the few things of hers I have even seen, let alone own. I've saved it for a special occasion and this has to be it. It's not every day, after all, you meet a Hollywood star. I smooth the fabric and pull at the slightly too-tight waistband. I've always fancied my mother to be my absent protector, and now Dom is with us too.

I believe we have a connection in common: your mother, Katherine Wilde. I am searching for her and if you are too, we need to talk.

The knowledge he was looking for her too is an enormous encouragement but something I must, for now at least, keep close to my heart and, as warned, undisclosed at all costs. I take a deep breath and with notebook and pen in hand, I open the broken door, stepping into what appears to be the seventh circle of hell.

Molten tomato, thick with the scent of burnt garlic, bubbles like lava on the hob as Ludo, apron spattered like a crime scene, stirs the spitting pot. But the carnage caused by Ludo's cooking isn't my only concern. I hadn't noticed earlier, rushing to keep up as he led the way out to the annexe, but the expansive kitchen is basically... well, it's filthy. The kind of uncleanliness that puts a previously starving person straight off their food.

'Ms Wilde, spot on time!' Ludo congratulates me. Then he pauses, scanning me up and then down before he adds, 'Although I see you have ignored my advice, yet again.'

I look down at myself. 'What?'

'Make yourself at home, Ms Wilde,' he instructs, shaking his head. 'Blythe will join us presently.'

He returns to his stirring and I put my notebook on the table, taking in the full horror of the grubby kitchen. As far from the gleaming surfaces I'd seen in the online sales brochure as it's possible to imagine. This is weeks of neglect, or maybe months?

'Sit!' Ludo directs.

I do as I'm told, a whiff of over-ripe fruit from the bowl on the table, turning my stomach. An overflowing bin by the glass doors is adding to the rotting smell and the sink next to Ludo is full of dirty dishes, and matched if not bested by the disturbing level of ingrained dirt on the countertops, the sun hitting them to fully illuminate the tide of stains. I'm not even *that* fussy, but this is beyond a few days of sloppiness.

I suppose the month since Dom's death could account for the seismic drop in care and attention, and Harry said the staff were recently let go, but this feels indicative of something endemic. A poison eating away at the Hoppers even before the shooting, perhaps? What had changed between them to sour everything so badly, even their beautiful home?

'Can I do anything?' I offer. 'Maybe clear up a bit?'

'No thank you, Ms Wilde, I'm coping,' Ludo replies, his tone indicating I've been critical of him personally, although it was a well meant, if clumsy offer. 'Help yourself to some water,' he suggests. 'Blythe will be us momentarily'.

I move seats to the end chair, where the water jug and glasses are placed, ready to pour.

'Not there!' Ludo calls over. 'Blythe always sits at the head of the table.'

I return to where I was, facing the garden, and pull the water jug closer. The jug, in the shape of a glugging fish, looks clean, the contents clear as far as I can tell. Slices of cucumber and a head of mint dropped into the fish's open mouth. Oh, and a black bug is floating on the surface. I hook it out and squeeze it between my thumb and forefinger, wiping the mess on my T-shirt whilst Ludo's back is turned.

Beside the water jug is an ice bucket within which, aside from a gallon of crushed ice, is a bottle of champagne, the brand familiar, although I've never been fortunate enough to try it. Even Harry draws the line somewhere south of that price point. I take it as a positive sign. The luxury I'd anticipated, finally in evidence.

Ludo, his face as red as his pasta sauce, glances over and notices my interest. 'You're a wine connoisseur, Ms Wilde?'

'Not really, but I know enough to recognise this is not a cheap bottle of Prosecco.'

'Indeed. Blythe's request. I'll open it as soon as she joins us.'

'Lovely. Where is she?'

'On the phone with her agent. Some exciting career plans afoot, I believe.'

'Isn't talk of a comeback a bit optimistic given the circumstances?' I ask, concentrating then on pouring from the overly filled water jug, the thimble-sized glasses pretty but hard to aim at, especially when a theatrically projected voice startles me.

'What *circumstances* might they be, may I ask?'

The jug still in my hand, I turn, slowly.

Blythe Hopper is barely ten feet away, water pooling at my feet and on the floor beside me as my grasp slips. 'I'm so sorry, I didn't mean—' I set the jug down with trembling hands. 'I—'

'So what circumstances *did* you mean?' Blythe asks, steel-grey eyes pinioning me to the spot. 'And I'd like a straight answer. Now!'

9

Any preconceptions I've had of the moment I properly meet with the great Blythe Hopper and begin our great collaboration, are swept aside. My terror suspending and extending the silence as I struggle to explain my faux pas. Hoping the last few seconds can somehow be rewound and I am the erudite professional author I long to be in her company. A career woman at the top of her game. Equal to and even surpassing expectations, instead of a clumsy mess who has already spoken out of turn and spilt water everywhere. 'Ummm, err...'

'Now would be good!' Blythe repeats, arms crossed, nails tapping. 'I want to hear what you mean by that comment, as if we both don't know.'

The Oscar-winning actress is dressed in a surprisingly unfussy way: an expensive-looking crisp, white shirt, unbuttoned enough to expose a single diamond strung onto a slim chain, matching earrings pricking her earlobes. Each stone, if real, several carats. Her hair, shoulder length and glossy, in shades of flax and gold, is now lightly waved to frame her face which is perfectly made up, as if she were due on set. Her tanned legs are covered by white, cotton, close-fitting trousers, slender feet pushed into nude heels. A navy blazer, hardly needed in this heat, is draped around her shoulders. She removes the jacket and clothes the dining chair at the head of the table with it. Long-fingered hands grasping the back of the jacketed chair as she says, 'I asked, Marnie, what *circumstances* you were referring to that might make my career plans... how was it you phrased it... *optimistic*?'

'No, sorry, it's just... Hi, I'm—' I hold out a clammy palm. 'I'm Marnie. Marnie Wilde.'

'I know who you are and that's not what I asked. You consider my career beyond redemption? Talk of a comeback deluded?'

'Sorry, no, of course not, it's just—'

'*Just?* Just?'

'Nothing. I'm sorry.'

'Not the most auspicious of starts, is it?' Blythe observes, plucking an olive from a glazed blue tapas bowl Ludo sets down before her as she sits; a neatly choreographed move. She then snatches the tea towel from Ludo's shoulder as he retreats and tosses it at me. 'Maybe you could mop up the spillage, before one of us slips up?'

'Yes, of course. Apologies again. You startled me.' I drop to my skinned knees and mop the floor.

'I startled *you*?' Her voice is shrill above me. 'Gosh, how very strange when I live here and you are my guest.' She pops in another olive as I surface. 'These are the good ones, Ludo, well done. Did you go to the farm shop on the high street?'

He grins, which is a first. 'Of course.'

'It's crazy prices, I know, Ludo, but so worth it.'

'I didn't mean—' I begin as I fold the wet towel and take it to Ludo who throws it on the floor again.

'You didn't mean... you didn't mean...' Blythe tuts. 'Have some backbone, Marnie. We both know what you meant. And Ludo tells me you arrived over an hour late this afternoon, with alcohol on your breath and looking like you'd been in some kind of a bar fight. Sit!'

'I was a tad late, yes,' I say, sitting on the edge of my chair. I reach for an olive and she pulls the tapas bowl towards her, out of my reach.

'And then you see fit to cast aspersions on my career plans,' Blythe says, sucking in another plump green olive. 'Before we have properly made our acquaintance?'

'I would have very much liked to earlier, but—'

'You arrived late and drunk and covered in blood!' Blythe roars, spitting out an olive stone which lands on the table. 'And tone down the perfume in future; I can barely breathe!' She holds a splayed hand to her face. 'Cheap stuff is so cloying.'

'It wasn't cheap!'

Ludo has his back turned, ostensibly stirring pasta into the pot of sauce, but I note the sly grin at my expense as he comes over and picks up the olive stone and lobs it towards the bin.

'I do apologise for the slight lateness, Blythe, but,' I reply, tilting my chin up. 'I certainly wasn't drunk or covered in blood. I actually tripped running for the Tube, but I'm fine, thanks for asking.'

Ludo raises an eyebrow at Blythe, but she doesn't seem to notice.

'OK, enough of the excuses,' Blythe says. 'Although another might be in order for that skirt. Ludo, did you not explain that I am very visually stimulated?'

Ludo nods then takes a long look at me and snorts. An actual snort.

'I like what I'm wearing,' I tell them both, smoothing down Mum's beautiful sewing. 'I'm sorry you don't, but you don't have to be rude about it.'

'I'm messing with you, Marnie,' Blythe says, and spits out a stone before popping in another of the olives. 'Can't you tell?'

I'm barely holding on to my temper but I resist the urge to cry; there's something cruel in those grey eyes that's hungry for fresh meat. If she wants a fight to amuse her, she can have one, but not yet. And not about Mum's beautiful skirt. It's perfection.

'Anyway, whatever you think of me and my fashion sense, I can assure you I am more than up to the job.'

'Yes, that's what that dreadful woman at the publisher's said. What was her name?' Blythe snaps her fingers and frowns.

'You mean Priscilla, my editor?'

Blythe looks at me blankly. 'Maybe... I'm not sure I believed a word she said,' she adds, before popping in another olive. 'Struck me as rather a false woman.'

'Priscilla's highly skilled, and dedicated to making your incredible life a bestselling memoir, as am I.'

'If you say so,' Blythe replies, affecting nonchalance despite the obvious spark my compliment has lit. 'But it was when—' She clicks her fingers again.

'Priscilla?'

'Yes, darned woman kept telling me... *Marnie is unreliable, Marnie is a mess*, then suddenly, you're the best ghost there is... Very mixed messages and of course, we all know your recent history with that so-called celebrity's husband. What was that dreadful TV program she was in called again, Ludo, something about dating?'

Ludo's shoulders shrug as he sloppily ladles pasta into bowls.

'If it helps to reassure you, Blythe, I can share some of the other names I've worked with, confidentially of course. But Priscilla is very discerning. She wouldn't take a risk with a prestigious name like yours, and neither will I.'

'I think we both know the woman was desperate to get me to

sign up to someone,' Blythe replies. 'And if you don't mind, I'll be the judge of your suitability.'

The bounce-back of my charm offensive smarts, but I get the impression Blythe is enjoying the verbal sparring match.

'Well, we both signed a contract as I understand it... so...' I shrug, chancing a grin as I stretch again for an olive.

There's a long beat, then Blythe pushes the bowl towards me. She's almost twice my age, and yet not old, just a different generation, and imposing as fuck, no doubt about that. But I actually quite like her. Although she's terrifying. And I enjoy a challenge as much as she appears to. It's good not to be a pushover with such a strong personality.

'Shall we have a glass of fizz now?' Blythe asks, lifting the dripping champagne bottle from the ice bucket and into Ludo's outstretched hands. 'Ludo, best glasses!'

With practised ease, her business manager/chef/pocket-size security guard and chief sneak, pops the cork and pours for Blythe first, and then grudgingly for me. The gold-rimmed flutes shimmer in the evening glow of a sunny day as we lift them and clink across the wide table.

'Let me just say, Blythe, it's an honour and a pleasure to be entrusted with—'

'Oh, for goodness' sake, Marnie, spare us both the bullshit!' Blythe interjects. 'This is transactional. Let's at least be honest about that much.'

'I don't agree.'

'Well, let me illuminate you. I know you're on a final chance from your editor and your screenwriting project is dead in the water.' Blythe sips her champagne as my mouth falls open to protest, but she's not done yet. 'You're behind on your rent and you haven't had a relationship in months, not since a handsome screenwriter who appears to have moved to LA to get away from you and now very much moved on. You're a mess, Marnie Wilde. A solid gold fuck-up.'

I slam my glass down on the table. 'That's personal and none of your—'

'So you're not denying it?' Blythe replies, smirking. 'Ludo found you on social media and put it all together, but pretty spot on by the looks of things.'

I stare at Ludo, who has paused by the table, pasta bowls in hand. 'That's a gross invasion of my privacy.'

Ludo has the decency to look embarrassed as he attempts a pained smile, but Blythe remains unrepentant.

'Is it?' she asks. 'Really? I mean, haven't you researched me and my husband? And before you answer that, Ludo saw your screen earlier.'

'Yes, of course, but you're my author; I need to know your story.'

'And isn't it also perfectly reasonable to check on someone I'm welcoming into my home? Bit like a those dating apps you're on? Might want to tone down the message a bit, or so I hear.'

Oh God.

'There was no need to snoop into my personal life like that, it has no relevance,' I tell Ludo as he puts the pasta in front of us.

'I think there is every need,' Blythe replies, her face now caught in a shaft of sunlight. 'I've granted you access to me and my home. I need to trust you, Marnie Wilde. And believe it or not, I'm not judging you. Not one bit.'

I sit back, feeling light-headed. 'And do you? Trust me?'

She sticks her perfectly straight nose in the air, highlighting a slight uptick by the nostrils. Forehead smooth, cheekbones raised. A version of beauty that must be a combination of top knife work and genetics. Either way, I am inferior, in every which way. Outgunned. Outsmarted. Out of ideas, if my challenge backfires.

I smooth Mum's skirt across my lap, Blythe looking at it again, a question in her frown.

'Mum made it,' I blurt out, daring her to be mean again. 'And I love it.'

Blythe leans back in her chair, contemplative, but no further comment is forthcoming. Then she surprises me, reaching out. I recoil, picking up the champagne glass to cover my reaction, but she only wants the bottle, lifting it by the neck, dripping, a chunky gold watch revealed beneath the turned back cuff of her shirt as she offers me a top-up. A mock and exaggerated shiver as the melting ice runs up her wrist, a charming move which makes me smile despite myself.

'To a successful collaboration?' Blythe suggests, the refilled champagne mesmerising as I regard her through it; a fuzzy version of something chilling but captivating. Like a jump-scare movie or a terrifying rollercoaster: heady and yet addictive.

'Actually, no. To the ugly truth!' Blythe announces, correcting herself and raising her glass to mine. 'May it all come out in the end.' Ludo's stare ignored as we clink glasses again.

10

Despite a rocky start with Blythe – affording her ample opportunity to put me well and truly in my place – I feel myself relax a little as the delectable champagne slips down. I've passed the initiation ceremony, I think. Not with flying colours, but I have redeemed myself.

Ludo places a bowl of pasta on the table for himself, and despite the lack of food hygiene, I look forward to tucking into mine. Blythe uses her napkin to wipe her fork clean and I follow suit. Ludo frowning across the table at me, but not her.

I'd hoped 'supper' would be a chance to chat, informally, but Blythe then picks up a remote and points it to the television on the wall behind me, the dramatic tones of the evening news blaring out dire warnings of drought and heatstroke.

'Wow!' I say, turning to glance at images of 'London Burning' in the heatwave. 'Those climate change deniers can't argue against this, surely?'

My comment is ignored so I tuck into a surprisingly good puttanesca – Ludo's speciality I'm advised by Blythe – then I listen to the back and forth between my fellow diners. It's an odd dynamic, more domestic than business. Puts me in mind of a married couple, me their disregarded child as they discuss some damp in an upstairs bathroom.

Blythe pushes her bowl away, her food untouched, and points the remote at the TV again, switching off the weather report partway through. The only sounds the birdsong outside and Ludo's slow but audible chewing. A chance, finally, to talk.

'Lovely evening,' I say, starting small.

Blythe fishes in her jacket pocket and pulls out a packet of cigarettes and a lighter, which she throws onto the table, startling me so I drop my filled fork into my lap, a blob of sauce tracking down Mum's skirt. *Damn!*

'You're very jumpy, Marnie,' she observes, lighting up as I rub at the orange stains with my white napkin.

'I'm fine, just...' I reluctantly give up on the mess and look up. 'Sorry, it's just such an honour meeting you.'

Blythe's clamped lips curve in a smile around the cigarette. She's far from immune to flattery, which is good. I can use that to my advantage.

'You're a fan of my work, Marnie?'

'Oh yes. Loved *Affairs of the Heart*.'

'Not my only role,' she replies, the smile gone.

'Sorry, that must be annoying?'

'No, I get it,' she replies, blowing smoke in my face. 'It's natural that's the one everyone references. I won an Academy Award for it.'

We run sweepstakes in our ghostwriters WhatsApp group about 'the first mention' of the slebs' biggest claim to fame. The winner so far was a one-hit wonder who referenced their dreadful earwormer in ten seconds. Shame I can't post in the group whilst I'm here. It would be a nice antidote to all this fawning.

'I'd love to see the Oscar statuette,' I reply, meaning it. 'Where do you keep it, in the toilet?'

'All in good time,' Blythe tells me. 'Ludo, will you top up Marnie's glass?'

Ludo sighs, then pushes the bottle towards me. I don't need asking twice, although I'm conscious Blythe's glass is still half-full and Ludo is only drinking water.

'Forty-four degrees tomorrow,' Blythe says, circling back to the weather as she smokes. 'Forty-four! That's like being back in LA, but without the smog.'

'Did you enjoy it there?' I ask, wiping again at Mum's skirt, the corner of my napkin surreptitiously dipped in my water glass. I rub hard, but it's not looking good, the marks stubborn, but at least the fabric is a print, and mainly red, although the largest blob of tomato sauce landed on a pure white flower.

'Enjoy Hollywood or the climate in LA?' Blythe replies, exhaling my way.

'The whole thing,' I reply, suppressing a cough.

'The land of dreams can be a cruel and unforgiving place,' she replies, tapping ash into her uneaten food.

The Hollywood I experienced in my brief time there last summer was seedier than I'd expected – homeless people living out of tents beneath billboards advertising billion-dollar movies – but I met some enthusiastic people who had the best of intentions. Or appeared to. But ultimately, I was shut out. Which did feel cruel. And unforgiving.

'I quite liked Hollywood,' I reply. 'And I found it exciting.'

'Oh, yes, it has its allure, clearly, but it's toxic beneath the smiles and promises.' Blythe replies, blowing more smoke my way. 'The best way to survive out there is to believe nothing and no one, Marnie. And be prepared to look after yourself.'

'Care to elaborate on your personal experience?' I reply, still battling the urge to cough as I crack open my fresh notebook and click on my pen, wishing the broken door was open enough to allow in a cleansing breeze. For this is it: the start of the process.

Blythe looks down at her bowl and taps more ash onto her uneaten pasta.

'You're not hungry?' I ask, looking at Ludo for some kind of reaction to the trashing of his food, his expression unchanged as he meets mine.

'I have been on a diet so long, I don't know how else to be, Marnie,' Blythe says, looking up.

'You don't need to be on a diet!' I tell her, ignoring Ludo's warning look. 'Your figure is incredible.'

'And that is precisely because I am.' She looks at her ash-covered food, thoughtful. 'When I arrived in Hollywood I was advised in no uncertain terms that if I were to stand any chance of getting representation or auditions, I needed to shed at least twenty pounds and hit the gym hard. It's been a life-long journey ever since.'

'Oh my God, that's—'

'Quite,' Blythe responds and exhales a curl of smoke. 'But you know, we accepted it back then. It was the early nineties. Different times, although... I don't know if it's any easier now, but I do hear more woman are standing up to it.'

'Yes, indeed. Is that why you left Hollywood in the end?' I ask, draining my refilled glass. I need to slow down on the alcohol, but it's so delicious, and the buzz is pleasant, and emboldening, unlike Ludo's stare, which I ignore. 'Because of the body image stuff?'

Blythe looks out at the garden. 'There were several reasons we came back to the UK, that wasn't one of them. We gave Hollywood too many years as it was.'

'Reasons such as?' I ask.

Ludo is sending me another withering look. I don't know what his problem is; I'm only doing my job.

'We will get to all that in due course,' Blythe replies. Then ignoring me to return to a previous discussion with Ludo. 'So, what thoughts about getting the gardener back? The grass is so long now.'

I jot a few things down in my notebook from the short exchange about Hollywood, whilst Ludo and Blythe debate whether the cost of help can be justified. The answer still being a firm no from Ludo who seems to be in charge of a very limited if unspecified household budget. The question is then whether they should continue to use the sprinklers to water the lawns, or turn the timer off and let nature take its course. The huge house and grounds are slowly descending into wrack and ruin, although the lack of funds is never directly mentioned, I guess on account of my presence, but also because of Blythe's declared disinterest in the 'tiresome' details. Ludo then offers to cut the grass himself and she tells him he better make a good job of it. The issue of a water shortage in the UK ignored. Then, as if on cue, the sprinklers kick in, dousing the lush grass.

Blythe returns her attention me, the cigarette ground into her food as she says, 'The lawns will be last to go, no doubt. The last to go...'

'The last of what?' I ask, but I'm ignored again as she stares into the distance. Ludo also avoids my questioning gaze as he chomps on a speared tube of pasta, his eyes cast down.

Being disregarded is all part of being a ghost, and often advantageous. If I could melt into the scenery, I would. The fly on the wall, although there are already too many of those buzzing around us and the food. But whilst I still have Blythe's company, if not full attention, establishing a few ground rules for our collaboration would be helpful. I have the opening chapters of the memoir to deliver 'ASAP' to Priscilla. Although my editor advised me they don't need to be beautiful, just *juicy*.

'So,' I say, clearing my throat, a piece of pasta regurgitated that I swallow down. 'How would you like to play this, Blythe?'

'Play what?' she asks, her gaze still towards the pool.

'The memoir,' I reply, trying not to sound like I'm stating the obvious. 'It would be good to make a start on the first interview. Maybe right now, if you—'

'Tonight, you mean?' Blythe snaps her attention back to me.

'Nice and relaxed, just a chat.' I laugh, although it's forced.

Ludo stands, the frown he wears more purposeful than ever, although I'm not sure I'm the cause of his annoyance this time. Blythe shakes her head at him as he removes the bowls, a silent exchange that I assume references an earlier conversation I wasn't privy to. He drops the crockery into the sink, a clatter that cannot have done the white bowls any good. Then his funny walk takes him out the kitchen at pace.

'Ludo has perfected the art of being rather annoyed with me about everything of late,' Blythe explains. 'But as I have told him many times, I decide what happens from here, not him. Well, as much as I can.'

'What's his objection to the memoir?'

'It's nothing personal, Marnie. Ludo has no beef with you; why should he?'

'No, of course not.' I close my notebook. 'I didn't mean that. But he's not happy you're talking to me, that's obvious. In fact, he told me he thinks it's a terrible idea.'

'What you need to understand is that Ludo is very protective of me. It's been a difficult time and he sees himself as my guardian angel and manager all wrapped into one feisty little permanently cross package of substandard service.' She laughs and I do too. 'I shouldn't be mean, Marnie. If he could whisk me away from all this, he would. But we are where we are. That's what I keep telling him. No one knows what's around the corner. We have to make the most of what time we have and I intend to do just that by righting a few past wrongs. Starting with talking to you.'

'Of course, that will be my honour, and I promise we will take this entirely at your pace. I normally start by—'

'Let me just explain how I see this working,' Blythe says, reaching again for the cigarettes.

'Yes, of course, great.'

She clamps another cigarette between glossed lips, the pucker unflattering, her lips feathering, but I also see the younger version. The one I've watched on screen many times, and now most clearly recognisable around those grey eyes, despite a few wrinkles. The playfulness, the knowing way she looks from me to the cigarette as her thumb clicks on the lighter.

She draws deep then looks past me again, towards the garden. It's all a performance, of course, but she's an Oscar-winning actress. And regardless of her comment, *Affairs of the Heart* was by far her most notable role: bit parts all she'd had before she went to Hollywood, and playing a 'tough mum' in a continuing drama all she got after she came back to the UK. Not exactly a stellar career, other than that Oscar winning role as a broken actress falling into prostitution and addiction.

Her love interest in *Affairs of the Heart* was played by an actor who, like many famous men of that era, has since toppled a long way from former grace, something else I intend to ask her about. The *#MeToo* stuff will add a modern element to the memoir, making it, as Priscilla loves to say, 'relevant'. Although it's far too early in our collaboration to broach anything as hard-hitting with Blythe. Her less than happy experience of Hollywood may have been hinted at, and it's certainly the prize Priscilla expects me to return with, along with the 'full deets' about Dom's murder, but for now, it's best I keep things light and, as we say in the ghosting world, *Let the sleb talk*.

'The thing is, Marnie,' Blythe continues, expecting me to pick up the thread I've dropped in my introspection. 'My priorities have changed since Dom's death. That's why I finally agreed to go ahead with this memoir.'

I snap back at the mention of Dom's name.

'I can't elucidate it exactly,' Blythe continues, blowing smoke towards the open patio door, where flies are buzzing in and out. 'But things have changed of course, profoundly.'

'What did your husband think about the idea of a memoir?'

'Dom hated the idea,' she responds, somewhat tersely.

'Really? Is that why you turned it down before?'

'God, no! I make my own choices, Marnie. But now I need to honour his memory.'

'Yes, of course.'

'Dom gave up everything for me, Marnie,' Blythe says, as if I've disagreed. 'His children, his home, his dreams. He has supported me through dark times as well as the good and whatever has come to pass between us in recent weeks, whatever betrayals, that does not change the fact I loved him and he loved me.'

It's a compelling performance, tears welling in her eyes.

'Right, yes, of course, betrayals?'

'Yes, Marnie. I have been betrayed many times. But Dom's memory is my focus. And he must be yours too.'

He is, very much so, but I can't declare that as yet, and as far as the memoir goes, no one is interested in Dom, other than the circumstances surrounding his murder. Blythe was and still is the star of this show. Her face on the cover. Her name below the title. The memoir has to be all about her. Including the *juicy* bits.

As if she's read my thoughts, Blythe adds, 'But let us not forget we need to also fuck the Hollywood patriarchy along our way, which has shat on us both from a great height, has it not, Marnie Wilde?'

'More than up for that!' I tell her, grinning.

She smiles and asks me for the ashtray, a heavy onyx one which is buried amongst a pile of magazines at the far end of the table. The scent of stale tobacco unpleasant as I stretch for it. I push it just short of her reach, making her stretch too. Maybe I'm better at the game-playing than I give myself credit for, an almost imperceptible nod as she rises from her seat to retrieve it, but again, it seems I've underestimated her as she says, 'The male lead, in your TV series that never happened...' Blythe clicks her fingers. 'Remind me, what was his name?'

I supply the arsehole's stage name, two syllables spitted out.

'Ah yes, that's right,' she says. 'Typical arrogant bag of shit. Pretty face and no talent and a wandering dick I hear.' She taps the cigarette, the ash falling on top of yesterday's filters. A chain-smoker. Which isn't ideal as I'm likely to be in her company a lot over the coming days, my dislike of passive smoke born of necessity, not preference. The doctor's advice is to avoid all stimulants, and clearly not heeded as far as alcohol goes, but I haven't touched a cigarette since I was fifteen when a few puffs sent me straight down to the ground, my first proper black out. I lean away from the second-hand nicotine and try not to inhale, the smell starting to make me feel weird.

'These powerful, potent men,' Blythe continues, exhaling . 'They still think they can ride roughshod over us with no consequence to their actions.'

'Yes, it's not great,' I agree. 'Wasn't your co-star in *Affairs of the Heart* another of that ilk?'

I'm struggling to dredge up his name and specific misdemeanour from the lake of research I've done. I flick through my notebook as if I might find it there amongst the blank pages. I've drunk too much champagne, my mind foggy with heat and carbs, my head spinning. I pull my chair back and fan myself with my napkin.

'Oh, he was a sweetheart,' Blythe tells me, waving away any potential rebuttal – or maybe just one of the many flies. Certainly not the smoke, oblivious to my aversion even as I cough. 'It was the system that broke him,' she says. 'You can't deny someone their true self and then expect it to turn out any other way than it did.'

I remember the details now. Not exactly a sweetheart. More a predatory paedophile.

'It's like the royals being told who to marry,' Blythe continues. 'You cannot repress true feelings.'

'Propositioning underage boys isn't exactly comparable to a royal divorce, if that's what you meant?'

She shakes her head as if she has no comprehension of my meaning. 'So tell me about this screenplay of yours, Marnie.' She leans nearer, cigarette in hand. 'I don't pretend to understand the concept, but it was almost at the point of being made, was it not?'

'Yes,' I lean away. 'Frustratingly close to cameras rolling when the news broke.'

'That's rough.' She sits back in her chair, offering me a cigarette as an afterthought, which I decline. She taps the packet on one end and then the other, round and round. 'Sad to think so little has changed.'

'Indeed.'

'Dom was an immensely talented screenwriter, but I'm sure you know that already.'

'Yes.' I swallow. 'I had heard.'

Heard? What am I talking about? I swallow again, but Blythe is in her own thoughts.

'His success was sadly all too short-lived,' she continues. 'But show business isn't a fair business, is it?' She looks at me.

'No, it isn't. So Dom was treated badly by Hollywood?'

Blythe drops the cigarette packet and looks directly at me. '*Dom?* Sounds as if you knew him?'

'No, sadly not,' I reply, annoyed I've sounded so familiar. 'But I'm a bit of a fan of his work. *The Man* was incredible.'

'Indeed.' Blythe regards me with an intensity I could do without, my face burning.

'So, tell me the secret to such a long and happy marriage?' I ask, changing the subject. 'I mean, for Hollywood it was quite remarkable, wasn't it, that you lasted almost thirty years, before his... before...' I trail off, having wandered again into dangerous territory.

'Yes, it was,' Blythe says, taking a final drag before grinding the cigarette into the over-filled ashtray. 'Quite remarkable.'

'So, what would you say was the key to sticking together?' I persist, unable to change tack from Dom, the hole I'm digging getting so deep, I'm about to fall straight down it.

Blythe is smiling, relishing my discomfort as she blows out the last drag of retained smoke before she replies.

'I'd say my tactic has been to ruthlessly dispose of everyone who has ever got in my way, Marnie. That's the key to success, not only in marriage, but in life. Take out your rivals. Swiftly and without compunction.'

11

Blythe throws her head back and laughs heartily, and for longer than is comfortable.

'I'm joking, Marnie, of course I am. You should see your face!'

I manage a smile, wishing in a way I'd accepted a cigarette. It would be a distraction from her comment, although completely inadvisable. I'd almost certainly black out. I reach for my champagne glass but it's empty. 'Is Ludo coming back to join us tonight?'

Blythe shrugs, noncommittal.

I'd assumed Ludo lived in, but I don't know that for sure and as the possibility of his return recedes, the hope he's around somewhere becomes stronger. It won't be dark for a while yet, but the isolation will surely intensify as night falls. Just Blythe and me here, together. Cut off from the rest of humanity.

I'd like to take a breather, stretch my legs, get some air, but there's no exit strategy that doesn't feel rude and I'm here to work. I consult my notes, searching for inspiration, Dom's name still standing out.

'What was he like – your husband?'

Blythe lifts her eyes to mine. 'I thought you knew all about him? Such a fan!'

'I've been researching you both, it does feel that way a bit, but of course I didn't,' I reply, hoping that is explanation enough. It's true, after all, I never met him, and as far is Blythe is concerned, I have no connection to Dom whatsoever. 'What was he like?' I ask, pushing away the recollection of Dom's email which appears again, fully realised.

'He was very handsome,' Blythe tells me, misty-eyed. 'Tall, dark, a man in his absolute prime,' she enthuses, her face lighting up. 'Brooding, successful, charismatic. I suppose I should have spotted the signs sooner.'

'The signs?'

'His depression. Anxiety too, *maybe*. And he was a heavy drinker.'

'Oh, I had no idea. That's so sad. Did he get professional help?'

She shakes her head. 'He barely talked to me about it, let alone anyone else. He was, ironically, always a closed book.'

'Why do you think that was?'

'Saw it as a weakness, I guess. Dom was old-fashioned. Didn't believe in therapy, or happy pills. He self-medicated: booze, bit of recreational drugs when we were in LA, nothing much. Everyone did it. No real harm. But after the move back here, his drinking, and his mood swings worsened. He certainly wasn't the man I married.'

'And who was the man you married?' I ask, looking up from my frantic scribbles. The contract stated no intrusive recordings, so I haven't got my phone out my skirt pocket. but I don't want to miss a sly smile or a raised eyebrow. Those *tells* often say more than the words themselves.

'Dom was a beautiful man, Marnie. With beautiful dreams. But life stripped him of those. Made him bitter and resentful, full of regret.' She looks up from the ashtray where she's rested a lit cigarette. 'I won't sugar-coat the past, Marnie. It's all part of mine and Dom's story and I shall be honest with you. But jealousy is never a pretty thing, is it?'

She twists her champagne flute, still half full, and smiles, clearly satisfied with her carefully worded, and quite possibly rehearsed lines.

I try to reciprocate the smile, but she has denied me the chance to ever meet Dom and ask him why he was looking for my mother. And yet she is claiming the moral high ground on account of her honesty and his envy. Not a trace of remorse, or even culpability for his death. Talk of honouring her husband's memory is mere lip-service to her narcissistic desire for attention. It's unsurprising, and yet hard to accept when she pulled the trigger on a beautiful man's life. The man I feel a deepening connection and allegiance to.

'So I assume there's a quid pro quo here?' Blythe asks.

'Sorry, in terms of what?' I ask, startled by her question. Surely she can't know the other reason I'm here? All I did was claim to be a fan of Dom's work, a very minor slip.

'In terms of the memoir, what else?' Blythe says.

'Right, yes, of course.'

'You're here for the scraps of gossip people will buy the book for, I assume, because they're vultures,' Blythe observes. 'Picking over a carcass, am I right?'

The analogy is jarring, but accurate. 'Yes, we will need to address recent events, in a tasteful way, of course, but I want to talk about your time in Hollywood, and your return to the UK. There's a lot to unpack in such an illustrious and eventful life.'

'Sure, but it's not going to be easy for me, Marnie. There are painful truths that I will share, but in my own way and my own time.'

'Yes, of course, Blythe, everything at our pace. I am sensitive to your grief, but as you said yourself, we have to make the best use of the time we have together.'

She fixes me with dry eyes that now look like charcoal in the evening light. 'This is a house of hope, Marnie, always has been, always will be. We deal with what comes but we never give up. Is that clear?'

'Yes, it is,' I reply, the first to break eye contact. 'Sorry.'

'Good! So let's see what comes, shall we? Both in terms of my future as well as the memoir. We must think positively. That's what I always told Dom. Or tried to.'

Fragments of the email float in the space between us again. The man here for a moment, then lost in the miasma as Blythe exhales. I blink, my eyes tired and sore from smoke. If he were alive, he'd have answered my replies. He'd have found a way to meet me, wouldn't he? But he's gone. Because of her.

'What was Dom working on, before he died?'

'How do you know he was writing again?' Blythe asks.

'Ludo said he was working hard, in the writing annexe.'

'Ah, I see. Well, yes, he was, but he was always his own worst critic. Fairly typical for a writer I guess. Fragile and yet full of ego.' Blythe's challenge is sharp.

'Yes, that's true, I guess, we are a mixed-up bunch.'

'Exactly!' she replies, jabbing the air with a pointed finger and leaning towards me. 'And I get it. The process, I mean. It's hard, mining the emotional truth, but that's always the seed. Take the kernel and then change the dates, names, set it on the moon or down a mine, in the past or future, but it's the truth that echoes, isn't it? *Boom!*'

I jump as she mimes an explosion with an outstretched hand. 'Right, yes, and I'd love to read some of his recent work. Was there a script in development I could take a look at?'

Blythe shrugs. 'I think I shall have to leave it there for tonight,

Marnie. I'm exhausted. Don't worry about locking the kitchen door after you; it's broken.'

Blythe stubs out the latest cigarette then takes the blazer from the chair and drapes it around her shoulders, commenting on how it's getting chilly although it really isn't, the heat still heavy. She places a hand to the back of the chair and grips on, making eye contact. I get the feeling I'm about to be the recipient of a carefully prepared exit speech.

'It's very empowering, isn't it, Marnie? Being young. All of life's adventures ahead of you. Everything to play for. Mistakes don't feel quite so final. Risks worth taking because you still have time, but none of us know how long we have. The clock is always ticking.' She walks towards the door, the one that leads back into the house, but then pauses and says, 'I think we both know I don't have the luxury of time. I'll see you in the morning, Marnie. Let's spend the whole day together, make the most of it. Sleep well.'

* * *

I linger a while at the kitchen table, making the most of a flicker or two of Wi-Fi signal and brighter light, downing Blythe's half glass of champagne as I check my socials.

Jake, so his Insta story advises, was at a Hollywood party last night. With *her*. The model slash whatever. I torture myself long and hard but resist a comment or a message. That's progress, of sorts. Isn't it?

The mosquitoes make a dinner of my ankles as they follow me down the gravel path towards the writing annexe, a harvest moon rising above The Towers as I wave the bugs away. A light comes on at the top of the tall tower behind me, bright as a beacon. A figure up there, moving around. I raise a hand but the light goes off. A silver spider's web stretching between the annexe door and the shadowy inside as I unlock it and rush inside.

I type up my notes at Dom's desk, Ernest looking down with what I interpret as approval. The darkness complete by the time I'm done, but I'm far too hyped from meeting Blythe to sleep. Questions and insects humming. And it's so hot in here.

What I could do with is another drink. Something stronger to settle me. Should have packed whisky not perfume. More in keeping with Ernest, and Dom. Although Ludo would have no doubt taken the opportunity to berate me even more if it had been alcohol I reeked of rather than the Aqua di Palma perfume Jake got me for Christmas, a parting gift.

I pour a glass of fizzy water and prop open the door with a convenient pebble, noticing the initials DFH are scratched on the underside. The Towers is now a homogenous outline of grey from my vantage point on the annexe's veranda. I can't work out how I feel being here, but as a writer, I guess I should try.

The best way I can describe it is I'm split into two parts. The part that wants to run from Blythe's company whenever I'm in it, her claims of only wanting the truth and the sick jokes about eliminating rivals distasteful and at times utterly chilling. And then there's the other part of me. The part that cannot leave until I have answers about Dom's search for my mother. The lack of clarity makes me restless, even as physical exhaustion slumps me down onto the outdoor sofa, eyes cast to a starry sky.

I have to know what Dom's plans were and why he involved me, that much remains clear, but then I realise something else. Something unsettling.

I've assumed until this evening that his interest in my mother was well-meant, even loving, but maybe I should question that. He was a depressive drunk, embittered and possibly controlling. I can't rule out the possibility he intended my mother harm, although what reason could there be for that?

Maybe he found Katherine Wilde after he sent the email and he'd told Blythe he was leaving her for my mother? Although how can that be possible when the email was sent after his death? How can any of it be possible?

I grab my notebook from the desk and return to the veranda, going over everything Blythe said, searching for different or extra meaning, then compiling a list of questions. As much as anything, to empty my mind of them.

Was Dom in love with my mother?

Does Blythe know that?

Could Dom have been my... birth father?

I haven't allowed myself to think that before, not in a real way, but it's the obvious question. And it explains Dad's reluctance to discuss my mother and how I've always felt distanced from the man who raised me. The feeling of connection to Dom is strong, but maybe I've manifested it through longing, much like the hankerings as a child for a different upbringing. The other side of the fence always greener.

There are so many maybes, buzzing around me like the drone of the mozzies. I slap one away and hit my hand hard against the arm of the plastic sofa. I squeeze my eyes tight against the pain, feeling the wooziness of a late night and too much smoke inhalation.

I don't really want Dom to be my dad. Missing him by two days would be horrendous, and anyway, Dad, my real dad, the man who brought me up, imperfect as our relationship might be, has been the one constant in my life. Rejecting him is an unkindness and therefore not an option.

Jumping three steps ahead, I stumble across another fear, one that sends me back inside. I turn the key and rattle the handle to double-check the door is firmly locked, heart bouncing in my chest. Because maybe the danger here is real, and personal. Maybe I am not the only one with secrets or prior knowledge?

What if Blythe knows I'm connected to Dom? She seemed to be pushing me on that. What if she accepted me as her ghost, not because she had no choice, but by deliberate connivance? What if I'm the fly, already caught in her spider's web?

The air in the annexe is a little cooler now than it was in the day, but I am covered in sweat. I scoop water onto my face from the kitchen tap and bathe my sore knees, splashing under my arms and around the back of my neck. Then I wash my feet. An awkward process with only the kitchen sink at my disposal, one leg then the other raised, my blisters smarting under the cold tap as I stumble and almost topple.

It's only when I'm ready for bed – Mum's skirt laid over the back of the desk chair, pasta stains worryingly stubborn despite a scrub under the tap – that I allow myself a final look outside, a sweating palm placed against the annexe's locked glass door.

The light at the top of the tower is still off, but there's another one illuminating the bay window at the first floor, a slender figure silhouetted at the middle of the three large panes. I gasp, stepping back into the swivel chair at Dom's desk, my handprint all that's left on the glass. I wait in the shadows, blood whooshing in my ears as I watch the bay window for movement, the figure now gone. Then the drapes are pulled across by a hidden hand, one rectangle of light obscured after another.

It feels as if Blythe and I are the only people left in the world, separated by the darkness. I check the door is locked, again, and crawl under the duvet, eyes wide open.

12

Mum and four-year-old me are in my bedroom. The one at the front of the semi-detached house where we lived as a family, until she left us. In fact, this is the day she left us. My bedroom looks out onto a sunny cul-de-sac and the window is open. It's almost summer and all is good. Her hand is protectively across me as I look down at the pots of flowers that line our front path. She's whispering something in my ear. A perfect moment, until Dad bursts in.

Heavy thuds at the writing annexe door wake me. The knocks imperative. A knuckle swung against the glass. Insistent enough to drag me from the dream, the duvet cover stuck to sweat-damp skin. I peel myself from the bed. More thumps as I stagger towards the person who has seen fit to wake me from the pleasure and pain of the past, knees groaning as if I were twice my age, the scabs cracking open, heels shaved of skin now blisters.

'OK, I'm coming!'

I pause at Dom's desk to check my notebook and laptop are both closed, aware of Ludo's previous observations but also his proximity through the glass door. I turn the key, the rabbit's amputated foot nestling in my palm, grey fur soft as velvet. *Poor bunny.*

'Ms Wilde, thank goodness,' Ludo exclaims, breathless. 'I was about to let myself in. Are you unwell?'

He's dressed head to toe in his favoured black: an archetypal villain. Or maybe one of those martial arts experts who drop down on ropes to swing through opened doors, except he's holding a spare key and was about to use it. I step into the gap, prohibiting any thoughts of entry despite the fact he has declared his intent to invade my privacy at will. It's blindingly bright, bars of sunlight crossing my exposed legs, the burn on my pale, freckled skin such that I touch the skin on my thighs below my T-shirt.

'I was asleep. And I'd appreciate it if you didn't just—'

'Are you aware of the hour, Ms Wilde? It's almost eleven.' He taps his ostentatious watch. A different one than yesterday's. This one is larger and blingy with what surely cannot be real diamonds? Is that a Rolex?

'In the land of the insomniac writer, that's not a particularly late rise,' I reply, although clearly to Ludo it's yet another bad mark against my name. 'Was there something urgent you needed?'

'Blythe is by the pool and waiting for you to join her.'

'*Now?*'

'If it's not too much trouble, Ms Wilde?'

'Yes, of course, I'd love to. Just give me a couple of minutes to—'

'I'll walk you over,' Ludo tells me. He takes a seat on the veranda, crossing one leg over the other before he starts picking imaginary lint from his dark trousers reminding me of Harry. 'She's waiting, Ms Wilde.'

I bash my calf on the corner of the stupid metal-framed bed in my haste to dress, a bruise blooming beneath the weeping graze. I could do with covering up my battered legs under trousers, but with a limited choice of outfits, and the time pressure of Ludo waiting, and Blythe apparently, I grab some dark denim shorts and pull them on over a navy one-piece swimsuit, wincing as the fabrics touch my grazes. I'm a terrible packer, chaotic and always forgetting the essentials. I'd prevaricated until the last possible moment, as per usual. But I'm grateful I brought the swimsuit. It's so hot! I add sunglasses and flip-flops, switch off my laptop, and avoiding my reflection in the glass, step outside and lock the door behind me.

Ludo's face falls as he looks up from the rattan sofa. 'That's what you're wearing?'

'It would appear so,' I reply, pocketing the fob with exaggerated care as I juggle notebook and phone. 'Shall we go?'

We head the thirty or so paces across the long grass towards the parasols, the walk sapping any energy reserves I've snatched in those elusive few hours of dream-fuelled sleep. The denim shorts rub at my inner thighs, my flip-flops flapping loudly against the sweaty soles of my feet. The predicted forty-four degrees is due later this afternoon, but it already feels more intense than yesterday, humidity high.

'There's a chance of thunderstorms,' Ludo advises when I comment on the heat. 'Should be dramatic over the heath, always is.'

'Yeah, right. Is that Blythe's room?' I ask, pointing behind us. The triptych of tall, mullioned windows on the first floor reminding me of last night.

'Yes, that's her suite,' Ludo replies. 'Why do you ask?'

'I saw a light on, quite late in fact.'

'Blythe doesn't sleep well, so quite possibly yes.'

'Well, yes, I'm telling you I did,' I snap.

Ludo's eyes widen.

'Sorry, I'm tired and hot. And the internet here is virtually non-existent, and even when it is, it's...' I say, glancing at my phone, '... annoyingly slow.' I take off my sunglasses and wipe the back of my hand across my brow.

'Why do you need to be connected to your phone?' he asks, apparently impervious to the heat whilst I can feel beads of sweat at my hairline. 'The contract you signed clearly states no social media or outside contact whilst you're here.'

I pocket the mobile. 'For my work, Ludo?' He looks at me blankly. I hold up my notepad. 'I'm writing my notes old-school in Blythe's presence, as requested. But I have to type them up and save them to the cloud and I need the internet for research purposes.'

'What kind of research?' he asks, glancing ahead towards the pool, as if he hadn't been snooping yesterday.

'It doesn't matter, I'll sort it. Let's just get over to Blythe, shall we, before I pass out? But I'd appreciate a desk fan, if you have a spare? The annexe is like a sauna.'

Blythe is reclining on a lounger, stretched out in a bright-red bikini and sporting a different pair of dark shades today: mirrored aviators this time. I dive into the blessed shade of the nearest parasol and flop onto the lounger beside her. My scratched sunglasses are obscuring everything a little, which makes her *slightly* less imposing.

'Marnie!' She leans across the table set between the loungers, a jug of iced water on the mosaic pattern, and a crime novel, the cover of which is a swimming pool with a dead body beside it. You have to admire Blythe's complete lack of tone. She clearly doesn't give a shit what anyone thinks of her. Her skin is slick with sun cream as her hand brushes my shoulder. 'You're alive!'

I draw back and attempt to deflect my recoil with a fake cough, hand raised dramatically to catch it.

'Are you unwell?' Blythe asks, covering her nose and mouth and glancing at Ludo. 'Your knees look infected, Marnie. A fever? Sepsis?'

'No, I'm fine, honestly.'

'Have some cucumber water,' she says, looking at Ludo to do

the honours. 'What a day we're having, almost as hot as yesterday already, and it's going to get even hotter!'

I gulp the iced water down, my pasty legs and scabbing knees angled away from Blythe's long, slim legs.

'Better?' She takes off her sunglasses and regards me with suspicion rather than concern for my health.

'Yes, much, thank you.'

'We're fine now, Ludo,' she says, dismissing him. 'Off you trot!'

We both watch as Ludo walks away, our gazes returned then to one another.

'Would you like a dip before we start work?' Blythe suggests. 'It's very invigorating. Might help with those too?' She points at my knees. 'The chlorine will smart, but it's antiseptic.'

'Oh no, I'm good thanks.'

'You can swim, I take it?' Blythe is looking over her sunglasses. 'You learnt as a child?'

'Yes, Dad insisted on it. We lived by the sea from when I was five, you see.'

'Then what's the problem?' she demands, looking at me, then the pool.

'No, nothing. Of course.'

I unzip my shorts and shove my sunglasses in a pocket then quickly run across the burning patio stones and into the water, submerging myself step by step, knees stinging in the chlorinated water, legs kicking out before I can think about Dom's floating body, or my imperfect figure in a swimsuit, or the sting of antiseptic. The pool isn't designed for lengths – a few strokes and my hand is touching the end – but my efforts are applauded by Blythe as I turn and swim back, the efficient technique I learnt as a child still there. I grin, waving as she waves back. What's that all about?

'You swim well, Marnie,' she observes on my return, my short, damp hair sticking up at odd angles so I scrape it back with a clawed hand. 'Here, use this.' She passes me the towel she's been lying on. 'Go on, I don't mind.'

'Thanks.' I take the damp towel, patting myself dry with a corner. I've always had a thing about sharing towels. It feels wrong. And also, why assume I don't mind? It's *all* about her.

'Your father was right to teach you,' she says, waving it away as I offer to return the towel. 'It's an important skill. You never know when you might need it.'

'Yes, true. Dad took me every Saturday morning for years,' I tell her, sitting down, and dropping the towel beside me. 'Until I lost interest when my boobs turned up.'

'You were a rebellious teen?'

'I think it was hard for both me and my father.'

'What happened to your mother?' she asks, as people often do. 'If you don't mind me asking?'

'No, it's fine, I don't mind talking about her,' I reply, ready with the same potted version I always share when people ask. Although this time, it feels different, every word loaded with extra meaning in light of Dom's email. 'My mother left us when I was four. I have no idea where she went or why, and that's about it.'

'Do you remember her?' Blythe asks, getting up to grab a towel from the low wall where it's drying, every bone in her spine visible as she smooths the crisped fabric over the lounger.

'I have only vague and unreliable recollections of my mother, sadly,' I tell her as Blythe lies back. 'Her name was, *is*, Katherine Wilde.'

I always mention Mum's name, just on the off chance. Six degrees of separation and all that, especially here, where Dom – also searching for Katherine and so recently – once lived, but as is invariably the case, Mum's name is greeted with a bemused shake of the head. Blythe looking, as most do, unsure what to say or do next as she turns away.

'It's OK,' I say, laying the towel over my lap and smiling. 'Can't miss what you don't really remember having.' Although it's not true and I am watching Blythe carefully throughout our exchange for any sign, however small, that my mother's name means something to her.

Blythe smiles back, then announces she's going for a dip herself. She descends the shallow steps with a poise I fear I sadly lacked, her body lithe, her hair slicked back. Her movements graceful as she glides up and down the pool, her long limbs fluid. When she emerges, skin glistening, it could be the opening scene of a Bond movie, another of Dad's favourites. The Sean Connery era. For a woman of fifty-seven she looks incredible.

'I'd love to hear more about how you and Dom met?' I ask, droplets beading her bronzed legs as she reclines in shades, like a starlet in Cannes, the only clue to her maturity a jawline less defined than it was in the corridor of early nineties photos.

'I first *saw* him at a film premiere,' she begins, adjusting herself on the thick towel-lined cushion, which looks considerably more comfortable than the bed I've been tossing and turning on all night. 'We met properly two months later.'

I'm tempted to stretch out too, but I'd be asleep in minutes. I push my swelling, hot feet back into my flip-flops, the patio burning hot, even in the shade, and grab my notepad from beside me. London is on fire and I'm burning too. I crack the spine to the page of notes I'd previously marked with a pen.

'Sounds a suitably glamorous meet-cute, a film premiere,' I prompt, squinting against the brightness as I remove my shades and jot down a few contextual details as reminders for later:

Pool, red bikini, film premiere meeting

'Not so glamorous for me.' Blythe laughs, outraged. 'I was waitressing. Pass me the sun cream, will you?'

I grab the bottle from the table and hold it out. Blythe has extended one tanned leg and is regarding it, the other also raised so the knee partially blocks my view of her face. She seems acutely aware of how she is positioned, a heightened consciousness – something I've observed in other celebrities I've ghosted, particularly actors. I suppose it's a part of the craft – very 'method' – but the seepage into real life exhausts me. She looks down at her bare, toned and clenched stomach, then takes the bottle and squirts sun cream across her skin.

'I'd arrived in Hollywood late September '92 on a three travel month visa. Trying my luck for a few months,' she explains, massaging the sun cream into her stomach and legs with flattened palms. Her nails are lacquered in a glossy red to match the bikini and her toes, but the mani is as amateurish as the pedi. I guess she's not at liberty to go to a salon, and I don't suppose she wants anyone coming to the house who might then sell a story. There's also one coarse grey hair on her chin which is highlighted by a shaft of illuminating sunlight. It makes me sad and also embarrassed for her.

'Like every other young and unknown British actress in Hollywood at the time,' Blythe continues, squirting more cream into her palm, 'I was putting myself out there in hope and sadly also expectation.'

'But you were already an established name though, weren't you?' I prompt, referencing her minimal credits on IMDb. 'You'd worked in the UK in the theatre, and some TV parts? You had a right to expect.'

'Yes, you'd have thought it stood for something, wouldn't you?' Blythe replies, setting down the cream. 'Unfortunately, I was made acutely aware of my dwindling shelf life.'

'That's crazy; you were still in your twenties!'

'Indeed, twenty-six, no seven, anyway, that's how it was back then, maybe even now. Then fast forward to the December, just a few weeks before the Academy Awards nomination announcements, and one night I was at that premiere.' I nod. 'I was earning cash-in-hand, and worrying that my visa was about to expire. Glasses on trays that made your arm ache and canapés curling in the sun that no one wanted. Circling round, over and over, and then I saw him.'

'Dom?'

'God, he was so fucking handsome, Marnie. I wish you'd met him. You two would have got on like a—' She stops herself and I realise I've been grinning too, both of our smiles slipping. 'Six foot two, in an Armani custom suit, white shirt, open collar, tanned. I knew I had no chance with a man like him, but of course I fell for him anyway, hook, line and sinker.'

'But you did have a chance? He liked you too.'

'Nope, he didn't even notice me. And anyway, he was there with his first wife, *Wendy*.'

A tiny piece of spittle appears in the corner of Blythe's mouth at the mention of Wendy's name. She sits up, wiping it away and neutralising her expression which had twisted unattractively. Then she pours another glass of the cucumber water and gulps it down.

'It was Dom's big night, you see,' she says, patting at drips of water that dribble down her chin and between her breasts, white flesh peeking from beneath her red bikini top as she adjusts it. 'His movie: *The Man*. Have you seen it? By far and away his best work.'

'I've only watched clips on YouTube. I couldn't find it anywhere else.'

Blythe shakes her head. 'Breaks my heart, it really does. It's a classic, or should be. It deserves an audience, even now. Well, to be honest, especially now.'

I'm not sure if Blythe means on account of Dom's death, or as a commentary on the underbelly of the Hollywood system in the early nineties. The film is about a man who is corrupted by fame as he shapes the career of a vulnerable starlet – but from what I saw, *The Man* is dated, with low production values, although the script was whip-smart and it was well acted by the female lead, Florence Saint John: the young actress who, in terrible dramatic irony, died at the Hoppers' Hollywood home during a wild party the following year. A very sad case of life imitating art.

'So good, isn't it?' Blythe continues, assuming my agreement. 'Dom was hotly tipped for an Academy nom for best original screenplay, but another film came out around the same time and the competing title was bigger in every way – cast, budget, director – so it got all the attention and then cannibalised every award going. There was widespread outrage at the snub, but I guess that's the luck of the drawer: one swims to the top, the other... but that premiere was Dom's night. He was going to be a star. Everyone thought it. I couldn't get near him. *Persona non grata* with my cheese and pineapple.'

'And Florence Saint John?'

'Yes, she was there, I believe.'

'She was the star of the film, wasn't she? And also tipped for super-stardom before she...'

Blythe shrugs. 'It was an ensemble cast.'

I make a note to dig a little deeper into the circumstances of Florence's death. Something about the way Blythe dismissed her starring role, which it really was despite the film's title, has aroused my curiosity. The male lead was a conduit to her, from what I saw, and the rest of the cast wasn't even that memorable.

'Wendy looked completely out of her depth at the premiere,' Blythe tells me, lying back. 'Didn't make any effort to fit in, as always. A little housewife, that's all she ever wanted to be.' She pauses, turns to me, my frowning expression reflected in her sunglasses. I rearrange my face into something more pleasant, taken aback by my unattractive scowl.

'Not everyone wants to be in the limelight, of course,' Blythe concedes, 'but that smallness of outlook was never going to be enough for Dom. He needed a challenge.'

'And along you came?' I smile. 'Definitely more than a match for him, I'm guessing.'

She laughs, hands spread in a gesture of *ta-da!,* her smile returning as she adds, 'Yes, for better or worse, he got me. We were happy for a long time, Marnie. Very happy.'

'So would it be fair to assume Wendy would have preferred to stay in the UK?'

'For sure! She was always bleating on about returning to London with the boys, which broke Dom's heart, of course. He loved his sons, would have done anything for them... but sadly, he lost them anyway.'

'Yes, so I gather. Why was that?'

Blythe takes off her glasses to clean them with a corner of the towel. No response forthcoming as she polishes each lens.

'Are you uncomfortable talking about Wendy and the boys, Blythe?'

'Of course not!' She looks at me directly, eyes narrow slits. 'Why would I be?'

'I suppose because the circumstances of Wendy's death were tragic and also somewhat unresolved. Some concerns raised at the inquest, I believe?'

'I see you are a student of Wikipedia, Marnie. Maybe widen your searches a bit? For instance, did you know that Wendy couldn't swim? And that she was taking a daily cocktail of drugs for manic episodes? None of that was reported, but it's true. Dom had been a saint to stay for so long.'

'Can I quote you on those points, Blythe? In the memoir, I mean.'

'Do as you like, Marnie. I have nothing to hide.'

'Must have been tough for Dom, though, to lose custody to Wendy's parents?'

Blythe nods. 'It broke him. Part of the reason he stopped writing for so long. But he wanted what was best for the boys, not him.'

'But surely the boys wanted to be with their f—?'

'It seemed as if Dom was being punished for loving me,' Blythe says, cutting across my question. 'As if he'd had to choose between us when the marriage was long over. He was consumed by the guilt; it ate him up.'

'Must have been a difficult time for you both. I mean, three stepsons would be a lot for anyone—'

'What are you suggesting?' Blythe asks, interrupting me. 'That I discouraged him from fighting for his boys because I didn't want them?'

'No, of course not. Only that I would have found it very hard, however much I loved their father, to take on another woman's child, let alone three young boys.'

'Yes, that's true,' Blythe concedes. 'But don't quote me on that. I'll sound like a heartless bitch.' She laughs.

'No, you won't, it's entirely understandable, but if you want me to, I'll leave that part out.' I place a question mark in my notes, knowing Priscilla will love it if I can somehow persuade Blythe to give her permission for the heartless bitch comment.

Blythe presses her toes into the striped towel again. 'Wendy clocked me straight away, that night at the premiere; I think she sensed a threat, kept glancing over at me. If looks could kill.'

The choice of words is jarring, as is her expression, even behind the mirrored glasses, but it doesn't perturb Blythe, still lost in the past. 'Dom always claimed our "first" meeting was at a Hollywood party,' she explains, 'and it was a better story, in fairness. But I worshipped him from afar after that premiere.'

'It does sound like a special night.'

'For him, yes, although bittersweet in retrospect. Dom clung on to the tail of that early predicted success for *The Man* for far too long. The Oscar rumours should always be taken with a pinch of salt – there are always snubs for reasons undeclared; you can't make enemies in Hollywood and get away with it – but in Dom's case, it was just bad timing. He truly believed it would happen, so when I won mine two years later, well, you can imagine...'

'Must have been hard for him, although I'm sure he was very proud of you.'

She shrugs. 'Anyway, I was still trying and failing to make it in Hollywood when I finally met Dom at a party the following February. 1993 was quite a year.'

'What was that like, the trying and failing, I mean?'

'Soul destroying. It was horribly competitive, amongst the younger girls especially. Open casting calls, the dreaded "let's talk over drinks"; a couple of call-backs were as good as I got. I didn't conform to the required image.'

'Your great age?' I quip.

'That was a factor, yes, but also in terms of the specific look they were after back then. I mean, there's always a look, but it was rigid in the nineties. Madonna or whore, that was about it, and I don't mean Madge.' She laughs. 'It was Dom who helped me hone my image to turn the tide in my favour. He suggested the name change too.'

I look up. 'Your name was his invention?'

'Yes. I was on about my third by then, all awful! He loved *Blithe Spirit* by Noel Coward. That's where it came from. We just adjusted the spelling, a Y instead of an I. The blonde hair was Dom's idea too, after he'd encouraged me to grow out the hideous pixie cut. Oh, and he recommended a personal trainer.'

'Sounds like Dom was quite the Svengali?' I reply, smoothing my short hair.

'I fell in love, Marnie. Hopelessly, deliriously.' She hoists herself up in the lounger and starts to rub sun cream into her shoulders although we're in the shade. 'I'd have followed him and his ideas to the moon and back. And he fell in love with me too. Love at first sight he always said, despite the fact I still carried at least ten of those excess pounds when he spotted me poolside at that party!' She shakes her head at the memory.

I resist the urge to draw my stomach in beneath the balanced notebook. 'None of that should matter, though, Blythe.'

'It shouldn't, but of course it does.' Blythe holds out the sun cream. 'You should be careful with skin like yours, Marnie. UV damage is so horribly ageing. We used to cover ourselves in coconut oil, can you believe it? Literally frying ourselves by the pool! But I've always had olive skin.'

I take the cream and rub some into the tops of my feet first, which are already red around the straps of the flip-flops, exposed where the shades don't quite meet, then I smother my nose. 'So, tell me about this party.'

'It was your typical Hollywood hills mayhem. Coke and cocktails, sex in the *many* bedrooms. Boobs out by the pool. Blow jobs in not so quiet corners. Deals made. Careers ended.'

Priscilla is going to *love* this. I scribble fast. 'How did you get an invite?'

'A film director I'd been working with invited me and my roommate.'

'So you'd got a film role by then?' I don't recall that on her IMDb, making a note to check. 'Amazing!'

'Yes, but sadly it all fell apart before it began, but what it did get me was an extension on my visa and an invite for me and Josie to that party. I felt like my luck was finally changing.'

'Josie? Another actress?'

'Sort of. Josie was a stunt double and we shared a condo.'

'Oh yes, there was a photo of the two of you, on a motorbike.' I point over to the house. 'In the corridor.'

'Arty was one of the few nice guys,' Blythe explains, again ignoring my questions.

'Arty?'

'The film director who took us to the party. Lovely man, but you could always trust a gay man in a way you couldn't the rest of them... None of us knew he had Aids, of course; it wasn't talked about openly back then.' Blythe swivels on the edge of her lounger, facing me, a relaxed pose, knees apart, and offers me a cigarette which I decline. 'He died tragically young. And he got me onto these,' she says, holding up the cigarette. 'Bloody cancer sticks.' She searches for a lighter on the table and the crime novel falls to the ground, lurid cover bent, the body disfigured. She lights up, puffing. 'Smoking was considered sexy back in the day. I could even blow smoke rings.' She hoots with laughter. 'Oh, that reminds me, you asked last night about seeing the latest scripts Dom was working on. Still interested?'

'Ooh yes please, I'd love to.'

'Great. I'm not sure what you'll think, but...' She waves her hand in the direction of the writing annexe. 'I still think the concept is amazing.'

'What was the elevator pitch?'

'For a series,' Blythe says, standing up and pulling on a billowing kimono, the folds falling loosely around her slim frame and narrowly avoiding the lit cigarette which she passes from hand to hand. 'Starring me, naturally.'

'Of course. A biopic?'

'Not exactly, but I'll let you make your own mind up about the treatment; it's interesting.'

'Sounds good. Is this the project you were talking to your agent about yesterday?'

'God no! James wants me to do more voice-over work. You know they'll pay you 15K to sound like you're having an orgasm over a chocolate biscuit?' She drops the cigarette into her water glass where it fizzles and dies. 'I've told him, I'm so over it.'

'Sounds like money for old rope.'

'Yes, that's what Ludo says too.' She slips on a pair of designer flip-flops, which put mine very much in the shade, then she pulls her wet hair into a silk scrunchie as she mutters, 'Some people don't know gold when they see it and you have to maintain standards. Anyway, I'll be interested to hear your thoughts on the script notes over supper. Can you read them by then?'

I stand up. 'I thought we were spending the day together?'

'My day started at 5 a.m., Marnie. I have a call with my lawyers, then I'll need to rest. Wish me luck!'

'Good luck!' I call after her, although I'm not sure how much my wishes are worth, or if I really mean them. Once I have what I need from her, they can lock her up and throw away the key as far as I'm concerned. Although that's a bit reductive. I wouldn't say I like her, but I do find her fascinating.

'Read the scripts!' she calls back. 'They're waiting for you on your desk.'

'But I locked the annexe door!' I call back, feeling in my pocket for the velvet fob and pulling it out, the bunny's soft pads resting in my palm. But of course, Ludo has a spare.

13

The scripts are indeed waiting for me on Dom's desk, dumped from a great height by the looks of things, a circle of displaced dust around them and some pages fallen to the floor. Their presence indicates two things: that it was pre-agreed between Blythe and Ludo that he should leave them here, and that, as suspected, Ludo sees fit to let himself in when I'm not around.

At least I had the foresight to switch off my laptop before I left, images of Ludo trawling through my entire search history crawling over me. It's bad enough my dirty undies are strewn across the bedroom floor, his beady eyes no doubt also falling on the overnight bag left open on the bed.

Mind you, he always seems reluctant to come in, so maybe his visit was brief, and there's nothing inside my bag except for the broken bottle of perfume.

My notebook, thankfully, came with me to the pool.

I lock the door again, despite the oppressive heat inside the annexe and the apparent uselessness of doing so. Dom's stiff cowhide chair creaking as Mum's skirt slips from the back of it as I sit down. The stains are even worse today, the sunlight highlighting the orange splodges, but tackling them will have to wait as I have other priorities. Namely Dom's scripts. The excitement of finally having something of his creation in my hands, eclipsing everything else.

There are roughly thirty or so unnumbered pages, but they are disappointingly amateurish in their presentation as I flick through. Dom hasn't even used industry standard software, the documents word processed. He'd been out of the game for a long while – stung by the loss of his boys and his career – and things have moved on immeasurably in that time, but sloppy presentation aside, there's precious little content either. No lines of snappy dialogue and crackling scenes. No signature acerbic wit as demonstrated in *The Man*. More a collection of thoughts masquerading as a partial for a six-part series about an ageing actress staging her comeback. No prizes for guessing who! An unsurprisingly meta premise that nevertheless does have some appeal.

Most of the typeface is annotated with red pen, as if Dom were still working on it, or perhaps he'd asked Blythe to read his work and she added the scrawled notes for his benefit? Blythe's not someone I'd go to for positive critique at such a fragile stage of a newish project, but she was his wife, someone to bounce ideas off and potentially a first reader, which begs the question: how much further did Dom take this? Because this isn't good enough. Not for my purposes. Not for anyone in the industry either. This isn't anywhere near ready to sub to agents or producers, even as a spec script. It's no more than an idea expressed via a disjointed collection of thoughts, which sketches out a thinly veiled pastiche of Blythe's life and early career.

I push away the messy pages, disappointed enough to pause in what had felt an imperative and fevered chase for information. Hopefully, this is, as Ernest would say, merely the tip of the iceberg. A saved dossier somewhere of Dom's more detailed plans and pages. I look up at Ernest but he keeps his counsel, the only witness to Dom's endeavour. Surely all those hours out here must have produced more than this shit first draft?

I will certainly quiz Blythe on that, although it seems I won't have the chance until this evening at supper. I suppose I could ask Ludo. He cleared out the shed and delivered these pages. Maybe there's a stack of notebooks and a hard drive somewhere filled with later iterations.

I spread the pages on the dusty floor, trying to arrange them in order, but the heat is making me feel weird. I unlock the annexe door, a welcome breeze rushing in which unfortunately then scatters the script pages. I gather them up and stand at the open door to cool down, the sky now leaden with the threatened storm which Ludo warned might be on its way. We could do with it to clear the air. If Ludo doesn't appear with the requested fan soon, I'll use that as my excuse to seek him out.

I wedge the door open with the scratched pebble, wondering at the initials, DFH. The marks were made with a pen, ink in the crevices. Dominic-something-Hopper.

Back at Dom's desk, I skim through the script again, attention caught by the last page which is headed *SYNOPSIS*. That's where I'd usually start, but hey-ho.

The synopsis is printed on the back of a handwritten list headed *Wardrobe* – top designers' names handwritten in thick, pink Sharpie underneath. I'm guessing these are Blythe's thoughts?

I secure the other loose pages with my laptop and study this one more closely. The pink ink has bled through so the typeface is partially obscured, but the synopsis looks much more professional in tone and presentation, although it's also the product of a printer that needs more ink, the font faint, the stupid pink list of designer fashion houses making it almost impossible to read the synop. I spin the desk chair round and hold the page up to the open door, seeking sunlight.

The premise of the series is set out clearly and succinctly. The actress's present-day situation – isolation and obscurity in her palatial London home – counterpointed with her arrival in Hollywood thirty years before. Dom's source material confirmed as very close to home, as if there were ever any doubt.

The theme is our actress's struggle against the misogynistic casting system and the bitchiness of the younger competition, women against women as well as the imbalance of power in favour of the studio, namely men. Also cited as motifs are the price of fame, the definition of success, and how long-term relationships between creatives can be a challenge. *Interesting.*

The synopsis then briefly outlines the first two episodes.

The opener is entitled, *Wanda.*

Our 'fictitious' actress, renamed 'Darcy Diamond' – *dear God* – meets a handsome screenwriter called David and his wife Wanda – *wonder who they might be?!* – their paths crossing at a film premiere where Darcy is a cocktail waitress and described as plump with short hair.

Episode one then focuses on the aftermath of *David's* first wife, Wanda's, tragic death. Wanda drowns in the pool at the couple's oceanside home, their three daughters – *that'll fool everyone!* – finding their mother in a tragic scene entitled, *Mummy is dead!*

For fuck's sake. My raised expectations take another tumble.

I put the synopsis page down and place my hand on top, the breeze getting up now.

I can only hope later versions have moved on both in quality, quantity, and from the uncomfortable similarities to real life. It's far too close to the bone to be seemly. I mean, it's all well and good pushing boundaries between fact and fiction, but Wendy Hopper *did* drown. Is that really where Dom wanted to go with this?

Making capital out of family heartbreak in a barely disguised version of his and Blythe's life together? Wendy was the mother of his boys, who are, despite his abandonment of them, still alive and well and I'd imagine, hugely protective of their late mother's memory now they are grown men.

I adjust my position in the leather chair and squint to read about episode two which in the synopsis is entitled *Lola*.

Darcy, having disposed of her first rival, *Wanda* – the drowning rumoured not to be wholly accidental – now worries someone else is a rival for her new husband's affections. A stunt double who is called Lola. Who will also need to be eliminated.

Shit! Blythe's friend and roommate in Hollywood was a stunt double. The woman in the photo. What was her name?

There's a final paragraph at the bottom of the page which has been almost obliterated by the soak through from the pink Sharpie. I get up and walk to the open door, holding the sheet up to catch more light. The emboldened line is a possible series title, the weight of its implied meaning punching me right in the solar plexus as I read each blurred word.

The Six Kills of Darcy Diamond: An Icon's Murderous Route to Fame

What the actual fuck?

I sag into Dom's chair, the synopsis page falling from my limp grasp to land in front of me on the desk, typed side up, pink ink turning dark red like spilt blood as my focus slips.

What is this? A chronicle of his wife's crimes? The same ones she alluded to in that so-called joke about eliminating her rivals?

I retrieve the dropped page and read again, noticing an even fainter line of print beneath the proposed title. The typeface gets lighter and lighter, the pink leakage darker and more obtrusive. I grab my pen and trace the words through, pressing on Dom's dusty desk to decipher each syllable.

> A darkly comic pastiche of an actress trying to make it big in Hollywood who picks off her rivals in a female revenge, anti-Hollywood, anti-love-rivals, pre #*MeToo* frenzy.

I wedge the synop page with the others under my laptop and pace the annexe, trying to shake the mix of fear and adrenalin as the potential magnitude of what I've read sinks in.

Was Dom trying to get a message to the outside world through these scripts? Or is my febrile and fertile imagination getting the better of me? Blythe gave me these pages freely and stated she has nothing to hide. Although she could easily have missed the reverse of that synopsis page; I almost did, the pink ink obliterating the printed side on first glance. And I have no reason to take her word at face value. I hardly know her. She could be toying with me.

'Everything OK, Ms Wilde?'

I jump. Ludo standing at the open door.

'Don't do that!' I tell him, hand clutching my chest to stop my heart bouncing straight out. 'You scared me half to death.'

'Sorry, I didn't mean to startle you,' he says. 'I've brought you this, thought it might help in the heat.'

I expect him to produce the requested fan, but instead he pulls a cling-filmed bowl of cut fruit from the carrier bag hanging from his thin wrist: mango, melon, strawberries and kiwi arranged inside. There's even a sprig of mint on top.

'Thank you, looks lovely,' I say, the bowl delightfully chilled in my sweaty palm. 'You want to come in?'

'No, thank you. I won't, but I hope you find it cooling.'

I peel back the clingfilm and bite into a ripe and tooth-numbingly chilled chunk of sweet melon, the juice dribbling down my chin. 'Mmmm. Delicious.'

'Good! Have you had a chance to look at those as yet?' Ludo says, gesturing past me to the script pages wedged under my laptop.

'The script that you left in my absence, after I'd locked the door?' I reply, swallowing a slippery slab of mango and leaving space for Ludo's explanation of his violation of my privacy.

'Yes,' he replies, flatly. 'The very same.'

I put the bowl on the desk and thumb the trapped pages. 'You sure you don't want to come in?'

'No, thank you. So, your thoughts on the script pages?'

'They're a little... underwhelming, on first glance at least.'

'I'd ask you keep that opinion to yourself, Ms Wilde.' Ludo advises pompously, then he produces a dust-encrusted, cheap-looking desk fan from the same carrier bag. 'And the fan, as you requested. Because we all need one, apparently.'

I smile and wipe my sticky palms down my shorts. 'Thanks, much appreciated.'

Ludo turns to leave, setting off back towards the house at his usual brisk trot, as if he were on a piece of elastic, pinging back. I step onto the sun-warmed veranda and call after him, 'Ludo, wait!'

The heat-dry grass digs into my bare feet, the sun searing as I catch him up. 'Do you know for sure that Dom wrote those pages?'

'Sorry, I'm not sure what you're suggesting, Ms Wilde?'

'I'm asking if there's a chance they are Blythe's efforts?' The thought only just formulating. 'I don't just mean the annotations. Pretty much everything I have feels... They just don't feel like they're the work of an experienced screenwriter, at least, not all of them.'

Ludo opens his mouth and closes it again, taking a step back. 'I don't want you to push Blythe on this, Ms Wilde. She's very fragile right now.'

'So I'm right, she wrote them?' I wait, but he remains tight-lipped. 'I'll just have to ask her myself then, won't I?'

Ludo sighs heavily. 'Anything I share is strictly between us, Ms Wilde. Do I have your word?'

'Of course.'

'Blythe has become...' He glances up to the bay window, all three panes closed, as are the curtains. '*Preoccupied*, shall we say.'

'So this is the hoped-for comeback; a star vehicle for her?'

'I believe so. And for the record, I don't know how much Dom contributed, but yes, the pages she passed to me are, I believe, more recent, although Dom was writing a lot before his...' Ludo clears his throat. 'He was definitely working on something, night and day. But I was not privy to the content.'

'OK, so this idea was his, but the pages I have are her execution?'

'That would be a fair summation.'

I knew it! Although the confirmation is still disappointing. Dom's presence receding once more.

'Blythe hasn't talked to me about it much,' Ludo says. 'But it's become... well, kind of an obsession. She was up late last night finessing these for you so please, be gentle in your feedback. And I didn't say a word!'

'Yes, sure.'

Ludo continues his fast walk across to the house and I return to Dom's desk, re-evaluating the script in light of its authorship. Any former worth, or lack of, evaporating now I know Dom's input was negligible, at least as far as these pages go.

And surely any idea of a comeback is madness? Blythe must see that.

Even if I could do something with these terrible scripts there's no way she can star in a TV series. They take months, possibly years to get made. By then, she will surely be locked up? There's hope and then there's downright delusion. I'm not the only sane one here, am I?

I plug in the fan and recycled air spurts out thick dust, as hot as a hairdryer; the pages of script scattering. I anchor them firmly with the bowl of fruit, the corners still ruffling as I eye them warily. They have betrayed me. Pulling a mean trick at my expense. Not Dom's work at all, although in a way that's a relief. At least he hasn't let me down, not as a writer anyway.

I open up my saved folder of research and update my notes with the information about the script – if you can call this mish-mash of ideas a script – only looking up to bat away a persistent fly. The reassuring familiarity of the keyboard diffuses some of my pent-up energy, if not the frustration that despite a flutter of excitement, I am no closer to Dom's trail than before. This is all about Blythe and her ridiculous ambition. Her flights of fancy taking precedence over all logic and reason. She is, as always, pulling focus, along with that buzzing fly. My host manipulating me and the truth until I can't see clearly. Am I here as her ghost, or to complete a dead man's work?

I pop in the last piece of mango and wipe my hands down my swimsuit, beneath which I'm sticky with sweat and fruit juice and outrage. The question of Blythe's motive for asking me here is perhaps the most troubling part of this latest development. Am I her memoir writer or a proxy screenwriter, or both? I guess the only thing I can do is arm myself with as much knowledge as possible whilst I'm here. The key to the present lying firmly in the past.

I hunt through my saved file of notes and the scribblings in my notebook for references to Blythe's friend and roommate. A stunt double, like Lola.

Josie Phoenix. That's her name! The real Lola. I grab my phone to research Josie, but the bars are of course, non-existent.

The signal kicks in as I walk towards the house, strengthening as I near the kitchen. I am in direct contravention of Ludo's rules about wandering around on my own, but he did say I could walk up to the kitchen if I needed anything, and I'm sure I can come up with an excuse if he spots me. I should have brought the empty fruit bowl to return.

The temperature has soared even higher, the burn of it intense on the back of my exposed shoulders as I glance into the kitchen. It's empty. Although Ludo and/or Blythe could appear at any moment. I open up a search engine, leaning my back against the sun-warmed brick beside the kitchen door – my thumb working with a satisfying efficiency as I type in Blythe's full name, plus *Josie* then add, *Phoenix*.

The photo of Josie with Blythe that I saw in the corridor, both women astride a motorcycle, fills my thoughts as I wait for the results to load. The bad wig. The wide smiles. Friends? Or maybe rivals? Those smiles were for the camera, and not one another, I'm sure of it. No warmth in them. No generosity. Two ambitious women in competition. So what happened with Josie? Was it just, as Blythe said, that they were both chasing down the few roles available and Blythe got her big break, whilst Josie was relegated to being her stunt double? Or did something bigger sour the friendship? They were both invited by Arty, the film director, to the same Hollywood gathering where Blythe met and fell in love with Dom. Was it do with Dom? That would also make sense. If they were love rivals too.

The search for Josie finally loads. The headline from the *Los Angeles Times* February 1994 the first result.

Death of a Daredevil Actress

It's a very different Josie who smiles at me from the photo that accompanies the report of her death. A younger, less knowing version than the motorcycle stunt woman, a mere girl in fact. Her smile genuine, and innocent, a real-life and very much alive crocodile, or maybe it's an alligator, in her outstretched hands. The circumstances of her untimely death, heart-breaking.

> Josie's beloved motorbike appears to have left the road at a notorious bend near Mulholland Drive sometime last Tuesday, local residents reporting loud unexplained crashes in the valley, the Hollywood hills searched in vain for forty-eight hours straight, before her crumpled body was located, coyotes prowling. Josie was a promising and talented young actress and stunt woman who had come to Hollywood to fulfil her dreams.

Fuck! This takes those script ideas beyond a comedic pastiche. This is real life tragedy, cut and pasted onto the page.

I check through the kitchen glass door again, but there's still no sign of anyone inside, so I return to the list of searches and click on an obit in Josie's local paper, back in her home state of Florida, lifting one foot behind me to press it against the sun-warmed brick for balance.

> Josie Phoenix was born and raised in Winter Haven and grew up wrangling alligators at her father's farm and ferrying tourists around the swamps. From there, she made her way to Hollywood to pursue an acting career, gaining a reputation for taking on daredevil stunts as a double for many well-known actresses. She died aged only twenty-three. Her short life, nothing short of spectacular. She will be much missed by her four siblings and grief-stricken parents.

I wipe away a tear for a woman I never knew who died almost thirty years ago, her life fuller than mine, despite her shortened years. What a woman.

A mention of the Hoppers draws my eye down to the last line of the obit.

> Actress Blythe Hopper, who worked with Josie most recently on the much-anticipated *Affairs of the Heart*, said that she and her husband are devastated to learn of the death of a close and trusted friend. 'Josie was a rare talent and my first friend and roommate when I moved to LA. I shall miss her smile, her warmth, her energy. Her legacy will be in the wonderful contribution she made to the film which we will complete in her honour.'

So they'd started filming, but it wasn't finished, and Blythe and Dom were already married. I check the dates and it all fits. The Hoppers were married in August '93. Josie died February 1994. And *Affairs of the Heart* was released later that year, just in time for an Academy nom, Blythe's Oscar won in early '95. I scan the rest of the search results, looking for more gold, but they are mash-ups of the same, more references to the *notoriously twisty section of road near Mulholland Drive*. That was where the Hoppers lived, and the venue of another tragic death: that of Florence Saint John in May '93.

The body count is stacking up, but no one seems to have linked these deaths, or suggested Blythe might have been in any way to blame, or indeed have a motive for wanting any of these women dead.

I'd say my tactic has been to ruthlessly dispose of everyone who has ever got in my way, Marnie. That's the key to success, not only in marriage, but in life. Take out your rivals. Swiftly and without compunction.

* * *

I run back to the annexe and review the script pages again, scanning every crap line of dialogue and clunky direction for clues about those three deaths: Wendy, Flo, and Josie. Three deaths in the space of a year. Two of them in two months.

Circumstantial evidence, but that seems like more than coincidence!

The notes written in Blythe's hand on the scripts turn my stomach in light of this new information on Josie's death. The red pen annotations and pink Sharpie wish lists expressing her feverish thoughts on how she might be dressed for what she terms, *the collision scene.*

> *Think Isadora Duncan, scarf wound round my neck (but not strangling me!), hair blown back. I'm wearing a Stella McCartney jumpsuit or maybe Victoria Beckham dress as I drive after Lola.*

Blythe even suggests what make of car she'll be driving in pursuit of 'Lola' who is riding her motorbike back down the twisty road after an assignation with David which was interrupted by Darcy's unexpected return. The camera cuts between Darcy's *beautiful red Camaro* and her love rival's motorbike, until the latter leaves the road on that notorious bend.

But surely if Blythe were in any way involved in Josie's death, she wouldn't be so blatant as to telegraph that to me, let alone the rest of the world? Unless her desire for a comeback has blinded her to all other concerns.

And it was Dom who came up with the idea, supposedly. The question being, why?

I sit back, trying to fathom his rationale.

Ideas have to come from somewhere, of course. Often long

buried in a writer's subconscious, so buried, in fact, it can seem as if they've come out of nowhere, even to the person writing them. I've done it myself: a name borrowed without realising it, a story twisted from fact but based on tiny nuggets of reality and then extrapolated for dramatic purposes. We writers mine our pasts, switching things up to remove ourselves and our loved ones from the narrative. The holy grail, as Blythe said, is the emotional truth. Universal. But he hasn't based this story on them; it *is* them, other than a few dreadful name changes, which I ascribe to Blythe, not Dom.

I used a real name once, by mistake, in a short story. Had it published in a magazine before I realised, which was unfortunate given it was Priscilla's name I used and I made her a total bitch, but the fact remains that the truth makes for the most authentic, emotive writing. The commonality of life's experiences – grief, love, regret, envy – ploughed deep for inspiration. The loss of a wife, a close friend, and the lead in Dom's film in quick succession, bound to leave a mark. But to include all three, so thinly disguised? What was he thinking?

But let's say, for argument's sake, Dom, not having written in decades, decides to use his wife's extraordinary time in Hollywood as his start point. A little too close for comfort in this substandard version, but this is Blythe's interpretation of an early iteration. He'd have moved it along since then. Made it thematic rather than biographical. His reaction to losing his first wife and custody of his children, plus two close contacts, packed away in his writer's bag and brought out decades later to facilitate Blythe's desperate and unseemly quest for fame and to get past his writer's block.

Yes, that makes sense. *Sort of.*

This is not a crisis of conscience, or some great confession. No one, not even Blythe, would have a framed photo of someone they murdered on their wall, surely?

I make a mental note to look for photos of Wendy and Florence next time I walk through the corridor of fame, although it seems unlikely they feature. It's all about Blythe. As is this pulpy version of her life. What I need are Dom's notes, and any later versions of the scripts, in *his* words. Not hers. She is not a writer like us. It's Dom's wit and keen eye that is lacking on the page. That's all. And I need to understand where he was going with this.

I take a deep breath and look up at Ernest, as if he might have an opinion, which no doubt he would if he were here. I guess my doubts and questions will just have to wait. This bloody heat is sending me crazy. My thoughts running away with me.

I set myself a task. Another read through before supper, but this time for a clear analytical critique I can present to Blythe. I have to go back with something. I need to find the positives.

The final scene of episode two is uppermost in the piled papers. This page has no dialogue, just a few lines about how the episode might finish.

> Darcy pulls up at the studio the day before Lola's body is found. Darcy admires her shiny red car but is sad that when she walks around it – I'm thinking in Louboutins and a skin-tight Versace dress – the red soft-top Camaro is sporting a dented fender and smashed headlamp. She sighs heavily and kicks the dent, smiling at the memory of something only she knows, the shot cutting away then to a coyote, prowling.

Shit!

I sit back, all attempts at logic or reason abandoned. Because I have no idea what I'm dealing with here.

Could Blythe Hopper, Oscar winner and narcissist, actually be a serial killer?

14

It's a little after six when I walk towards the kitchen again, empty fruit bowl in hand this time, as well as my notebook. The sun is hazy, day turning slowly towards a long evening, a slight breeze running through the trees that shiver behind me, although it's still unbearably hot. So hot, I've thrown on my denim shorts again, teaming them with a loose-fitting blouse. Another charity shop find and a favourite of Jake's. Mind you, Ludo will sneer at whatever I wear and I can't hope to compete with whatever designer outfit Blythe has chosen. But in the grand scheme of things, what I'm wearing is the very least of my concerns as I contemplate supper with a psychopath.

The trees that line the drive the other side of the lawn – poplars, or maybe cypresses – are crazy tall but still dwarfed by the tall tower, its long shadow engulfing me in much-appreciated shade, sweat beading already. The benefit of a recent if disappointing shower already wearing off in the humidity, although I shiver like the trees, the thought of seeing Blythe again stopping me just shy of the kitchen door. Ostensibly, to check my phone, but more, if I'm honest, because I have no idea how to face the woman I now consider, in my wilder moments, to be involved in up to four deaths: Dom, Wendy, Josie and Flo.

I lean my back against the brick wall as I did earlier, one flip-flop pressed to the wall, voices coming from the kitchen as Blythe and Ludo bicker. Dark clouds are gathering again. A storm still brewing. Portents of doom. And however much I've tried to convince myself otherwise, I cannot persuade myself those three women's deaths are all entirely coincidental.

There are sadly no further updates from Jake in LA on Insta and no emails from Harry or Priscilla to delay me, the blanket ban on communication observed to the letter. Unless the signal isn't strong enough to send or receive emails, even here, by the house.

A deflating but obvious realisation hits me. So blindingly obvious I could kick myself for not putting it together before. Dom's email didn't reach me until two days after his death, not because he was sending me messages from beyond the grave, but due to the dodgy Wi-Fi! A boring and unromantic explanation, but the most likely reason for the delay. I've idiotically, or maybe wishfully, half believed he was a ghostly protector, when the email was simply stuck in Dom's Outbox. I can't believe I've been so stupid.

I'm about to go into the kitchen, unable to put off the inevitable any longer, when Blythe raises her voice, intoning her anger. An actress projecting.

'I don't need your opinion, thank you, Ludo! I have had it in spades and it's not helpful.'

I step back from the door, although they appear not to have noticed me, too wrapped up in the heated exchange to consider my arrival. Ludo's response, if there is one, too quiet for me to catch.

There's a short pause, then Blythe shouts, much louder, 'I may as well give up now according to you! Locked up here with your utter negativity. If it weren't for Marnie's presence—'

The sound of my name sends a shock wave through me,

straightening my back so I stumble, a series of trips as I back away, my flip-flops the culprit. I place a hand to the warmed brick and steady myself, then I edge nearer again.

'So, what exactly is your problem with her being here, Ludo?' Blythe demands. 'Tell me!'

I'm right beside the door now, chancing my luck, but Ludo has his back to me, his hands in the sink, yellow washing-up gloves up to his bony elbows, whilst Blythe is pacing, still on the bikini and kimono combo.

'I am only trying to protect you, Blythe. This is far too risky a game. You're playing with fire!'

'Sometimes I think it's you I need protecting from!' she replies.

'I'm not the one you need to worry about, Blythe,' Ludo tells her, scrubbing at the dishes so suds fly. 'She's been asking me all sorts.'

'So what if she does ask questions?' Blythe says, by the table now, only a matter of meters away, but back turned. 'I want her to ask! That's why she's here.'

'You don't need her; you have me,' Ludo replies, rather pathetically.

'Yes, I have you,' she says. 'Thanks for reminding me.'

I straighten up and march purposefully towards the door, stepping inside in time to see Blythe leave the kitchen via the corridor, kimono flapping and no indication she's seen me. 'Hi, Ludo, am I OK to come in?'

Ludo's recovery is impressive. He spins round from the sink, gloves dripping and declares, 'Ms Wilde, you are here at the appointed time, a miracle!' Then he glances at the clock. 'Or maybe a tad after.'

I hand him the emptied fruit bowl. 'It seemed like you two were having an argument.'

'Not at all,' he says, staring at the door to the corridor which Blythe left open. 'No argument.'

'Oh, I definitely heard raised voices.'

'It's a frustrating legal process, Ms Wilde, and a worrying one,' he says, dropping the returned bowl into the murky water. 'But we must all continue to hope for a miracle, even at this eleventh hour.'

'Is that what it's going to take?' I ask, his current mantra of hope at odds with Blythe's criticism of his negativity.

'We shall see. Now do please sit down, Ms Wilde. I'll just...' He clears a space for me at the table, removing a pile of folded towels. 'There you go.'

A glossy magazine is placed at Blythe's favoured position at the head of the table, open to an article about the lady herself. I pull it closer, excited to read, although the photo of Blythe is less than flattering. She is seated by a window, the light from behind subdued, her skin chalky and pale. She looks older than in real life, and terribly sad. The shout line trails *A Star's Twilight Years*. Dom's *reclusiveness* and Blythe's *former fame* also standing out as I skim-read. It's reductive and unkind. Blythe cannot be pleased.

Ludo snatches the magazine away and closes it.

'Hey, I was reading that!' I tell him, looking up.

He places the magazine out of my reach, scooping up some crumbs with a curved hand then dropping them into the other palm to throw them at the overflowing bin. 'I'd prefer you didn't take things that don't belong to you,' he says. 'Or eavesdrop.'

'I wasn't taking it, just looking, and I wasn't eavesdropping, I was invited for supper!'

'How long were you there?'

'Not long.'

'Good,' he replies. 'And I'm afraid supper is running a little late.'

My stomach growls in protest. 'Anything going begging in the meantime? All I've had is fruit and if my blood sugar drops, I tend to...' I mime a dramatic fall from the chair, the back of my hand raised to my forehead as I stop myself from actually toppling over sideways. It was meant to lighten the mood, but I do feel a bit weird. 'Carbs are best, or—'

'I can offer a cup of tea, Ms Wilde,' Ludo suggests, frowning at my antics. 'Maybe a biscuit if I can find one; neither Blythe nor I indulge.'

'Thanks, a biscuit would be good and tea with sugar. Will Blythe be coming back soon?'

Ludo fills the kettle before he replies. 'She will return presently, I'm sure. She needs to change for supper. It's part of her ritual, makes her feel better. As I think I told you.'

He sets a plate of promising, if melting, chocolate digestives on the table. 'Not the case for you though, Ms Wilde? You prefer a more casual look?'

'Yes, I do.' I bite into a biscuit to stop myself saying more. It's soft and past its best. I try another – the same. I check the packet and they're wildly out of date, but I'm starving so I cram in another, despite the fact the chocolate is developing a white bloom and I've dropped crumbs down my white top.

'When I was eavesdropping...' I venture a cheeky grin through the mouthful of claggy biscuit. Ludo side-eyes me. 'I heard you say you were protecting Blythe, what did you mean by that?'

'I'm not sure I understand your meaning?' he asks, dropping teabags into mugs he then brings to the table.

I swallow the chewy oats with some difficulty. 'I understand your reluctance to talk, she's your employer, but it's got something to do with me, hasn't it?'

'Don't flatter yourself, Ms Wilde.' Ludo opens the fridge, sniffs the milk and grimaces, then hands the carton to me. 'And for the record, Blythe is a lot more than my employer.'

'Is she?' I ask, eyebrows raised as I spoon in damp sugar from the bag Ludo has plonked down in front of me, a tablespoon sticking out. 'How so?'

'Not in the way you infer with that look,' he says, 'but yes. I'm all she's got.'

Ludo sits in Blythe's chair, contemplating his black tea and waving away the milk when I push it closer. Probably a wise move. There are sour clots now floating in mine. I pretend to sip, lips clamped.

'Why not help me to help her, Ludo?' I suggest, wiping my mouth with the back of my hand. 'I honestly want to, if I can.'

'I'm not sure that's in your power, Ms Wilde. Unless...' Ludo stares into the garden.

'Yes?'

'No, it's nothing, not my place to say.'

'Is this to do with the scripts?' I swallow, the sour taste now in my mouth although I didn't allow any of the milky tea to pass my lips.

Ludo shakes his head. 'It's Blythe's story to tell, when she's ready. *If* she's ready.'

'What story? The memoir, or the scripts?'

He gets up and walks back to the dishes, his hands gripping the edge of the enamel sink as if he's clinging to the side of a sinking ship. 'Like I said, I think this is all a terrible idea.'

'Why though?'

'Blythe isn't in the right place to make good decisions about what to share, that's all.'

'Why?'

He turns to face me, his face animated in a way I haven't witnessed before, eyes wide and mouth filled with spittle as his words trip over one another. 'Isn't it obvious?! She's wild with grief, terrified of the future, tortured by what happened to Dom. She has to live with that, but she can't. It's the worst timing. This is all a huge mistake.'

'Were you here the night Dom died?'

'No, Ms Wilde,' Ludo replies, eyes narrowing. 'I most certainly wasn't and I don't much care for the insinuation.'

'But you were in the photos as Blythe left the police station.'

'Blythe called me and I arranged a solicitor who organised bail. We emerged to a barrage of unwanted cameras, reporters jostling her. It was awful.'

'Thank goodness you were there! You're her rock, Ludo,' I reply, turning on the charm. 'Whatever would she do without you?'

He smiles. 'I'm not saying that, but it helps me sleep at night to know she's looked after.'

'So you live in?'

'Mostly, when I can.'

'And everything falls to you, from watching Blythe to cutting the grass?'

'What is this, Ms Wilde, an interrogation?' He attempts a laugh. 'I thought Blythe was your interviewee, not me?'

'Sorry, I'm just curious. You're clearly very important to her.'

'Who else is going to keep this place going?' He gets up and slides a dishcloth over the counter beside the piled dishes. 'As I say, I'm all she has left and I'll be here for as long as she needs me.'

'But surely this isn't what you signed up for, as her business manager?'

Ludo sighs heavily, abandoning the cloth for a tea towel and drying up dishes with little enthusiasm. 'Blythe has been very good to me over the years, Ms Wilde. She took a chance on me when no one else would, and now... I owe her, that's all, nothing else. And nothing romantic, if that's what you're still hinting at with those animated brows.'

I adjust my expression, always an open book. 'She took a chance on you, how?'

Ludo eyes me, mouth clamped tight.

'It's fine if you don't want to tell me, I'm sure I can look it up.' I hold up my phone. 'Good old Google will provide!'

His eyes widen again. I'm onto something.

'I lost my first job, at a wealth management company, many years back. It was a misunderstanding, a genuine mistake in accounting that was... unfortunate and misinterpreted. Anyway, for a young man it was very... Blythe was a client and she stuck with me when others didn't and now I will stick with her, and I do it gladly.' His back straightens, the tea towel that had been circling a plate, now still. 'The greatest honour of my career is to be her manager. I'm only sad it's come to this, but I shan't desert her, not ever. I'll be here to the bitter end. And beyond, if needs be. I hope that satisfies you of my reasons for being protective, Ms Wilde? Purely out of concern for Blythe. Nothing else. Nothing sinister. I know how you writers look for motives, dark deeds, secrets lurking, but you'll find none here.'

I make a mental note to look up the 'genuine mistake in accounting'.

'Yes, of course, but surely, it's a matter of days now until she's charged? It's been over month since Dom's death.'

'Let's just wait and see, shall we?' Ludo says, glancing towards the corridor. 'Blythe remains confident of her legal team, so I suggest we follow her lead.'

'Confident about what, getting away with murder?'

Ludo scowls then turns away, pulling a pan from the cupboard. 'I need to get on with supper; maybe you could leave me to it for a while?'

He fills the saucepan with water, the clattering noise precluding further chat, but I stay put, smiling at him to ease my continued presence. I don't want to appear bullish, but this may be my best chance of getting to the truth of their argument. I just need to convince him of the value in talking to me. Because his denial has only convinced me more that there *are* secrets to unearth.

'You do understand that even if I don't write Blythe's memoir, someone else will? It won't go away, Ludo, unless she pays back the advance?'

He spins round. 'That's a possibility, about the money, I mean?'

'Of course. If the memoir doesn't go ahead, she will have to give back what she's been paid so far. It's in the contract, didn't you read the Ts & Cs?'

'I see,' he says, eyes cast down to the grubby floor, a pair of tongs in hand. 'In that case... Although I'd still prefer Blythe to wait until she can be more... *circumspect*.' He catches my eye, an eagerness in his as he waves the tongs. 'Do you think you could delay the memoir, Ms Wilde, even by a few weeks? It would be so appreciated. Blythe needs that money, but now is such a tricky time for her to be talking to you.'

'What are you afraid of her telling me, Ludo?'

He blanches. 'I have no idea what you mean by that.'

'If you want my help, you have to give me something in return.'

'Are you trying to blackmail me?'

'Come on, Ludo. Help me out. I won't say a word to Blythe, I promise.'

He drops the tongs on the counter and lights the hob with a match, the roar of a flame under the pan filling the silence. Then he crumbles a stock cube into the water, my expectations for dinner tumbling as they are for this conversation. Any candour I'd established melting along with that stock cube.

'I really must insist you allow me to get on,' he says, leaning round to pluck a mouldy lemon from the fruit bowl on the table. He inspects it then lobs it with impressive accuracy over the table and into the overflowing bin, before taking a replacement lemon, firm in his palm as he tests it. Ludo slams the hardened fruit on the worktop, then selects a knife from the magnetised panel on the wall, the paring blade passing through the tough skin like a scalpel cutting through flesh, the slices paper-thin.

I get up, sensing the futility of pressing him further. The sour milk I tried so hard not to swallow, sloshing around my stomach in a worrying manner.

'What time shall I come back, Ludo?'

'Maybe around seven?' he replies, still slicing, his snub nose crinkled as the zesty oil is released. 'I'm sure Blythe will be ready to join us by then. We were planning on G&Ts as an aperitif, if that suits?'

'Sounds great.'

I'm negotiating the broken patio door when I drop my last, deliberately casual question, tossed over the right shoulder of my embroidered top, my freckled skin pink beneath the chocolate stained white cotton.

'I meant to ask, do you know where Dom's laptop is?'

Ludo turns, knife raised. 'Why do you ask that?'

'I'm thinking there'll be a stack of scripts held on his hard drive. Would be great to check through the iterations, to compare stylistically as well as content. You said he'd been working on them for months. He must have produced more than I've seen?'

'Well yes, but—'

'And if I'm to perpetuate some hope of a comeback, however misguided, I'll need more to work with. I could maybe extend the window for delivering the first chapters on the memoir, as you suggested, if you were able to help me find those copies?'

He stares, looking unconvinced.

'Should I ask Blythe about the laptop instead, Ludo? Explain I'll need it to work on the scripts...'

'No, Ms Wilde, I'm afraid that won't be possible, sadly.'

'OK, then you need to help me.'

'I can't.'

This is getting tiresome but I force my frustration down. 'I understand you might be reluctant to hand over something of Dom's without Blythe's permission, but I promise she won't know, I'm used to keeping secrets and—'

'No, you don't understand, Ms Wilde.' Ludo raises a hand, the paring blade reflecting the evening sun leaking in from the garden, a crow squawking loudly in one of the tall trees as the blade flashes its warning. 'Dom burned everything. Razed it to the ground, including the laptop. A terrible bonfire. His life's work went up in flames the night he died.'

15

A circle of scorched earth marks the site of the bonfire. The spot located, as Ludo advised, just beyond the swimming pool. In an area of the garden hidden behind trellis. A productive patch filled with raised beds and sweet with lavender. A thriving bed of brassicas is beside me, rainbow chard still sprouting. Reminiscent, incongruously, of the vegetable bouquets they sell in the Sunday market near my flat. Life born of ash. And death. Although I have no idea if the mulch of a man's life's work is good for veg growing. I just paid my five quid at the market, then watched lovingly as Jake threw the ruby red and verdant green chopped chard into a stir-fry. The closest I have ever come to asking someone to marry me.

The fire damage certainly hasn't helped the fruit trees in this secluded corner of the garden, the branches charred. Ludo said the bonfire was threatening them when a concerned passer-by alerted the authorities. The smoke was spreading, a thickness to it that drew two fire engines. The first crew broke through the gates to find much more than an unwise bonfire as they tumbled into the garden. What Ludo told me about the bonfire is consistent with the accounts I've read of the night Dom died. But Ludo, like the reports, kept very much to the bare facts, loyal as always to his employer.

The blackened tree trunks border the same section of wall I ran my hand along street-side as I tried to find my way in.

A sudden yearning to be on the other side of the boundary wall pulls at me, the sense of confinement claustrophobic. Or maybe it's the drastic means by which Dom's entire body of work was destroyed that's urging me to get out, while I still can. The uselessness of my search reinforced by that pile of ash. Nothing to show for all that creative endeavour other than a few mangled scraps of plastic and metal.

There must be backup copies somewhere though, surely? In the cloud. Although Ludo said his understanding was that the bonfire had immediately followed a mass digital cull.

'There's nothing left,' he told me before I came out here to see for myself. 'Not one copy of anything he was working on. It seems an extreme reaction, granted, but Dom was a passionate man with violent tempers. Frankly, it doesn't shock me that much.'

I run the point of my flip-flop through the ashes, the soot getting under my toes as I ponder what on earth made Dom destroy everything in such a dramatic and final way. However theatrical his tendencies, something must have triggered this over-the-top gesture after months of obsessive writing? Had Dom come to a realisation too awful to face? The same one I've recently been terrified by. His wife's past too horrific to fictionalise. But if so, why on July second and not any time before?

The Hoppers clearly had their ups and downs, but stayed together for three decades, through success and obscurity, and a move from the sun-drenched hills of California to the perennial mizzle of London, this current heatwave an anomaly. It was a show-business marriage that endured despite Dom's demons, his bitterness at his thwarted success sending him down a spiral of drinking and self-pity that kept him from writing for years. So what changed in that regard too? Not only in the weeks before his death, when he'd been writing night and day, but specifically on the second of July when he lit a match and razed everything he'd laboured over to the ground? The same day he ended up dead. Why then? That's the key to all this, I'm sure of it.

And within that is the solution to another conundrum too. Because Dom was looking for my mother, his email said so. So that must have some bearing on this too.

And there's another major concern, one that I've tried and failed to set aside ever since I read the scripts' proposed series title: *The Six Kills of Darcy Diamond: An Icon's Murderous Route to Fame.*

Six kills.

And I know of only three. Plus Dom's, but that was afterwards.

Which means there are at least three more tragic deaths that I'm yet to uncover.

I stare at the pyre and ask all these questions and more. But there's only one that I whisper aloud.

'What happened to make you burn the lot, Dom? What the fuck happened?'

Only the tips of my green toenail polish show through as I kick my way through the ashes in my blackened flip-flops, hoping that, phoenix-like, Dom's thoughts will rise up and share their secrets, but of course there's nothing left here. Not even a curl of smoke to offer me a signal. Maybe Ludo was right. There are no dark discoveries to be made. Only sad losses and petty jealousies and my wild imagination filling in the gaps. *Wilde by name and wild by nature.* That's what Dad always used to say to me, the meaning changing according to the nature of my transgression. Sometimes benign and indulgent, sometimes weary and resentful. But always Dad. Constant, loving. *My* rock.

I look over at the house, the tower looming even larger from this perspective. Did Dom look up at it too as he added fuel to the fire, knowing Blythe was up there and would see the flames, then come running to the beacon he'd lit? He should have run himself, as far and as fast as he could. Whilst he still could. Maybe he did and Blythe stopped him with that bullet. Maybe she will do that again. To me.

I take out my phone, hand trembling. No signal. Of course. But I doubt I would call the police, even if I could. The lack of means is a convenient cop-out. I have to get some answers first. And let's face it, if I was going to report anything, it would have been on receipt of that email from a dead man. The mere fact of its existence – two days after the sender's fatal shooting – potentially significant.

I thought about reporting it, often, but even if the police took me seriously, there's literally nothing in Dom's message that would have made any difference to what had happened. He was already dead. An irrefutable fact, much as I'd have loved to think otherwise.

Plus telling the police, or anyone, would have put paid to me following the trail. I couldn't risk my best chance yet of finding my mother, Katherine, but should I report my concerns now, whilst I still can?

I look at the non-existent bars of signal and kick again at the pyre.

All I have are suspicions and *feelings*.

If only that email had come two days earlier. *Two days*. The story of my life. Two days until my screenwriting debut would have begun shooting and I'd at least have been paid. Two days that an email failed to send to me due to lack of decent Wi-Fi. A message that could have changed everything had I been able to speak to Dom, but instead it got stuck in Dom's Outbox as he worked in the black hole known as The Writing Annexe. But what was he working on? His escape plan, or his wife's greatest role? The terrible truth he'd lived with for too long finally rendered into a decent script to end his thirty year drought, but to what end? A parting shot or a parting gift? A confession of her terrible deeds, or merely suspicion? Maybe he'd only just put it all together as he neared the end of the process and the dreadful truth dawned? Dom making connections to deaths he'd mourned and never suspected were anything but accidental and unconnected, until that fateful night?

I replied to Dom's email, of course, several times, knowing in my heart it was useless, those headlines of a fatal shooting in Hampstead, barely noticed two days earlier, then suddenly all I could see. A stark reality I couldn't believe. I even contacted Dom's agent, James Langley, to see if he had heard from Dom. He's never responded, probably assumed I was a crank or a reporter scratching around for a quote. Like Ludo, James' loyalties clearly lie with his biggest client: Blythe. Dom barely getting a mention on the 'Talent' page of JL Assoc.

I kick at the pyre, harder now, dust clouds rising up. I'm so close to the truth, I can feel it. I'll talk to the police. Tell them everything, once I know it. But not yet. There's no need, Josie Phoenix died decades ago. I can't save her, or Wendy Hopper, or poor Florence Saint John – which reminds me, I need to find out more about the circumstances of Flo's death, as well as looking into any other suspicious deaths that might be linked to Blythe. Then when I do go to the police, I can report fully and frankly everything I know, presenting myself as a credible witness.

All I have so far is my research – facts which are all in the public domain – and a few pages of terrible script written by a mad woman obsessed with her comeback. Far short of evidence of any actual wrongdoing, but enough to need to know more. Because Blythe is capable of murder. That's fact. She killed her husband.

The love of her life. And despite Ludo's claims of her being grief-stricken, I've seen little remorse.

I swat a mosquito as it draws blood, attracted by the fruit trees no doubt, which despite the fire are laden with apples and plums that are splitting in the heat and falling to the ground. I squash the offending gnat, its innards spilling out as I press it between thumb and forefinger, a jagged line of red smearing the tattooed heart that forever beats on my forearm.

You're a terror, Marnie-Moo, Mum says, surprising me with her sing-song chatter.

The image of my mother often returns, fuzzy, but reliably there, but to hear her voice... That's a surprise.

I close my eyes, concentrate. Will her to return. The diminutive, softly spoken woman with auburn hair and freckles, like me. Same pale skin, same curves, same brown eyes. Katherine, or *Kate* as Dad called her with a smile in his voice that departed the day she left.

I am standing on the windowsill of my bedroom in the old house. I'm four and I'm flying. The window is open, but I'm held safe in my mother's arms. It's the last day I ever saw her. I squeeze my eyes tighter as the image escapes me. I pull it back. Like watching a movie. Intense, and yet dream-like. My mother isn't with me now, she's below, walking down the path towards a man who is definitely not my father. Dad is shouting, maybe at me, but he's not beside me, his thinning hair what strikes me as I look down on him. But that's wrong: I'm seeing him as he is now, not then. I wave and the man with Mum looks up and he's not Dad, but Dominic Hopper – tall and dark, like a thousand other men. Millions, in fact. Smartly dressed, in black trousers and a sweater, the outfit taken from a photo I saw of him with Blythe, back in the UK, when she was up for an award as the matriarch in a continuing drama. One of those tacky televised ceremonies where the skirts are too short and heels too high, drinks flowing, the carnage reported the next day in British tabloids. But Blythe was resplendent in an Oscar-worthy gown on the red carpet, Dom in a jumper at her side. And she didn't win.

Now I hear Dad's voice. His shouts coming loud, frantic calls to stay back from the edge. Screams bounce round my head and yet the sounds are detached from the images. There were tulips and daffodils in pots lining the front path. Pots we had planted together, my mother and me. I watch her drag her case down the path until the tall man I see as Dom takes it from her and she climbs into his sleek, polished car.

Her name was Katherine Wilde and she iced Bakewell tarts and sewed skirts with pockets in, mostly by hand but sometimes on an old machine with a foot pedal that she pushed down with her plump, bare toes. She called me sweetie. Let me try the machine, just the foot pedal. The needle was too dangerous for little hands. And now I've ruined her skirt with my stupid clumsiness, and I still haven't found her.

All I know is I have to stay and see this through to whatever conclusion there is. I'm sick of waiting for answers that never come. Tired of living on hope that one day Mum will return for me, which she never has. Who does that to a four-year-old? I'm thirty in a few months. Not a child, but forever one inside. I can't move on and I can't stay stuck in the past forever. I'll turn into a madwoman like Blythe.

Blythe startles me, appearing round the clematis-choked trellis. She is barefoot, and still in the bikini/kaftan ensemble. She carries the wide-brimmed sunhat, placing it on her head as she looks at the remains of the long-dead bonfire, then at me.

I poke the edge of my flip-flop at the pyre again, disturbing it. My feet are filthy. 'Why would he destroy everything he'd written, Blythe, after all his hard work?'

Blythe shakes her head, the same quick dismissal I've witnessed her send Ludo's way many a time. But I'm not him. I'm Katherine Wilde's lost daughter and I'm here for answers.

'Something must have made him do this! What was he afraid of, Blythe? Something in the scripts he'd discovered that frightened him, was that it?' As soon as the challenge is out I regret it.

'*Afraid?*' Blythe repeats. 'What of?' She looks at me, aghast, waiting for a response I cannot form. 'I've come down for a swim, Marnie, not to elicit more drama.' She massages her temples. 'I have a headache after those bloody calls with my lawyer.'

With that, she turns and walks towards the pool, the hat blocking my view of her expression as she retreats.

I follow, arriving as Blythe slips off the animal-print kaftan, allowing it to slither like a snakeskin by the edge of the pool, then she walks into the water and begins carving smooth strokes to the end. I step into the shallows by the steps, washing my dirty feet in the clear water, reminded of that image of Dom's blood, the one I've quite possibly invented: crimson seeping through the blue and spreading like the soot from my feet.

There were no witnesses to that final argument, or none that I know of. Ludo said he wasn't here that night, but he could be lying. Either way, all I have is the woman currently floating on her back in the middle of the pool, the water lapping at fronds of blonde hair that radiate like a halo. And even when I do broach the subject of Dom's murder and the reason for that, will she be truthful? Does she even know what the truth is any more?

It's only been a month, but memories are notoriously unreliable, the past reinvented to fit our needs. I know that more than most. My mother the cake baker, seamstress, a warm fuzzy presence, when she was likely much more, and less, than that. We all do it, airbrushing over the memories we don't like and painting in more flattering strokes for those we've loved and lost.

Even if Blythe wants to capture the past in her outstretched hands as she paddles the water, eyes closed against the sun, it may well elude her. Is she thinking of Dom? Reinventing him too? Remembering the good and forgetting the bad in their marriage?

Like the stitches in the home-made skirt, Mum is true and firm. Straight and narrow and beautiful and crazy and perfect. But she's not. She left me and I've ruined her skirt. We are all broken. All messed up.

Blythe pulls herself upright and walks towards the steps, then past me, emerging from the sparkling pool, her blonde hair scraped back with clawed nails, droplets falling from her bronzed skin to the hot paving like dissolving diamonds. The narrow footprints she leaves soon erased by the heat, the water cooling as my feet and ankles, now cleaner, remain submerged.

But you can't wash away the past. It's there. And I will find it. Whatever the cost.

I step in the last traces of Blythe's footprints, following her to the loungers, my feet wider and longer than hers and leaving a dirty trail.

'I need some answers, Blythe, or...'

My head swims, a step back as I right myself.

'Or what, Marnie?' she asks, a hand shielding her eyes as she looks up at me.

'Or I'm going to the police with my concerns.'

16

'Care to explain exactly what those concerns may be?' Blythe asks, getting up to grab a rolled towel from a stack by the loungers and patting her legs dry. 'And why you are threatening me with the police?'

'No, I, it's—' I'm back on the window ledge of my childhood bedroom, the world spinning beneath me. Nothing to stop me from falling. Blythe's voice imperious and yet distant. It must be the heat, but I'm in real danger of passing out on the hot slabs which now burn my drying feet.

'I'd like to know what exactly you are accusing me of, Marnie,' she says, stretching out on the lounger, a hand shielding her eyes as she surveys me, the damp towel in her lap. 'I am already known to the police and I'd very much prefer not to spend another night in a cell. Are you all right there, Marnie?'

'No, nothing, it's just...' I stumble forwards and fall onto the lounger beside hers.

'Is it the heat?' she asks, scowling at me.

I nod. 'Yes, and seeing the bonfire...' I take a deep breath. 'It made me think more about what happened that night, and how terrible it must have been.'

'Dom died, Marnie. What else do you need to know? The police are fully aware of the situation, I can assure you.'

'Yes, of course, sorry. It's just... Did you mean to kill him?'

I hold my breath and wait, about to retract the question, or pass out beside her, one or the other, when Blythe swings her legs round and sits up, meeting my eye. For a split-second, I consider sidling two steps to my right and submerging in the water. Might solve a multitude of problems; likely I'd pass out, maybe drown? I doubt Blythe would rush to save me. But then something unexpected happens that shocks me out of my light-headiness. Blythe starts to cry. Tears falling so fast, it surely cannot be a performance? The grief I've been looking for finally demonstrated. She pulls the towel up to her face and sobs into it. A grief too raw and private to interrupt. Although, basic humanity would dictate I do something. I lift my hand, but drop it as she wipes her eyes and looks up. At least it's stopped me spinning out. I'm fully in the moment.

'I'm sorry, Blythe. I shouldn't have asked if you... I didn't mean to be insensitive.'

'No, you should ask, it's your job.' She shakes her head, dabs her face again, then runs a finger under each eye. 'You need sun cream, Marnie,' she tells me, donning yet another pair of fabulous shades, these ones pink-hued, the sun cream held out to me. 'Your nose is burning horribly.'

'Oh, right, yes,' I reply, blindsided by the sudden change in her mood. 'Thanks.'

I rub in the proffered cream, then sit back, knees raised, mirroring Blythe. The lack of eye contact is helpful. Like those conversations Dad and I used to have in the car. The excruciating ones which were only possible as we both faced forwards: like the one when I'd had to tell him I'd started my period, or needed a bra, or was broken-hearted over a smelly boy who'd had his fun by the sea then buggered off home a week later without a word. The kind of conversations I'd imagined Mum would have handled so much better if she'd been around. She'd have taken my hand and told me all girls went through this. It was normal. Not my fault. I wasn't a disappointment or a 'stupid girl' who'd had to be taken for the morning after pill in the local chemist where Dad had peeled a tenner from his wallet before he sent me inside. An embarrassment to a man of his standing. A man of the law.

'Dom had been drinking a lot that day,' Blythe begins, startling me with her circle back to what I'd thought would remain an unanswered question, my pulse quickening. 'His alcoholism, which it was, despite his denials, became the root of many arguments. Not the cause, but it exacerbated the tensions.'

'Yes, I can see how it would do that. I think my grandmother was the same.'

I catch her eye then Blythe turns away, staring at the pool. A leaf has fallen in, several now I've noticed. There's a net by the side, filled with them. Another of Ludo's duties, I guess, like the rolled towels and kitchen suppers and guiding his client through a crowd of waiting photographers.

'Dom being drunk was sadly very much the norm,' she continues. 'But that evening...' She looks at me. 'The second of July...'

I nod. 'The night he died.'

'Yes, the night he...' She swallows. 'He was much more drunk than usual. Picking fights over nothing. He threw a plate at me during supper, Marnie. Straight at my head.'

'That's... Did it hit you?'

'No, I ducked; not my first time, sadly.' She gives a sad laugh and sits back, reaching for her cigarettes on the table between us. 'I left him to calm down and went up to the tower. Did some yoga, a spot of meditation, felt better, until I saw the smoke drifting across the garden.'

'The bonfire?'

'Yes, the bonfire.' She lights the cigarette, the flame held on the lighter afterwards, flickering by her cheek for a second or two. 'I ran straight down to him, of course, tried to reason with him, but it was too late. He'd burned everything by the time I got there. Even threw in his laptop.'

'Why would he do that?'

Blythe inspects her bare feet, pulling at her toes and sucking on her cigarette. 'He'd sent a series treatment to our agent, unbeknownst to me. It was the first thing Dom had written in a very long time, and even longer since he'd submitted anything. I wouldn't have shared it at such an early stage. Dom was far too fragile, and I could have murdered James for the brutal way he rejected him.'

I wince at Blythe's unfortunate choice of words but if she notices my reaction, she gives no sign.

'A fucking compliment slip, Marnie! Three words written on it: "Not for me!". Can you believe it? I don't think he even read it.'

That is brutal. 'Why the snail mail?'

She exhales stale smoke and glances across. 'I think it was about me not knowing he'd shared it with anyone, until he had good news.'

I nod, clearing my throat, although I wonder if that's true. 'So that's what set Dom off on his quest to burn everything: a brutal rejection from his agent?'

'James was never known for his people skills,' Blythe explains. 'And as I've told him now myself, it's a brilliant idea, but I'm wasting my breath. James wouldn't know a decent script if it hit him between the eyes. The man's a joke.'

'But he's your talent agent too, isn't he?'

'Unfortunately, he is.' Blythe stubs out the cigarette in a drying puddle of pool water before she stretches her legs out and closes her eyes.

'Sorry, but why would you and Dom both sign to this man if he's rubbish at his job?' I ask, thinking of Harry more fondly than usual.

Blythe takes off the pink glasses and opens her eyes. 'James was the only agent who offered to represent us after we returned to the UK.'

'But you're an Academy Award winner!'

'Yes, I am aware, but unfortunately, or fortunately at the time, I guess, James didn't know the score because he has no connections in the US.'

'The score about what?'

'I need to rest now, Marnie. Just for a minute. Get rid of this awful headache. It's...' She grimaces. 'It's actually a pretty bad one.'

I study her face for signs of a performance, the diversion a little too convenient, but she looks in genuine pain. She starts to massage her temples, then her skin loses all colour and her eyes roll into the back of her head, a hand falling over the side of the lounger.

I spring up. 'Oh my God! Blythe, are you OK?'

I gently shake her shoulder and wait, hand on her thin arm. Should I do something? I thought it was me going to pass out and now—

'Marnie?' She opens her eyes and looks at me. 'What happened?'

'I think you blacked out for a second. It's this heat. I felt funny too.'

'Yes, it is the heat. You're right.'

'Can I get you anything? Water? Paracetamol?'

'Ludo knows what I need,' she whispers, hand touching mine as I pull away. 'Ask him to be quick, Marnie!'

I run barefoot towards the kitchen, breathless as I tell Ludo what's happened. His face falls and he volleys questions at me as he grabs a pot of pills from the cupboard and hastily fills a glass with tap water.

'Is she conscious? How long was she out for?'

'A few seconds. Maybe more. What's wrong with her?'

'It doesn't matter!' he shouts, running ahead across the lawn and calling, 'Blythe, are you OK? Blythe, talk to me! I'm coming!'

Her throaty cackle is reassuring as I catch up with them by the pool. She's still lying down but pulls herself up on the lounger as I approach.

'You need to come inside,' he's telling her. 'I can help you upstairs.'

'Calm down, Ludo, I'm fine!'

She takes the water glass Ludo holds out, then the tablets, which he drops into her open palm, two of them, blue with orange centres. Like no prescription I've ever seen.

She swallows the pills. 'You should see your faces! It's just a headache.'

'You need to rest, Blythe!' Ludo barks, then frowns at me as if I'm to blame. 'I'll ask you to leave, Ms Wilde. Blythe needs her rest.'

'Ludo, it's fine. *I'm* fine.' Blythe points me back to the other lounger. 'Come, Marnie, sit with me again. And, Ludo, please stop staring at me and go back to whatever atrocity you are preparing for supper. I'm fine, I promise. No drama, OK?'

I snort at the lack of self-awareness from our consummate drama queen, but it's good to have her back. Which is kind of an odd thought, but she's why I'm here.

'What are the pills for?' I ask as Ludo reluctantly turns to leave.

'Headaches, as I said,' Blythe tells me, waving him away. 'Oh, and there's something else Ludo found me,' Blythe whispers, leaning closer, conspiratorial as Ludo walks off. 'I'll have to ask him the name; they're very good.'

'I prefer not to take tablets if I can, but thanks.'

'No, they're diet pills, Marnie. Doctor in the US prescribed them when I couldn't shift the weight. Ludo gets them online. They suppress appetite.'

I swallow the hurt, or try to. 'No, thank you.'

'They're natural supplements,' Blythe says, lying back and closing her eyes. 'Ludo knows the guy who imports them. Mind you, he knows everyone.' She glances at me. 'Anyway, tell me, what did you think of the scripts?'

She waits, taking my silence the wrong way as she adds, 'I know Ludo told you I wrote them, Marnie. I'm not a writer, don't pretend to be, but the idea… it's strong, yes?'

'It's interesting,' I offer, still stung by the offer of diet pills.

'I knew it!' She claps her hands then rolls onto her side to face me, one small breast protruding more than the other in the tiny bikini as she cups her chin and digs an elbow into the cushion, propping herself up. 'So, how can we make this happen? What do you need from me, more ideas?'

'I guess but… I'm sorry, Blythe, don't you have more pressing concerns?'

'What could be more pressing than you and me working together on something that could be a game changer for us both?' she says, eyes bright. 'Come on, Marnie. Let me worry about the other stuff. What do you say?'

I imagine her delivering a similar pep-talk to Dom, goading him into the ill-fated project. A Lady MacBeth, urging him to seize the crown.

'You think I'm mad,' she says, turning away to inspect her cleavage, although she's so thin, it's mainly bone. Too thin in my opinion.

'No,' I lie, but maybe I do. 'Is this why you accepted me as your ghost? Because I have screenwriting experience and you want me to finish the scripts?'

'Oh, don't flatter yourself!' Blythe snaps, getting to her feet and pulling on the kimono. 'I'm sure you're not the only ghostwriter with ambitions to be a screenwriter.'

'*Ambitions?* I had a series commissioned. And what about the memoir? I'm here for that payday, not some pipe dream of a comeback.'

'You should be thanking me!' she says, shaking out the damp ends of her hair. 'I'm an Academy Award winner, as you said yourself. This could be the making of your washed-up career.'

'Hang on a sec!'

'And don't write me off as the lead, either!' She jabs a finger my way. 'I know you think my plans are... What was the phrase you used? "A bit optimistic given the circumstances," but I have something up my sleeve that could change everything.'

Blythe struts towards the house, kimono flowing behind her, hat on. An impeccably timed exit and before I've had chance to question what exactly she has up her diaphanous sleeve that will allow her to star in a television series of her questionable past, rather than end up in prison.

'G&Ts in thirty!' she calls back. 'And bring the scripts! We need to start fleshing out the other episodes if we're to get this project off the ground.'

17

I set aside, for now, the memoir writing, my head full of questions about the scripts as I head back to the writing annexe. As preoccupied with the idea, it would seem, as Blythe is. The past more present in those pages. The key to everything, I fear, as I sit at Dom's desk and open up my saved files again.

The deaths of Wanda (Wendy) and Lola (Josie) are the subject of the first two episodes, in that order. At least according to the synopsis of the proposed six-part series. The working title – *The Six Kills of Darcy Diamond: An Icon's Murderous Route to Fame* – indicating there are four more episodes, and therefore four more 'kills'. The question being, who are those other dead women? I have one potential name, that of the young actress Florence Saint John, found dead at the Hoppers' home after a party in May 1993, but that still leaves three blanks to fill in.

I scan the script pages again, something about a scene in the first episode I want to quickly check before it's time for the promised pre-supper G&Ts.

In the outline of that scene – it's barely more than a scribbled note, in what is now confirmed as Blythe's hand – there's mention of Darcy/Blythe auditioning for a *big* role. No detail other than that, although I assume it's referencing the lead in *Affairs of the Heart*, the film that won Blythe an Academy Award in 1995. The scripts never seem to stray far from Blythe's past and it is her biggest role by far.

It could be nothing, but I can't shake the feeling the proposed scene holds extra significance. I make a note to raise the audition process with Blythe when I get a chance. Dig a little deeper into the events surrounding it and ask if there was much competition for the part.

I also need to do more research into any other suspicious deaths connected to the Hoppers, potential 'kills' for those remaining episodes, including the full story of Flo's death, which appears to be by suicide.

I reluctantly close my notebook and take it with me as I make my way to the house. The thought of a stiff drink most alluring.

Blythe's laughter floats out the broken patio door this time as I approach. She's seated in her usual place at the head of the table, the sliced lemon Ludo was prepping earlier, along with a bowl of melting ice cubes and a bottle of craft gin – plus a litre of tonic water, low calorie of course – set out before her. The colour is high on her prominent cheekbones, a contrast to her blanched complexion when she'd zoned out by the pool. The flush a product of a contouring brush, perhaps, although another reason then becomes apparent.

'Marnie, come join me!' Blythe raises a huge crystal glass in her hand, the iced contents sloshing around, her eyes unfocused, smile wide. She's already well on the way to being drunk, if not arrived at that destination.

'Sorry, I'm a bit late,' I tell her as Ludo turns from the pot he's stirring and scowls. 'I was reading over the scripts and lost track of the time.'

'See, I told you she was busy working!' she tells Ludo, as she waves her G&T towards him, a spillage slicked across the table. 'Get this woman a large drink!'

I sit in my usual spot and accept the strong liquor which Ludo mixes with tonic and a side of disapproval. I take a restorative gulp of juniper and quinine, the tang of lemon reminding me of the amaretto sour in the pub, which feels like a lifetime ago. I set my notebook aside for now, pen balanced on top, savouring the drink.

'So?' Blythe prompts. 'What's your verdict on the scripts?'

'The problem is, Blythe, well, a couple in fact—'

'Oh, don't give me problems!' Blythe says as she shakes her head, the loose waves she's run through her hair flicking side to side. 'Give me only solutions, Marnie.'

'O-kayyy,' I reply, smiling. I quite like this smashed version of Blythe. A little less imposing, her lipstick more on the glass than her lips, her usually perfect hair mussed up, which also softens her features.

She's cinched in her waist with a leather belt, the buckle a designer logo. The dress is clearly designer too, in an exquisite floral print of pinks and blues and greens. Gucci or maybe Versace? The neck plunges to that tiny waist, the bodice fitted. You'd have to be underweight to wear the size she fits, the bones across her breast anatomical. I pull at my dress, debating the ethics of taking her up on the diet pills. It's the same dress I wore yesterday and it feels cheap and tight and very inadequate in comparison to hers. I gulp more of the G&T. It tastes a bit odd, probably that hardened lemon Ludo sliced. Past its sell-by date.

'OK, so yes, in my opinion,' I say, taking another quick sip despite the taste; vaguely chemical, on reflection, and dusty? I inspect the glass. 'Although it has to be said, my opinion isn't worth that much.'

Blythe nods, a little too easily for my liking.

'Right, well, I feel it's a problematic premise.'

'*Problematic?*' Blythe repeats, loudly. 'I thought you liked it?'

It's true, the idea is daring and therefore exciting, but there are obvious and troubling issues that I can't set aside.

'The resemblance to real events and people...' I swallow. 'Many of whom seem to be... well, they're dead, and in tragic circumstances. It won't sell, not in today's mindful and sensitive to—'

'Jeez, this again!' She slumps back in her chair, drink in hand. 'I'll say the same to you as I said to my tone-deaf agent: if they're dead, they can't sue us.' She catches my eye, then Ludo's. 'Oh for fuck's sake, I'm joking! We change a few names and locations to keep the lawyers happy, big deal! It's an easy fix.'

'Possibly,' I reply, taken aback by her no-fucks dismissal. 'But even besides that...'

Blythe raises an eyebrow. 'There's more?'

'The meta version of a well-known celebrity has been done before,' I reply, the alcohol helping, as is the return to my screenwriting persona, which I do enjoy.

'So has everything,' Blythe counters. 'There are only seven ideas, or is it five?'

'Yes, and although it's still a very popular format, especially as a means to reinvigorate a big name such as yourself, it's not exactly ground breaking.'

'Look at Matt LeBlanc...' Blythe says as she lights a cigarette, exhaling smoke before she adds, 'It did him no harm, did it?'

Blythe's fame is hardly in the same league as a former star of *Friends*, and the differences between truth and pastiche were more clearly defined in that series, which is kind of where I would take this script, if it were mine, and if it weren't for the fact that those dead women are *real* people who had tangible connections to the Hoppers and died in very dubious circumstances which are more than alluded to and in a less than sensitive manner.

'Legal concerns aside, there are victims here to consider...' I deliberately use the term victims, allowing a pause to gauge her reaction as I take another mouthful of the G&T. Surely even Blythe can see the questionable morality of exploiting these women, even if their names are changed?

Blythe says nothing, staring into her drink.

'It would be helpful, maybe, to address those worries sooner than later, Blythe? See if there's a way around this?'

'So you *do* want to work on the scripts with me?' she asks, sitting straighter. 'Is that what you're saying?'

Is that what I'm saying? This could be, as Harry suggested, a way back into scriptwriting. '*Maybe?*'

Ludo joins us, sitting beside a grinning Blythe and clearing his throat before he says directly to her, wooden spoon in hand, 'Do you really want to delve into those past matters now, Blythe?'

'Now is the only possible time!' she replies, snapping at him. 'Who knows what the future holds! We cannot all be cowards, hiding in the shadows, can we?'

Ludo swivels round to exclude me from their discussion, his back to me as he half whispers, 'Some matters are best left in the past, Blythe, are they not, for all concerned?'

Her expression turns thunderous. 'Don't you have a pot to stir elsewhere, Ludo?'

He jumps up as Blythe slams her drink down, dropping his wooden spoon, which he retrieves, taking it straight from the floor to pot.

'You have to be ballsy in this game, Marnie,' Blythe tells me. 'And I'm nothing if not that, so yes, fuck it, let's go there!'

I swallow, looking at Ludo in a rare moment of solidarity. I hadn't actually agreed to anything. My 'maybe' taken as confirmation.

'The story has to be handled carefully, of course,' she concedes.

'Victims honoured, as you say, names changed to be less recognisable, to protect the guilty as much as the innocent.'

I laugh, no one else joining in. 'Oh yes, sorry, of course. Yes. That's the very least we should do.'

Blythe nods at me as she spins a finger in the air, returning Ludo to his pot stirring. 'And as for my "predicament", as Ludo likes to call my potential incarceration.'

'Oh yes?' I ask, surprised she's even acknowledged the possibility.

Ludo's stirring slows, his interest as apparent as mine even if he daren't look over.

'My defence lawyer, Roland, has been pushing me again for my... "rationale," as he calls it... and whilst I've maintained my counsel, a loyalty to my beloved Dom to consider, I have to look to my future now and...'

She glances at Ludo's back, his shoulders raised, body stiff, his attention on the conversation at the detriment of what smells like burnt rice.

'Anyway, we shall see!' Blythe declares, startling me, my glass slipping from one hand and half-caught by the other. It's not an issue, it's almost empty, but my heart bounces along with the crystal tumbler as it hits the wooden table and rolls towards Blythe.

'I've told Roland to come over tomorrow and I'll try to explain it all,' Blythe explains, trapping the glass. 'The extenuating circumstances I have decided to share could make all the difference to the charges. I think the term he used is "extreme emotional provocation".'

'Abuse?' I ask, looking up from the dregs of ice and lemon I'm scooping from the table, the favourable opinion I've formed of Dom challenged yet again. I see him very much as a kindred spirit and on my side, despite the fact I already know he was a far from perfect father and husband. But if he was abusive towards Blythe then that changes everything.

'I'd call it more violent tendencies maybe...' Blythe replies, contemplating the glass and then me. 'Let's not make a big thing of it now. In fact...' She glances at Ludo. 'Why don't you sit in on the meeting tomorrow morning with my lawyers, Marnie? Save me saying everything again, which I find exhausting. Roland always asks me the same things about ten times, anyway.'

Ludo is staring at us both now.

'Yeah, that would be great, thanks,' I reply, hardly believing my luck.

'Good, because tonight, I don't want to think about any of that. I just want to drink until I forget. You'll join me in getting absolutely hammered, won't you, Marnie?'

'Absolutely!' Another offer I'm very happy to accept.

She refills my glass and we toast, a little heavy-handed on her part so she laughs and says, 'Oops!'

* * *

Ludo's risotto is of course a disaster. An inedible stodge he scrapes from our bowls straight into the bin. Dull thuds as it lands in amongst the rotting fruit in heavy clumps. Even I couldn't stomach it and I'm starving.

'Let's have buttered toast!' Blythe proposes. 'And scrambled eggs!' she declares, as if she's just invented the delicacy. 'Do we have eggs, Ludo? I fancy eggs!'

Poor Ludo. Despite everything, I do feel sorry for him: the ignominy as he shoves the ruined pan in the washing-up bowl and starts over is heart-wrenching.

Blythe tells me to bring my refreshed drink whilst Ludo 'crashes around', her opinion expressed loudly as an egg rolls from the counter to smash on the sticky floor. We exit the chaotic scene, Ludo's expression murderous as I chance a final glance back.

'Where are we headed?' I ask as Blythe leads the way along the photo-lined corridor.

She's even more drunk than I'd realised, dislodging a frame and sending it crashing to the floor.

'Fucking hell!' she says as I stoop to pick it up, a smiling chocolate Labrador staring back at me from behind the glass, younger Blythe's arms around its neck.

'He was my LA baby,' she says, stroking the dog's smiling face gently with the pad of her forefinger. 'Best boy ever. He adopted me, not the other way around, but I only had him a short time.'

'He's gorgeous. Was he... I mean, what happened to him?' I literally cannot deal if she's killed a dog. I'm out of here.

'Old age,' she says, looking rather sad. 'We knew it wouldn't be that long when we took him in from the coyotes. I think in some ways, he was the only reason we stayed as long we did.'

'Why did you leave Hollywood?' I ask, re-hanging the frame and adjusting my opinion with it. Surely anyone who loves a stray that much can't be all bad? 'I mean, you'd won an Oscar.'

'Yes, I had, and on that note, onwards!'

Blythe forges ahead, although her progress is somewhat erratic.

'Isn't it so very strange that frame and fame are only one letter apart?' she observes, stopping again. It amuses her a lot, her laughter over the top to the point of hysteria. Then she heads off once more, still weaving.

The hallway opens out in front of us. Magnificent and yet so old fashioned. The kitchen is much more modern, and the corridor which links the two the same, but the grand entrance hall remains imposing, dominated by the equally grand staircase. What I don't know is where the access to the tower is located. Somewhere way above, I guess, up that red-carpeted staircase.

'Impressive, eh?' Blythe observes, spinning a full three-sixty, which is remarkable given her drunken state.

'Certainly is.'

The Towers must have been a massive step up from the Hoppers' marital home in Mulholland Drive, which was gorgeous and clearly in a prime spot, but much smaller. I found some photos of it online, from an old magazine article, the spread taken just before the Academy Awards – Blythe reclining by the kidney-shaped pool, the Hollywood sign visible in the distance. Dom was blurred out in the background, a fuzzy silhouette, and the house, one-storey, wasn't even half the size of The Towers.

Maybe that was part of the appeal of the move, and also an effort to build some bridges with Dom's boys who were already living over here. Although waiting for a stray dog to die first doesn't suggest the Hoppers' priorities were with Dom's sons.

'I know it's terribly vain,' Blythe says, picking up another framed photo, this one on a table in the hall, then handing it to me. There are a few frames dotted around, along with lamps and small vases and trinket bowls. This photo, in an ornate silver frame, is of Blythe, naturally, with a handsome if somewhat sleazy looking man in his mid to late forties, whom I recognise as the male lead in *Affairs of the Heart*. The one she claimed was vilified for no reason other than his closeted sexuality. 'But I do love these reminders of better times,' she tells me. 'Well, in some ways I do.' She leans in, breath pure alcohol, and taps the man's face, a little clumsily. 'There were precious few good men in Hollywood back then,' she says, taking the photo and placing it back down, the frame falling over. 'Everyone out for themselves and what they could get. Soon as you met someone, they'd be sizing you up, see if you were worth fucking, or rather, worth *fucking over*. You had to stand up for yourself, but if you did...' She trails off, eyes unfocused.

'You were fucked either way?'

'Yes!' She laughs loudly, then the smile drops and she links arms to march me across the hallway, half of our G&Ts sloshed onto the rugs and marble as we make our way into the sitting room.

It's an enormous room with a gorgeous view. The evening sunlight pouring in through a wide bay window, beyond which is the long sweep of front lawn, dropping down to the courtyard I came in through, and then the busy road, and finally Hampstead Heath. Or rather the entrance to it, a thicket of bushes and trees all that's visible from here. But it's not the lovely proportions of the room, or the view that draw my gaze, but rather a statuette on a plinth positioned in front of the window where it is bathed in golden sunlight.

'Oh my God, Blythe, your Oscar!' I run towards it, then stop, afraid I might knock it over.

Blythe beams, lifting it with both hands to place it in mine as if it were a baby.

I weigh the Oscar in my palms. 'It's so heavy!'

'You try carrying it round all night!' Blythe exclaims, delighted.

'I'd probably have dropped it, or left it in the loo.'

Blythe laughs, but I hand it back before I *do* drop it.

She caresses the smooth surfaces then places it down on the table. A thing of beauty to be worshipped, as it should be. Pride of place. I'm surprised it's taken her this long to show me, although her expression is not pure joy, more complex emotions buried beneath the smile; hard to read but there. And she's left fingerprints on it, or was that me?

'It was upstairs in my bedroom until recently,' she says. 'But Ludo brought it down, to cheer me up.'

She makes it sound like she's the victim here, not Dom, but I'm still dazzled by the reality of that gold statuette and what it signifies. Ever since I decided to become a writer, I imagined myself holding one.

Best Original Screenplay. Marnie Wilde.

'Quite right,' I reply, still starstruck by the glimmer of reflected glory. 'This needs to be seen. It's incredible, Blythe. You're incredible. Best Actress. That's something to treasure.'

'Well, it was a long time ago now and no one sees it but me and Ludo. And now you.'

'Thank you for sharing it with me.'

There's a rare and awkward silence as we stare out at the view. A pink sunset in the distance, as if the rest of the world was on fire.

'C S Lewis supposedly based Narnia on Hampstead Heath,' Blythe says, setting her drink down beside the Oscar, the statuette wobbling alarmingly. I reach out to steady it.

'My dad used to read C S Lewis to me at bedtime,' I tell her, the memory a comfort as is the secured statuette. I can't believe it's a real Oscar, and I've held it. 'I've always thought those stories of snowy forests were why I wanted to be a writer. Silly really.'

'No!' Blythe counters, eyes wild as she grabs my arm, my heart tattoo squeezed so it bulges. 'Dreaming big brings big things, Marnie. If you take nothing else from me, learn that. Whatever I've become, whatever is yet to come, at least we dreamed big.'

I step back, extricating myself from her tight grip. Her dramatic plea has come out of nowhere. And I don't like her touching me. A burn where her hand was. I move away, walking slowly round the room, a palm across the back of the white sofa which I recognise as the same one she was seated on for that unflattering photo in the magazine left open on the kitchen table.

'You must be sad to be selling this place.'

Blythe smiles. 'Let's not pre-empt that quite yet, shall we?'

'Oh, I thought I saw The Towers was for sale. Is that no longer the case?'

She dismisses the question with a flick of her hand. 'Money is such a bore, isn't it? I leave all that to Ludo. But there may yet be a way to sort out this mess.'

'You mean the meeting tomorrow with your lawyer?'

'That, and other plans afoot.'

'The scripts?'

She falls into the squashy sofa without reply, her legs lifting so I fear for a moment she might topple over backwards, imagining her slender frame slipping between the cushions in an absurdly comedic way.

I take the other sofa, the opposite side of the fireplace, the remains of my G&T downed as I sit. Annoyingly, whilst I had the forethought to bring my drink, my notepad is left on the kitchen table, where Ludo can peruse it at his leisure.

'Where you going?' Blythe asks as I get up.

'Just to get my notebook.'

'Oh, leave that!' she says.

'I won't be a moment.'

'Leave it!' she tells me, raising her voice.

There's a beat when the room stills.

'I told you, Marnie. Tonight isn't about the memoir; you won't need to take notes.'

I've never been a fan of directives. But this is her house, so I guess her rules. Although the force of her instruction was unwarranted, and her unpredictability worries me.

I sit and she smiles, having got her own way. 'OK, but we cannot abandon the memoir altogether, Blythe. We've signed a contract.'

'Sure. What do you think of that?' she asks, glassy eyed as she points at a painting above the fireplace.

I look up, confused, then stand to study it properly. It's an enormous portrait of Blythe, arresting and colourful, partially abstract and in profile, head and shoulders. The features are recognisable but they're undefined, and distorted as the profile is blurred by the merging of a thousand tiny multicoloured butterflies that scatter from Blythe's face, filling the right-hand side of the canvas. The technique is intricate, and the way the artist has obfuscated the line between portraiture and abstraction through tiny dots of paint, undoubtedly accomplished. There's something magical about it, and it's clearly the work of a gifted artist, but it's also got elements of the grotesque. As if it's threaded through with an unpleasantness you can't see until you look more closely.

'I'm not much of an art buff, I'm afraid,' I reply, still transfixed.

'Me neither, but the artist is rather collectible now, or so Ludo tells me.'

I read the signature. *Caroline Costello 2006*. 'Is she well-known?'

'Not really, but death seems to up your currency.'

'She's dead?' I ask, spinning round.

'Yes, not long after she painted that,' Blythe tells me, draining the last of her drink.

'Wow, right.' Another victim? Although maybe Caroline Costello was ninety-six and died in her sleep, but I add her name to my list, in my head at least. The actual list is written in the back of my notebook which is still left, with Ludo, in the kitchen.

I edge towards the door.

'Come!' she says, recalling me to the painting as she gets up. 'Stand by me. Tell me what you think.'

Blythe's features melt into the canvas as I stand shoulder to shoulder with its subject, the winged retreat from her smile disfiguring the painted version into a sneer.

'Is it maybe an allegory for something?' I ask, focusing on the colours, the artist's signature, anything rather than Blythe who is staring at me now. 'Icarus, possibly? Melting wings as he got too close to the sun, like your relationship to... maybe fame?'

'How clever you are,' Blythe says, clapping as she did earlier when I swam. 'Clever little Marnie. Working it all out. And now it's way past time to get this hideous thing down!'

She steps forward and then raises onto her bare toes, hands held aloft, gripping the bottom of the canvas as she attempts to remove it from above the fireplace.

'Be careful!' I say as I quickly put my glass on the floor. It looks as if she's about to lose control of it and I have visions of her head breaking through in a bizarre tableau of life imitating, or rather *inhabiting*, art, but we manage to bring it down to the stripped floorboards between us, dust all we're covered in. Blythe leans the canvas against the wall, the portrait facing the tasteful wallpaper.

'Should have done that a long time ago,' she says, brushing her hands clean.

'You don't like it?' I ask, doing the same.

She retrieves her drink from beside the Oscar and tips the melted ice into her mouth. 'No, I hate it. Always have. But Ludo will know someone who can take it off my hands. Ready for another?' She crunches the ice between her teeth and looks at my empty glass on the floor. 'Silly question, eh? You could have drunk Dom under the table! I'm a terrible lightweight these days.'

She grabs my glass and heads to the open door, calling out, 'Ludo! Lu-do!!! Where are you?'

'How did the artist die, do you know?' I ask, afraid of the answer. 'Natural causes, or—'

'Poisoned,' Blythe replies, Ludo arriving on cue to take our empty glasses. 'Same again!' Blythe instructs Ludo. 'And check the date on that tonic; it tasted odd.'

I'm consumed with a spluttering cough, tempted to go with the convulsions and throw up the G&T I've already drunk on the rug. 'Poisoned, by whom?!' I ask as Ludo scuttles away to mix us another odd tasting drink. 'I mean, by what?'

I cough again, wiping phlegm onto the back of my hand,

although it's far too late for my splutters to be of any use in ejecting anything toxic. I've ingested a goldfish bowl of odd tasting liquid, which is now coursing through my veins.

'Are you OK?' Blythe asks, watching me with undisguised revulsion. 'Do we need a bowl?'

'I think maybe I do,' I say, rushing out.

I run across the hall and down the corridor, then without a word to a startled Ludo, I lean over the kitchen sink where I swill my mouth under the running tap three times, dress soaked from the bounce back. Ludo watches my performance without comment. I spit over the dirty dishes. But I can't make myself throw up, despite my retching, and I'm being ridiculous, aren't I? Ludo mixed the drinks, not Blythe. But poisoned?!

'Are you quite done?' he asks, leaning round me to turn off the tap.

'Think so,' I tell him. 'That tonic was definitely off.'

He shrugs and returns to the toaster, two slices popping up. I'm glad to see my notepad appears undisturbed on the kitchen table, at least, my pen still balanced on top.

'Maybe you and Blythe should stop drinking now?' he suggests, quite reasonably in the circumstances, especially as Blythe then arrives looking very much the worse for wear and demanding to know if I have a stomach bug she should avoid?

I rinse both the gin glasses thoroughly in fresh water and lots of washing-up liquid, washing up the dishes I spluttered over as a conciliatory gesture to Ludo whilst assuring Blythe I'm fine now, although I have no idea if I am. Does poison wash away? It could be in the gin, or even the melted ice! I open and sniff the bottles on the table as Ludo cracks eggs into a pan. My concern shifting to him, one eye on his movements in case he slips in something other than the grind of pepper he's now adding, reminded of Blythe's comments about his access to pharmaceuticals.

But I'm overreacting, aren't I? About everything. That artist woman probably died of food poisoning, and Blythe's pills are for headaches and weight loss and not in our drinks anyway. The tonic is three months after all. I sniff the gin again and decide it's worth the risk. I need another drink. A bloody strong one.

I hand Blythe a glass at random, and she seems to have no qualms about taking either and then a large slug.

I hook out my slice of lemon as a precaution and contemplate my third supper prepared by the archetypal bad guy who may or may not be spiking our drinks. Oh, to be back home, half-naked on my sofa watching crappy daytime repeats of detective shows where lemons are injected with arsenic!

Over the replacement supper, which is almost as dire as the discarded risotto – rubberised eggs and limp sliced bread with low-fat spread, every mouthful sniffed and eaten with caution, as if that would help – Blythe regales us with stories of her Oscar win. Not so much the night itself, which she skims over despite my prompts to 'tell all', but more the 'circus' that ran up to it.

She talks between mouthfuls, not of the rejected eggs, but rather spooning in peanut butter from a jar she found at the back of the cupboard after declaring Ludo's cooking inedible. It's nice to see her eat something at last and also fabulous to hear of the excitement and 'great deal of fuss' when she was nominated. She clearly lapped up the attention it brought, stories a-plenty and which I suspect Ludo has heard multiple times, and yet he encourages her in the tales as much as I do. I make notes as I eat, glad of some decent fodder for the memoir, if not my empty stomach. Envying the spoons of thick, creamy peanut butter that stick to the roof of her mouth so she washes it down with the G&T. She is even more drunk than before, but at least she's finally eaten something.

'And Dom?' I ask, still scribbling as I chew on the charcoal toast, gritty between my teeth. It's possible he did take the chance I stupidly gave him to read my notes, and in particular my 'potential kills' list, but he seems the same as ever. Distrustful and inscrutable.

I catch Ludo's eye across the table, both of us distracted then as Blythe pushes the jar of peanut butter away, her eyes narrowing in response to my question.

'What about darling Dom?' she demands, chugging her drink back and slamming the glass down.

'I guess it was tough on him, that's all I meant,' I say, leaping to his defence. 'After he'd been snubbed by the Academy a couple of years before, I mean.'

Blythe shrugs. 'Swayitgoes.'

She's definitely hammered, despite the peanut butter.

'Yes, I guess it is the way it goes, and he certainly looked very proud of you in the footage I've watched of your acceptance speech.'

She shrugs, dismissive. 'Appearances can be...' She clicks her fingers. 'Swatstheword?'

'Deceptive,' Ludo suggests, wrestling the gin bottle from her hand.

'Oh, that reminds me,' I say as they exchange angry glances, Ludo taking the gin to the pill cupboard where he stows it away. 'I was going to ask who the man clapping beside Dom is?'

Blythe frowns at me and shrugs. 'Clapping where?'

'When you gave your Oscar acceptance speech. I watched it on YouTube. I assume that was the director of *Affairs of the Heart* that you'd thanked, what was his name?'

Blythe looks directly at me, eyes glassy but cold. 'Producer, but he's not worth talking about, and on that note...' She pushes up from the table and stands unsteadily. 'I think I'll call it a night. Suits at ten.'

'Sorry?'

'The lawyers arrive at ten sharp,' Ludo tells me as he clears the table. 'You're invited, remember?'

Blythe is halfway across the kitchen when she stumbles, swearing as she lands in a crumpled heap.

Ludo rushes to her aid, that same look of concern as he had earlier when she was poolside and needed her pills. But this is the drink talking. How embarrassing.

'Is she OK?' I ask, Blythe's eyes closed as she catches her breath.

'She's fine,' he replies, tersely. 'How much gin did you put in that last drink?'

'Don't blame me!'

Blythe bats his hand away and manages to get up without his help, although with some difficulty, a hand to the table as Ludo guides her back to her chair. She's more drunk than I'd realised, lurching again as she pushes him away.

Ludo catches up with her back by the door and takes her elbow to guide her out into the corridor, his comments whispered low so I don't catch them. But her reply is loud, echoing after them.

'It's up to me how much I drink on my meds! You are a stupid little man who should know better than to question me. Do you hear me? Do you? I'll do what I want, say what I want, invite who I like into my home, and ask those to leave I want to! Maybe you!'

I follow them down the corridor, hanging back as they make slow progress. Blythe is still chiding Ludo, although she cuts a pathetic figure.

Ludo then helps her up the stairs, her beautiful, floaty dress caught under her bare feet. She grabs hold of the ends and tucks them into her belt, Ludo steering her up each tread. A very different woman than the one who'd attended multiple Oscar parties and enjoyed all the perks of her short-lived super-stardom. Ten stylists had crammed into her Hollywood hotel room, she'd told us, and she'd worn a million pounds worth of rubies to match her red satin Valentino dress. I've watched her acceptance speech over and over. She thanks everyone, but especially her beloved husband, tears of pride in Dom's eyes as he leads a standing ovation, and yes, that producer beside him, who was clapping even harder. What was his name?

'Leave us, Ms Wilde!' Ludo scolds, shooing me back down the stairs. 'Go back to the kitchen, I'll see you there!'

* * *

I scan for photos of Wendy, or Flo as I wander back slowly. But there are so many frames, it's dizzying. I must be drunk too. Worries about Ludo's pharmacy of pills returning, my head fuzzy and my vision blurred. I am looking now for the photo of Josie and Blythe riding on the motorbike, but I can't find it. I stumble on, head swimming, then run towards the kitchen, eager now to escape to the annexe before Ludo returns.

I gather up my belongings but drop my notebook, the spine cracking, the list at the back exposed as it hits the floor. I grab it and am about to leave when I notice the cupboard where Ludo stowed the gin bottle is slightly ajar.

I reach in, a moment's hesitation as I assess the likelihood the craft gin may be laced with arsenic or diet pills or God knows what else. It would be such an easy way to poison someone. The alcohol covering the taste and smell and I'm guessing hard to trace in an autopsy. My knowledge is coming again from the period crime dramas I love, and Dad's penchant for old movies, so not necessarily accurate, but I know there are poisons that are virtually undetectable.

I don't recognise any of the brands of pills on the shelf above the alcohol, some supplements, some more official looking, prescription drugs I assume, and the labels all in Blythe's name.

I hear Ludo's funny walk approaching so I tuck the gin bottle under my elbow and head out the broken patio door, but not quickly enough.

'Ms Wilde?'

I don't stop or look back, even though he calls after me again. Night is falling fast and I want to be alone, just Ernest and me and a bottle of gin, making sense of it all. If that's possible.

* * *

I lock the annexe door and wedge the swivel chair against it, only then stealing a glance back to the house. My breath catches in my throat. Ludo's there, of course, looking at me. But thankfully, he has remained at the kitchen door and not followed me over. I've no idea if he can see me, or the wedged chair, but right now, I don't care. I need that security if I'm to stand any chance of getting some sleep.

I take my laptop into the bedroom and close that door too, relieved to be away from the exposure of all that glass at the front of the annexe. The feeling of surveillance, however, is hard to shake.

If Ludo walks over, knocks the annexe door, I'll ignore him and feign sleep. I don't trust him. Or his so-called altruistic motives for looking after Blythe, who is clearly a sick woman. Maybe because of all those pills?

I open up a new Word doc, vigilant to any sounds of his approach and hoping to lose myself in my work as I often do, the gin at my side, regular swigs taken as I attempt a potential opening chapter to the memoir, which is still my only source of income and therefore requires my attention.

Writing has always been a good way to distract myself: from Mum, Jake, and the endless search for professional and personal fulfilment. And those chapters won't write themselves. Priscilla wanted them ASAP.

My idea is to open the memoir with the pre-Oscar frenzy. It's glitzy and a good contrast to Blythe's present circumstance. I type up a few ideas for Priscilla, but my email fails to send, of course, and I find my thoughts returning to Dom instead. Because, despite appearances, it sounds as if pride wasn't what he'd felt at all as he applauded her Oscar win. According to Blythe, he was jealous of her success. Not exactly a loving or admirable response, by maybe understandable?

I backspace on the chapter one title I'd just thought of – *Golden Years* – and re-type as *What Price Fame?* because I'm now wondering just how far Blythe is prepared to go to recapture the glint of gold that radiates from that statuette. And also how far she pushed others in that endless pursuit, especially Dom in the period immediately prior to his death. He burned those scripts for a reason. Maybe it was Blythe's terrifying pursuit of the drug of fame that pushed him to obliterate the meta idea rather than the dubious quality or even the potentially inflammatory content of those scripts? He must have thought his idea good to share it with his agent, so why back away from it?

The scripts are the real reason I'm here, I'm sure of it. To facilitate Blythe's deluded but all-consuming desire for a comeback role. Whatever the price. To her. To anyone. There is nothing she won't do to reclaim her fame. Including throwing Dom's reputation to the wolves to paint him as an abusive partner to secure her freedom. Maybe tossing me on the bone pile afterwards.

And as for Ludo, he has his own agenda. One I am yet to uncover, but which troubles me just as much as Blythe's motives, if not more. I push the gin bottle away but it's almost empty, my head heavy as I lay down on the uncomfortable bed beside my laptop, eyes immediately closing. As if I'm drugged.

18

It's a recurrent dream, or rather nightmare. I am on a ledge, but this time I am up in the tower room. I have no clarity of what that room is like, just the open window as I step out. Then I'm freefalling.

The suits, as Blythe referred to her legal representatives, are due on the dot of ten, my phone alarm waking me with barely twenty minutes to spare. I hit snooze, still sluggish and sweaty when it goes off again nine minutes later. My head like lead.

After a quick dribble of a shower, I spray a liberal amount of deodorant under my arms and boobs – vague warnings about it not being a good idea in intimate areas stopping me from emptying the whole can over myself – and pull on last night's dress.

It is less than fresh, but the buttons are not quite such a stretch this morning. The bonus of an empty stomach, I guess? I've barely eaten since I arrived and for someone who usually grazes 24/7 to keep my blood sugar up, it's taking its toll, my hands shaking as I run them through my hair. Or maybe that's a hangover? Or something else, like poison?

I pull on the Dr Marten boots, mainly to annoy Ludo as the flesh on my heels is still raw, but my knees are scabbing over nicely in the heat. I check my reflection in the glass door, wheeling away the chair I wedged against it last night.

My ensemble is far from formal attire, but surely Blythe must have greater concerns for today's meeting than what I'm wearing? Stupid, how I crave her approval. But Ludo is the same, the pair of us vying for her faint and rare praise. Her fragility scares me, though. Whilst Ludo revels in it. A concern about him I cannot shake, along with this hangover.

I hope to God Ludo's not complicit in her frailty, all those pill bottles lined up in the kitchen cupboard for him to play with.

But today isn't about any of that. It's about a legal miracle, which is surely all that can save Blythe from prison?

I leave on the dot of ten. The blinding sunlight taking a sledgehammer to my shrivelled brain. It had been the early hours, maybe gone two, when I'd woken from a deep stupor and finished the bottle of gin. The opening chapters of the memoir abandoned in favour of research into the artist who painted Blythe's portrait: Caroline Costello.

My notes on Caroline, extensive and handwritten, were virtually indecipherable when I read them back in bed this morning during that alarm 'snooze'. It seems that as my alcohol intake increased, my ability to write legibly diminished. God, why did I finish the bottle? Although I did find out a lot more about Caroline, and Flo, none of it less than disturbing.

Suffice to say I now have four potential victims on my list. All young women associated with Blythe. And although there's no suggestion of anything suspicious on her part – at least, none that I can find, and I looked hard, battling intermittent Wi-Fi and increasing drunkenness – there's space for doubt. Lots of it. Rational explanations and something much darker competing inside my thumping head.

Wendy's death by accidental drowning for instance, was vociferously contested by her parents, who said she would never have taken such risks with her own life, leaving the boys motherless.

And Flo's supposed deliberate overdose at the Hoppers' party a month later was also questioned, at least by her partner – an older actress who died a few years back at a great age – who saw no reason for Flo to end her own life, in fact, quite the opposite. Flo's loving partner was quoted as saying Flo was very excited about a future movie project. Whilst Flo was described in less than complimentary terms by the media as a 'selfish diva' who squandered her prodigious talent. Her bisexuality also referenced in negative terms.

Intolerant attitudes in the early nineties certainly didn't help Flo's cause. Her stellar performance in Dom's greatest work, *The Man* – the film completed before Blythe met Dom in Hollywood – also summarily overlooked by the Academy. Salacious headlines about Flo's partying and promiscuousness concentrated almost solely on the fact she dated – shock horror!!! – both men and women.

She was a gorgeous young woman of twenty-two; why shouldn't she have some fun? But clearly nineties Hollywood couldn't handle the fact she was bi. I sincerely hope it would be a non-issue in our so-called progressive society, but of course, that's wishful thinking. A depressing reminder of how far we still have to go.

There's something else about Flo I found out last night that niggles again as I near the house, causing me to pause my previously purposeful progress.

Flo's death in May 1993 was only a few months after the Academy snub in late January, and it must also have been around then that the announcement came of the surprise casting of Blythe as Julia in *Affairs of the Heart*. A role which Flo had been widely tipped as the favourite to fulfil. I can't pin down the exact dates all these years on, there seems to have been some delay in filming for *Affairs of the Heart*, a bit stop-start, but there can't have been long between those setbacks and Flo's death. So was Flo depressed about the Oscar snub, or the news she'd lost her next starring role and chance for a nom to Blythe, or maybe both? And would that be enough of a reason to take her own life? A cocktail of drink and drugs found by her bed in the Hoppers' guest suite.

Maybe if Flo had just found out about the recasting when she went to the Hoppers' house party she might have confronted Blythe and they argued?

I check the time on my phone and run towards the house. My last-minute entrance is deliberate, to avoid Ludo excluding me from the meeting, although I'm cutting it fine now. I hurtle into the kitchen just as a loud buzzer sounds from down the corridor. My arrival executed to perfection. Ludo barely acknowledges me, his funny walk turning into a half run as he sets off towards the imperative sound.

I follow, keeping him firmly in my sights, keen to see where the control panel for the gates is housed. But that ploy is scuppered as I'm intercepted by Blythe who has descended the red-carpeted stairs, cutting me off with a hand to my arm.

'Marnie, good morning!'

She's transformed from the drunk struggling to get up each tread last night, now resplendent in a turquoise trouser suit and matching heels, the jacket draped over her shoulders despite the heat, a plunging cream silk cami beneath.

'How's the hangover?' Blythe asks as she peers at me over dark glasses. 'Mine is fucking horrific.'

'Yeah, not great,' I tell her, taking my glasses off and tucking them into the neckline of my dress. 'I swiped the gin and finished the bottle as I worked.'

'Wow, impressive!' she replies. 'We both need full-fat Coke, and a couple of codeine.'

'No codeine for me. Makes me pass out.'

I kick myself as soon as it's out my mouth, thinking of Flo, found naked and unresponsive, spreadeagled across the guest bed surrounded by pills. But at least Ludo isn't here with his medicine cabinet of sweeties. I've annoyingly lost track of him.

'Suit yourself,' Blythe replies, dabbing gloss on her lips with her little finger, the tube then returned to her trouser pocket. 'You kids shake these things off so much more quickly than I seem to these days. Mind you,' she looks me up and down, 'that dress and boots ensemble is enough to give anyone a headache.'

I can't help but smile. 'You look gorgeous, by the way.'

She smiles too, then pushes the glasses up her nose and straightens her back. 'Got to present myself as something worth saving, haven't I?'

Ludo emerges from what I assume is a cupboard behind a door to the left of the front door, then, stepping aside for Blythe to frame herself in the stone porch, we wait. Blythe takes off the tortoiseshell sunglasses and shakes out her hair, flicking at the curls and twirling a couple before smacking the newly glossed lips as two men walk up the long drive.

Leading the way is an exceedingly tall man in a pinstripe three-piece and with a Draculin widow's peak. A younger man carrying a briefcase trots along behind.

'Roland!' Blythe exclaims, stepping forward. 'How wonderful of you to come at such short notice. I so appreciate you making the time for me.'

They double air kiss.

'Blythe, darling, you look incredible. How are you holding up?'

'Oh you know, better for seeing you.'

'Roland Penny, this is Marnie Wilde,' Blythe says, pushing her hair back with the sunglasses.

Roland Penny looks me up and down and delivers his verdict: a sneer. He is clearly a man used to being in discerning company, his suit cut so sharp it almost outdoes his scorn. I recognise his imperious features from the photo on his firm's website, but in person he is even more annoying than the smug thumbnail suggested. Impressive, sure, but not attractive, nor pleasant I'm betting.

He gives an obsequious bow which annoys me even more than his smacked-arse face. 'And might I ask why you are here, Marnie Wilde?'

'Marnie is sitting in on our meeting,' Blythe tells him. 'Full access, for the memoir she's ghostwriting for me.'

'Memoir?' Roland looks confused, as if an unpleasant smell has entered his orbit, which would be difficult given the cloud of cologne that envelops him. 'I don't think so, Blythe.'

'Well, I do,' Blythe counters, my heart swelling at her show of loyalty. 'Is that a problem, Roland?'

'Frankly, yes. Our conversations must remain confidential, Blythe. And, Marnie, I would also suggest you abort any thoughts of a memoir, at least a published one. Under the terms of the very delicately negotiated bail conditions I managed to ensure, at great personal and—'

'Roland, it's fine,' Blythe tells him, a hand on the soft wool of his suit jacket sleeve. 'Let's go into the dining room and discuss over coffee. Ludo, we will also require full-fat Coke and paracetamol for our younger guest who is "hanging".' Blythe throws the air quotes out with crooked fingers and an assassin's smile. *Traitor!*

Roland's entourage of one, a younger man than his boss by a decade or two – bright-red face and curly, blond hair – transfers a laptop case from under one arm to the other as he steps inside. Hampered also by the briefcase Roland left on the floor for him to pick up, he eventually clamps an A4 notepad beneath a roll of puppy fat. He's probably a similar age to me, but he has that boyish quality he will likely one day cash in by snagging a younger wife and several kids, a second chance at all the things he's given up to trail after Roland until he's a fully-fledged wanker with his own protégé. Charles, so he tells me through somewhat gritted teeth on account of the chinned notepad, is actually much nicer than his boss, waiting for me so we go in together. Ludo heading to the kitchen for coffee and coke and pills as instructed.

The dining room is dominated by a polished mahogany table even larger than the one in the kitchen. There are twelve matching chairs around it, six each side and two carvers. Blythe sits at the head, naturally, Roland to her right, Charles and I flanking them and opening up our notebooks at the same time on opposite sides of the table. Charles offers me an endearing smile and mouths, '*Snap!*'

'Marnie and I are actually working on a couple of projects together,' Blythe tells Roland.

Roland stares at me over his rectangular glasses. 'May I ask what else aside from the ill-advised memoir is in the pipeline?'

'A scripted series,' Blythe replies, 'and she has of course signed a stringent non-disclosure agreement, which Ludo drew up.'

'We will need a copy of that NDA,' Roland tells Charles who nods and writes it down, his boss's tone such that I assume Ludo's competence is in question. 'And please make a note that I have advised my client against this, strenuously.'

'You're a screenwriter?' Charles asks.

Blythe and Roland are discussing an email exchange from the CPS, which I try to tune into whilst nodding at Charles who replies, 'That's so cool.'

Charles is clearly in awe of Blythe too, and our lavish surroundings, looking about him, mouth open. His suit looks like it's a size too small, his shirt collar cutting into his neck and I spot a bead of red on the white collar where he's cut himself shaving. Or maybe he popped a spot.

'Yes, I wrote a script that was bought by a big Hollywood

producer,' I tell Charles as Roland shakes his head at Blythe. I'm missing what they're discussing, and quite why I feel the need to impress the man-child, I have no idea.

'Amazing! Is it on Netflix?' Charles asks as the table falls silent.

Everyone looks at me.

'The series didn't actually... It's still in development,' I explain.

'Oh shame.' Charles looks disappointed. 'Maybe next time.'

'Yeah, maybe,' I tell him with an aggressive tilt of my head as Ludo walks in with a tray of coffee. 'It's pretty common for productions to be put on hold.'

'Marnie and I are currently writing something very thrilling,' Blythe informs everyone. 'We're super excited, aren't we, Marnie?'

I nod, tentatively. 'Sure, but it's early days.'

Blythe frowns and Roland looks less than impressed. 'I hope I don't need to tell either of you,' he says, directing his comments at me whilst looking directly to Blythe; a performative parent scolding their spawn for the benefit of the gallery. 'NDA or no, you should not be discussing, let alone *publishing* anything to do with your case, Blythe, which is why—'

'We haven't and we won't, at least not yet,' Blythe assures him, sipping her black coffee. Her cup poured first by Ludo, of course. 'Not until this all goes away.'

Roland inhales his disbelief, eyebrows raised, accepting a coffee too.

I could do with the promised full-fat Coke and paracetamol but there's no sign of either on the tray. Just the weak coffee that Ludo slugs into my cup, the last to be poured and barely half a cup left, and the crappy biscuits I was given before, now fanned on a sticky plate no one is bothered about as it's passed round. Except for Charles, who eyes them greedily, his hand reaching out then pulled back as he clocks his boss's eye roll.

'And I'll need to see the publishing contract for this memoir,'

Roland replies, looking at me. 'Charles, make a note to get onto Blythe's publisher. The name of the contact there is...?'

'You mean my editor?' I ask. 'She's called Priscilla Bower.'

Charles writes Priscilla's contact details down as I dictate them. Then Harry's. I'm sure they'll both be delighted to hear from this self-important prick, but I guess it'll show I am still here and working hard on the memoir. I'll send Priscilla my further thoughts about those first few chapters later, Wi-Fi permitting. Maybe ask if she can send an advance on my fee then I can forward it to my landlord's bank account. Show willing. Although the first email still hadn't sent last time I looked.

'Ludo will have been very thorough in the terms of the NDA,' Blythe tells Roland, looking at Ludo, who is retreating from the room, fast. 'He's nothing if not a man of details.'

'Well, that's a matter of opinion,' Roland replies, then winces as he takes a sip of his coffee. 'And a heads up would have been useful, Blythe. You said nothing about any of these writing projects when we chatted last night.' Roland frowns at me. 'And have you given any more thought to dispensing with Ludo's questionable services?'

Charles and I both look at the door, left ajar.

'I've told you, Roland, that's off the table, indefinitely,' Blythe replies, palms slammed down flat. 'You have no idea how much his loyalty has meant to me this past month.'

'Right, but to be clear,' Roland adds, fountain pen in hand as he surveys us each in turn, ending with me. 'None of this conversation is to be repeated beyond these walls. I can't have anything leaked that may prejudice my client's defence and that includes any projects in the works, scripts or otherwise. Is that clear, Marnie?'

'Crystal,' I reply, closing my notebook and raising my hands in surrender.

'It's not a joking matter,' Roland says, eyes narrowing. Then to Blythe: 'The terms of your bail clearly state—'

'Yardi-yardi-ya!' Blythe interjects, waving away his objections. 'It's all fine, Roland. Marnie knows the score and as we're on your time, which *I* pay for, through the nose, can we please get started? Do you have any updates for me after our discussion yesterday?'

'Not exactly but...' Roland looks at his subordinate. 'Charles has a few ideas to present to you on possible defences, don't you?'

Ah, so Charles is not only the donkey but also the fall guy, his already reddened cheeks turning a deep cerise as he clears his throat and finds his place in his notes with a pointed finger before he begins.

'Our best hope, Mrs Hopper, would be a partial defence. That's different to a complete defence, such as self-defence.'

Another cough, the finger threading down the page as if it belongs to a child learning to read.

Roland's eyebrows migrate north and I stifle an inappropriate snort.

'As you have already confessed to the murder of your husband, Dominic Farnsworth Hopper...' Charles says.

Farnsworth? That's a new one on me. I surreptitiously open my notebook and make a note of the name on the corner of a random page. The same initials as the ones scratched on the bottom of the pebble I've been using as a door jamb: DFH.

'...we cannot enter a Not Guilty plea,' Charles continues. 'That's not an option.'

Blythe sighs. 'I already know all this, Roland. Give me solutions!'

'Just hear him out,' Roland says. 'Go on, Charles. And please, do cut to the chase.'

'But if successfully argued, a partial defence could reduce the offence to an act of voluntary manslaughter.'

'What does that mean?' Blythe asks, echoing my thoughts. 'Is this the extenuating circumstances we talked about, Roland?'

'Possible partial defences,' Charles continues, reading from his script, 'may include killing in pursuance of a suicide pact—'

'This is a waste of my time!' Blythe says. 'Dom would never have done anything like that!'

'Quite,' Roland says, looking less than impressed with Charles, even shushing him when he threatens to pipe up again. 'So, we are left with two other partial defences, Blythe. Either diminished responsibility or—'

'I'm not going to claim insanity and end up in some institution for the rest of my life, I've told you that!'

'Of course not,' Roland responds evenly, showing impressive restraint as Blythe unravels. 'Diminished responsibility requires medical evidence, a four-stage test. As I've said before, it's really not an option for us. So our best hope is loss of control.'

He nods at Charles to go on.

'To quote from the CPS guidelines, Mrs Hopper, that's the Crown Prosecution Service who will decide on the charge—'

'Yes, Charles, I think we all know that,' Roland snaps.

'Right, yes, sorry...' The finger is back, tracing along his lines of notes. 'The common law defence of provocation was replaced with sections fifty-four and fifty-five of the—'

'Charles!' Roland interrupts, a palm held up. 'In plain English, as discussed. Get to the relevant point of law. Pronto!'

Charles scans his notes. 'It applies to defendants charged with murder, let me just...'

'This is tiresome, Roland.' Blythe massages her eyes so her mascara is smudged as she stares at her potential saviour. 'You still think I'll be charged with murder?'

'Yes,' Roland replies, flatly. 'There's no other possible outcome.'

'But I thought...' Blythe rubs her eyes again, a single tear tumbling down her already stained cheek. 'You said there was hope? You said last night that I had to think about it carefully, but there would be a way forward.'

'Yes, a way to reduce, mitigate, but not to *eradicate* all charges.' Roland rubs his eyes too. He must witness this kind of desperation and delusion a lot, waiting for his clients to absorb the magnitude of their situation. 'Listen to Charles. All is not lost, not yet.'

'The loss of control defence has three components,' Charles continues. 'Loss of control is the first component.'

'Which means what?' I ask.

Everyone turns to me as if I've just apparated into the room. 'I'm sorry, but if shooting the man she was married to for thirty years isn't loss of control then what is?'

'There needs to be sufficient evidence to convince the judge based on certain criteria,' Roland explains. 'Or else everyone who committed a crime of passion would be given a free pass, wouldn't they?'

'A qualifying trigger is the second component,' Charles pipes up, finding his voice now. 'The third component is an objective test. The trial judge should consider the three components sequentially.'

'What does that all mean?' Blythe asks, echoing my thoughts. 'What test? I'm completely lost. I don't even know what the first one was now.'

'The legal technicalities are our concern,' Roland assures her, patting her hand. 'What I need from you,' his voice softened to silky-smooth as he squeezes her fingers tight, an enormous diamond on her engagement finger which I haven't seen her wear before, cutting into his large hand. 'is for you to supply me with your rationale for your actions on July second.'

Blythe pulls away. 'And if I do – tell you exactly what made me do it, I mean – will that help?'

'Depends what it is. And frankly, still no guarantees, but I might successfully argue for a reduced sentence.'

'Oh great! So whatever I say, it's a custodial sentence?'

'Yes,' Roland says, deadpan. 'You have confessed to a crime which carries sentences of up to life imprisonment. Even I can't change the law.'

'There's definitely no way I'd be able to stay here?' Blythe asks, looking around the oak-panelled dining room, the view taking her, and my following gaze, towards the garden and then in the direction of the pool. 'I'm hardly a danger to society, am I? Maybe I could do some community service? Pick litter in one of those terrible tabards.'

Blythe clearly hasn't accepted her situation, nowhere near.

Roland shakes his head. 'I would hope to get the charge reduced, and you could be out in twelve, even ten years. A lot of life still ahead of you.'

Blythe shakes her head, another tear falling. 'That doesn't work for me, I'm afraid. You'll need to think again.'

Roland sighs audibly, and I don't blame him. Blythe's utter lack of remorse or culpability, or even sanity, is staggering. She seems to think her former A-lister status and dwindling but relative wealth will grant her some kind of special dispensation. And it clearly won't. The law, as Roland has said, is the law. For everyone.

'I need you to help me to help you,' Roland tells her. 'Something concrete I can go back to the CPS with other than the usual domestic strife. It's not enough, Blythe. You confessed to the first responders, the gun still in your hand... Oh, and on that note, any recollection as yet where the weapon went after that? It would help your case to surrender it, even at this late stage.'

Charles and I exchange glances.

'If I knew where I'd thrown the gun, I'd have told you, wouldn't

I?' Blythe challenges. 'My husband was in the water. I panicked and dived in after him. You know all this!'

'Quite, but as discussed, Blythe, the search of the garden was extensive. God knows how I swung house arrest with the murder weapon unaccounted for. Anyway... to get back to the matter in hand...'

Isn't the gun's whereabouts the matter in hand? I exchange another look with Charles who expresses his solidarity with stretched eyes.

'So, as we discussed, Blythe,' Roland presses on. 'Even given Dom's violent moods, we don't have a valid defence against an imminent murder charge. I need something more... specific. And – how shall I put this? – compelling. What do you think sparked his anger that day?'

'The rejection,' I say, the words out before I've thought them through. 'From his agent. Of the scripts. James Langley. That's why Dom lit the bonfire.'

Blythe catches my eye. 'Are you going to let me speak, Marnie, or is this your show?'

'Is that why he threatened you?' Roland asks, ignoring her dramatics.

Blythe's reddened eyes dart to mine again, avoiding Roland's inquiring stare. Is she angry that I spoke up, or for what I said? I'm more concerned that her lawyer, on Blythe's payroll, is leading his witness. Urging her to not necessarily tell him the truth and nothing but the truth, but rather the most useful thing to build his defence. Surely that's not ethical legal practice? Although, I guess it is his job to ensure his client fully understands the consequences of her secrecy.

Blythe rubs at the mascara previously transferred to her hands, a thumb licked which she then pulls against the black tracks under her eyes. 'What do you need me to say, Roland?'

'Just the truth,' Roland replies, looking at me. 'You're amongst friends here. People you can trust. This will go no further, for now.'

Charles is still writing furiously as Roland continues to coax.

'Let's go back to this rejection. What was it about the news which affected him so badly, do you think?'

'I guess the manner of it, very brutal, but his drinking didn't help, of course. He was already in a foul mood because I'd said there was no way I was going to get rid of Ludo.'

'Oh?' Roland says, catching my eye. 'Why did your husband suggest that?'

'Same reason as you, I guess.' She pulls a tissue from her jacket sleeve and wipes her nose. 'Dom was always suggesting it. He said he could manage our financial affairs, that we didn't need Ludo on our payroll or in our lives. I refused, of course. Ludo is non-negotiable as I've told you, many times.'

'Yes, and I have told you that I have grave concerns about Mr Villander.'

Charles and I both look at the slightly open door and I swear it moves a little. If Ludo's there, just the other side, he *must* be able to hear this. Charles' eyes widen again.

'Anyway,' Roland says, 'let's get back to the argument pre-bonfire. Is there anything else I should know?'

'No,' Blythe responds.

Roland, experienced cross examiner that he clearly is, waits.

'OK, if you must know, he said he was leaving me, but he always said that.'

We meet glances again, Charles and I, unlikely allies. Dom *was* leaving her. I *knew* it. For my mother, I bet. If he'd found her by then.

Blythe notices the exchange of looks, and adds, 'It was an empty threat.'

'OK,' Roland replies, pulling hard at his fleshy earlobe. 'I'm not sure this is that helpful. Maybe if we go back to when you went up to the tower room?'

'The tower room?' Charles echoes, looking up at the ceiling, an ornate wood panel.

'We have a floor plan on file which shows the access and layout,' Roland advises Charles, brusquely. 'Do carry on, Blythe.'

'I read a little, and did some yoga, meditation, anything to disperse the bad energy after our fight over supper. It's such a beautiful view from up there. You can see for miles and miles. Which was making me sad, to be honest. We'd been forced by our creditors to market the house a few months before, as I told you Roland, and I knew that was getting Dom down. He always said the only way he was ever leaving The Towers was in a—'

Blythe catches herself and wipes her eyes then blows her nose.

'My husband saw himself, his... status, I suppose... as wrapped up in this house. Leaving it would be a final admission of defeat. He resisted to the very last, but we had no choice but to sell. We've been on borrowed time, financially I mean, for a few years, although I hadn't realised *quite* how tight things were until Ludo recently explained to me, after Dom's death.'

'The accounts literally beggar belief,' Roland responds, eyebrows lifted. 'Anyway, The Towers hasn't sold to date?'

Blythe shakes her head slowly. 'It's a bad time to sell, so I'm told. They keep asking me to reduce, but you have to know your worth.'

'And to clarify,' Roland continues, making a note in a dossier he opens up. 'The property is solely in your name, always has been?'

'Yes, that's right. But as I always told Dom, what does it matter who pays for what?'

'But it did matter?' Roland prompts. 'To Dom.'

'It certainly all came tumbling out during that argument: how I'd emasculated him for years, despite the fact I'd taken that awful part in a continuing drama to pay for the house renovations and kitchen extension he wanted. And I'd literally begged James to take Dom on as a client. That certainly backfired.'

'Yes, but let's fast forward to the bonfire of the vanities,' Roland suggests, clearly familiar with the Hoppers' ongoing marital grievances.

I'm impressed by Roland's reference to Tom Wolfe's great American novel, the lawyer's knowledge of eighties literary satire surprising. Or maybe he'd meant the religious practice of setting fire to objects that symbolise one's sins.

'Stupidly, I thought at first it was the gardener burning leaves,' Blythe says, 'which was ridiculous; we'd had to let the man go months before. Then when I saw that it was Dom feeding the fire, I panicked.'

'So you ran down to him at once?' Roland asks, as dispassionate as if he were checking a shopping list.

'Yes, at least I wanted to, but I couldn't get to him. I've told you all this.'

'The locked patio doors from the kitchen,' Roland prompts. 'The ones you shot at to get out.'

I look up and catch Charles's shocked expression, both of us agog. Blythe must be a crack shot to aim at such a huge pane of glass and only shatter the lock.

'I meant to ask, did your husband deliberately imprison you often?' Roland asks.

'No, never, at least, not intentionally. Dom was a stickler for locks, carried keys everywhere, often locked the annexe when he was in there. Said he needed his privacy.' She glances at me and I feel for the rabbit's foot in my dress pocket. 'I got a spare cut, just in case he fell down drunk or something, but I respected his space.'

'Right, but the front door must have been unlocked because the emergency services came through that?' Roland says.

'Yes, I suppose so.'

'So you could have gone round that way?'

'No. There's no access that way. Only through the house,' she says, leaning back and placing a palm across her forehead. 'You have a floor plan, as you said yourself.'

'Yes, of course, I'm sorry to be pernickety, Blythe, but every detail could be vital.'

'I don't know what else I can say. I shot the lock off then I ran to the smoke, tried to reason with Dom as he was feeding the flames, which were alarmingly high by then. We argued, he was vile to me, cruel. Isn't that enough?'

'No, it's not,' Roland says, leaning in. 'Vile in what way?' Blythe shakes her head. 'I need his cruel words, Blythe, every single one. If I am to have any chance of helping you. Do you understand that?'

Blythe wipes her eyes, too upset to speak. But she's a good actress; it's hard to separate out what's real emotion and what's a performance for her rapt audience of three, maybe four if Ludo is on the other side of the door, as I strongly suspect he is.

'You're doing so well, Blythe,' Roland says, encouraging her. 'Just keep going – all the way to the bitter end – then it's done and we can start to build a defence.'

She sniffs and pulls her cigarettes from her jacket pocket. Roland takes the lighter from her shaking hand, holds a steady flame as she places her hand on his and draws deep. She exhales, then takes a long, rattling breath before she finally speaks.

'When you find out the person you love more than life itself believes something so utterly abhorrent of you, so heinous you can barely believe it, how do you ever recover?' Roland shrugs, not here for the performance it would seem. 'Well, I'll tell you,' Blythe says, glancing at me. 'You don't.'

The room is utterly silent, no movement other than a creak the other side of the door.

'To try and compute that the man you have adored, worshipped even, has believed this dreadful thing about you for all these years... It's very hard to see a way forward at all. We had reached a point of no return.'

Roland leans in, strong jaw softened, voice like melting chocolate as he speaks to her, Charles and I disregarded.

'Blythe, I know this is terribly hard for you,' he says, squeezing her hand even tighter this time. 'But what was it Dom said that upset you so much you saw no option but to use that gun?'

'I can't!' she says, shaking her head and pulling away. 'I just can't.' Then she leans towards Roland, her face an inch from his, her voice chilling as she adds, 'And I suggest you don't push me again!'

And with that, Blythe forces her chair back, an awful screeching sound as it scratches the wooden floor before she strides out the room. Almost taking out Ludo who is, as suspected, the other side of the door.

Roland gets up too, gathering his belongings and readying himself to go, apparently unfazed by the drama or Blythe's final threat. He even manages a wry smile as Ludo makes his excuses about coming in to collect up the cups.

I make a quick decision. Lurking after Ludo has left. Roland will be gone soon and with him, any opportunity to say what I now feel I must.

'Roland, I was wondering if I might have a quick word, in private?'

He glances at Charles and nods, sending him on his way, briefcase, laptop and the chinned notepad taken with him. I close the door and lean against it.

'Yes, Marnie?'

'It's just, these scripts of Dom's...' I say, walking to the table. 'The ones he burned the day he died.'

'Yes, yes, I'm aware.' Roland's tucking his pen in his silk-lined jacket and appears much more interested in the Mont Blanc flower being uppermost than what I'm saying.

'Right, yes, it's just that Blythe has already shared some of the content with me, and they are very close to—'

'I thought the scripts were destroyed in the bonfire?' Roland asks, glancing up at me. 'The laptop too. All versions culled. I would strongly advise that you desist from working with Blythe on anything for the foreseeable.'

'Yes, right, it's just... Blythe wants to recreate the idea, which is based on her life, but what I find troubling—'

'*Troubling?*' Roland is ready to leave. In fact, he's halfway to the closed door. 'Be specific please, Marnie, and succinct. I have a murder charge to fend off and I'm afraid any idea of Blythe's to star in a screen version of her colourful life would be inadvisable and frankly hugely optimistic.'

'Right, I was just wondering if maybe the Hoppers' past is reflected in the scripts? A kind of confession.'

'Confession of what?'

'Right, well I don't know exactly, but there are a few characters and plot points that share striking similarities with... well, dead women.'

'Dead women?'

'Yes, like Dom's wife, Wendy, and a stunt double of Blythe's called Josie Phoenix, and the actress who starred in Dom's film *The Man*, she was called Florence Saint John. All of whom died in tragic circumstances in the early to mid-nineties.'

'That's quite the list, Marnie,' he says, his tone patronising. 'Of deaths which happened thirty years ago.'

'Yes, but there was another, more recent death.'

'How recent?'

'2006.'

Roland looks unimpressed.

'A woman called Caroline Costello. She painted a portrait of Blythe. She died of a severe nut allergy. Anaphylactic shock, maybe deliberately poisoned, although I haven't finished my research on her as yet.'

As I say it aloud, an image of Blythe spooning in peanut butter last night comes back to me. I gulp, audibly. Am I being ridiculous?

'OK, Marnie, can you email me all this?' He hands me a business card taken from a small wallet inside his jacket pocket. 'But I do have a defence to put together for my client, which has to be my priority.'

'Yeah, sure, of course, I'll email all my notes and the links.'

He leaves and I slump back down in my chair and write up what I can remember of the intricacies of the meeting.

It's only as I close my notebook that I remember the dodgy Wi-Fi in the annexe. *Urgh!* It's like when there's a power cut and you keep trying to switch on lights. I will try to email Roland all those attachments, but there's no guarantee when it will reach him, if at all.

* * *

'What was that about?' Ludo asks. He's in the hallway, by the open front door.

'Nothing. Have they gone?'

'Yes, just left.' Ludo glances outside, as I do, the drive empty. 'This is looking very bad for Blythe, isn't it?' he asks, his face tight with worry.

There seems little point either of us pretending he hadn't been listening at the door and must have heard everything, but I'm surprised by his openness. 'Yes, I agree, but maybe if she can tell

Roland what Dom said to her just before she–?' I stop, watching for his reaction. 'You've got no idea what it is?'

Ludo shakes his head, giving nothing away. 'No, and there's no point speculating, Ms Wilde.'

'No, guess not, but we could anyway?'

Ludo remains tight-lipped, suggesting I make myself scarce for a while whilst he checks on Blythe who has gone upstairs to lie down. He runs halfway up the red carpet, then he stops and looks back down. 'Ms Wilde, was there something else?'

'Sorry! Still got this hangover. It's making me slow.'

'There's everything you might need in the medicine cupboard. Same one where we keep the gin. I know you don't mind helping yourself.'

* * *

I swear the gallery of Blythe's smiling face is more macabre each time. I half close my eyes against the pain of a pounding head and the rubbing boots as I run back through the corridor, the brightness of the kitchen also too much. It reminds me of an operating theatre, especially with those sharp knives on the wall. I grab a glass of tap water and stand at the broken patio door, gulping in fresh air. The lock is neatly sheared off. A single gunshot. Perfectly aimed.

Whatever Dom accused her of that night it was clearly enough of a 'trigger' to make Blythe mad enough to kill him, and then refuse to say why all these weeks, even to save herself a few years in prison. I can't think of anything that awful. Except maybe I can.

19

After the intense meeting with Blythe's lawyers, I am completely wrung out. The heat, and the remnants of the gin hangover – the worst I've ever had apart from after that misguided night of margaritas with Harry in Hollywood – manifesting as not only a pulse-pounding headache, but also waves of rolling nausea that threaten to spill over into actual vomit. I return to the annexe to rest and regroup, eschewing Ludo's offer of codeine – it does make me pass out, but also, I'm not taking anything pharmaceutical from him – and just about manage to kick off my boots and crawl into bed before I do throw up. I hate being sick. And the nausea is also a sign that I should rest or I'll definitely black out. Something I have an unfortunate tendency to do, often at the most inopportune moments. Like that night of cocktails with Harry, immediately after we'd taken our relationship from strictly professional to a brief and thankfully one-off attempt at shagging. Maybe Harry is gay, or just didn't fancy me? He didn't seem that disappointed, more concerned. Probably just a nice guy.

Goodness knows how Blythe must be feeling after last night's drunken excess, followed by Roland's stark warnings this morning.

She killed Dom, she's not denying it, never has, but she's finally having to face up to the consequences. A custodial sentence of a decade, maybe more. The chance of a few years knocked off, not enticement enough to break her silence on what Dom accused her of that night. Must be pretty bad to keep it a secret. She's fifty-seven, so she could be in her seventies by the time she's considered for release. An old lady. If she makes it to that point. I can't see prison life suiting her. She's a rare orchid. I'd imagine they get stamped on pretty quickly in places like that.

I peel off my dress under the duvet. That chilly warning Blythe gave Roland not to push her has sent a shiver through me, despite the heat. Blythe might not have fazed Roland, he's probably seen it all before, but the menace in her voice, and the way she looked at him, freaks me out. I'll send that email to him, attaching my evidence, as soon as I'm feeling a bit better. The email to Priscilla still hasn't left my Outbox, so it's irrelevant for now.

I roll on my side and bring my knees to my chest to counteract the sickness, picking up the pages of script I grabbed on my way to bed. The mattress is an undulating sea of questions. I need full-fat Coke, dry toast and my own bed. I need answers. I need not to puke if at all possible. I need Wi-Fi to whisk those chapter ideas to my editor and to send Roland my thoughts on the dead women.

I hold the scripts above me page by page, squinting through one eye. It's not what's been written so much as the missing episodes and their kills that consumes me. I guess they'll reveal themselves as Blythe and I collaborate further, although maybe she won't want to work on the scripts, or the memoir, after that dreadful meeting with Roland. I could be on my way home today.

The prospect of leaving is both a relief and a massive disappointment. Because I haven't found what I came here for.

I drift off with my phone in my hand, Dom's email open, his words filtering into my dreams, my mother there too. A happy family of three until the darkness spins me round and I'm falling from my mother's arms into a void. Dad's voice is so angry, telling me I'm a huge disappointment. I don't deserve a mother. I'm why she left. It's all my fault!

I wake with a start, a page of script stuck to my face, a bunch of questions buzzing round my aching brain about long-dead women. Wendy, Josie, Flo, Caroline... maybe even Katherine Wilde. Although I push that last thought down. I can't think of my mother as dead... Hope must prevail. Or what was the point of me coming here? Earning some money, I suppose, although that has fallen way down my list of priorities. Which feels wrong. I still have a contract to fulfil, if I can, and a fee to earn.

A fat bluebottle dive-bombs me. I sit up and grab the pages of scripts, rolling them into a tight wad. My aim alarmingly effective as I spatter the fly, white sheets sullied by the bloodied mess. I need coffee, and to calm down. Then I need to get back to the job I am being paid to do. I pull on a T-shirt and get up.

* * *

The desk fan Ludo brought me whirs noisily beside my mug of instant coffee as I finish the first chapter of the memoir and whizz it to Priscilla, or at least try to. How I am supposed to work with no reliable internet connection, not to mention the perennial heat? I unlock the door and prop it open with the scratched pebble, DFH, no sign of anyone up at the house as I stick my head outside.

The tiny fridge isn't exactly well stocked, but I deserve a snack after all my hard work. There's a tiny block of cheap waxy Cheddar which I chomp through with some dry crackers that were in the cupboard.

Dad's voice is the one that comes to me as I work out my next move. The distraction of writing only keeping other thoughts at bay for so long.

You can't ever go wrong with the facts, Marnie. No one in their right mind can argue against those.

I scan down the list of kills in my notepad. Four dead women: Wendy, Josie, Flo and now Caroline. What connects those deaths, other than the Hoppers? And why would Blythe want them 'disposed of'? She'd need motive and means.

Wendy wanted to come back to the UK, threatening to take Dom's boys with her, which I guess could have provided a motive to kill her, to keep Dom Stateside, but it's hard to see Blythe as a doting stepmother. And she wouldn't have known Dom would lose custody.

Josie Phoenix, what motive is there for killing her? An affair with Dom, maybe? Or because Josie was an actress too, so perhaps competition?

And Florence Saint John. That's hardly straightforward either. If Blythe was offered the starring role in *Affairs of the Heart* after the favoured choice for the role tragically died, then that's kind of fair enough. But if Blythe somehow knew the part was hers if Flo was out the picture and helped make that happen, that's something entirely different. Maybe Flo confronted her about rumours of Blythe stepping in and Blythe took matters into her own hands?

Then there's Caroline Costello. Poisoned according to Blythe. Which is a perturbing way to put it, especially as the 'poisoning' was due to a severe nut allergy and knowing Blythe's predilection for peanut butter, but obviously I need to know more.

The buffering on my laptop has finally been replaced by the results of the search I typed in. I scan down and click through to a newspaper report on the inquest into Caroline Costello's death, and there's a photo.

'Ms Wilde?'

I spin round in the chair to see Ludo is standing outside the open door, his hand raised, finger crooked as if he's contemplating knocking on fresh air.

'Ludo! Don't creep up on me like that!' I pull the T-shirt down over my knickers.

'Sorry to make you jump, Ms Wilde. You were so engrossed in your work; I didn't like to interrupt.'

I glance at my open laptop, the page on Caroline still open. A photo fills the screen. Caroline, blonde, slim, attractive, is flanked by two very familiar faces, Dominic and Blythe Hopper, at an exhibition of Caroline's work in 2006, in Fowey, Cornwall. The same year Caroline died. No way Ludo hasn't seen it; he's only two steps away.

I point at Caroline's smiling face. 'You know anything about the artist who painted Blythe's portrait?'

He shakes his head. 'I'm sorry, should I?'

'Blythe said you might sell the painting for her.'

'Did she?' Ludo asks, his habit of answering questions with one of his own starting to annoy.

'She did. Said you'd know someone. You always do.'

'I haven't discussed that with her, but if she wants me to, of course I will.'

'And Florence Saint John, does that name mean anything to you?' I ask, closing the laptop before I join him at the door.

He shakes his head. 'Should it?'

'She was in Dom's film, *The Man*. He must have talked about her; she died at their house in LA.'

'They never discussed Hollywood, either of them. The most I've heard in years is what she's been saying to you, and frankly, it worries me.'

I step back. 'Do you want to come in, have a chat about your concerns?'

'No thank you, I just came down to see if you need anything.' He eyes the crumbs scattered across the desk. 'A dustpan, perhaps?'

The cheek of the man! He's not exactly an exemplary housekeeper.

'No, I'm fine thanks, although it would be helpful if you could tell me more about the Hoppers buying this place. Blythe said you worked some kind of magic with the finance.'

Ludo stiffens, his back straight. 'I don't see how that's any of your business?'

'My dad is a solicitor so I have a pretty good grasp of what's ethical and what's not, Ludo, but I can ask Roland if you'd prefer.' I grab Roland's business card from my desk and brandish it.

Ludo blanches. Dad is a divorce solicitor, not a conveyancer, but Ludo doesn't know that. Does he?

'It was standard practice, back then,' he says, kicking at the pebble. 'Five, even six times earnings. Nothing irregular, I can assure you.'

He turns to go, but I stop him with another question.

'Have you seen Blythe since this morning's meeting? It really took it out of her.'

'Her welfare is my concern, not yours,' he says, staring at me as he rocks on his expensive loafers. 'I'll let you know when she's ready to see you.'

And with that he leaves, halfway across the lawn before I have a chance to reply. I watch his retreat, his fast walk less funny now, a worrying thought formulating.

Maybe I've been so preoccupied with the dead, I've neglected the living.

20

Ludo Villander is a made-up name. Of course it is!

I could kick myself for not checking before, but once I've reconciled myself to the oversight, it's only a hop, skip and jump – or rather a few judicious clicks and annoying waits for internet – until I am reordering my saved folder of notes to create a chronological timeline of Ludo's past dealings with the Hoppers.

Ludo's real name is Luke Wiggins, the discovery of which makes me snort over Dom's desk. I find this nugget via a trawl back through 'Ludo's' employment history, the search for information frustratingly slow until I decamp onto the veranda and hold the laptop above my head every time the signal wavers. It's not a reliable system, but the email to Priscilla that was stuck in my Outbox until now, finally sends, so that's a small win. I will send one to Roland soon, but I don't want to overwhelm the system. It's Ludo/Luke I'm interested in for now.

Luke Wiggins worked as a trainee accountant in the early 2000s for various firms, never lasting more than a few months. The last company who took him on are still known for their impressive roster of well-known writers, actors and musicians. A wealth management accountancy service.

There's even a photo of Dominic and Blythe with a very young-looking Luke/Ludo at the firm's summer party in 2005, the trio looking very cosied-up, and Luke positively beaming as they raise their champagne glasses for the camera. It's an obscure trade publication and no client names are credited, for confidentiality I guess, but thrilling to see the three of them together.

Luke Wiggins left – or was he pushed? – that same year to set up a company with Dom called Farnsworth Wiggins. Which explains why I hadn't stumbled upon this treasure trove in my previous searches for Dominic Hopper. Dominic Farnsworth Hopper: DFH.

September 2005 was when the Hoppers bought The Towers according to Land Registry, so I'm assuming Ludo's services were soon deployed to hand them the method if not means by which they bought a house which was by all accounts, well beyond their means. Blythe's inflated income used to get the loan, and thereby emasculating Dom, as she'd told Roland. Ludo's creative accounting skills implemented to the max. I think it's a sound hypothesis and explains why the Hoppers, or at least Blythe, cosied up with Ludo so readily.

Farnsworth Hopper has two directors listed at Companies House: Luke Wiggins and Farnsworth Hopper, i.e. Dominic Farnsworth Hopper. A shell company, I assume, although I'm not entirely sure what that means, other than shady.

Ludo admitted he'd lost clients due to a genuine mistake in accounting that was... unfortunate and misinterpreted. But that Blythe has stuck with him. Now I am beginning to see why. Ludo's silence clearly needed about an arrangement that suited them all. Ludo's willingness and skill in creative accounting, used to project earnings that never came through. But does that explain Blythe's loyalty over so many years since and especially now the house is to be sold? And why did Dom and Ludo fall out when they were former partners in crime?

I take my laptop back inside before I'm spotted waving it in the air and sit at Dom's desk, staring into space until the screen darkens. My reflection startles me when I mentally return to the room, the otherness of my features jarring. But there's something else that pounds out a drumbeat in my chest. Something I can't quite get back to, but also can't let go.

Maybe it's the certainty that by knowing all this, I am in more danger than ever.

I need to talk to Blythe about her relationship with Ludo, but how do I raise that without also alerting Blythe and Ludo to my discovery of his reinvention? They are clearly as thick as thieves and Ludo is always there, lurking. I'd thought of him as the victim here, under Blythe's tyrannical reign, but is it the other way around? Is he blackmailing her? What dark secrets are buried here at The Towers and is it wise to go digging, even if knowledge equals danger?

For now, I compose an email to Roland setting out my concerns, and attach everything I have found about those dead women. Better to be safe than sorry.

I go outside again and stand on my tiptoes on the veranda, laptop held aloft until my arms ache so much, I think I might pass out. But it's worth it as I hear that whooshing sound. All emails sent. The opening chapter now with Priscilla and my 'evidence' with Roland. It's a bloody miracle given the size of files I sent him on those dead women, but for better, or worse, it's all out there now. Although whether Roland will take me seriously, or even have time to read my long email and sift through the links and attachments, remains to be seen.

The annexe is hotter than ever as I go back inside.

I need to get out of this cabin, and not just onto the veranda, but to properly stretch my legs. This is my third day here and I'm starting to go stir-crazy. My hangover has lifted and I'm restless in mind and body.

The trouble is, my options are extremely limited, especially if I'm to abide by Ludo's folder of rules and I really don't want to cross him. I flick through the binder, looking for any leeway. The washing machine and dryer in the garage are available to me, a small key slipped in the plastic wallet on the page headed *WASHING FACILITIES: IF NEEDED*. It's not a very exciting excursion, but good to be out of the writing annexe for a bit. There's something about this place that unnerves me. Ghosts of the past disturbed by my footfall.

The thing I'm not admitting to myself as I gather up dirty laundry, and pull on a pair of shorts is this expedition is about a lot more than a leg stretch and a clean set of clothes. It's also an exercise in finding an escape route. Because the point at which you need one, is often far too late to start looking.

The only route to the garage is through the house. I know this from Blythe's testimony to Roland. I head to the kitchen, keys jangling in my shorts pocket, no signs of life as I approach the patio door. It seems lax not to have fixed the lock, it's been over a month. What if the weather turns? Thunderstorms are forecast, flash floods too. And the kitchen gives full access to the rest of the house. Anyone could wander in, but nothing here conforms to the expected rules, and those high gates do make it very hard to gain entry. I call ahead as I go in, '*Hello?*'

The kitchen is empty. No reply to another tentative greeting as I enter the corridor, washing cradled before me. 'Hello? Blythe? Ludo?'

There must be a hundred photos lining the long stretch of white walls. Maybe more. I hadn't thought about the symmetrical pattern, too caught up in either studying or avoiding Blythe's smiling face, but the arrangement of the frames suggests they were all put up at the same time. Ludo's methodical work, I assume? Designed to massage Blythe's considerable ego, much like the prominent display of her Oscar statuette. Although the amount of dust the frames have accumulated suggests they've been here a while longer than a month.

As always, it's unnerving to be surrounded by Blythe's gaze, my footsteps echoing, but I force myself to study the images more closely. Searching for familiarity, and possible victims.

The faces I recognise immediately are the ones famous to me, snapped at celebrity gatherings. A premiere with a director known for his blockbuster movies, a dinner party with at least three Oscar winners. Then I notice a gap, like a missing tooth in an otherwise perfect smile. I free up a hand from the bunched washing to touch the space, a pair of black lacy knickers dropped in the process. The chalky white paint is a little darker where the frame was hung. The spot where the photo of Josie Phoenix with Blythe was displayed now empty.

I retrieve the dropped knickers and move on, the hallway flooded with sunlight, my flip-flops bouncing across the marble, slip-slap. The front door, as it often is, has been left wide open, but there's no sign of anyone on the drive. I leave my laundry by the front door and take the opportunity to try the door beside it. A coat cupboard, but no sign of a way to release the gates, just an old-fashioned bell system for when the house once had servants: very Agatha Christie.

I glance up the stairs, the red carpet rising in an enticing manner to the first floor. It's very quiet. Blythe's likely still resting after that trying meeting this morning. It would be a massive invasion of her privacy to disturb her, even a polite knock at the door a bit much, but as Ludo isn't around for some reason... Should I be the one keeping an eye on her?

I balance on the first stair, looking up, but I can't see much more than before. I take another step and another, halfway up the flight before the full length of the landing is visible. I'm guessing Blythe's room is behind the double doors at the top. That would tally with where the large bay is, overlooking the back garden. I go up one more tread, my right flip-flop catching a stair rod. My foot twists, wobbling alarmingly, a soft thud as the flip-flop hits each tread before it lands at the bottom.

I hobble back down and retrieve it, taking it as a sign that I should leave well alone.

I half expect to find Ludo on the walk down the drive, Blythe's manager waving at me wildly and demanding to know what I'm up to. But birdsong is all I can hear as I make my way towards the garage. I pause, enjoying a momentary sense of freedom, along with the intense afternoon heat, reminded of sneaking out of school between lessons, the days long, beach calling.

The clothes held tight in my freckled arms, dried sweat rising from them and scenting the heat, the mid-afternoon sun high and beating down on the back of my neck, I cautiously take the steps down to the courtyard. The crevices behind my knees are slick with perspiration, my feet slipping in my flip-flops. The tattooed heart thumps dark red on my forearm. The scratch from the bramble outside the gates almost healed over as the serpent hisses.

I'd always planned a full sleeve when funds allowed, but it's been over a decade since that serpent. My first ink, at the tender age of seventeen, was so painful it almost put me off forever. I'd claimed I was eighteen, doctoring my date of birth on my library card as parental consent was required. Which surprised me given the casual set-up of the seafront parlour that smelt of lentils and burning incense.

'Why on earth would you do that to yourself?' Dad had demanded, jabbing at the still-sore initials carved amongst the cherry blossom on my ribs just beneath my bra. K and H. I'd got sloppy about covering up the reddened skin, the tiny crop top I'd chosen that day advertising my rebellion to the world, and of course to my vigilant father. It had hurt like hell getting it done so close to the bone. But the pain was worth it. That tattoo was about more than defiance. It was about Mum and me, not Dad. Her initials. That's what I told him, insubordinate in the face of his anger and disappointment. I'd wanted him to witness my act of abandon. Otherwise where was the rebellion?

'This might be the stupidest thing you've ever done, Marnie,' he told me, and there was already a high bar with drunken nights out and unsuitable boyfriends. 'Senseless!' he called it. He even swore, and Dad never did that. 'You don't have a bloody clue about your mother, Marnie. Not a clue! What were you thinking getting those initials on your skin like that?!'

'What was I thinking?! I was thinking that as you've hidden every single card she ever sent me—'

'What? You found those?'

'Yes, all signed by her, and I'll find her too. Then I'm the fuck out of here.'

I'd thought for a second he might share something, *anything* about her. I would have seized on it and treasured every detail, but all he said was, 'She's dead to us, Marnie. That's all you need to know. Dead to us.'

Then he stormed out, robbing me of the chance to do so myself.

We are fine these days, Dad and I, but I wouldn't describe us as close. How can we be when so much is off-limits? It's exhausting holding it all inside. Like stoppering a shaken bottle. Even a tiny leak and the cork explodes, everything rushing out and spraying us in a sticky mess it would take forever to clear up. It's better to say nothing, that's what I've learnt, but it's come at a price. As if I'm not being true to myself, or Mum. Dad makes me a liar as I deny my feelings to preserve his. Ten things stacked underneath the one thing I *can* say, another brick in the wall we're building between us. The burden too much alone.

The concrete steps are baked with days of heat. I take a final glance behind me to the house as it disappears, then I pick my way down the last few steps, rye grass tickling my bare legs as I enter the courtyard.

Ahead of me are the gates, and beyond them, freedom, and in spite of all my resolutions and need for answers, I'm taken by a sudden urge to keep going. Through the gates. Down the road. Anywhere but here.

I am going to do it. I have to. There's too much danger at The Towers. I am going to run away.

21

I drop the sweaty pile of clothes and run towards the solid wooden gates, fists hammering and nails clawing at the sliver of a gap between them, all my efforts met with total intransigence. The gates are an impenetrable obstacle. It's futile, but I won't give up. Can't. Despite every logical bone in my body – or at least the few I inherited from Dad – telling me it's a waste of physical and emotional energy. I pound and kick and grasp, as if I might break through the thick wood or prise the two halves apart, or somehow scale a ten-foot-high barrier overgrown with a tangle of brambles.

The gates win, of course. It was always an unfair fight. All I gain is bruised knuckles and a tight chest, breathless and frustrated as I give in and peer through the tiny gap. There's no one passing by, not even a curious dog walker. The reality is that without someone buzzing the gates open from inside the house, there's literally no escape. And I've possibly broken a toe, a dark purple bruise blooming on the big toe of my right foot.

I cast around for an alternative means of escape, but the boundary walls are as tall as the gates, if not taller, and the exit at other side of the house is blocked by the writing annexe, which seems a crazy spot to build in, given it means there's no vehicular access up to the house. I'm guessing Roland parked outside on the road and slid through the small gap with Charles, as I did. But that's not really sustainable, is it? What if the Hoppers had needed a furniture delivery, or an ambulance? Which they did, although the one that took Dom away had to park behind the gates, hence those photos of the body being stretchered out.

I just don't get it. Why build the writing annexe there, right in the way, when there's extensive grounds with plenty of sites to choose from?

Maybe that's one of the reasons why The Towers hasn't sold, the weirdness and neglect, although if you can afford the seventeen million price point, you can probably fold in the cost of tearing down a wooden structure and fitting new gates that fully open.

I kick the gates in protest, left-footed this time and half-heartedly, a final act of desperation before self-pity consumes me. I'm stuck here. No personal freedom, beholden to my inhospitable and murderous host.

I'm not usually one to cry, I didn't shed a single tear in front of Jake even when he told me it was over two days before Christmas and thrust my perfume, which I chose, under the tree, but as I struggle to come up with my next move, a sob threatens. Ludo hasn't wanted me here from the start, although that does mean he would let me out, if I asked him. But then I leave here with nothing. No answers. No memoir. No payday, and therefore no home. Oh God, this is a nightmare. I can't leave.

I head back across the courtyard, gathering dropped laundry as I go. I have no enthusiasm for the washing now. It's unimportant. But without it, I've lost purpose. I climb back up and slump down on the top step, then let go of the dirty clothes, watching them tumble down to land in a heap at the bottom. The resultant pile could easily be mistaken for a body. A maudlin thought, but that's how I feel.

I pull my phone out my shorts pocket, more for something to do than expecting signal, but for the first time in days, all the bars of signal are back! I check on my emails first – no response from either Priscilla or Roland – then I open up my social media apps, studying an annoying post from Jake about a Mexican meal I bet the model-slash barely ate. I drag myself from that, eventually, and scroll through my phone contacts, tapping the one at the top. If there's no answer, I probably *will* cry. Maybe I'll cry even if he does answer. I'll know at the sound of his voice.

'Hello, Marnie, how's it going?'

I clear my throat and inject a jokey tone. 'Great! I'm at a very swanky house, Dad.'

He laughs at my use of his vernacular. 'Good, I'm pleased the job is going well, but I won't ask who the celebrity is, or you'd have to kill me.'

I try, but can't laugh at our usual joke, my voice cracking as I reply, 'Yeah, right.'

'You OK, Marnie-Moo?'

'Yeah, all good.' I swallow. 'Dad?'

'Yes, love?'

'No, nothing.'

'What's happened?'

The inference stiffens my shoulders, pulling them back. Not, *Are you OK, Marnie?* Or, *Can I help, love?* But, *What have you done this time?* Or at least, that's what I hear.

'Yeah, all good, Dad. I haven't fucked up, you'll be pleased to hear.'

'No, of course you haven't, but please, don't swear.'

'Sorry, Dad.'

The silence stretches out between us. I wait for him to say something, which he eventually does, commenting on how hot it is.

The washing sits at the bottom of the stone steps as we discuss the forecast, the tumbled fabrics now even more reminiscent of a mangled body through the blurred focus of my swallowed tears. My imagination takes me down after them, a slow motion reel of my head hitting each concrete step, blood on the weeds, both legs breaking, then my back, skull fractured.

Dad is saying something about his neighbour in the flat above. How they've been in hospital with heatstroke after falling asleep on the beach. He is saying goodbye then. The call ended.

I don't think I've ever felt quite so alone.

I go down and collect my clothes, then traipse back up the steps. Tears swiped away. No point crying when there's no one there to comfort you.

* * *

The key I attached to the fob unlocks the side door of the double garage, a single bulb activated as I go in. There's enough space in here for two vehicles, but it's stuffed instead with a jumble of gardening equipment and patio furniture. No one uses their garage for cars, but it does confirm neither Blythe nor Ludo seem to have one.

Straight ahead is the washing machine, beside it a tumble dryer, both industrial sized and covered in patio cushions, clouds of dust and cobwebs engulfing me as I remove the mildewed cushions and open the top-loading tub to drop in my clothes. My blasé attitude to Ludo's lengthy page of instructions about the tub is regrettable as I study the incomprehensible dials, a family-size bottle of detergent in hand that was on top of the dryer. I open the crusted screw-top lid and pour the pungent blue liquid in, selecting a programme at random.

The wind catches the open door, a strong gust bending it back on groaning hinges. I close it, feeling safer for the privacy it provides. But I won't lock it. That would send a signal, should Ludo come looking for me. As if I'm up to no good, which I'm not. Not really. Although I do intend to have a look around whilst I'm here. Pass the time, if nothing else.

The large up-and-over double door is rusted shut, or locked. Maybe both. Either way, it's not budging, despite my best but frankly puny efforts.

I'm guessing the laundry facilities are housed here so the domestic staff could take care of sheets and towels without disturbing the Hoppers, a duty which now must fall to Ludo, although it doesn't look like he's been down here in a while, the pool towels reused, I guess. *Yuk!* I lift the top loader's lid to check on my clothes and am hit with a blast of steam. Everything I brought with me, other than the T-shirt and shorts I'm wearing, is slopping around in the soupy blue hot water. If it shrinks them to dolls'-clothes-size, I'm completely buggered, but it would be the loss of Mum's skirt that would slaughter me. I've never worn it before; it's far too precious. I was afraid I'd drop something down it, which of course I now have. I press buttons on the dryer for when I need it, but that seems completely dead.

A wave of light-headedness washes over me. Panic about the skirt, maybe, or maybe something more? Like poison? I hear Dad again, the voice of reason.

Stop it, Marnie, you're spiralling. And then, as if he were right behind me, *Just like your mother.*

I've never heard him say that last part before. I'm sure I'd have remembered if he had.

I swoon, alarmingly. It feels like the top of my head is coming away from my body and floating towards the cobwebbed rafters. A decapitated Marnie, free-form, about to disengage from consciousness. A switch is about to be turned off in my brain; darkness coming. I grab onto a metal shelf unit and take deep breaths, holding on. Fighting the urge to pass out.

I've fainted before in a garage. A school 'friend' if that's what you'd call her, describing the whole scene with not a small amount of zeal and in lurid detail as everyone at the ad-hoc party gathered round me after I regained consciousness. She'd loved the drama, regaling me with a full description of how my head had bounced off her parents' garage floor and that I'd made some 'weird' noises, and 'writhed'.

I was only saved from a cracked skull by my bobble hat, which Dad had insisted I wear to the sixteenth birthday party as it was mid-winter and in a garage. The pom-pommed monstrosity had been something of a talking point before my unfortunate faint. Which was why I'd kept it on, playing up to the joke which was then at my own expense.

Dad was called and took me straight to the hospital where I was tested for everything under the sun – drugs, drink, and finally something called *petit mal* which is a kind of epilepsy. I'd worried not so much about what was wrong with me, but how I'd looked when I was passed out. Had my face looked funny? My tongue lolling as I frothed at the mouth? What had I said, if anything? I still don't know. I kept to myself at school after that, just in case. But I heard the rumours, noted the stares. The joke still on me, but definitely no longer funny. I hadn't wet my pants, that was a lie.

This garage floor is way too dusty to sit on, but my legs are about to give out. Head below heart, that's the advice Dad and I were given by the consultant. It apparently sends the flow of blood back up, or something like that. And not to drink to excess, or smoke, or generally neglect my own care.

I lie on my side, resting on my cheek, the floaty feeling intensifying. Sometimes, I can hang on, if I try hard, pull myself back from the brink. Often it's too late.

The last time it happened was the day after Jake left me. I was on my way to the toilet when next thing I knew, I was on the bathroom floor. I have no idea how long I was unconscious. That was a wake-up call. I'd had the best part of two bottles of cheap red and nothing to eat all day. I registered with a doctor in the new year and the *petit mal* prognosis was amended to 'absence seizure'. Which I quite like. As if I can disengage at will. I was also advised again, a dozen or so years on from the A&E visit, to cut down on alcohol and generally take better care of myself. Hence the attempt at a healthier new me – the odd bottle of red aside. I need to try harder. Bad, Marnie. *Very bad.*

Feeling slightly better, I dust myself down, a stack of folding chairs catching my eye behind a round plastic table. If I can sit quietly for a few minutes, I'll be OK to walk back up with the washing once it's done. The drum rattling as the spin cycle kicks up a gear.

I pull the table out to access the chairs stacked behind it. The tremor in my hands and buoyant feeling in my legs making every movement hard work, like I'm simultaneously walking on the moon and wading through water. It's a liminal state, often detached from reality. As if I'm watching a film I'm starring in.

We had a cheap patio set just like this one when I was a kid. Before the move to the flat, on the estate where families lived. Orange squash in plastic beakers. Burgers in buns and ketchup jammy from sitting in the sun too long. A dripping cone from the tinkling van, an ice pop from the freezer. Funny how clearly I recall those meaningless details and yet Mum's face is obscured. Her laugh, though, comes through loud and clear. I recall the day I danced for her, in and out of the sprinkler in my Minnie Mouse swimsuit. *Marnie-Moo, ever the clown.* Sometimes, the memories are more real to me than the present.

I pick up a folded chair, the rusting spring resistant as it bites back, my finger trapped inside. I yelp and extricate myself, determined not to be beaten despite the throbbing pain. The chair springs open at last, but with such force I almost lose my balance. A patch of the woven plastic seat eaten away.

I scream and drop the chair but manage to avoid the contents landing on my foot. A dead mouse in its tiny nest. I step back again, my right leg connecting with something very hard and very pointed. The offending item, a hoe that's hanging on the wall at my calf height, then falls, hitting my Achilles with such force I open my mouth to emit an even louder scream, which never comes.

Then everything goes black.

* * *

I wake to see Blythe's face is thrust into mine. She's crouched down, prodding my fleshy thigh with a pointed fingernail. 'Marnie? Can you hear me? Oh thank goodness, you're alive!'

'What happened?' I ask, squeezing my eyes tight, then opening them.

'I assume you passed out,' she says. 'Is that something you do often?'

I sit up. Head aching. No bobble hat this time to cushion my fall, a bump on the back of my head that's soft and painful when my fingertips find it. I think of the frothing mouth, the lolling tongue. 'Was I out for long?'

'No idea, I just got here,' she replies, looming over me as she straightens up. 'Do you need anything?'

'No, I'm OK.' It's a lie; my head is throbbing.

'You think there's a dustpan somewhere in here?' Blythe says, hoisting herself to sit on the workbench at the back of the garage. 'See if you can find it, will you?'

'Sorry, what?'

'For that!' She points at the chair on its side, the mouse nest beside it. 'It's freaking me out. Can you deal?'

I hold on to the wall, then a mower as I locate the dustpan behind it, the shelf-life on Blythe's concern shockingly short. I could well pass out again. Although usually once I've fainted, I'm over the worst. Like a reset button, my GP told me. A warning sign to rest up. I should lie down though, and I'll need to sleep it off for a while. It can take days to get over a bad episode. But I don't have that luxury here. Already put to work by Blythe as I scoop up the mouse and its nest.

'There's a black plastic sack over there,' Blythe directs, hoisting her feet up on the bench. 'Use that.'

It's behind the hoe I bashed my leg on. I move the offending item aside and untwist the top of the sack one-handed, not easy, head spinning as I tip the dustpan towards it. Blythe watches appalled as the long-dead mouse slides off for its last adventure, followed by its home.

'So are you going to tell me what happened?' Blythe asks, lowering her feet now it's safe to do so. She's dressed casually in white jeans and a candy-stripe shirt, teamed with box-fresh white trainers.

'No, honestly, it's nothing. I've barely eaten since I got here and I've done it before, but not in a long while.'

'Mmm... that'll be your blood sugar...' she replies, no offers of refreshments forthcoming. 'I actually came down to tell you Ludo thinks it's time you leave.'

I snap my head up from the contents of the black bag, spots appearing before my eyes. 'Leave The Towers?'

Blythe jumps down, a hand to my shoulder as I sway. 'You sure you're OK, Marnie?'

'Yes, I'm fine. Do *you* want me to leave?'

'No, not me,' she replies, twirling a lock of glossy hair. 'But Ludo is quite insistent.'

I pull the chair nearer to the sack of rubbish and sit down before I fall down. 'I didn't even know Ludo was home. The house was empty.'

'Oh, really? He's been buzzing around me like a bad smell since that meeting, and I'm afraid the upshot was I promised him I would talk to you.'

'Did he say why?' I ask, my attention diverted back to the contents of the bag.

'He said you're asking too many questions.' Blythe brushes down her jeans. 'Poking your nose in where it's not needed and damaging any chance of a defence.' She raises her hands in surrender. 'His words, not mine.'

'Am I?' I ask, taking deep breaths as I get up and the dark spots return. 'Asking too many questions?'

'Not as far as I'm concerned. What have you got there?'

I hold up an ashtray I've pulled from the rubbish sack, a twin of the onyx one Blythe used at the kitchen table and almost too heavy to lift one-handed. It's partially wrapped in a navy cashmere sweater, moth-eaten and studded with paperclips and bits of fluff as it hangs from the battered ashtray.

'I assumed Ludo would have disposed of the rubbish from the annexe rather than dumping it in here,' she comments, taking the ashtray and pulling paperclips off the sweater which fall, pinging to the floor. 'Always half a job with Ludo.'

'The bins are overflowing in fairness,' I tell her, holding up some paperbacks I've unearthed: Hemingway, Fitzgerald, Steinbeck. The yellowing pages are blighted with coffee stains, or maybe whisky rings, stale cigar smoke released as I flick through. It feels as if Dom has stepped out of the past and into the garage with us. Is it too much to hope I might find a script amongst the discarded ink cartridges and old receipts for printer paper? Or notes in the margins of the battered copy of *Gatsby* he clearly loved, also one of my favourite books. We truly are kindred spirits.

'Well, that's really no excuse for dumping it all in here,' Blythe says, tossing the ashtray back into the sack and narrowly missing my hand. 'Can you stop rooting around in there, Marnie? It's just rubbish.'

The dead rodent has unfortunately fallen on top of what looks to be potentially the most intriguing item. A stuffed A4 padded envelope that is welded to the base of the bag by something sticky which has leaked from a broken coffee mug which explains the sour smell. I pull at a corner of the jiffy bag, shaking off the clinging mouse.

'Give me that!' Blythe snaps.

I manage to avoid her grasping hand and also get a better grip on the package which is not as light as I'd thought it would be, the contents then tipping out and hitting the concrete floor. A photo frame, just like the ones in the corridor, lands face down, glass smashing, bits of broken plastic fracturing between us as we both jump back.

I grab for the photo, but Blythe gets there first, peeling it from a shard of lethal-looking glass and holding the print above her head as I reach up.

'What is it?' I ask, tiring of her childish antics. It's as if we're playing netball, but she's so much taller than me I don't stand a chance. 'Blythe, show me!'

She lowers the photo and studies it briefly, then throws it back in the rubbish. Twisting up the top of the plastic sack. 'It's nothing, just rubbish, as I said.'

'Mind if I take a look anyway?'

I untwist the top, half expecting her to wrestle the black plastic sack from me, but I guess that's not her style, her arms folded as her keen gaze meets mine. 'Do what you want, Marnie! It's inconsequential.'

I'd anticipated the photo would be the missing one of Blythe and Josie, so I'm ready with a volley of questions about why it had ended up in here and the circumstance of Josie's death, but the discoloured image is not the one I expected.

Four people, two men and two women, face the camera in a line. I recognise three of them instantly. The fourth is also vaguely familiar, although I can't place him. They are grouped on a length of red carpet, behind them a wall-sized poster for Dom's film.

'This was taken at the premiere of *The Man*?' I hold the photo up to Blythe.

Blythe turns away, a slight shrug, her face pale under the yellowing bulb.

On the far left there's Dom's first wife, Wendy, looking, as Blythe described her, extremely uncomfortable to be in the limelight and wearing a navy, low-cut maxi dress and kitten heels, the dress a bit tight and slightly too short to be elegant, the heels too low to flatter her legs. She's attractive in a homely way, but her smile is forced and therefore unconvincing.

Beside her, and taller by a foot, is her then husband, Dominic Hopper, basking in the glory of his big night, his navy tux cut beautifully to define his masculine frame, his dark hair slicked back and aviator sunglasses on. He's devilishly handsome, but carries his confidence a little too knowingly, his expression verging on arrogance.

To his right, diminutive Florence Saint John, female lead in *The Man*, is scene-stealing in a strapless, black, taffeta dress, her platinum-blonde hair faultlessly styled in a classic Hollywood chignon, her smile putting everyone else's in the shade, even Dom's. The camera adores Flo. Terrible to know she would be dead only a few months later.

The man to Flo's right, the one I can't quite place, is older and much less photogenic. Overweight and scruffy, he is in his late forties, maybe early fifties, thinning hair pulled back in a scraggly ponytail which presumably is compensating for his lost youth, as is his leopard-print bomber jacket.

'Who's that joker on the end?' I ask, holding the photo by a corner as I point him out. 'He looks ridiculous with that stupid ponytail.' I laugh, but Blythe's expression remains cold.

'Give me that!' she says, making me jump as she snatches the photo from my hand and drops it on top of the rubbish, twisting the top of the sack.

'You don't want to keep it as a memento of that first meeting with Dom?' I ask.

'No, I do not,' she responds. 'I told you, he didn't even notice me that night. This means nothing to me. Nothing! What are you doing now?'

I've retrieved the broken frame from the floor and am attempting to unhook the rusted metal catches to open up the back, careful to avoid the sharp edges of broken glass.

'Dad used to replace school photos with the latest one,' I tell her, 'but he'd always slot the previous photo in the back. I thought maybe... Oh, it's empty.'

Blythe opens the rubbish sack wide and glares at me. I drop everything inside, glass, frame, a piece of card backing. She gathers the edges and begins to tie a knot but then she opens it again and extracts the photo with fingertips. I assume she's changed her mind, wanting to preserve that memory after all, but she rips up the glossy print and drops the pieces like falling confetti back into the bag. Then tying a double knot.

'Right!' She brushes her palms clean. She glances at the open door, tugged back and forth by the wind again, the sky grey. 'Looks like the heavens are about to open, you coming?'

'So you don't want me to pack my bags and go?'

'No,' she says, looking down at me as if I'm crazy. 'That's the last thing I want, and I told Ludo the same. That's what I came to tell you. To ignore him. You're my guest and we have matters to attend to, OK?'

'Right, thanks. I'll just wait for my washing to finish.'

She nods, then she's running across the courtyard, rain pelting down.

I wait until I'm sure she's not coming back before I carefully kneel down, mindful of broken glass, and pick out the confetti pieces of photo to pocket them in my shorts. Then I start sifting through the remaining contents of the sack just in case I missed anything of note: old biros, paperclips and a stapler, a coaster and block of blank Post-it notes, and even a pair of reading glasses – everything fuzzy when I look through them. I lay the moth-eaten sweater on my lap as I sit back on my heels, bashed Achilles protesting. Dom's sweater is curled beside me like a faithful cat, the sack now emptied. No script notes. No old diaries. Not even a scribbled idea. Just that photo which incensed Blythe so much she tore the glossy paper to pieces with the sheer force of her anger.

The rain continues, still torrential as the washing cycle completes, drops throwing themselves like pebbles against the garage's roof. I chuck Dom's sweater over my thin T-shirt and grab the sopping washing from the tub, locking the door. I'm soaked through even before I start running.

I fly in through the open front door, dripping on the marble, flip-flops sliding around as I jog across the hall and down the corridor, skidding to a halt in the kitchen where Blythe is seated at the table, smoking, her startled expression turning to distaste as she takes in my dishevelled appearance.

'Good grief, Marnie! You're soaked. And why are you wearing Dom's sweater?'

'Sorry, I thought it might help in the rain.' I shake my short hair like a dog, hands filled with wet washing.

'And what's happened to all your clothes?' Blythe asks, exhaling smoke.

I look down. No idea what she means. I'm wearing the same shorts she saw me in a few minutes ago; and isn't it obvious why they are now wet? Except that's not what she'd meant. The realisation dawning that the wet washing I grabbed from the tub and then ran with, is now a livid shade of pink. The bright-red fabric my mum sewed into the petticoat of the dirndl skirt has bled into everything. But worse than any of that, it appears the skirt itself is damaged beyond repair, the lacy hem ripped and the floral top layer distorted and shrunken, the pocket hanging off.

'Oh dear,' Blythe comments. 'Ludo didn't tell you the washer is a bit unpredictable these days?'

'No,' I swallow hard. 'His folder of rules didn't cover that.'

'Well, if you need to borrow anything of mine, let me know,' she says, stubbing out her cigarette. 'Although we're hardly the same size.'

I'm such an idiot. Why did I wash Mum's skirt, and in a machine I don't know or trust, or shouldn't have if Ludo had bothered to warn me? Even the splodges of greasy pasta sauce would have been better than this. It's ruined. Forever. And Ludo is an utter bastard setting me up like this. What's his problem? This is deliberate sabotage. Deliberate cruelty, in fact. He knew I was down there. Probably watched me carry my precious few clothes down the drive and he did nothing except spill poison in Blythe's ear to get rid of me. Well I'm going nowhere!

I hold the skirt to my face and press it to my closed eyes. I don't deserve Katherine's belongings. I don't deserve *her*. My mother. But I'm damned if I'm leaving without finding her, or at least what Dom's connection to her was.

'And as if your day couldn't get any worse, I have some bad news,' Blythe announces, getting up.

'What?' I ask, in no mood for her dramatics right now.

'You'll be sorry to hear we are without Ludo and his culinary skills tonight,' she says, opening the fridge door and peering in as if it's the first time she's ever done so, the contents mystifying. 'He left us something cold, apparently, but God knows what.'

'He's not coming back?'

'Not tonight,' she says, pulling a face before she closes the fridge door. 'I thought it best I keep you two apart, in view of his comments. So, it's just us girls, OK?'

'Yeah, sure.'

I guess it should be welcome news, but much as I dislike Ludo, and distrust him, especially now, his presence has oddly been a reassurance. Something I've only realised now he's gone.

'I have a nice bottle of rosé chilling,' Blythe tells me. 'And apparently, there's bread... somewhere.' She looks round, at a loss in her own kitchen. 'Be a nice chance to talk freely, don't you think? Without him poking his nose in where it's not wanted.'

'Yeah, sounds great,' I reply, forcing a smile. 'I'll go and get changed, or try to.' I hold up the dripping washing. 'Might come back in a swimsuit!'

* * *

Dad always says you can only get wet once, but I'm soaked through to my knickers by the time I reach the shelter of the annexe. I spread the pink-hued washing around the veranda where it's protected from the worst of the storm, then unlock the door and go into the bedroom, shivering as I peel off my clothes and underwear whilst the thunder rolls around overhead, flashes of lightning crossing the annexe's shadowy walls. It's so gloomy in here. Even in the glass-fronted room, it's almost dark. Ernest looks down on me. I'm shivering in my dress now, which is all I have that's dry, and that's a miracle as it was kicked under the bed and missed the wash.

And that's when I remember I've left the photo pieces in my shorts pocket. I retrieve the pulped mess, saving what I can as I deal out the pieces of confetti on the desk.

Dom's face and the other man's head are the best preserved. The women now blurry and decapitated. Dom's sunglasses and the smile are appealing, whilst the other man, whom I still can't place, is doughy and sweaty, grey hair pulled into a mid-life crisis ponytail. Does he not know it makes him look like a dick?

And that's when I finally place him. He's the man applauding beside Dom in the video clip from when Blythe won her Oscar. Blythe had looked every inch the star as she ascended the steps in her red Valentino gown, thanking 'the two men who made this happen' as they led a standing ovation. Both men back-slapping and high-fiving each other in an over-the-top, scene-stealing way.

Greg Chaplain. That was his name.

He produced *Affairs of the Heart* as well as Dom's movie, *The Man.* That's why he was at the premiere of *The Man* with Wendy, Dom, and Flo. And clearly a good mate of Dom's too. I couldn't place him at first, the Oscar night tux taking a few years off him.

The storm is crazy now, lightning forking and rain thrashing, the guttering bubbling over. I grab the washing and stuff it into my bag, then type Greg Chaplain's name into Google. The room is lit with nature's electricity, the internet kicking in too. A coincidence no doubt, but I'm grateful for a rare moment of connectivity which I leap on, my searches confirming that unlike the other three people in the photo, Greg Chaplain is alive and well, if twenty pounds heavier, at least, and still very much a power player living and working in LA. A multimillionaire, no less. A big man in every sense, with his third, no, fourth wife on his arm just last week at the premiere of his latest blockbuster. One of those terrible franchises that inexplicably does well despite plot holes the size of a small country. He's seventy-four now, so he was only forty-three in that photo. Younger than I'd thought.

The signal dies as the power cuts, the gloomy annexe plunged into near-darkness in the middle of the afternoon. I walk to the glass door and look at the house, also dark. The sky is like night, the only light coming from my laptop as the battery keeps Greg's Wiki entry on screen.

I make some handwritten notes as I wait for the power to return, playing jigsaw puzzles as I piece the photo together, some of the confetti crumbling in my fingers like a tissue run through the wash. Some pieces missing, like Flo's face.

I hold the fragment of Dom's and Greg's faces closer so I can look into their eyes, or rather sunglasses in Dom's case. An unsettling flutter in my stomach as I study Greg's features. He's not an attractive man; in fact, there's something quite repellent about him. A perniciousness I'd picked up in the Oscar night clip too. His behaviour inauthentic. Maybe that's unfair, he's a famous movie producer, with the attendant ego, but I'm sure not every big player is like that. The ones I met in Hollywood seemed genuine people.

I click between his Wiki page and other photos. Comparing Greg now with the younger version of him in the scrap of photo. He definitely reminds me of someone; I just can't place who.

Never mind. Probably nothing. Like the guy I asked out when I was drunk because he was the double of Harry Styles. Spoiler... he wasn't. But there's no wish-fulfilment in terms of Greg Chaplain's ugly face. Far from it. It's as if I don't want to know where that feeling of familiarity is derived from, even as I scratch at my memory, trying to make the connection.

22

The storm has passed, or at least the rain has, for now, hammer-grey clouds lying low above the tall tower as I walk over for supper with Blythe, just 'us girls'.

Blythe is already seated at the kitchen table, hunched over a notebook and scribbling furiously. There are two, maybe three, flies buzzing around, the rain leaving behind not the desired freshness but muggy dampness. I wave away a persistent bluebottle that's intent on my right ear, the drone maddening as it makes another swoop past, whilst I wait for some acknowledgment of my presence from my host.

Blythe looks up at last, pleased to see me. 'Marnie!'

She is dressed impeccably, of course, in a floral, low-cut number with a matching head scarf, soft waves spinning from beneath the tied silk. Perfection, except for the scowl that then blooms as she adds, 'Oh dear, is that really all you have to wear?'

I look down at my creased dress and dirty flip-flops.

'Yes, your machine has ruined everything else.'

'I could maybe find you a loose blouse and slacks, although they're all much—'

'Don't worry, I wouldn't want to ruin anything of yours.'

She nods, thoughtful, then recoils as I sneeze. 'Is it a cold, do you think? Or flu?'

I do feel a bit crap now as she's asked, but I'd assumed it was the after-effects of blacking out.

'Nothing a drink can't fix. You said something about a bottle of rosé?'

'Oh yes, I did. Sit down and I'll—' Blythe frowns as I sit beside her. 'Not there! There!' she tells me, pointing me halfway down the table. 'I'll just finish this thought then we'll brave some of Ludo's cold supper and have that glass of wine, but please, keep your distance, just in case you're infectious.'

Blythe returns to her notes, right hand curved around the colourful notebook.

I take the seat she suggested, two away from hers, watching the storm through the broken door as the rain starts again, painting the garden into a blurred watercolour, the wind rattling the glass.

The thought that Ludo is out there somewhere, at liberty despite his underhandedness, whips up something akin to jealousy as I wait for Blythe to finish whatever she's so intent on writing. Nasty little man, ruining my clothes. I slouch in the dining chair and rub at my running nose. Blythe glances up at me, lip curling. She definitely won't survive a prison stretch if a potential cold freaks her out this much.

'Shall I open the wine?' I ask, tiring of the wait. 'Let it breathe.'

'Nope, almost there! And it's rosé, not red. It's chilling.'

'Right. What are you working on?'

Blythe closes the notebook, the cover a print of exotic birds in jewel colours.

'I journal,' she replies in that annoying way of turning a noun into a verb. 'Find it's very useful to order my thoughts. I encouraged

Dom to do the same, but he never did. Is rosé OK, or would you prefer a red?'

'I'll drink anything.'

Blythe nods and takes a bottle of pink wine from the fridge, uncorks it and pours two large glasses. She hands me one at arm's length. 'Cheers!'

I reciprocate the toast from down the table and take a large gulp of the chilled and fruity wine. With Ludo not here, my concerns of being poisoned, by him at least, can be set aside, although he did prepare the cold supper. *Damn.* And isn't it Blythe who's the poisoner with peanut butter? I gulp more wine, confused.

A rumble of distant thunder adds gravitas to the scene, which I could do without, but Blythe seems in good spirits. Until I sneeze again, her hand covering her nose and mouth as she leans away.

'I'm super germ-phobic, I know,' she explains, jumping up.

She fetches salad bowls from the cupboard and piles them with leaves from a shop-bought packet.

'It comes from years of trying not to get sick mid-role,' she explains. 'If the star goes down, so does the production.'

'I guess that was especially so for *Affairs of the Heart*?'

She slides the salmon onto the leaves with a spatula. 'Why do you say that?'

'Because you were the star!'

She smiles over her shoulder. 'Yes, I was. And I did not want to fuck that one up, we all knew it was something special.' She waves the spatula around, glancing over again before she adds, 'I really wanted the part, Marnie. I knew it would be... significant. You get a feeling sometimes, that this is the one. Something defining.'

'Yes, I'd imagine you'd have gone to great lengths to secure it.'

Blythe stares me down, the same look in her eye as when she'd told Roland not to push her any further. I gulp my wine and wait whilst she grinds pepper over the food, but I'm determined to press on now I've started.

'I hadn't realised until recently that Florence Saint John was the first pick for that role.'

Blythe slams a bowl of salmon and leaves in front of me.

'I wouldn't say first pick, Marnie. She was considered, then eliminated.'

A fork follows, dropped from too high so it bounces off the table and narrowly avoids my leg before it lands on the floor. I pick it up and wipe it on the hem of my dress as I contemplate the salmon. The leaves came from a sealed bag so they should be safe to eat, but they might also be contaminated from the fish which is leaking juice. But I'm so hungry I could cry!

'She died at your house in LA, didn't she?' I ask, spearing some of the dry salad. 'Florence, I mean.'

'Do you mind if we don't talk about suicide over supper?' Blythe asks, pushing her fork into the fish to flake the orange flesh.

'Sure,' I cover my mouth as I chew. 'Sorry.'

I watch to see if she eats any fish, but she abandons the fork and picks up her wine, a crash of thunder making me jump, whilst she appears to barely notice it.

'It's surreal, being tended to by a Hollywood star during a wild storm,' I say, gingerly touching the tip of my tongue to a tiny flake of salmon. 'Like an old film.'

'Yes,' she replies, a smile drawn from her pink glossed lips. 'Must be.'

She drinks her wine down to the last drop. I'm tempted to do the same as another rumble closes in, plump drops landing on the glass doors and dampening the floor inside now, a puddle collecting. The wine is good, and restorative, but I try to sip, not gulp. I have a feeling I might need my wits about me tonight. *Just us girls.*

'I *will* talk about what happened back in Hollywood,' Blythe tells me, mashing the fish with the back of her knife as a flash of lightning forks the sky, 'but it won't be easy, so please, be patient.'

'Oh, right, yes, of course. I understand. Let's make sure we circle back to that big audition, though.'

Blythe looks straight at me. 'Why would you mention that?'

'It was in the scripts, that's all, sounded kind of a big deal.'

She shakes her head and pushes her chair back, scraping the legs on the tile floor as she stands.

I *knew* there was something significant about that audition. It raised a red flag when I first read the script notes, and again now.

'Why don't we watch the storm from the sitting room window,' Blythe suggests, refilling our glasses to the brim. 'It's always dramatic over the Heath.'

'Not from the tower?' I suggest, imagining the view from up there would be even better and then regretting my hasty suggestion. My vertigo has kicked in even at the thought of it.

'No,' she says, headed for the door. 'The sitting room for now. But maybe later, Marnie. Maybe, later.'

* * *

'I lived on a dull suburban estate as a child,' Blythe begins as lightning cracks the panoramic and frankly biblical sky. She's standing in front of the sitting room's picture window, holding court and taking me back much further than I'd asked her to, although I dutifully make notes. This might make it into chapter two, and you have to let the slebs talk.

'No one in my life had any real drive, Marnie. No ambition. Well, my mother, I suppose, but she was a dreamer and often absent. I always wanted to get out, make something of myself. Be famous!'

'But isn't fame often a curse?' I ask as my stomach lurches unexpectedly.

I've never liked storms, the sky riven with splinters of light, but the salmon was definitely on the turn. Not that I ate much. Barely two mouthfuls. Is that enough to be poisoned? Probably. I place a hand on my gurgling tummy.

'Fame isn't always a curse,' Blythe responds, seemingly oblivious to my queasiness, 'but, yes, it's addictive. One taste and that's it, no going back to obscurity, I'm afraid. It's a drug. Never enough. Dom was the same.'

I'm struck by her candour and self-awareness. Her floaty dress is see-through as she is backlit by the flashes that threaten to break through the glass and strike her skeletal body down. An x-ray as she bares her Faustian soul.

'The summer of '76 was a drought,' she says. 'Six weeks of no rain, then when it finally broke, the whole street was out, neighbours running up and down, splashing in the puddles as if it was the best thing to ever happen to them. I felt very separate. Better than them, if I'm honest. How about you, Marnie, were you a happy child?'

I look up from my notes. 'I wasn't *unhappy*,' I offer, 'but I don't think of my childhood that fondly. I missed my mother.'

'Not all mothers are worth missing.'

'No, I guess not. What was yours like?'

'In and out of our lives. A failed actress as well as a failed mother. Sixteen when she fell pregnant. Not a planned pregnancy, or that wanted.'

'Was that why you decided not to have children yourself?'

'You assume it was a choice?' Blythe snaps, slumping down too close beside me on the squashy sofa, her qualms about potential germs dampened by the alcohol intake, I assume. She drains the remains of her wine, ahead of me now, my glass set on the edge of the coffee table which is covered in magazines and newspapers.

'And I *am* a mother,' she says, raising her empty glass.

'You have a child?' I ask, blindsided by the revelation.

'I've mentored many young actresses in my time,' she explains. 'That's valid mothering, isn't it? Or do we still have to be defined by narrow stereotypes in these supposedly enlightened times?'

'Yes, of course, sorry, I misunderstood.'

The storm is retreating a little, the sitting room still dulled though by the encroaching twilight. I look at the back of the canvas leant against the wall by fireplace, splodges of paint on the reverse.

'That painting...' I gesture towards it, my other hand finding the list in my notebook where Caroline Costello's name is the fourth one down.

'Yes?' Blythe asks, leaning even nearer so I can smell the wine on her breath.

I close the page. 'I researched the artist, out of curiosity.'

'My goodness, you have been busy,' Blythe says in a less than admiring tone as she leans back. 'Ludo said you were grumbling about lack of internet and yet you are always somehow connected.'

'Yes, it has been tricky, but I was lucky and found a sweet spot. Enough to establish the cause of Caroline Costello's sudden death.'

'I told you, didn't I? A severe nut allergy,' she says, then tries to drink her non-existent wine. 'Top up?'

'Yes, thanks.' I swallow the last mouthful and pass her my glass as she gets up. My stomach definitely feels unsettled, but wine should help. 'Oh, didn't we finish the bottle?'

'Plenty more where that came from!' Blythe responds, headed for the door.

'It's so strange about Caroline,' I continue, getting up. 'Her sister said—'

'You spoke with her sister?' Blythe asks, turning back at the door and glaring at me. 'When?'

'No, this came from the local paper.'

'Really?'

'Yes, apparently the sister testified that Caroline was always careful to the point of obsession about any hint of nuts in her food, cooked everything from scratch and she carried an EpiPen, which was never found.'

'I suppose it only takes one lapse,' Blythe replies, holding up the glasses. 'I'll be right back. You stay here.'

True to her word she's soon back, but sadly not with the promised wine.

'I was thinking about the script,' she says, sitting beside me and opening up the journal she'd been writing in at the kitchen table, the one with a cover of exotic birds. 'You mentioning Caroline has given me a brilliant idea for episode four.' Blythe clicks her pen and starts to write.

'Oh, yes?' I ask, nervous where this might lead. She seems wired, and erratic.

'Just a sec.' The writing is too small to read, her spidery strokes unsettling as they criss-cross pages, no adherence to the lines. 'The Cornish setting would be very picturesque, don't you think?' Blythe circles something in the journal with a pressed fingertip, eyes bright as she looks up. 'You know, the tropey thing of the penultimate ep coming from the husband's POV?'

I nod, gulping. 'Sure.'

'It's been done to death of course,' Blythe continues, 'so how about we slide Caroline and the Cornish stuff up to ep four, mix things up a little bit!'

'You mean use Caroline's death as inspiration?'

'Well, now you've suggested it...' Blythe leans back, closing her notes.

'I didn't suggest anything of the—'

'It could be a pivotal moment, Marnie,' Blythe interjects, leaning closer again. 'Imagine the intrigue... does he stay with his wife or go to his lover? The classic conundrum. It works so well, don't you think? The Cornish Affair could even be the title of that ep.'

'And you'd be OK with that, referencing an affair?'

Blythe nods. 'I've moved past it, Marnie. The hurt and the pain. I had no choice at the time and it was a long time ago now, seventeen years.'

I stare at the back of the canvas. 'Did you suspect an affair when you sat for her?'

'I didn't. Sit for her, I mean. Dom gave her photos and clips of film after we'd been to an exhibition of her work on a weekend away. But I had no idea. About any of it. Not at first.'

'How did you find out?'

'Oh, he got careless,' she says, closing her eyes briefly. 'Kept disappearing off to Cornwall "to write". Stupidly, it was me that encouraged him to go. He'd been so down after the move back to the UK, although it was him who wanted The Towers, pushed so hard, said it was the only way. I had to find the means to make it happen. Then he says it's easier to write by the sea, gone for days at a time. Never showed me what he was working on, claimed it was a work in progress. Turns out he wasn't working on anything but *her*.' She gestures towards the turned painting. 'Had the cheek to give me that. It's not even that good!'

I swallow, wishing I had that top up of wine.

'I understand now why you hated the painting, Blythe, but why have it on your wall all these years?'

'Dom and I never discussed Caroline. It was just easier that way.'

'Right... God, I mean, I'm not sure I could internalise all that.' If indeed, that's what she did. Or maybe she found another way to exact her revenge.

She leans against the sofa cushion, reflective, the journal closed on her lap. 'One does what one needs to do in order to survive, and to preserve what we love. You'll feel the same when you fall for someone as hard as I fell for Dom.'

The assumption I haven't experienced true love is annoying, but I let it go. Who knows if I loved Jake? I was broken-hearted when he ended it, still am. I know that much.

'But to forgive an affair, Blythe, and say nothing?'

'I said plenty to her, believe me!' She pushes herself up. 'Red OK this time?' Blythe heads to the door in another impressively straight line given how much she's put away.

'Yeah, sure, whatever. Thanks.'

'Ooh, and I've just remembered!' she says, pausing at the door. 'Ludo said there was bread to go with the salads, a nice French stick. We could have chunks of that with our wine, soak it up. What do you say?'

'Sounds good,' I reply. Empty stomach grumbling.

'Ooh, and I'll grab the jar of peanut butter,' she says, eyes bright. 'It's always been my guilty pleasure.'

23

Even the great Blythe Hopper, narcissist in the extreme, couldn't be that brazen, could she? Mentioning peanut butter moments after a conversation about her love rival who'd died of a severe nut allergy. *It's my guilty pleasure.*

I can only hope it's a case of my overactive imagination making wild leaps. My opinion on that varying the longer I have to think about it. Which has now been quite some time. Must be at least ten minutes.

Blythe told me to stay put, but how long does it take to open a fresh bottle and cut some bread? I have so much to ask her. So much she has promised she will now tell me. The confetti pieces of that photo uppermost in my mind as I contemplate what this evening might bring, and what I should focus on. My aim is to patiently guide her towards the one question that truly matters to me: how Dom knew my mother.

I circle the Oscar statuette, studying the contours. It's so beautiful. It can't have been an easy decision for Blythe to leave Hollywood behind and all that glitz. Or easy for Dom, even if his writing was going badly and Blythe's acting success hadn't continued as hoped. Which is surprising given the Academy Award win, although I have heard it's not always a golden ticket. But doubly so as Greg, a top producer, was good friends with the Hoppers. I mean, why not continue that mutually beneficial collaboration? Sure, *The Man* tanked, but not because it wasn't good, and Blythe had won Greg's next film a top accolade.

No, something must have happened to cause a rift. That friendship turning to the hatred I witnessed as Blythe looked at the photo of Greg with Dom, Wendy and Flo. But who incited that look of pure venom?

I flick through my notebook for inspo on Greg Chaplain, but I need the saved file of notes and links on my laptop, which is in the annexe. I take out my phone, mindful of Blythe's imminent return as I refresh my memory of Greg via an article I found earlier about *The Man*, the signal good in here. Greg and Dom are both quoted as using the term 'dream team' in reference to their collaboration. The best of mates.

Sounds like Greg dropped his 'mate' like a stone after *The Man* failed to live up to the hype, then he moved on from Blythe too, despite those shows of camaraderie at the Oscars in '95. So what happened between Greg and the Hoppers to cause such a permanent rift after Blythe's win? Blythe replaced Flo in *Affairs of the Heart* but she did a good job for Greg didn't she? Her performance won this beautiful Oscar!

I tiptoe around the statuette again, studying it from all angles, but afraid to pick it up in case I drop it. I can totally envisage Blythe being a diva on set, but is that enough to get her blacklisted from not only Greg's future projects, but all of Hollywood? Or was it something more fundamental which ruined her chances? Something that happened in the audition that coloured everything that came after? But that makes no sense as she bagged the part and then totally nailed it.

These are questions I cannot hope to answer. Not alone. But I will ask them of Blythe. They're important. Not least for the memoir, a response from Priscilla buzzing into my Inbox right on cue. My editor is happy. She loves the opening chapter and wants more.

I prowl the sitting room, then decide to go in search of Blythe, as well as the promised wine. She's been gone too way too long now.

* * *

There's no sign of Blythe in the kitchen, but I can see she's passed through, a freshly opened bottle of red on the side, a glass beside it with only drops of the Montepulciano at the bottom, the French stick she mentioned, on a wooden board beside the red. I lift the bottle to the light; a third is missing. *Go, Blythe!*

But where is she? Collapsed in a heap somewhere?

The storm is gone for now, the sun setting in shades of orange and soft pink behind the burnt trees, silhouettes dappling the lawn. I scan the kitchen for more clues. The cupboard where the pills are kept is again slightly open, overly stuffed with bottles. I inspect the contents, reading labels, but I still have no idea what they all are, and what, if anything, is missing.

I grab a wine glass from the drainer and sniff the opened red, drowning my mounting concerns about poison in gulps of the warming Italian as my stomach growls. The salad bowls are still on the table, my fish less than half eaten whilst Blythe's is mashed into a gelatinous lump on top of wilting salad leaves. Hardly tempting, despite the hunger pangs, but there is that fresh loaf on the counter, the end torn off and beside it, a knife smeared with crunchy peanut butter.

I eat a chunk of plain bread by the patio doors, a slight breeze coming in but nothing much, the heavy heat of earlier now returned. The breadcrumbs land in the puddle by the door. I scan for any sign of Blythe's floaty dress down by the pool, or signs of life in the writing annexe. My laptop is password protected, the door locked, but nothing feels sacred or private, as if Ludo's disappearance, rather than reassuring me, has lifted the lid on a can of worms, maggots crawling out.

I open the flapping door and call Blythe's name into the twilight, clouds gathering over the house as fat drops hit the patio. This weather is crazy, so changeable, the rain tumbling hard and sudden, as if a tap were turned on and filling in the gaps between the puddles around my feet. She can't be out there in this, can she? Or maybe she's left The Towers too, and I am alone here. With the other ghosts.

I retreat to search the house, flip-flops slapping down the corridor as I hold my red wine steady and run, calling ahead, 'Blythe?' Then from the bottom of the stairs, 'Blythe, you up there?'

The front door is locked when I try it, which is unsettling but maybe as we're here alone Blythe thought it was best. I drink down to the bottom of my glass and go back into the sitting room. The room is desolate, the storm raging over the Heath. I carefully balance my empty glass by Blythe's Oscar, then head back into the hallway, knowing there's nowhere left to go but upstairs.

The red carpet is spongy beneath the rubber of my flip-flops, the gold runners gleaming as I make my way tread by silent tread, careful not to trip this time.

The first-floor landing curves further round the stairwell than is visible from below. A polished banister leading me towards the set of closed double doors at the top, which I believe to be the entrance to Blythe's bedroom.

A film of dust from the banister coats my fingertips as I pause, white streaks down my dress when I wipe my sweaty hands. Dust is mainly dead skin, or so I've been told. Not sure by who, but it's stayed with me. This place must have been sliding into disrepair for a long time. An allegory for a failing marriage and even before that, the Hoppers' stalled careers. Affairs, tragic deaths and lost dreams. Blythe said their marriage weathered many storms, but at what cost? And how did she persuade Dom to come back to her when he'd found love with an artist in a beautiful part of the Cornish coast? If Dom truly loved Caroline, why didn't he have the balls to stay with her, unless that's exactly what he'd planned to do? Before Blythe stepped in and dealt with the situation.

I back away from the double doors, afraid now what this woman is capable of. I'm not ready to go in, not yet, and anyway, this a good chance to have a look round, see what's behind the other doors.

I find piles of towels and sheets pushed around a water tank behind the first door I try. The next one opens to a guest suite, the distinctive red and pink modernist painting above the four-poster bed recognisable from the sales video. I haven't seen or heard of any prospective buyers since I arrived, and can't imagine they'd be impressed by the neglect that has occurred since that video was filmed. The guest room is tidy enough but similarly dust-filmed when I run my fingers over the bedside tables. The drawers all empty.

A second guest suite, azure blues and greens, is also unoccupied, but a third, all white, is clearly in use, items left out, although there's no reply as I call a nervous greeting. I inspect the clothes neatly folded on the bed. A black polo top and skinny jeans: Ludo's trademark. Then I open the wardrobe and find at least a dozen tops and jeans, all identical black, and on the shoe rack below, seven pairs of Ludo's favoured Gucci loafers are lined up with such precision, he might have used a ruler.

I have my favourites too, even bought the same top twice in case I ruined one, which I did, but this is bordering on OCD.

By the bed is a smartwatch, charging, and a plastic dental case, inside which is a moulded mouthguard, the same kind of splint Dad wears for teeth grinding, and a plugged-in phone charger snaking up from the wall socket. There's also an overnight bag in the en suite, packed with a few clothes: toothbrush and a can of hair dye inside the leather washbag when I unzip it. The shower is stocked with shower gel from Molton Brown and the bathroom cabinet stuffed with expensive cologne and moisturisers for male mature skin. There's also one of those nose-hair shavers.

I creep out, closing the door. Ludo's room reminding me of the deserted shipwreck Dad was fascinated by... the *Mary Celeste*.

The only doors I haven't tried are the double doors at the top of the stairs, where I'm faced with the same choice as before. To go in, or leave well alone.

I press myself to the gap and listen, but all I can hear are my own breaths, shallow and too loud. I knock, lightly, but there's no answer. A stab of panic in my gut at what that signifies. Blythe is clearly in a very difficult place, her husband dead, her freedom at stake, and she has been drinking heavily and may well have taken a cocktail of Ludo's pills on top. Time could be of the essence if she's in trouble, and I'm the only one around. I pull down both handles, parting the doors and peering into the darkness beyond.

It's an enormous room, the bed across an expanse of thick carpet. The curtains on the far side have been drawn, the rain loud against the obscured windows. It's a circular bed, something else I recall from that sales video. I mean, how could you not remember that? It screams Hollywood glamour, but that's not what strikes me, my eyes adjusting to the lack of light and widening in horror.

'Oh my God, Blythe!'

My first thought is of Flo and what the papers said about how she was found when the poor cleaner went in the morning after the party to clean her room.

Blythe is naked too, a bare leg peeking out from beneath silk sheets, her left arm lolling over the side of the round bed so her fingertips are touching the thick cream carpet. A bottle of pills has fallen, the contents sprayed across the wool tufts just beyond Blythe's reach. They look like tiny blue sweets. On the table beside her is a bottle of champagne, tipped on its side, the rug soaked with the spillage as I step on it, barefoot now, flip-flops cast aside in my panic.

'Blythe, it's Marnie! Can you hear me?'

She hasn't stirred, mouth slack. I crouch down and press my cheek to her open lips. 'Blythe?'

Is she breathing? I have no idea. I feel her wrist for a pulse and find none.

Panic hardens in my chest, images of Flo Saint John stronger now than ever, that Hollywood party scene rushing at me. The reports of Flo's death feel frighteningly real, or surreal, as this cannot be happening on my watch. A film star dead. Me the only witness. The only suspect? I grab my phone from my pocket, then Blythe sits up with a gasp.

I scream, backing away, my phone falling from my slack grip.

'What the fuck are you doing in here?' Blythe roars.

'Oh my God, I'm so sorry. I thought—'

'You thought what?' She cinches the sheet around her protectively. 'Give me some credit, Marnie. I'd never leave a scene before it's done; that's very unprofessional.'

She's half joking, I think. Her tone razor-sharp.

'No, sorry, I'm being dramatic, forgive me.' I retrieve my dropped phone. 'You were gone so long, I thought... Doesn't matter what I thought.'

Blythe arches a brow. 'I needed a lie down, Marnie. One of my headaches.'

She scoops up her phone from beside the bed where it's charging.

'Did you call anyone, Marnie?' she asks, glancing up from the screen. 'Police? Ambulance?'

'No. I was going to, but no.'

'OK, good. Now fuck off!'

Cheeks flaming, I grab my flip-flops and stumble out and then down the stairs, tripping in my haste and flying forwards. My heart leapfrogs as I fight gravity, landing awkwardly in a heap at the bottom, my ankle bent beneath me, my right wrist taking the brunt of the impact, flip flops thrown across the hall.

'What now?' Blythe calls down from the top of the stairs, sheet wrapped round her. 'Marnie, what are you doing?'

'I'm fine,' I say, getting up and testing my wrist. 'Nothing broken.'

'Wait for me downstairs while I dress!' she tells me. 'And try not to have another disaster in the meantime! In fact, you can make yourself useful and tidy up the kitchen, it's a pigsty!'

Forty-five minutes later Blythe finally joins me in the kitchen. She looks drawn, despite the refresh of make-up. I heard her on the phone when I crept up the stairs ten minutes ago to see if she was ever coming. She was talking fast and for her, quietly, so I couldn't hear a word through the door.

'You OK?' I ask. 'You were a while.'

'Takes longer every day to look this good,' she tells me, only half joking.

'I thought I heard you on the phone?' I ask, wiping the drainer now all the dishes are dried. I haven't found the right homes for everything, but they're out of sight at least, and the result is a vast improvement.

'Another call with Roland, tiresome man. Pushing me again.'

'Oh?'

She shrugs. 'I've told him my thoughts and he has shared his.'

'Right, well, I've been busy clearing up in here, as instructed!'

I've actually enjoyed the displacement activity. It's been calming as well as distracting, although I'd thought she would be more appreciative of my efforts, her attention elsewhere. Maybe on that call.

She's changed into a long, seventies-style skirt, a floral, fluid top arranged over her slim frame and to expose one shoulder, a different but matching scarf tied around her head, the loose waves invigorated, lip gloss reapplied. Her feet are bare, but it looks as if she's matched the toenail polish to her outfit, a deep plum that's been freshly, if messily, applied. I'm guessing forty minutes went into her styling and five on the call.

The sad thing is, she still looks dishevelled and tired, despite all that work.

'So!' she announces, spinning round and finally casting an appreciative eye over the kitchen. 'You have worked wonders in here, Marnie.'

'Thanks. And I am so sorry about earlier. I shouldn't have barged into your room like that, but you did give me a fright.'

'No matter,' she says, ignoring the implied question. 'You definitely didn't call anyone, no 999 call?'

I shake my head, wondering if I should have seeded the idea help is on the way, especially as she seems so keen to know it isn't.

'Good,' she says. 'That's good. Now where's your phone?'

'My phone?'

'Yes, that thing your generation is permanently attached to.' She extends a palm, upturned, shaky, but insistent.

'I told you; I didn't call anyone. I promise.'

'Yes, and I believe you. But I would like to remove all distractions. I assume you're OK to be parted from it for just one evening?'

'Yes, of course, but I won't be recording you. Here, I'll switch it off if you'd rather?' I take my phone out of my dress pocket and press the side buttons until the logo fades. 'There, done!'

Blythe reaches out and quick as a flash grabs my phone.

'Hey!'

'I'll just drop it in here,' Blythe says, opening the drawer by the hob to reveal a mess of random things. 'Remove all temptation. OK? We have much to discuss!'

A glint of metal at the back of the drawer stops my heart. Blythe notices my reaction, smiles and then removes it and tosses the item in the air.

My relief is palpable as she catches the corkscrew with surprising dexterity and then throws it to me. Needless to say I miss the catch, the metal clattering to the kitchen floor.

'Oh, Marnie!' she says, laughing. 'Grab that and I'll find a rather special bottle that I think might be more befitting of this momentous occasion.'

'Momentous?' I repeat, picking up the corkscrew.

'Yes!' she says, laughter fading. 'Most definitely a day I have been waiting for. You too, I believe? As my ghost, I mean. The "tell-all" memoir!'

Blythe's grey eyes are as dark as I've seen them, the lines around them deep grooves.

'Right, yes, of course!'

'Good! Now, let me find that '93 I've been saving.'

Blythe crouches in front of a built-in wine rack that sits neatly between the fridge and a larder cupboard. 'Ah this is it!' She slides a dusty red from the bottom shelf and presents the label to me.

The variety is one I haven't heard of, the year 1993, as stated.

'Is that a good year?' I ask as I hand her the corkscrew.

'I guess you could say it was the very best and the very worst,' Blythe says, clearly relishing the intrigue as she uncorks the bottle at the table. 'But definitely the start of our story. Will you just excuse me a moment?' She hands me the opened bottle. 'I just need to check my phone. I left it upstairs. Only place there's reliable 5G in this fucking mausoleum when the wireless router is unplugged!'

'You unplug the router?'

'Oh yes, all those tiresome spam emails and crank calls. I only switch it on when absolutely necessary. Such a distraction.'

Well, that explains one mystery!

* * *

In her absence, I pour the aromatic red, my hands shaking. I can't believe Blythe pulls out the connection unless she needs it. It doesn't make sense. Another oddity she waved away with a flick of her hand before she left, as if it was perfectly normal and fine to be so selfish.

The 1993 wine has depth, but I prefer something easier to drink. Like the Montepulciano she'd already opened. Probably cheaper, less classy, but eminently more palatable. But what's troubling me is not the wine itself, but why this is an occasion worthy of uncorking a thirty-year-old bottle. What does Blythe have planned for this evening? A trip down memory lane to that year? Which is what I signed up for, but not a wholly enticing thought given her erratic mood, and I don't like being without my mobile phone.

I sidle up to the messy drawer and with a quick glance to the open door, pull it out. I saw her drop it in here, but I can't see it. I take my eyes off the door and put my glass down to check again, sifting through the mess with increasing alarm.

'Right! Where were we?' Blythe asks, startling me.

'Everything all right, with the call?' I ask, closing the drawer behind my back and handing her a glass of the '93.

She drinks deep so her lips are stained purple as she comes up for air, one hand holding a phone. 'No, not really. So as I suspected, it would seem there is literally no time like the present!'

She drains her filled glass and with a pointed finger moves me aside, opening the messy drawer to drop in my phone, before sliding the draw shut again with force.

'No time left at all, not really,' she says, ignoring my dropped jaw. 'So I suggest we make a start. As I said, much to tell! Shall we?'

24

Blythe leads the way down the corridor. She's weaving from side to side. Hardly surprising given we're on the third bottle of the night, the '93 sunk whilst she'd recounted a story at the kitchen table about a wedding anniversary party at The Towers when Dom had scared their guests by firing a gun into the trees. A gun they'd smuggled back from the US. The same one, I assume, she killed him with. I didn't ask. The story amusing her almost as much as it terrified me. I should never have surrendered my phone, my eyes travelling to that drawer at every chance, but there's been no opportunity to retrieve it. Not without her knowing.

Currently it's taking all her concentration just to stay upright. Her expression glassy as she regards me over her bare shoulder. I'm beginning to wonder if the promised candour will materialise before the next 'headache'. Maybe the night will be less significant than promised. Or maybe she's only just got started. I'm not sure which I'm hoping for, although it feels as if the stakes have somehow been raised by that call from Roland. The 1993 wine just a small part of a much bigger performance.

'Ludo is OK, isn't he?' I venture as she staggers on. 'I mean, he will come back at some point?'

'Oh, for God's sake, Marnie, stop worrying! Ludo is fine.'

It's crazy how much I miss the security of having my phone. If I can distract her, maybe get back to the kitchen, to that drawer? I don't want to aggravate her by asking for it back, but if I could sneak it into my pocket...

'Oh, I left my notebook in the kitchen! I'll just grab it,' I tell her, doubling back and heading straight to the messy drawer.

'Oh, Marnie,' Blythe says, startling me again. 'You really cannot bear to be without it, can you?' She snatches it from the drawer, my arms too short to grab it from her longer reach.

'Hand it back at once!' I tell her, fed up of this now. 'This is ridiculous!'

'I agree.' She smiles, then to my horror, she drops my mobile straight into the sink, where it submerges in the greasy dishwater I'd failed to let out.

'What the fuck, Blythe?! Are you crazy?'

* * *

Blythe's back in the corridor by the time I catch up with her.

'Why would you do that?' I ask, brandishing my dripping phone. 'I need it for work! I switched it off in front of you, and I told you I hadn't called anyone. What the actual fuck, Blythe?! That's my property!'

'Soz,' she slurs, reeling as I grab her arm to halt her. 'I do tend to act on instinct, Marnie, but we're so limited on time, aren't we, sweetie? Don't try and switch it on! Let it dry out first.'

'Why do you keep saying we're limited on time?' I ask, pocketing the ruined phone. 'What's happened? Is this to do with Roland's call?'

'See that?' she points wildly round to the gallery of framed photos. 'I should have taken them down the second Dom put them up.'

'I thought Ludo hung the photos?'

'No!' she replies, eyes wide. 'Dom did *aallll* this.' She sweeps a pointed finger round and loses her balance, a hand to mine to steady herself. 'You know what was there?' She looks in the direction of the missing photo.

'I think it was of you and your friend Josie?' I say, pulling free of her grasp. 'Where's it gone?'

'Disposed of. And high time.' She brushes one hand against the other as she did in the garage, but with less coordination. 'Shall we proceed, Marnie?'

The line she takes, if one were drawn out of the corridor and across the hallway, zigzagging from one side to the other. I'm getting a very bad feeling about tonight, especially Ludo's unexplained absence. Blythe is drunk, manic, untethered, but vigilant. Her eyes unfocused and yet always on me as she spins and turns.

'Sorry, Blythe, I really need to pee, I'll head back over to the annexe quickly then join you in the—'

'Upstairs!' she says, stopping me in my tracks. 'First door on left. Use the guest en suite.'

'Right, sure, thanks.'

I was hoping to get back to my laptop, send a message to Harry, or maybe Dad. But maybe this is better.

I head straight to Blythe's room, but the phone charging by her bed, my main hope, is now gone. I run out of her room and check the stairs, empty, then, bypassing the first door on the left, I go into Ludo's room at the end. Searching drawers, then pockets in the hung-up jeans, finding only receipts, paper ones, and lots of them—

'What are you doing?' Blythe asks, flinging the door wide open.

I pause, caught in the act yet again. 'Where is he, Blythe?' I ask, slowly turning to face her. 'Is he... harmed?'

'He's at his mother's if you must know,' she replies, leaning against the open door which moves with her so she stumbles.

'Looks like he left in a hurry, and without his bag.' I point at the en suite.

'Ludo travels light. Two of everything. Saves packing.'

'And what about these?' I hold up a wad of receipts retrieved from his pockets: meals in expensive restaurants, a hotel that I know for a fact is three figures per night because Jake took the model-slash-bitch there when they were last in London. A paper trail of Ludo's excess. Blythe the payroll provider. 'Were these jaunts with his mother too? Ludo has expensive lifestyle tastes for a lowly washer-upper?' I suggest.

'Give me those!'

I hand them over and she looks at them briefly, then drops them in a wastepaper basket by Ludo's empty desk.

'I'd like to leave now,' I tell her, as calmly as I can. 'We can talk another day, when you're less—'

'Less what?'

'I'll come back tomorrow. Promise. Can you let me out the gates, please?'

'You're not leaving, Marnie,' she says, staring me down.

'Only for tonight. Grab some rest, clean clothes, then I'll come back, OK? I think I do have the 'flu.'

'You're not going anywhere!' she shouts, her voice projecting with such force, I step back, bumping into the bed.

I'm terrified of her now, no doubt about that, but also I've never been one to be told what to do. It's a red rag. Or, much as Dad would always say on parents' evenings, or swimming lessons, or when I got fired from a Saturday job at the local supermarket for insubordination, *Marnie doesn't respond well to orders*. I push past her but she grabs me and pulls me back into the room, shoving me towards Ludo's bed. It's a shock to be manhandled in that way, but I still try to reason with her as I land heavily on the bouncy mattress.

'Blythe, please! This is ridiculous. I'll come back tomorrow, first thing, I promise.'

'I need you here now,' she says, leaning over me.

I dig my heels in the mattress and back away towards the pillows, noticing something stuck in the back of her waistband, the rain slung hard against the window as she moves towards it. A phone, nestling just below the silk top. If I can get to that, I can summon help, alert the police to my concerns: about Ludo, and heck, myself too. I've had enough of this. I want out. It's escalating way too fast.

I get up and lunge for the phone but she dodges out my way and then she slips, hitting her head against the desk and landing in a heap.

'God, Blythe, are you OK?' I lower a hand to help her up. 'Are you hurt?'

She lifts her head, a strange smile as she reaches round and pulls out what I'd thought was a phone and points it at me. A gun.

'What the?!'

'I'm sorry, Marnie,' she says as the ornate light fitting above the bed – a kind of modern but retro arrangement of glass baubles – reflects pinpricks of light off the metal in her hands. An incongruous disco light strobing the white walls. 'But I can't let you leave.'

'Blythe, please!' I raise my hands, backing away. 'I honestly thought it was a phone. Please don't shoot me, I'm not even thirty!'

I would laugh at the absurdity of it all, except I know for a fact she's killed at least once, and it feels increasingly likely this whole evening has been designed to ensure whatever else she has to tell me remains eternally between us. Including getting rid of Ludo, his clothes beneath me as I cower on his bed. But then I spy something else, a sliver of silver between the pillows. My eyes dart to the window and Blythe follows my gaze. I take my chance and grab Ludo's laptop, opening the lid and tapping the track pad. And that's when Blythe fires the gun, straight up at the light fitting, glass shattering across the bed, and then at the laptop screen as I scream and roll onto the carpet, reeling from those bullets, so close to me. I'm trapped in this room, the glass-strewn bed between me and the door, Blythe's maniacal gaze following me whichever way I look and the gun still pointed at me. The missing gun. The gun that killed Dom. The gun she kept hidden from the police, despite Roland's warnings to surrender it, for her own good.

'Look, I'm really sorry, Marnie,' Blythe says, remarkably calm. 'I shouldn't have done that. I do tend to act first, think later, as I said; it's the creative in me. You get that, don't you? Don't you?!'

'Yeah, sure.' I swallow. 'I get it. Course.'

'Good. Now let's go back down to the sitting room where we can talk sensibly. There's so much I need you to understand. I promise you will want to know. Then if you need to leave, you can use my phone, call an Uber. Okay, sweetie? All good?'

'Yeah, sure,' I reply, my voice small and shaky. 'All good.'

25

The sitting room is painted in shadows, a fittingly eerie backdrop for such an auspicious and yet bizarre situation. The lamps Blythe switches on pool light on the seating area by the unlit fire. She directs me to sit on one sofa as she sits on the other. The storm whirls around The Towers with a ferocity I pray will soon pass. My nerves are shot. The bass of distant thunder not helping one bit, but there are two potentially positive developments. Blythe seems to have sobered up a little, and the gun is tucked back into the waistband of her skirt, out of view.

I suppose I could have tried to snatch it as we came down the stairs, but when a gun is pushed between your shoulder blades by a madwoman, it's tricky to imagine how to get a hold of it without being killed. My main aim was not to trip and spook her into a false move. And now it's to keep her talking as I work out how to either escape, or summon help.

'OK if I go to the window, get some air?' I ask.

She shrugs, but the gun comes out again.

I walk slowly to the bay window, craning to see the Heath. A reminder that life is out there: cars climbing the hill, dots of activity in the distance, and a lake with flapping waterfowl which is obscured by the line of trees. I lean against the window and surreptitiously try the latch but I can't work it out.

'It was the view that swung it for me,' Blythe says, standing beside me and tucking the gun away. She unlatches the window, opening it just a crack, cool air flooding in.

'And what about Dom?' I ask, pushing the glass to see if it will open further, which it won't. 'Was The Towers his price for the move from LA? I'm guessing it was you that wanted to leave?'

Blythe raises a salute. 'Clever little Marnie. Adding two and two and making five. Yes, it sweetened the deal for him, although he hoped to see more of the boys, which sadly didn't happen. Wendy's parents had besmirched his name.'

'That's a shame.'

'More than a shame! It killed him. Tore him apart!'

Dom hadn't exactly rushed to build bridges with his three sons. It was twelve years after Wendy's death when they finally moved back to the UK. But I keep that thought to myself. The crazed look in her eyes a constant warning, but if I can keep her talking, calm her down, maybe I can work out a way to survive the night.

'It was *so* out of our price range, of course.' Blythe tells me, then she frowns, as if she's confused. 'I don't know exactly what Ludo and Dom cooked up, but we took a chance on my future earnings which proved... optimistic, shall we say?'

'You must have been offered roles, though?' I point at the Oscar statuette.

She snorts. 'You'd have thought so, wouldn't you?'

'But surely Hollywood was still where you needed to be?' I start backing towards the door, slowly. 'I just don't get why you wanted to leave after everything you'd achieved?'

'No, I don't suppose you do,' she says. 'Where are you going, Marnie?'

'And Ludo,' I ask, pausing. I'm closer to the door now than the window. 'What was his price for the fraud that secured the loan to buy The Towers?'

'It's a little more complicated with Ludo, but I wouldn't call it fraud. He's always had my best interests at heart. Sit down, Marnie! I won't ask again!'

I return to the sofa as instructed, but I need to get to the annexe. I've never used my laptop to call 999, but I guess it's easy enough? A thought then occurs, and falls like a stone. Maybe Roland has told her about the email I sent him with my suspicions. My 'evidence' that she's a psycho serial killer.

Blythe sits facing me and tucks her bare feet beneath her skirt. 'Are you OK, Marnie? You're white as a sheet.'

'Yeah, I'm OK,' I reply, the question at odds with the threat of that gun, out of sight, but there when she needs it.

'It's always chillier this side of the house. I used to joke that this room was haunted, but sometimes, I do feel that the past is more present than the... well, recent history, I guess.'

'How do you mean?'

'Dom and I have lived on dreams, Marnie. Broken ones. Oxygen to us at times, but...' She stares at the coffee table between us, covered with newspapers and magazines. Then, without warning, she passes a hand across it and sends everything crashing to the floor.

I scream, pushing myself into the sofa as if it might swallow me up, Narnia waiting on the other side of the deep cushions. Blythe shakes her head at me, then drops to the floor and rummages through the mess, finding a pack of cigarettes. Her thumb spins the spoke wheel on a gold lighter and then she raises the flame to the cigarette clamped between her lips.

I slip off my flip-flops, ready to sprint, my stomach in knots as I swallow vomit. I just need one moment of opportunity, praying it will come before the light-headiness that now threatens. If I pass out, I'm done for. I'll wake not in Narnia, but... well maybe nowhere at all. Oblivion. The end. I've never believed in an afterlife. Ghosts, maybe, but nothing profound. I try to quieten my thoughts, focusing on Blythe as she sits on the floor and smokes.

'This house was meant to be a fresh start,' Blythe says, an ashtray pulled into her lap. 'The problems came with us, of course. I don't know why we expected anything else, but we did. Well, *I* did. Dom had perfected the art of sticking his head in the sand, as always.' She taps ash on her skirt rather than in the ashtray. 'We'd been living *way* beyond our means in Hollywood, lavish parties which Dom justified as a good investment to increase our connections, which they didn't. I gave it ten years after the Oscar. Ten years!'

She looks at the plinthed table where the Oscar statuette is displayed in all its glory, my wine glass beside it. Then she staggers to her feet and picks up the glass, throwing it to the floor. I gasp. But she's not done. The Oscar held above her head and then flung to the floor, shards of gold exploding everywhere.

'Oh my God, Blythe, that's—!'

'A fake?' she asks, removing the cigarette from her lips. 'Yes. It's our second, no, third... The staff, so bloody clumsy and then you have to pay them to keep quiet.' She prods at the pieces of gold painted plaster with a bare foot. 'I think Ludo bought this one on eBay. Quite a good one; heavy.'

'Where's the – the real one?' I stutter, picking up a chunk of the base that so nearly hit my foot. The paint is only a thin layer. Pure lustre, but no depth.

'A Saudi collector, I believe,' Blythe responds, kicking at the broken pieces.

'Oh yes?' I palm the piece of heavy plaster.

'Gave Ludo a fraction of its worth,' she tells me. 'Appropriate, considering I was paid half of what my male co-star was for *Affairs of the Heart*. The first replica was light as a feather. All Ludo could get in a rush before Dom started asking questions, but my husband *had* to have a new kitchen, to distract him from everything we'd left behind, as if this house wasn't enough already.'

'But to sell your precious Oscar! Surely there was another way?'

'There was always something, Marnie. This place is a money-pit. My Valentino gown, the one I wore at the Oscars,' I nod, recalling how incredible she'd looked. 'That paid for the construction of the writing annexe.' She laughs, a hollow sound. 'It's like this place is cursed or something. I don't even want to live here, but obviously, I am unable to leave!'

'But you are selling, aren't you?'

'Oh, God, you still have no idea of any of it, do you, Marnie?' She shakes her head. 'It seems Ludo's fears were rather unfounded and I had such high hopes for you. Well, for both of us, but of course that dream is over. And no, I can't leave The Towers. I just marketed it to keep my creditors off my back.'

'I don't understand.'

She falls onto the sofa and taps the space beside her, dipping her head to make eye contact as I reluctantly join her. 'Don't you see it yet, Marnie? Why you're here with me, at the very end of our story? Well, almost.'

She reaches behind her and lifts the gun out, looking at it.

I raise my hands, cowering away from her. 'Blythe, please don't kill me!'

She laughs. 'I have no intention of killing you, Marnie. I just need you to do as I say, is that OK?'

'I don't know anything, Blythe, and I don't want to. I just want to leave. Please let me go home and I'll never write a word about you, I promise. Someone else can ghost your memoir, and the script. Or not. Either way, you don't need me.'

'Oh but I do, Marnie. And you need me, to help you find your mother. Isn't that why you came here?'

'My mother?' I sit up straighter. 'What do you know about her?'

'Oh I know plenty about Katherine Wilde.' Blythe leans in, her breath hot. 'I know where she is, Marnie. She's here, close by.'

26

It's the ultimate irony: the one thing I've longed to hear all these years and now I'm about to be killed for knowing it. For the fact Blythe knows about my mother, Katherine Wilde, claiming she's close by, almost certainly means my mother is dead and soon, I will be too.

The realisation of these terrible truths is awful, of course, but it also removes all jeopardy. What do I care about the gun, or escaping? Better to be dead than live with the knowledge I've wasted the last twenty-five years yearning for someone I'll never get to see again. But survival is instinct, and therefore impossible to resist.

I take the shard of gold plaster from my pocket and throw it at Blythe's stupid head as hard as I can. Then I run.

I'm out the sitting room and halfway across the hallway when she fires the gun again. I cover my ears and then my head as the chandelier way above me shatters, glass raining down.

I open my eyes and realise I've fallen to the floor, ears ringing, pain searing through my left heel. Blythe watches as I tentatively pull a large piece of glass from my foot. Blood pours from the wound. A slice of flapping skin then caught as I try to put weight on it. I cry out.

'Can you walk?' she asks.

'I'm not sure.'

'Let's try,' she says, pointing me back up the stairs with the gun. 'You need any help?'

I shake my head, the crimson carpet absorbing my bloodied trail, the pain each time I put my left foot down, unbearable. If only I hadn't kicked off my flip-flops back in the sitting room: an ill-judged move. Like so many I've made. The piece of fake Oscar bounced off her, not a mark to show for it. I've always been rubbish at throwing.

We go through the double doors into Blythe's bedroom, a plethora of discarded outfits littering the carpet that I didn't even notice before. Puddles of silk and georgette, shoes with glittering heels and satin straps cast aside. I'd thought she was dead from an overdose earlier. Now I wish she had been.

She tucks the gun into the back of her skirt, which swirls as she spins and pirouettes towards the bay window. 'It's a wild night, Marnie.' She lifts a latch and opens one pane so the wind whistles in.

I limp nearer, hand outstretched for that stowed gun, dropping it to my side as she gives me a quizzical look.

Blythe goes to a wardrobe on the far side of the room, reaching up to retrieve something that looks like a book, high on a shelf.

I could take my chance now, dash back down the red carpeted stairs, but there's no way I can outrun her, not now I'm injured. And she's a crack-shot. I cast around again for Blythe's phone. But still no sign of it. Maybe it's in the drawer of her bedside cabinet? I should have checked that.

'Sit!' she tells me, waving me towards the circular bed. 'You're bleeding on my shagpile.'

I pull myself onto the high mattress so my feet are over the edge. It feels like the flap of skin is about to detach, blood pouring warm over my right foot as I rest the left one on top of it. Blythe sits beside me, the gun hampering her as she opens the book, which is an old-fashioned photo album. A pretty one too, padded pink candy-stripe. She hands it to me, open to the first page.

'You *did* have a child?' I ask, amazed to see a much younger, tired looking Blythe, cradling a newborn baby. They are in a hospital bed, a band on Blythe's thin wrist. 'But I thought—'

'Read the caption,' she says, voice softer now. 'Go on.'

The handwriting is faded. I squint and read: London, 22nd January 1994.

'You had a baby the same time as my mother, is that how you know her?' I ask, trying to make sense of the photo in light of the fact Blythe denied ever having a child.

'Not *a* baby, Marnie,' Blythe says, taking the album back and turning to the next page. She hands me the album again.

This photo is of a little girl in a garden. Gap-toothed and grinning. And the hand-written caption says, *Marnie. Aged two.*

'Where did you get this?' I ask, recognising the garden at the old house, and the tiny watering can I'm holding in my chubby hand. 'Did you take it from my mother?'

'No, I took that photo myself, on a visit.'

'No, that's not... No!'

'I'm your mother, Marnie,' she says, turning the pages in my trembling hands.

I'm sitting at the patio set in the next one, drinking orange squash, I look about three, a woman beside me, in an enormous hat.

'Why are you in this photo?' I demand, holding the album up to her.

'Because I'm Katherine Wilde,' she says. 'And I am so very happy to finally be able to say that to you, my darling daughter.'

I'm on my feet now, despite the white-hot pain in my left heel. 'No! That's not true! You said you didn't want to be a mother! You said that was a narrow definition. You said you knew where my mother is and that she's close by!' I lower my voice and narrow my eyes. 'What did you do to her, Blythe? Did you take this from her when you... When you hurt her?' I shove the album into her hand.

'No! What are you talking about? This is me, with you, in the hospital.' She splays the album to the hospital photo again, jabbing at the woman's face.

'You told me you didn't want a child!'

'It's true, I didn't, but sometimes, we women have no choice.' Blythe speaks as if she's giving a magazine interview, or we were still compiling her memoir which now feels so unimportant, it's ridiculous. 'And this one,' she holds the album in front of my face, 'was taken when you were four, on my last visit.'

It looks like me, in my bedroom at the old house, but that doesn't mean that she's... that Blythe is... Oh God.

I want to run, but I can't move, can barely breathe. The pain and confusion rooting me to the cream carpet which is soaking up more and more of my blood. I take the album from her and stare at the final photo with its faded writing: *Marnie, aged 4*.

'This isn't true. It can't be! You're delusional, deranged!'

'No, I'm not,' she says, as if she were being perfectly reasonable.

Blythe's long, skinny toes are now buried in the carpet as she stands before me, lines furrowing her usually smooth brow. Her eyes flashing a warning. '*I'm* Katherine Wilde. Your mother. You have to believe me.'

'No, I knew Katherine!' I say, hobbling back to the bed and sitting on the edge. 'She was short and curvy, dark hair. She baked cakes and made her own clothes. She was not you!'

I sound ridiculous, I know I do, but it's true. Mum iced Bakewell tarts and called me sweetie. Like Blythe did earlier, but it's not a unique affectation. And Mum was a homemaker, a good one. She's one hundred per cent *not* Blythe Hopper. The antithesis of her. And anyway, Blythe was living in LA.

'I gave birth to you on the twenty second of January 1994. I named you Marnie. You were born in London, at St Mary's. Where the royal babies are born. It was an easy enough birth. Not that I have anything to compare it to, but bearable.'

I pull my feet up, wincing as I push myself into the middle of the now bloodstained bed. 'I grew up with a mum and dad. I remember them both.'

'Your grandparents. Not that Mum was around that much, for either of us. I wanted different for you. But I had no choice. I'd told no one, you see, and I had to get back to LA, to Dom, to the film set. To save my career and my marriage.'

The storm is building, crashes of thunder overhead. But I'm not afraid. Not of her or even the gun, only of what she's saying. Because this cannot be. It just can't. And it's so hot, so unbearably hot. I slide off the bed and limp to the window, try to open it further, but the old-fashioned latch defeats me again. Blythe takes over, twisting the catch and opening it wide, the wind wrenching it from her hand. I lean out, rain bathing me as the gravel rushes up towards me. I could jump, but it's so high, I'd break a leg, probably both, or my neck. And even if I somehow survive the fall, I can't run; my foot is bad, *really* bad. I squeeze my eyes tight against the pain and the vertigo and a memory returns.

I'm with Mum, back at my bedroom window in the old house. And oh my God, I fell from the ledge! Is that right? Or are my thoughts spiralling? The pain, Blythe, the gun, the drop... it's making me panic. But what's even more scary is some of what Blythe's just told me is starting to make sense. I sink down to the carpet and breathe. Wait for the facts. Wait for Dad's logic and sense. It's there. In me. Somewhere. Come on, Dad. I need you. Now more than ever.

But is he my dad?

He's old enough to be my grandfather, but it isn't only his age that is consistent with Blythe's narrative. I don't mean the jigsaw puzzles or Dad's conservative attitude to my tattoos and fifteen-year-old me coming home drunk, but also the distance that he placed between us. Loving, but not parental. But I *knew* Mum. She was there, until I was four. And that woman wasn't Blythe. I pull myself up on my good foot and somehow stagger back to the edge of the bed.

'I saw my mum leave. She got in a car.' I look at Blythe, pacing before me. 'With your husband.'

Blythe frowns. 'That man was a driver, Marnie. The studio sent a limo. It took me straight to the airport. That was the last time Dad let me visit you.'

'OK, say that's true, which I don't believe it is, then tell me... who is the woman I recall being there until I was four? Because it sure as hell wasn't you!'

'Your grandmother, as I've said. And frankly, not a good person, Marnie.'

'Oh for goodness' sake, this is crazy!'

But my protests are fading, because the woman I have thought of in that scene, walking to the car, Dom waiting, is already changing. Her flat shoes growing heels as she clips down the path, the dark hair lightening to blonde, the tall, dark man waiting for her no longer in a cashmere sweater like Dom's, but a chauffeur's uniform. But Mum was a good person. She was. I won't have Blythe say otherwise. Or erase her from my past.

'I should have tried harder,' she's saying. 'I know that, Marnie. Visited more often, especially once we were back in the UK, although that was forbade. I don't blame your grandfather, not really. He did a great job with you – well, he did his best. Mum, on the other hand... she was an actress too. A failed one, I should say.' She looks up, eyes narrow. 'That skirt of yours... Hers, I assume? I recall her dubious taste in fabrics.'

'That proves nothing.'

Blythe shrugs. 'Look, I'm not trying to justify myself, but I want you to know one thing. Whatever Dad's told you about that last visit, it's not true.'

'What are you talking about?'

'You don't remember?'

I shake my head, although I do, or some.

'You were only four, but already feisty, with an iron will.' She laughs at the recollection. 'You wanted to see the shiny car that had arrived for Mummy, so I lifted you up on the ledge in your bedroom and opened the window so you could wave me off.'

The memory rushes at me again, even clearer now. I'm stood on the ledge, looking down on the limo and the driver. Blythe comes out the front door and down the path. I'm crying. Calling to my tall glamorous Mummy to look up, but she doesn't. Not once. So I lean over and the ground rushes towards me, head spinning. Then Dad is there, pulling me back from the brink. His firm grasp saving me from a disastrous fall, his shouts to her filled with anger and recriminations. 'Your daughter could have died!'

What kind of a mother lets a four-year-old stand on a first-floor ledge? No wonder Dad told her never to come back. She was a positive danger. Still is.

'He stopped me ever seeing you again,' Blythe hisses. '*Bastard*.'

'Don't call him that!'

I lunge at her and her hand goes to her back, retrieving the gun. She points it at me on the stupid round bed. There's blood everywhere. All mine, from my foot.

'You claim I'm your daughter and then you threaten me with a gun? You don't have a maternal bone in your body, never have! Go on then, do it!'

'I wouldn't ever hurt you, Marnie-Moo,' Blythe tells me, empty hand outstretched. The affectation jars, for so many reasons. The photo album has fallen onto the bed between us. The hospital photo displayed.

'Is that the same lie you fed Dom, just before you killed him, and my mother? Promising you wouldn't hurt them either!'

'I am your mother and I love you with all my heart!' she screams, eyes flaming and mouth twisted, gun shoved in my chest. 'Don't you get it?!'

I sit back, heart thrashing as my lacerated heel takes my weight, a hand to the silk sheet, warm blood oozing. I can't pass out, I can't pass out.

'Whatever I have done,' Blythe says, her delivery measured as she regards the gun, now shaking in her hands, 'was always out of love.'

'That's a great speech, Blythe. Shame I don't believe a word of it.'

Blythe takes a deep breath. 'I have so little time left. Believe me when I say—'

'Oh, for God's sake, Blythe! Is there no end to your lies? You're not dying!'

'All I want is for you to accept me before it's too late.'

'You don't care about me. Only yourself.'

I regard her, dispassionately now, assessing every detail as she cries, oh so beautifully. It truly is an Oscar-worthy performance, her chin slowly lifting, eyes wide, a perfect tear sliding down, just to add some authenticity.

Her features are perfect; mine are not. She is slender, I'm curvy. I cannot and will not find any comparison with this woman, but the more I resist, the more I see the possibility. A careless, self-centred, ruthless, reckless, ambitious woman. Not so different to me, but so very different to my quiet dad. Poor Dad. Three generations of feckless dreamers in his life: wife, daughter, granddaughter.

I blink away the fear of the truth as more blood leaves my body through my heel.

'It's a lot to take in,' Blythe says, now recovered from her crocodile tears. 'And you don't know it all, not yet. Come on,' she tells me, headed towards the door. 'I think we need some air.'

I limp down the stairs, the gun at my back.

The rain is slowing now as we reach the broken kitchen door, but it's mad to go outside barefoot, in the sodden garden with an open wound, but nothing about this night is anything less than crazy and who knows, maybe I can get to the annexe and raise the alarm. Tell the police a mad woman who claims to be my mother is about to kill me.

If I make it that far.

27

If it weren't for a gun between my shoulder blades, I could maybe appreciate a late summer's evening as the clouds clear to reveal a glorious sunset, but I can barely put my heel down, even the wet grass painful to touch.

'Put your foot in the water,' Blythe says as we finally reach the pool. 'The chlorine will help.'

We sit on the edge, my blood threading through the blue as I ease my foot in, eyes squeezed tight. The cut stings so much I reel, pulling in sharp, cool air.

'Does it hurt a lot?' she asks.

'Yes, and I need medical attention.'

'Oh dear,' she says, looking at the water. 'I can't allow that, not yet.'

The parasols are down, the loungers empty except for the rolled towels. Ludo must have placed them there before he left, *if* he left. Blythe gets up and grabs one, then lifts my foot out the water by my ankle, raising it on the rolled towel. I steady myself, resisting the urge to lie back on the cooling slabs.

'Better?' she asks, sitting beside me.

I nod. 'Some. But I will need it seen to, professionally, Blythe; I've lost a lot of blood.'

She shakes her head. 'Sorry, not quite yet, OK?'

A real mum wouldn't risk their child's life. Dad never would. This woman is a monster.

'So, tell me this,' I say. 'How did you get hold of those photos?'

'What is *wrong* with you, Marnie?' Blythe's lips are translucent in the twilight, her expression unfathomable. She draws a deep breath. 'I've told you. I am Katherine. Or I was.' She sighs heavily. 'Katherine Wilde was the name I was acting under before I went out to LA. I kept reinventing myself, new names, new looks, but I kept a British passport as Katherine Wilde. For anonymity as much as ease of travel. And I also wrote that name in all your cards, in case you wanted to find me.'

'I tried to find her,' I say, still rejecting her version of the truth. 'After I found those signed cards.' *Katherine Wilde (Mum) x*

She places a hand on her heart. 'It meant a lot when I heard you'd changed your name from Smith to Wilde when you turned eighteen. It felt like you were coming back to me, then the years went by and...'

'Heard from who?'

'I called Dad, every now and then. One time he was angry you'd had a tattoo.' She smiles. 'And then I saw your TV series was announced in The Hollywood Reporter, and I was so proud of you, Marnie. A screenwriter!'

'Then why not approach me long before this?'

'I suppose I was afraid of rejection. I'd endured enough of that, but then of course recent events have forced my hand.' Her blonde curls catch the moonlight now reflected in the water, her eyes bright. 'You like the name though, don't you? Wilde. It's a good one, appropriate!'

'Hate to break it to you, but Wilde's not *that* unusual a name.'

She laughs. 'You're right, it's not uncommon, but great to hear you have searched for me. I hoped you might be looking.'

I turn away from her smile. Now is not the time to bond over lost chances. And no wonder Dad went mad about the tattoo. He was right, I knew nothing, a stupid, made-up name inked as initials over my ribs. I'll get that changed, if I get out of here.

She massages her temples, and sighs.

'Are you claiming you're dying then?' I ask. 'No time left, so I fall into your arms, reunited at last?'

'No, but we do have limited time.' She looks at her wrist, but neither of us is wearing a watch. 'Roland said to expect the police within two hours, maybe less.'

'They're going to arrest you, tonight?!'

'I guess?'

It's a lot to take in, the shock of her imminent departure, on top of all this. 'So is that why you decided to tell me everything tonight? Not that I believe you!'

She nods. 'It was always my intention, that's why I insisted on you as my ghost.'

'No. I pushed to be here, you didn't want me, I was forced on you!'

Blythe smiles. 'Priscilla was very resistant to you when I said I'd agree to the memoir, but only if you were my ghost,' she explains, confusing me again. 'Kept shoving other names at me, for weeks. She said you are unreliable. A liability, in fact. I knew my girl would be a firecracker.'

'I'm not your girl!'

'Well, anyway, I held out for you and she agreed, in the end. I sent you the email from Dom as extra enticement, in case it was needed. And so you'd feel it was coming from you, not me. I needed to be in charge of the when and where, you see.'

'You sent that email?'

'Who else? He was dead by then!' She raises her hands, nonplussed. 'Worked though, didn't it? I'm only sorry it's taken his death for me to pluck up enough courage to face you. That's unforgivable, but still, that's what I'm asking for. Your forgiveness. And in return, I am gifting you something very special.' She tilts her head. 'My story.'

I get up and limp across the patio, Blythe watching me. I don't want to write the memoir, or the scripts. I just want to get out of here.

And then I'm running, fast. Ignoring the pain, lit like a terrible fire in my foot. If I can get to the annexe, lock myself in, maybe I can summon help. Because I don't trust her that the police are coming. She's a pathological liar. It's my only chance of surviving. Unlike my poor mother, Katherine, who, according to Blythe, is somewhere close by.

A shot rings out, a murder of crows squawking as they take flight.

I stumble. Then nothing.

28

Hemingway is looking down on me, hard rain falling on the flat roof of the annexe, the clatter loud. I'm not dead then. That's something.

'You OK?' Blythe asks, somewhere above me. 'Marnie, can you hear me?'

I open my eyes fully. 'Why are we in here?'

'I dragged you in out of the rain. God, you were heavy.'

'You shot me!'

'No! For goodness' sake!' she says, blonde hair flicking into view, then out again. 'I fired into the trees and you had another seizure. Do you take meds? You need to, Marnie. Mine really help, well, sometimes.'

I roll over and pull myself up, lean my aching back against the wooden wall by the closed door, my bare feet out in front of me, dirt and dried blood caking them. Is that sepsis setting in? Or gangrene? Trench foot? I can't look at my heel. I'm soaked with blood and mud and rain, and bone-tired, light-headed, dry-mouthed. But she had the chance to kill me and didn't. That, at least, gives me hope.

'Little late for motherly concern, isn't it?' I ask. 'And they're not seizures. Not like that, at least.'

'*Petit mal*,' she says, nodding as she crouches down in front of me. 'It's the same family as epilepsy. It's often genetic. My mother had a neat line in fainting too. I always assumed it was a cry for attention, a little too convenient at times. Like when I showed up pregnant with you.'

'I need to—' A wave of nausea consumes me. 'Can you open the door? I might throw up.'

Blythe looks at me with horror, then steps over my legs and kicks the pebble into place to keep the door ajar, the wind in my face as I drag my bottom across the floor to breathe in fresh air.

'You should get yourself checked out, Marnie. Epilepsy is not something you can ignore. You shouldn't drive either, you know that? Half the time, I honestly think I might just drop dead with these headaches. Then I'm passed out, like you.' She clicks her fingers. 'Out like a light. That's what happened when I was upstairs earlier.'

'I don't have epilepsy,' I say, tired of her dramatics. She isn't dying and we all have our private battles. 'It's called absence seizures.'

'Much the same,' she says as she paces around me. 'And you drink way too much; that's not good for you.'

'So do you!'

'Fair enough!' she says, giving me a disapproving look. 'I was only trying to help.'

I shake my head to clear it and try to join the conversation where we left it earlier, outside, in the rain, with my dead mother. 'So I guess Dom is my father and—?'

'Dom? If only!'

The rain is hitting the veranda. The hammering sound familiar when everything else has shifted, my world rocked and spinning on a different axis.

'But he must be,' I say, my eyes closing. 'He's a screenwriter.'

* * *

'Marnie, stay with me!' Blythe is kneeling beside me, holding my chin up from a puddle of rainwater on the veranda. Her hair is wet, and she looks so much older. She gets up and goes inside, then sits at Dom's desk, in his swivel chair, moving it from side to side.

'Tell me everything,' I say, limping back in and sliding down the wall. 'Please, I need to understand. Before it's too late. I'll believe you this time, I promise.'

'It's not an easy listen, Marnie. You sure you want to know?'

I've spent my whole life being denied answers. It can't be worse than the void I've filled with drink and Jake and work. I see Jake's beautiful face as I close my eyes for a second. I loved him. I *think*. I certainly wanted to. More than anything. 'Tell me everything. I need to hear it.'

Blythe smiles at my apparent acceptance of her truth. Although I'm not there yet, not by some way. But I want to hear what she has to say, whilst I still can.

'I'd almost given up on Hollywood before I met Dom,' she begins, a glance up at Ernest as if she's telling him the story. His inscrutable smile her only reward as I rest my chin on my chest and try to stay conscious. 'I told you before, auditions were near-on impossible to come by and when I did, everyone was younger and more beautiful.'

I look up, struck by the sadness in her voice. It all comes from a place of selfishness and vanity, but even so, a rare moment of insight.

'I was not far off your age. You're twenty-nine, that's right, isn't it?'

I laugh in disbelief. Wouldn't a real mother, even an errant one, know their only child's age without checking? 'Yes, thirty in April.'

'Hardly old of course,' she says, 'but for an actress, even nowadays... The thing is, Marnie, and my mother told me the same, there are three roles for women.'

'And clearly you didn't want to play the mother?'

Blythe ignores my cutting comment, swinging the creaking chair from side to side. Looking at her is making me horribly nauseous. I close my eyes as she continues to talk.

'It was such a male-led industry. You had to make the right connections.'

I sit up. 'You only dated Dom to further your career?'

'No! I mean, yes, in a way, but I soon fell hard and fast. I loved him, Marnie. Everyone did, he was so handsome.' She looks at the gun in her hand. 'Josie, my housemate, the stunt double.' I nod. 'She had a thing for him too.' She smiles at the memory as if it's benign. 'They'd met on the set of *The Man*; Josie was Flo's stunt.'

'Small world.'

'Oh, you have no idea, Marnie! Anyway, the party where I first met Dom – not counting the premiere – it was at a Hollywood producer's house.' Blythe leans forward. 'Are you listening?'

'Yes, Greg Chaplain's house, I assume?'

'Yes,' she replies, spinning away from me.

'Can you keep still or I'll definitely throw up.'

She spins back and plants her bare feet on the floor. They're muddy, like mine, but she's not bleeding, whilst a dark-red stain is spreading around me on the wooden floor.

'Greg's house was incredible, the party wild!'

'Sounds fun.'

'Dom was talking to Greg by the pool,' she says, scowling at the recollection. 'Word was Greg was onto an exciting new project after *The Man* had been snubbed for awards, and he wasn't one hundred per cent about his female lead.'

'Flo?'

Blythe glances down at me and nods. 'Flo was a brilliant young talent, but volatile, and as for her private life...' Blythe raises a brow. 'Anyway, I got talking to Dom and he introduced me to Greg as his "best friend and collaborator" and it felt like the start of something amazing. Do you know if there are cigarettes in here?'

She opens a desk drawer then closes it.

'No, I don't think so.'

'Anyway, Greg took my number, said we must chat, once he'd sorted out a few things with Flo. He was tied to a contract with her, but if he could see a way out, he'd love me to audition. I guess at that point, I should have seen the warning signs.'

'What warning signs?'

'Marnie, if I am to tell this story right, can you please allow me to do so? You sure you don't have cigarettes in here?'

'No, and you shouldn't be smoking either.'

She shrugs. 'I started to date Dom after the party and things got pretty serious between us, and fast. He'd virtually moved into my condo within a month. We couldn't get enough of each other.'

'What about your flatmate Josie?' I ask, the urge to tease out the story ingrained after all these years of ghosting. And I want to know every detail. If we have time.

'She moved out.'

'Poor Josie.'

'Anyway,' Blythe continues, frowning down at me. 'Dom called Wendy to say goodnight to the boys every night. He was a wonderful father. Then this one night about a month later he called as usual and she was hysterical. Said she knew he was with me, not working with Greg as he'd told her, Greg knew nothing about it. She said the boys were upset. Needed their father. The boys weren't even there, staying at a friend's for a sleepover. She planned the whole thing to emotionally blackmail him. I begged him not to go, but...'

Maybe it's the rain, or the cool air, but my brain clears a space, just enough for me to realise where this may be going.

'I got a call from Dom in the early hours,' she tells me. 'Marnie, are you still with me?'

'Yes, sorry.' I snap my eyes open. 'What happened?'

'I drove straight to the beach house,' she says. 'He was back in the water, holding on to her.'

'My God, what had happened?'

'An argument that got out of hand, that's all. Anyone, given that level of provocation— He only held her under a matter of seconds.'

'Oh my God!' I sit up, or try to. 'Dom killed her!'

'An accident.'

'But you married him, a matter of months later, even after that?'

'I was in love, Marnie. Desperately. And we were so happy.'

'Happy? How?'

'We partied a lot and we buried what happened to Wendy – well, as much as we could. Until...' Blythe stands and paces, in danger of tripping over my feet in the confined annexe.

'Until what?'

'Greg Chaplain had got in touch. After we'd met at the party. Said he wanted to speak with me to discuss Flo's "imminent departure" from *Affairs of the Heart*.'

Blythe's cobbled together script pages are on the desk, tucked beneath my laptop, The Audition Scene highlighted on page twenty. And here we are, back at that moment.

'We met at The Hollywood Roosevelt. May 9th, 1993. Greg was sitting by the pool,' she says. 'Shorts and shades, grubby little man.' She shivers dramatically. 'I talked to him about the part, he seemed keen for me to have it. Said he'd been concerned about Flo's state of mind on *The Man*. She wasn't reliable, and her sexuality was a concern, publicity-wise.'

'*Seriously?*'

'Marnie, please, I cannot be responsible for nineties homophobia right now. Can I?' She draws breath. 'Greg suggested we went up to his suite and run a few lines of dialogue.'

Oh God.

'I was worried, of course,' she says, picking up on my reaction. 'I'd heard the stories, it wasn't *that* unusual, sadly, but nothing specific about Greg had reached me. We'd only met once before, at Greg's party, but Dom still liked him. Spoke highly of him, in fact. Dom urged me to go there. I think he felt it might help his career too. I was nervous, but it was the biggest audition of my life. I didn't want to mess things up like Flo clearly had. The fact I was there suggested to me she was out the picture, which wasn't actually the case, not yet.' Blythe catches my eye. 'Anyway, Dom trusted him, so I did too.'

I don't like where the story is going, not at all. But I'm jumping ahead. I lean into the breeze coming in off the rain, breathe it in as waves of nausea consume me. I retch onto the dusty floor then sit back against the wall again, but Blythe, still pacing, remains oblivious.

'Do you know The Hollywood Roosevelt, Marnie?' Blythe asks, startling me. 'It's right opposite the Dolby Theatre, heart of Hollywood.'

'Yeah, I saw it when I was there,' I say, recalling the neon sign as I gulp in rain-soaked air through the wedged door. 'It's beautiful.'

'Yes, I'd always thought so.' She inhales, then sighs. 'After I left Greg's suite, I couldn't go home to Dom. I knew it would taint everything, bleed into our innocence.'

Innocence? He'd recently killed his wife. But there's a realisation dawning now, of what went on in that suite. Possibly equally as horrific. I try to push the thought down, not wholly successful as I prop myself against the door, my throat filling with bile.

'I didn't know what I'd say to Dom, you see, how I'd be, after what had been done to me... so I walked, the full-length of Hollywood Boulevard, or it felt like it. Up and down, every bloody star's name under my feet. Don't know how many. Then I called Josie and she arrived in a cab, took me to her crappy little condo, got me into a bath and poured a very large drink. Listened to me cry. Held me.'

'That was kind.'

Blythe shrugs. 'Josie had her moments.'

'So he... Greg Chaplain, he—?'

She nods. 'He raped me. Twice, in fact.'

'Oh my God, that's awful. Did you report him?'

She shakes her head. 'Not to this day, and I never will.'

'But you have to, don't you?'

'No, I don't!' Her eyes flash with anger.

'Sorry, I don't mean to victim-blame.'

She nods. 'Everyone knew stuff like that happened, of course, but no one said anything. And the chance of me making a charge against a man like that stick... You must know the odds, Marnie, they're totally stacked against us women. Besides, I'd washed away all the evidence. It would be my word against his. He's a powerful man. To this day.'

'Of course, but how could you still take the role in his film, after he—'

'Because I'd bloody earned it!' she tells me, eyes wild. 'Of course I fucking took it. You've no idea the lengths I'd gone to!'

I push myself closer to the door, thinking of Flo and what Blythe may have inadvertently just admitted to. Was she instrumental in Flo's dismissal, maybe even her demise? 'I don't think I could have worked with him. That's all I'm saying.'

'*Judging me*, more like,' Blythe tells me, voice raised. 'But you weren't there, Marnie. You don't know what you'd have done. And then of course I found out I was pregnant with you. Just before I married Dom and just as filming was due to start.'

So there it is. *Boom*. A sucker punch in the gut. I'm a child of rape. But I can't accept that, not yet.

'But why would you assume the one time you... I mean, Greg—'

'Dom had a vasectomy; he didn't want any more kids. He never even knew you existed! I don't think he'd have married me if he did.'

I am still processing that when another, awful, nauseating truth hits me. The photo, in the garage. It was *me* that Greg's stupid fat face reminded me of.

'So that's why you rejected me. I'm a constant reminder of the man who raped you.'

'No!' She sits beside me, our backs to the wall, me nearest the door, her arm around my shoulders. 'I never blamed you for who your father was. Please don't think that, Marnie.'

'But it's true, isn't it?' I shrug her off; everything about her repugnant. 'Abandoning an innocent child!' I pull myself to my feet and hobble to the door, looking out at the driving rain. 'But working with your rapist every day, that was just fine, apparently?'

'No! I kept away from Greg, made sure I was never in a room with him on my own.'

'And Flo?'

'Flo was a disaster waiting to happen, and after what I'd been through to get that part, I couldn't take any chances. Marnie, wait!'

I've staggered two paces, the rain soaking my back as I turn to face Blythe, now framed in the door.

'If you were pregnant, you'd have shown. You acted scenes in your undies, nude in fact! You're lying, Blythe. This is all lies!'

'I was so skinny, I didn't show at first, but I knew it was untenable. Although I never considered aborting you, you must know that. Then Greg had a heart attack two weeks after we started filming. He needed surgery. Production was put on hold, they kept it quiet, so easy to get cancelled last minute, you know that. Anyway, I told Dom I'd use the break in filming to go home, visit Dad for a few weeks, hopefully stretch it to a few months. I didn't really have a plan. You were due in February but arrived three weeks early, helpfully. So I was back home ready to resume filming just in time for Greg's new start date, but I'd been away from my new husband for too long.'

'Dom suspected something?'

'No, he was dealing with his own shit. The Wendy stuff... Dom was... struggling, so he distracted himself.'

'And he never noticed a baby bump, before you left?'

'We weren't particularly intimate, shall we say? I couldn't...Not after. Not for a long time. Can we go back inside, please, Marnie? This rain.'

'So you gave birth and then went straight back to filming with your attacker as if nothing happened? My God, you even thanked Greg in your speech. He was there, at the Oscars with Dom, giving you a standing ovation!'

'Oh yes, I did that, because I was fucking traumatised! Oh and did I mention when I came home from having you, I found Dom fucking my best friend in our pool?!'

'Josie?' I ask, swallowing.

'The same. That was a fantastic homecoming! I was postnatal, still bleeding and swollen, bandaged up and trying to hide it. Only to find him with my best friend! Ironic, eh? Especially as I'd got Josie the work as my stunt double because I felt guilty about me and Dom taking over the condo. I hated that publicity photo after that. The one of us on her motorbike; Ludo said you'd seem overly interested in it so he took it down.'

'I sensed something was off between the two of you.'

'I should have taken it down years ago,' she says, nodding, 'but I wouldn't give Dom the satisfaction of knowing it rattled me. It's a bloody miracle my car didn't go into the canyon as well!'

'You deliberately ran her off the road!'

'Did you not hear what she'd done?'

'And Flo, what did you do to her?'

'Flo only needed the means, Marnie. The rest was down to her.'

I lock eyes with Blythe, the rain a curtain between us, the falling darkness too, my head floating away from my body as I comprehend that my worst fears are true. I close my eyes tight, willing myself to stay in the moment, and that's when we both hear the unmistakable sound of the buzzer at the gates being repeatedly pressed.

'Move!' she says, gesturing with the gun. '*Now!*'

29

The staircase up to the tower room is hidden behind a secret panel on the landing, next to the linen cupboard. You'd literally never know it was there unless you saw the narrow door springing open at Blythe's deft touch.

I go up first, the open treads in the tightly wound spiral staircase inducing the worst vertigo ever. Well, almost. That moment on the ledge aged four just about tops it, but if it weren't for Blythe behind me, gun pressed into my waist, I'd never make the climb. I even forget my wounded foot until we reach the top.

The circular room is bigger than I'd imagined – rugs and a yoga mat on the floor – my relief at being on solid ground tempered by the realisation of quite how high up we are, the view stretching for miles and miles, London lights twinkling. It's like being in a luxurious cable car, and I swear it's swaying in the storm, or maybe that's just me. If it weren't dark, which helps a little, I'd surely pass out. I force myself to search the view for signs of help arriving, and thank God, it looks like it has.

There are two cars parked outside. The headlamps of one

pointed directly at the unanswered gates. A second vehicle behind. Blythe must see them too.

'Sit down, Marnie; you're bleeding on the Persian rug!'

There's a curved window seat. Upholstered in red satin and strewn with jewel-coloured silk cushions, the ceiling draped in similar tones. It's like a Sultan's tent. And a bookshelf built into the wall below the windows facing me as I sit. It's mainly lined with yoga manuals and self-help books. Guided meditation and CBT for Dummies. But one shelf is taken up with journals, the years written on each spine, and the covers beautiful prints of palms and waves and wildlife, including the exotic birds' notebook she was scribbling in earlier.

'So where had we got to in my story?' Blythe asks, as if we are still working on the memoir that I'm certain I will now never write. Because this is it for me, I'm sure of it. The end. Unless help arrives soon.

'Josie's and Flo's deaths?' I suggest, although that's not a good idea. I need to tread safer ground.

'Oh, yes,' she says, pulling out the journal marked 93/94. 'Let me find the page...'

The entry she's handed me is written in the same spidery hand I saw earlier as Blythe scribbled away at the kitchen table and in the sitting room. No wonder she was protective of the tower room. Her whole life is stored up here. Crimes journaled for posterity, which I'm imagining is where we're both headed. She points me to a line, about halfway down the open page, headed, February 5th 1994. 'Read!'

I was red-eyed and jet-lagged, bleeding and sore, breasts leaking milk. They were in the pool, doing it. My husband and my supposed best friend, Josie.

The prose is bad, but the quality of the writing is not my major concern. I skip ahead, the intimate details of that encounter explicit and excruciating, it's clear Blythe was furious.

Then Josie left. And I went after her. Dom had pleaded with me not to, but I had the car I'd hired at the airport. A lovely little red Camaro. It was nippy. Soon caught up with her motorcycle even though she was crazy fast. It was late, no one else about. We were going around this corner and—

'Did you even try to get help?' I ask, looking up. 'They might have been able to save her if she'd been found sooner.'

'No way I could get involved!' she replies, as if it's obvious. 'They'd have known I was there.'

'Did Dom suspect what had happened?'

'Maybe, but like I said, he'd perfected the art of sticking his head in the sand and I knew what he'd done to Wendy so—'

'You blackmailed him into silence?'

'Of course not! That was his choice. The man was always a coward. And if you're crossing names off your list, Flo was very much a joint effort and mainly his idea, well, mine too, but we did what was needed, together.'

'Oh my God,' I push the journal away. Ludo must have seen my notebook and the list of potential kills and reported back. 'You're both monsters!'

'I thought you'd be more grateful for me sharing my story! Isn't this exactly what you need for a bestseller?'

'I don't want any part of this,' I tell her, even as I ask, 'So what exactly happened to Flo?'

'We both agreed she had it coming. She'd been a nightmare for Dom on *The Man*, he blamed *her* for the nomination snub, her behaviour and her dubious personal choices.'

'So you disposed of her by spiking her drinks or something?'

Blythe sighs. 'It's easy to judge, Marnie, but consider what it was like for us. Trying and failing to catch a break. Flo was on a self-destruct trajectory anyway, we just helped her get there a little sooner. I needed that part, Marnie. It was mine once she was out the way, and we hoped it would help Dom too, with Greg.'

'Must have smarted, to never work again in Hollywood after all that effort,' I say, forcing the words out. 'Why was that?'

'Because I tried to warn others, about Greg. I thought I was doing the right thing for once, but it cost me everything. The phone literally stopped ringing. Dom was broken by it, couldn't understand why his former friend still wouldn't return his calls, despite that glorious night at the Oscars. Dom blamed me entirely. Said I must have upset Greg. He couldn't write a word, not for years, but eventually, he began those scripts.'

'But then he got scared of the truth coming out, that's why he burned them?'

'No! He wanted a comeback as much as I did. That's why he shared them with our agent. He was more keen than I was at the start.'

'So it was the rejection that caused the argument?'

Blythe nods. 'In part, but yes, Dom was keen to bury the past. He always was a coward, like I said. And nasty. And wrong.'

'So what exactly did Dom accuse you of that you still won't share with Roland. Being a serial killer?'

Blythe shakes her head. 'For goodness' sake, Marnie. I'm hardly that!'

'It can't be anything worse, surely?'

'Well, it is! Much worse! That my own husband would think I'd —' She stops, shakes her head.

Blythe's hate is fathoms deep, reflected in the deep pools of her dark grey eyes as she casts them down to her shaking hands, then up to meet mine. The silence hangs heavy, yet below us, there are loud sounds, crashing in. I chance a glance. A car is revving its engine, lights bright and a thud at it hurtles forwards, and breaks through the gates.

'I couldn't deal with the betrayal of trust,' Blythe tells me, ignoring the commotion outside. 'To think my own husband could believe me capable of... Not after all his betrayals that I forgave. Josie, and then that episode with Caroline.'

I want to ask about Caroline's death, of course, but it's pretty obvious it was down to Blythe and anyway, there's no time. Two cars are in the courtyard now, flooding the small space with their full beams, splintered wood crunching beneath tyres, gates hanging, car doors opening, people spilling out, then boots running up the drive.

Blythe looks at me, fear flashing across her features as a siren starts up. A marked car is speeding along the road towards the house, another behind it. They park behind the smashed gates.

'You're right Blythe, we don't have much time. What did Dom say before you shot him?'

'I... I can't say what he accused me of, Marnie. Not even now. But I wrote it down. Made myself do it, in case.' She hands me the 2023 journal. 'It's the last entry. Read it!'

I place the journal in my lap and turn the exotic birds' cover. Then I turn the pages until I reach the last one with that spidery writing and I read, incredulous.

'What?' I look up at and she nods, then covers her face, the gun pressing into her cheek. 'Why would Dom think that of you... *Why*?'

She sobs. No performance this time, she's bereft. Her voice cracking when she replies, 'Because Josie told him that it was true!' she says, wiping her face with her free hand, make-up smudged, eyes red. 'Pillow talk. All those years ago. When I'd confided in her and I'd thought she was kind, as you did. Then the second I was out the picture she slept with my husband and even worse, told Dom I'd willingly had sex with Greg to get the part. *Bitch!*'

'And Dom believed her? Oh my God. That's awful.'

I read the last line again, still disbelieving of Dom's awful words the night he died, written in Blythe's shaky hand.

You're a second rate actress who spread her legs for a role and then won a fucking Oscar for it.

'I knew it was over between us then,' Blythe tells me, sniffing. 'Whatever had happened in that Hollywood hotel room thirty years before, was back by the bonfire and it would always define us. I couldn't see any other way to end it.' She looks at the gun. 'But I also knew I had to find you and somehow atone for not being in your life. A chance to say how much I love you and tell you my story before it's too late. To try, if I can, to make it up to you with this gift of my truth.'

'Gift? This isn't anything I want! This is nothing to do with me!'

I throw the journal at her and it lands on the floor.

'My name still carries weight, Marnie. You said so yourself. You should be grateful!'

'No, I really shouldn't! And this memoir is never happening!'

The sound of heavy footfall running up the stairs distracts us.

'They're here,' she says, picking up the '93 to '94 journal and tossing it to me.

I don't want it, but Blythe is waving the gun wildly and now there are shouts to stand clear.

Blythe raises the gun and I react, holding the journal to me as protection.

Then a shot is fired. Ringing out through the tower walls like a bell being struck.

Deafening. Final.

30

TWO DAYS LATER

My mother is dead. There's no doubt about it. Her brains and blood spattering the windows and cushions of the tower as she raised the gun to her head and pulled the trigger. And yet forty-eight hours on, I still can't believe she's gone. She was such a life-force. Such a presence. Her face staring back at me from the blackened window as I sit on the last train to Brighton.

Am I seeing the resemblance now because I'm resisting it at all costs, or is the sheer exhaustion of the last two days taking its toll? Those final moments will never leave me. The relief of seeing Roland running up the spiral steps behind the armed officers. Then abject horror as I opened my eyes and realised what Blythe had done.

'I couldn't have saved her,' I told them as I held on to her hand under the blanket. But I still don't know if that's true. I was a coward. I saved myself, and something else.

I turn from the train window, fiddling with my cuff. I miss having a phone, mine still drying out on my sunny desk by the balcony. It is ruined, of course, along with so much else. The train is quiet, just the drinkers on their way home from a night out. An empty cider can rolls down the aisle. I sip a G&T, my second can, and will away the journey whilst also wishing it could last forever. Rain tracks down the window. Another reminder of that awful night.

I should have told Dad I'm coming, but maybe it's better this way. I've ignored every message since I called him from the police station. I need to see his unfiltered reaction as I tell him the whole story. Because my only hope is it was just that: a story.

And every day there is more. The latest that Ludo has been arrested.

Roland has tried, in his patronising manner, to keep me informed. Thank goodness he took my email seriously and alerted the police. Shame he also told Blythe of my suspicions. All that guff about how she was about to be arrested: another lie. And another reason I continue to doubt much of what she told me. She was a pathological liar. Never letting the truth get in the way of a good story.

I open my bag, the exotic birds journal inside: 2023. Beside it another notebook, plain black: 93/94. No one missed them in the mayhem. The bookend journals stuffed beneath the blanket I was offered, then into my bag before I left the annexe. A victim, injured and traumatised.

The on-call doctor at the police station superglued my heel back together, but it's still painful to walk. I promised I'd get it checked out, but I haven't. I took an Uber from my apartment to the railway station. The riverside glass box is still mine for a few more days, maybe weeks, if I can spin out the inevitable. I have savoured the solitude. A locked door. A comfy bed. The rain shower rinsing off the smell of that cramped police interview room, but I knew I'd have to make this journey sooner than later.

* * *

Brighton's streets are stuffed with revellers, music drifting from a club and temporarily obliterating the roar of the sea. It's a song that Jake and I loved. Our song. Then further along the esplanade, as I limp heavily, a door opens to a trendy looking hotel. Fairy lights and velvet chairs, softer music in there. I could order a cocktail, rest up, get chatting to the bartender, but the door slams shut. Closing time.

I cross the road and make my way slowly up a side street, the incline slowing me down even more, as does my heavy overnight bag. I never travel light. A reminder of that steep climb up to The Towers the first day, those moments of indecision when I might not have gone there at all. But I had to have my answers, still do.

Dad's flat is there now, the sea behind me as I cross the road. I last visited at Christmas. The buzzer loud in the quiet street. It takes a while for him to answer, but that's not unusual and it is way past his bedtime. He sounds confused, but I imagine he's been expecting me.

The hallway is narrow and scruffy, a bike against the wall. Dad still rents his first floor flat, as if he can't quite commit to the permanence of the move, and he's careful with his savings. I guess it comes of being the only reliable one around.

I climb the flight of carpeted stairs. Dad is waiting at the top.

'You're limping?' He reaches out for my bag. He looks old. Saggy, like his pyjamas.

'It's nothing, and sorry I couldn't call; my phone is broken.'

'No worries,' he says, going inside. 'You're here now. Cup of tea?'

The flat looks exactly as it always does, the furnishings comfortable but old, the surfaces clean but not spotless. He does his best, but he's also looking older than I recall, the stoop more pronounced.

I fall into an armchair and ease off my trainers, then raise my left foot on the table, waiting for the lecture. This isn't the first time

I've turned up in the middle of the night with a tale to tell. But never quite such an extreme one.

When I see Dad's face properly as he carries in a tray, it's full of sadness not reproach. I'm not the fuck-up this time, my hands shaking with relief as he pours from the familiar teapot.

Tea, always his answer. To everything he's had to deal with in the absence of anyone else to alleviate the burden of caring for me. He hands me the same mug I've drunk from more times than I could count.

Yesterday's newspaper is on the coffee table. The headline is about Blythe's death. It's a big story. Not least because of the remains they've found under the writing annexe.

'How have you been, Marnie?'

'Why didn't you tell me, D-ad?' I stumble on the last word.

He sips his tea. 'Dad is still fine. Always will be.'

'So it's true?'

'I don't know what she told you.'

'That she was my mother. That you raised me, but you're my grandfather.'

He taps the newspaper, opens it up to the next page. Inside is a photo of Blythe, beside it a drone shot of the flattened annexe and a white tent over it. The police think the remains are my grandmother's body. Ruby.

'They say she might have gone there to ask Blythe for money,' I comment.

'Addiction does terrible things to people, Marnie.' I think he means my grandmother's alcoholism but perhaps he means Ruby's addiction to fame. Ruby was 'a failed actress', according to Blythe.

He taps the newspaper again; it's starting to annoy me. 'But she didn't deserve this, clearly.'

'No, of course not. Did you know she might have visited your daughter?' It still feels odd, an adjustment needed even as I say 'daughter'.

'No, I had no idea,' he says, his eyes wet as he looks up from the newspaper. 'I knew Hannah had her issues, God I knew, but I hadn't seen either of them in years.'

'Hannah?' I ask, then I nod, remembering that was Blythe's birth name. Hannah Smith.

'But to do that to her own mother,' he says, nodding too. 'Mind you, I was worried enough to keep her away from you.' He catches himself. 'Doesn't matter.'

'Blythe told me about the last time she visited. I don't think she would have wanted to hurt me. She just didn't think.'

Even as I say it, I wonder if it's true. The lurch I then experience, catching me out like a misstep in a dream. Blythe was selfish, careless, leaving in a limo when she should have been watching her child. Abandoning me like she did the scene of Josie's 'accident'. Flo, too, 'a joint effort' with pills and booze supplied by the Hoppers and the left rest to 'chance'. Then Caroline, her severe nut allergy used against her so wickedly, I'm certain of it. And my grandmother, Ruby. Who came looking for her daughter and some help. And Wendy, who loved and lost! Too many deaths to be computed, or coincidental. Whatever Blythe may have told herself and then written in her journals, she's a serial killer, and sadly, so is Dom, implicated in at least two of those deaths. Maybe more?

'Why would she do that to her own mother?' Dad asks, tears in his eyes as he picks up the newspaper and studies the grainy photos. 'It's her, isn't it? It's my Ruby. Under a bloody shed, when I've thought that maybe one day, she might find her way back to us.'

'I'm so sorry, Dad.' I shiver at the thought of those bones beneath where I'd slept. No wonder I had nightmares.

Dad's grief is acute. My throat fills too, stoppered with pain.

Fragments of clothing were found, very like the skirt I handed in. It's her. We both know it.

'I'm sorry I was such a pain in the arse,' I say, trying to lighten this horrendous moment.

'Your grandmother idolised you, always said you have a creative mind.'

'I remember her being kind to me,' I blurt out, thoughts becoming words. 'And she iced cakes and called me sweetie. I'm so sorry she died that way.' I look at the newspaper, wondering how she did die. What Blythe did to her. Or maybe Ludo took care of that one? He always resisted stepping inside the annexe. No wonder they couldn't sell The Towers.

'Ruby did her best to help raise you,' Dad says. 'Until a chance of a part came up, and she'd be gone. We didn't see her much after your third birthday. I'm surprised you remember her at all.'

'I recall fragments, but Blythe's final visit is clearest.'

'Yes, on her way back to Hollywood. I told her never to come near you again. I'm sorry if that was the wrong call, but you almost died.' He gets up and takes my mug. 'Do you want something to eat? Toast?'

I shake my head, filled up enough already – with questions and recriminations I can't share because of course it was the right call.

'You could have at least told me who she was,' I say, following his slippered shamble into the kitchen. A gull screeches outside. 'I searched for years. It was all-consuming. You could have saved me that, given me some answers.'

'And now you have them, and do you feel any better?' A challenge in his tone as he loads the mugs into the dishwasher.

'At least I know.'

'Look, I'm sorry. I admit I've made mistakes. But I honestly did my best.'

He sets the programme, wipes the counter. That will most likely be all I'll get. More than I expected.

He says goodnight and tells me my room is ready, has been for the last two days. I curl up on the sofa and sleep the sleep of the dead.

31

The journey into London the next morning is uncomfortable. The heat, the proximity of so many people, it makes me light-headed and panicky.

I want to shove everyone out the carriage when the doors open at each interminable station. I need space. I need solitude. I need to be able to breathe. I found and then lost my mother in a few short hours. My grandmother too. My biological father, Greg Chaplain, is a misogynist monster. A rapist. My mother, a serial killer. Dom, Ludo, all complicit, although to what extent I still don't know, not fully. I cannot process even a sliver of all that. So I push it down with anger I cannot allow to surface, because I am not her; I can't be. Not in any shape or form.

Fear turns into a small, hard ball that swells and blooms and threatens to explode until I open another can of G&T and drink it straight down. So what if it's too early? So fucking what fellow travellers who stare and judge? The phone Dad leant me, his ancient Nokia, rings loudly. They all hate me. I don't care.

'Is that Marnie Wilde?'

The detective I emailed my Dad's number to this morning

informs me the list I shared has now been processed, but as they are all historic cases, some going back at least three decades, I shouldn't expect to hear anytime soon.

'These things tend to take a long time, Marnie. But thank you for all your help. The journals in the tower and your research will also be taken into account. But a lot of it is circumstantial.'

I quip that I know how it works, I've seen the television shows. The detective sounds confused and ends the call. My humour clearly not to her taste, or to my audience on the train, the woman opposite scowling.

I unzip my bag and pull out the bloodstained journals.

I thought I'd surrender them, anonymously, once I was done reading them. But this is my life, my story. I'm not ready to share it.

* * *

My apartment is as I left it and it's very nice to be back home. At least, it's home for now. I can't think beyond the next hour, minute. Day. But I guess I'll have to. Soon.

I check my emails and amongst the spam and demands for rent, Priscilla and Harry have both sent their condolences. It would be unseemly to pry, Harry says, but he asks for my thoughts on a posthumous memoir, when I'm ready, and said how much they both loved the first chapter.

I shower and change, grab a cereal bar, down a glass of water and make the call I've been putting off.

'Are you OK?' Roland asks. His voice not so different to the one he'd deployed to try and coax Blythe out of her circumspection that day in the dining room. I bristle at the recollection of the danger he put me in, telling Blythe of my suspicions, but then I recall his hand guiding me down the spiral staircase after he'd prised me away from my mother's dead body. That was genuine, and helpful, and I am grateful for it.

'Yes, I'm fine, Roland. I just wanted to say a proper thanks for, you know, being there.'

'No need, but I'm glad you called, Marnie. I was about to be in touch. Might you come in, to my office in town, at your earliest convenience?'

32

A WEEK LATER

As the bus enters the prison on this hot August afternoon, I think of Lenny, the bank robber whose memoir I almost ghosted. He'd invited me to visit him in Wakefield, another high security unit. With Lenny, it was the jibes from my fellow ghosts on WhatsApp about my 'prison boyfriend' that settled me on a firm No, but this time, I accepted the invitation without question, although I'm wondering now if that was a mistake.

HMP Bronzefield is in Ashford, Middlesex, a journey of an hour by train from my London apartment. I can call it *my apartment* again now, which amongst a field covered in cow shite is the one ear of golden corn. I've earned it. That's what I tell myself, over and over. Until I hear Blythe's voice, saying much the same. I mostly shut out the intrusive thoughts of her. With wine. And cigarettes: a new and dirty habit.

I haven't told Dad about my recent inheritance, or the prison visit, or the smoking. Just that I'm fine and taking a few days off work to 'reassess my options'. I should also stop calling him Dad, but Grandad doesn't feels right so it ends up as a stumble between the two.

I've spent some of my recent windfall on a few bits for the apartment. A potted plant, a new sofa. It was shocking how little I had to show for a decade in London. Clothes, shoes, a lot of empty bottles.

An unwise air fryer purchase to my name now, and a SodaStream. I'm thinking about a sewing machine next. Even ran the idea past Dad, who laughed and said I'd never use it. We talk most nights, conversation not exactly free-flowing but he likes to know I'm OK and I guess I am, mostly.

One thing I *have* decided is I'm going to make a proper stab at the screenwriting. The trust fund which Roland described as a 'modest amount', will tide me over for a few months, maybe more, although I am burning through it fast. Blythe's debts will eat up any sale value when The Towers finally sells, which it will at the reduced price, but she had secretly deposited money into a trust fund for me every year since my birth. I guess I should be touched, or maybe have refused to take her blood money. But pride comes at a price, one I've witnessed and do not wish to pay. And when the inheritance runs out, ghosting is still good honest work. I'll keep Priscilla on-side, pay my dues, but I'm not writing Blythe's memoir. I've been clear about that. I just hope Harry has finally got the message.

He's asked to meet for lunch, trailing some 'exciting news', which is probably a pack of lies, the memoir the only reason for the 'slap-up meal', but I'm curious enough to be tempted by his invitation.

* * *

The bus doors open and we spill out: kids, mothers, lovers, friends. I open my handbag to the female guard, pleased I've followed the rules for once – coins for a hot drink, two forms of ID, one with a photo on it. Greg Chaplain's doughy face pops into my head, unbidden. My throat fills with saliva. I swallow and smile at the guard who waves me through.

There's a long list of prohibited items on the prison website, some of which make sense – explosives, metal nail file, tools – others which surprised me – chewing gum, wax, toys. It's sad to think of kids coming here, but maybe they don't mind. Children are resilient, remarkably so. There was an article on the BBC website the other day about children of rape. We are to be officially recognised as victims. With accordant rights. Access to counselling. I couldn't read it all. Denial is my friend. I'll unpack it one day.

The press have hounded me for a comment about my past, my name now forever linked to a suspected serial killer who was once a Hollywood star. I have my suspicions that Priscilla, maybe Harry too, deliberately leaked the information I'm Blythe's daughter to create buzz for a tell-all memoir they hope I'll still write. I crave obscurity, anonymity, distance. For a while at least. I've had enough of fame. It's toxic in my experience. Addictive too. Like love.

Jake messaged me yesterday. Two words. Let's talk.

Of course I said yes, I'd love to see him when he's back in the UK.

A pat-down comes after the airport-style scanner, hands in the air as I experience the closest physical contact I've had in months. Then I'm in a large visiting hall.

The smell is institutional, stale and unappealing, the furnishings functional. There's a tea bar at one end where volunteers take our coins in exchange for a milky brew I can't stomach. I've barely eaten since I saw Blythe's brains spattered on the tower room windows. Which means I've finally lost some weight.

The doctor told me I'll need to lose more to reach my target BMI. They're judgmental fuckers, aren't they? He's also prescribed some anti-seizure meds and told me to give up the booze. I've told him to fuck off, but not to his face. That would be rude.

Prisoners and guards start to arrive, pairing up visitors with their loved ones like a shit reality dating show. As always, I'm the last to get picked. Then I see him, accompanied by a guard. His funny walk instantly recognisable. But the expensive loafers are gone, a tracksuit and trainers replacing the designer gear, a grey parting spreading through the black hair. When they found him in his ex-council flat, he had seventy-six unboxed pairs of Gucci loafers in his front room. *Seventy-six!* I mean, if you're going to embezzle your client for almost two decades, do better than shoes! Oh, and he had a Lamborghini in a lock-up, never been driven.

Ludo's bank account was barely healthier than the Hoppers. Her ever-faithful business manager protecting not only his employer and unwitting benefactor, but also, I suspect, his grubby involvement in the concealment of my grandmother's body. Oh, and a much younger boyfriend he'd been wining and dining of late who had a nasty gambling habit and expensive taste in hotels. I can't shake it all down in my head. It won't fit. Too many jagged edges. Maybe that's why I'm here, but I don't want to hear Ludo's excuses. They won't wash with me. In fact, I don't even know *why* I'm here.

'Thinking of going somewhere, Marnie?' Ludo says as I turn on my sore heel.

'No,' I reply, the terrible tea catching in my throat.

'Then shall we do this?' he suggests, sitting down.

I take a seat the other side of the table and drop my gaze to my hands, nails inspected one by one. I've booked a mani, and pedi. And a massage. A whole spa day, in fact. I deserve it.

'How are you, Ludo?'

'Oh, you know,' he says. 'Not great.'

There's a commotion near us. A guard intervening in a domestic. The table is turned over, the prisoner removed.

'Always drama everywhere you go, Ms Wilde,' Ludo observes as the wife/girlfriend who just gave her husband/boyfriend a slap is dragged out.

'And what about your decision to put me out in the writing annexe! How sick is that?' I blurt out, before I forget to ask. 'No wonder you wouldn't come in!'

'I'm sorry about that, Ms Wilde. I was... unsure. But I thought by keeping you slightly separate, I was protecting you.'

'Bullshit! Protecting yourself more like. Why am I here? What do you want?'

'To assure you face to face,' he glances round. 'That your secret is safe with me.'

'What does that mean?' I ask. 'I've nothing to hide.'

'I understand from the police they have Blythe's journals from late 1994 to 2022. They are keen to read 2023. But the first half of 1993, and specifically the time of your rather unfortunate conception, is so far not troubling them, especially as I told them Blythe most likely found it far too painful to write about her annus horribilis. In other words, I know you have them and why.'

'You knew about me? You knew everything, in fact?'

'Let's just say I made it my business to keep abreast of things. So you have those two missing journals, I assume?'

Fuck! I really should learn that I never get invited anywhere without an agenda. 'What do you want, Ludo, in exchange for "my secret" as you put it?'

'My understanding is...' He looks heavenwards for inspiration. 'One additional task is still to be taken care of.'

'I've got literally no idea what you're talking about.'

He leans in. 'Your list, Ms Wilde. Six kills. One of which...' He glances around. 'Remains outstanding.'

'Oh no, no, no, no... NO!'

The guard's attention falls on us as I get up too fast and my chair crashes over.

'You owe it to your mother, Marnie. It's what she would have wanted.'

'I am not my mother's daughter!'

'No?' Ludo smiles.

I'd tell him to fuck right off, but I'm already out of there.

33

ANOTHER WEEK LATER

Harry is at the same table as last time we lunched together. The day we discussed the possibility of me writing Blythe's memoir and I was convinced I had received an email from a dead man. Back when I half wondered if Dom was my father, searching for my long-lost mother so we could have a tearful family reunion. The magnitude of the truth overshadows all my wild imaginings and stamps on them. Being back here, white table cloths and chandeliers, feels wrong. It's too bright, too intrusive, recognition in every stare as I cross the crowded dining room, whispers behind every glass. I turn to leave but Harry spots me and beckons me over.

Head down, I walk fast. The headlines are just as salacious as they were two weeks ago, but at least they are getting farther apart, and Blythe's no longer on the front page. But they don't know the half of it, not yet. And the one thing they will never know, if I can help it, is that Greg Chaplain is my father. Even Dad doesn't know that. It's my secret, and unfortunately Ludo's too, his discretion bartered for a promise. One I have no intention of keeping. I mean, what can he do from inside? Nothing! I *hope*.

Although aren't there ways of getting a message out of prison?

Ex-cons paid to kill to order? These are the kind of thoughts that keep me awake at night. Or maybe that's just the copious levels of serotonin, post-sex, as I stare at Jake sleeping beside me. His face is so beautiful I want to cry. Sometimes I do, although he woke up the other night and told me to stop being weird.

The actress-slash-model was a psycho, apparently. I've told Jake that's doubtful, and having met a real one, I should know. He's only over for a few days. LA is chewing him up and about to spit him out. He needed to see me. Needed a break. I've explained it does that to people, because, yes, I'm the fucking expert. But of course he has no intention of giving up his dream, or heeding my warnings.

I arrive at Harry's table and we air kiss.

'My darling, you look like you've been run over by a truck,' Harry says, holding me at arm's length then releasing me. 'Did it also reverse back over you?'

'Thanks! I'm just tired.'

'Yes, "tired"!' he says, air-quoting. 'How's the beautiful disaster doing?'

'Jake's good, thank you; it's just casual, as I told you on the phone.'

Harry's blunt good humour is just what I need. I even manage to laugh, coaxed into it by his upbeat prattle about how too much sex suits my figure whilst he pours me a glass of the chilled champagne he's already ordered. The most expensive on the wine list.

'What are we celebrating?' I ask through a reviving glug.

'How about a complete reboot of the memoir?'

'Oh, for fuck's sake, Harry!' I bang down my glass. 'I've been very clear, so if that's all—'

I'm on my feet as Harry reaches out and grabs my wrist. I startle and pull away.

'Marnie, please,' Harry says, looking uncomfortable. 'It's me; I mean no harm.'

'Sorry, still a bit jumpy.'

'Of course, of course, please sit.'

I ease back into the chair and drink my champagne.

'Good, and maybe the revised figure I have from Priscilla will also help, it's seven-fucking-figures, darling!' He raises his glass to mine.

I suppose I should be annoyed that Harry isn't taking my hard No for an answer, or respecting the trauma I've been through, but seven figures. That is exciting news.

'How come the sudden hike in advance?' I ask.

Harry smiles. 'With you writing this memoir, it has *huge* potential. I mean, how many more skeletons do you think are in the proverbial family cupboard?'

I try, and probably fail, to conceal my annoyance as Harry references my grandmother's death and makes fun of it. But I know he means no harm. 'The answer is still no; it's too close to home. I'm her daughter, she killed lots of people. Including my grandmother.'

'I totally respect that. But I would not be doing my job if I didn't pass on the fact there's also oodles of interest in an option to develop the book for screen.'

I make a show of indifference, but it's bravado. 'From whom?'

'You name it, darling: Netflix, Disney, Paramount, Apple, Sony.'

'Wow!'

'Indeed, double wow. You'll retain full creative control, of course.'

'Right, and if I did say yes…' Harry grins. 'A big if! But if I did, I would prefer a novelisation. With names changed and scenes, you know, reinvented? With the same fat fee attached of course, you said seven figures?'

Harry smiles and raises his glass. 'That's my girl! Welcome back, Marnie. It's going to be a wild ride.'

34

TWO YEARS LATER – HOLLYWOOD ROOSEVELT HOTEL, LA

The pool I lie beside is quintessential Hollywood glamour. Fringed parasols over candy-striped loungers, loud music pumping out, palm trees beneath a cloudless blue sky. Sun so bright, I can barely see without my new designer shades in place – rose-tinted, naturally. It's the pool Marilyn Monroe famously posed above, looking cute and sexy on the diving board. The Hollywood story is rarely less than poetic. Funny how it retains its hypnotic allure when we all know it's a pile of crap.

'Can I get you something from the bar?'

I look up to a server who is impossibly beautiful. White blazer, long, dark legs, white trainers, shorts. She could be an actress, and probably is.

'A mojito, virgin please. Oh and I'm meeting someone soon.' I point to the shaded tables beyond the pool. 'Can I get it over there, somewhere private?'

'Of course, coming right up.'

When it was suggested I fly out for a crammed week of meetings, I insisted I stay in this hotel. Much to the disgust of my US screen agent, Riley.

'You wanna stay near the studios, honey, not on the Boulevard – that's for the tourists.'

I have my reasons, but I'm glad I've spent the week here. It's lovely. Black and white framed portraits of movie stars outside the elevator doors. The Hollywood sign on the hill as I look out my tenth-floor window, the Dolby theatre way below, where the Oscars are presented, although they started out here, in this hotel, in 1929. And the year of Blythe's win, 1995, they were held at the Shrine Auditorium. I'd thought to take a walk out there, snap a selfie for posterity, but when I checked on Google it was a cab ride... So I followed all those stars under my feet instead. Walking up and down Hollywood Boulevard, in my mother's footsteps.

The back-to-back meetings have been full on. Brunches, coffees, cocktails – virgin for me, though definitely not for Riley. She could have drunk me under the table, even back in my drinking days, yet she still rises at dawn to go over options and clauses on her treadmill in her glass office. She knows my priorities and she's with me all the way. It's a good feeling.

We've held out on early offers, despite Harry's qualms. A gamble, but Riley is right. By valuing ourselves highly, our currency has soared. Something Blythe touched on too.

I find myself coming back to my mother's words as much as Dad's these days. I've decided to embrace my legacy; it was part of the reason I wrote the book, or at least that's what I tell myself, and the crowds who gather at bookstores and literature festivals to meet the daughter of a serial killer seem to have no qualms about my material. It is my story to tell, no one else's. May as well own it.

Nice to be in demand for once too. A refreshing change from being oh-so bloody grateful, but that's what a number one *New York Times* and *Sunday Times* bestseller does for you. And there's no doubt that post *#MeToo* Hollywood has helped my generation, although I'm not pretending all is well in the land of dreams. Riley and I left a couple of meetings shaking our heads. But we've met enough good women, and men, to have a great choice of who we work with. A choice! Wow, how times change, all because of one book. Blythe was right; her story has been a gift.

My Mother The Serial Killer: The Six Kills of Blythe Hopper by Marnie Wilde has sold over a million copies, so far. A golden ticket which demands attention, but maybe my success is also to do with me carrying a different mindset now. Not just the confidence success brings – I ignore Jake's messages, mostly – but that I've finally 'got my shit together' in my thirties. At least, that's the vibe I promote, explaining on chat shows how I've found my peace through a search for the truth. The book's strapline offers an enticement in its disclaimer: *The truth? You decide!* I like to think of that as my Get Out Jail Free card. Dad and I always loved a game of Monopoly. But I often cheated.

There's been a lot of speculation about the parts of the novel that are real and the parts that are made-up, the gaps troublesome to some. Not least, the identity of the author's biological father. Most assume, without much thought, that it's Dom. I mean, we're both screenwriters and why would you think any different? But the *real* fans have written long posts about a shadowy figure in Blythe's past that I vaguely reference in the final chapters. A big Hollywood player. Who is he? Did Blythe have an affair with him? Is he... the sixth kill? Everyone loves to guess. But my publisher's legal team have crawled over every page, making sure I'm untouchable. Making sure *they* are untouchable. The disclaimer on the front is matched by a much longer one inside the cover that states most clearly this is a work of fiction. But we all know the very best stories are based in fact. I'm just amazed Greg's name has never come up. I guess people are still scared of naming and shaming such a powerful man.

Priscilla and I settled on *autofiction* in our developmental editorial meetings: a combination of autobiography and fiction. And it's written in third person, to distance myself with the pronoun *she* not *I*. Basically a cop-out, but I'm not sure I could have written those final scenes otherwise. It would have killed me.

My drink arrives. A very pretty, but alcohol free Mojito. Ah well.

I'm a Hollywood cliché, straight out of therapy and onto the plane, sipping my delicious virgin cocktails and making connections at the local AA meetings. It's amazing who you bump into as you say 'Hi, I'm Marnie, and I'm one year sober!' But I'm also a screenwriter. Who has just one book to her name, but a very successful one that everyone wants to adapt for screen.

There are *never* any guarantees in la-la land, of course, but Riley has built up a groundswell of support that I've consolidated during this week, turning on my British charm which they find 'super-cute'. I hope my mother is looking down on me with a smile. And I hope I'm about to make her very proud. It's an odd wish, given what she did, but doesn't every child dance to make their mother happy?

The detective still investigating Blythe's potential crimes is not a fan of my book. And sometimes, when there's space in our sporadic conversations, a figurative crackle on the line, I swear she knows something, maybe everything. Like the last time we talked, just a few days before I flew out here, when she told me to be careful. She said I owed no one anything, especially Blythe. She said I am not my mother's daughter, I am my own person. I make my own choices.

I knew I liked Detective Chowdery, right from the moment she offered me a cigarette in that interview room. I still smoke. But then, none of us is perfect.

Blythe would have loved the attention the book has had; it was what she'd hoped for. Her big comeback. She only gave up on that dream after Roland told her he'd been alerted to some serious concerns and the police were on their way. Blythe knew the moment she killed her beloved Dom that it was over, but dreams can be stubborn. They get inside you. She held on to hers until the last possible moment. I think she'd have hung on to it forever if she could. Dom wanted it too, not just as much. He burned everything. So I guess he was scared of the truth, which I totally get. But maybe he was finally facing up to the fact that his screenwriting career was over.

A short, balding man with a goatee and a paunch walks in and speaks to the beautiful server who then walks him to my table, tucked away from view in a shady corner. Every cell of my being crawls at the sight of Greg Chaplain, all three hundred pounds of him. My biological father. Except he's not my father. That's the man who stepped up and raised me, and who now lies in the graveyard beside his long-lost love, Ruby. If I do this for anyone, I do it for him. Not that Dad would have wanted me to. That's why I've waited until now. Two years since I sat across the table from Ludo in that noisy visiting room and he asked me to make good on the sixth kill. And Ludo hasn't let up since, with a monthly email, carefully but clearly worded.

> You have to visit the producer, Marnie – for your mother. It's down to you, or he gets away with it.

I've wondered a lot about that. The getting away with it part.

Did Blythe ever consider revenge, or Dom? Dom must have hated Greg. The man who'd fucked his wife, even though Dom believed Blythe had capitulated to get the role of a lifetime. Dom had a temper, but also a guilty conscience about Wendy, and maybe Flo too. But the man was a coward. So I guess that answers my question.

But what about Blythe herself? She had decades to call Greg

out. She tried to warn others, and that got her cancelled. But she couldn't face reporting the rape. Was that for my sake or hers? Or because she knew it was likely pointless, as she said.

Greg waddles towards me with a cigar in his flaccid lips. I feel sick, swallowing hard and opening my expensive designer bag to take out the gun and slip it into my lap under the table.

Sadly, I don't have the poetry of using Blythe's gun. That was whisked away from the crime scene in an evidence bag.

I purchased this one at a dodgy roadside armoury, the fake forms I'd downloaded laughably bad, but it's almost as easy to buy a gun out here as it is getting an underage tattoo back home. Not so easy to fire, but I've practised squeezing off a few rounds at a local range whilst Riley reviews the day's meetings. I'm not a crack shot like my mother, but good enough to press it into Greg Chaplain's fat gut and pull the trigger.

Maybe I should have chosen somewhere more remote, no witnesses. But I am wearing a *very* large sunhat, although I am signed in as a resident, and staying in the best suite on the tenth floor. God, I'd make a useless assassin.

I glance over at the recumbent, bikini-clad wannabes. They must have seen him make his entrance. An old man. But a powerful one. A man who can make or break careers. He's never apologised, or admitted to what he's done; in fact, he punished my mother for challenging him even in the smallest way when she'd tried to warn others. It makes my blood boil all over again as this monster nears my table.

My face is hot, hand slick as I hold it out to greet him, not a flicker of guilt or even recognition in his expression.

'Marnie Wilde, what a pleasure. No, don't get up!' Clammy skin presses to my cheek, low slung ponytail swinging round. 'Wow, you look like your mother!' he says, pumping my hand. 'Gorgeous, just like her.'

Aside from my now bleached hair, I really don't look like Blythe, but neither, thank God, do I look like him. I am young, powerful. I am *New Hollywood*. Quirky, individual. And I still have all my tattoos, including the initials on my ribs which I decided to keep. The full sleeve I planned is also almost done, with a ruby shining bright on my shoulder.

'You remember her as beautiful?' I ask, swallowing.

I have conversations in my head where I hate Blythe and then I watch her on screen and she is incandescent.

'She was a firecracker! And a fabulous actress.' He orders a whisky, straight up, from the server who has waited patiently for his acknowledgement of her presence.

'So you read my book?' I ask, as he sits down, thighs spread wide.

'Yeah – well, my assistant did. She loves it! Loves you!'

'Right, I see.' I feel in my lap and wrap my hand around the cool metal.

'Oh, honey, I know the hook and that's all I need to know!' Greg says, sweating. 'Six kills, one left to do. And about that... I don't think an ambiguous ending works for me; the punters need to get what they paid for.'

I squeeze the gun so hard, it hurts, my finger curling into the trigger. 'They do?'

'Yeah, we need closure,' he suggests. 'Justice seen to be done.'

'Yeah, yeah, totally agree,' I reply, the metal hilt reassuringly cold.

'One of those female, anti-revenge flicks that are so popular right now,' he says, not a word of thanks to the server when his drink arrives.

'Excuse me,' I call after the server.

She turns, smiles then scowls at him. Good for her!

'You want another?' she asks me.

'No, thank you. I wanted to ask, are you an actress?'

'Yes,' she says, laughing. 'How did you guess?'

'Well, this is Hollywood,' I say, ignoring Greg's drumming nails. 'I'm a screenwriter. Marnie Wilde.'

'Wow! Yes,' she says, grinning. 'I've read your book, it was great!'

'Thanks, let's talk, before I leave. I'm discussing an adaptation.'

'Sure, fantastic, thanks, Marnie!'

'So I take it from that, we have a deal?' Greg asks, watching the actress's arse as she walks away. 'We can discuss casting later.'

I adjust the gun in my lap, metal catching the sun and blinding me. 'Not so fast.'

This day of reckoning – as old as I am, maybe older – is for all the women who couldn't speak up. Who thanked Greg, and others like him, for awards they had won in spite of him, and for those who allowed a clasped thigh beneath a dining table without protesting, not out of cowardice but knowing the system was stacked against them if they made a 'fuss'. It's for women, and men, who stood frozen and scared and appalled in the face of abuse. Who said nothing because they had no way of knowing it would be heard, or believed.

But I have agency. Thanks to those before me. Women like my mother. Who tried their best to speak up, regardless of the personal cost. I don't for one second condone Blythe's terrible deeds, but for that much, I'm grateful to her.

'Do you see that room up there?' I ask, pointing to the tenth floor. 'I don't know if it's the same suite, of course, and I'd prefer it not to be in retrospect, but I thought by being here, with me, it might you know, prick your conscience a little, Greg?'

Greg pulls on a cigar, ignoring the no smoking signs, clouds of noxious smoke surrounding him. 'Sorry, honey, what's that?'

'You raped my mother in this hotel thirty-two years ago, give or take.'

He looks at me and I slide the gun into his eyeline.

'What the fuck is going on here?' He pushes his chair back and it falls over as he gets up.

'Sit down!' I tell him. 'Sit the fuck down and listen!'

'What do you want?' he asks, Adam's apple pulsing in time with the pumping music that covers our exchange. Fear is radiating off him, as well as the stink of smoke and sweat. He's seventy-six years old, only a few years younger than my dad was when he died last year. My *real* dad. This man is nothing to me. Certainly not worth years of my life behind bars. But I came here to finish a job and it's long overdue.

Greg rights his chair and sits down. 'I don't want any trouble, Marnie.'

'No, but I've a story to share, Greg. One I hoped you'd recall, or maybe have at least read, but you don't give a shit, do you?'

'Listen,' he says, leaning in.

'No, you listen, Greg! I've met with talented creatives this week, who love my work. Love me. The script I plan to write of the book you haven't even read will be a ballsy, no-holds barred exposé of nineties Hollywood and it has every chance of being made. It's still crazy odds to beat, I know that. Most projects never get off the ground, but yes, I have a good feeling. You, on the other hand, will not come out of this well.'

'So, what do you want?' he says, sneering and sweating. He knows what he's done, but still thinks he can buy his way out of his past. 'Name your price!'

'So you *do* remember?'

'I'll ask again, Marnie, what do you want?'

But the thing is, now he's asked, I don't know. I honestly don't have a clue. Him dead? That's what I'd thought, but maybe not. I certainly don't want to kill him myself. Then it comes to me. In the form of the beautiful server who is strolling past.

'Ready for more drinks?' she asks, catching my eye.

'Um, no thanks, but... Sorry, can you just come here a sec...?'

I turn to Greg, and despite the light-headiness that has descended, I manage say to him, 'I want you to thank her.'

'Who?' he asks. 'Your mother?'

'No,' I say, looking at the beautiful server. 'This young actress who has come to Hollywood with a dream and served you with grace despite your appalling lack of manners.'

I smile at her and she smiles her confusion back, Greg's sweating face sneering.

I press the gun into his thigh beneath the table and he mutters a thank you under his breath.

'Not good enough!' I tell him.

'Thank you very much,' he says, looking at her, then me.

'Better,' I tell him, opening my bag and sliding the gun inside. 'And now I want you to fuck off, Greg, so she can sit down.'

She looks at me with amused confusion, then smiles.

'Get up, Greg!' I tell him. 'I need to talk this stunningly beautiful and I don't doubt talented if overlooked young woman about a part in my screenplay. One I don't think you're going to enjoy that much when you finally get to see it. It's a kind of female revenge fantasy. With less of the fantasy. Because the truth is so often stranger than fiction, don't you think?'

ACKNOWLEDGMENTS

This is my fifth published book so I have thanked many people in the past and they deserve my thanks again, because being a writer may be a solitary occupation, but bringing a book to readers requires a team of creative passionate people to whom I am eternally grateful.

My editor, Emily Yau, for her encouragement not only for this book, but for my development as an author, and the whole team at Boldwood, including my copy and proofreader, cover design, publicity and marketing, audio, and the visionary Amanda Ridout who has created an egalitarian and award-winning publishing house I am proud to be a part of.

My agent, Hannah Todd, who always says, 'Shall we hop on a call?' whenever I need her. Her enthusiasm and advice hold me up and keep me grounded. Her patience and kindness are invaluable to me, always. And thanks to the whole team at Madeleine Milburn who are without exception, brilliant, including Maddy herself who I also owe a huge debt of thanks.

To my fellow authors and friends, Kate Riordan, Hayley Hoskins, the Ladykillers, Gloucestershire Writers, and all my colleagues and writers at The Novelry who are never more than a message away with support and understanding.

And the brilliant booksellers and festival organisers who support *The Assistant* and all my other books, so wonderfully. Also, my fellow crime writer, Jackie Kabler, my 'partner in crime' at many events, and Jane Bailey, friend and fellow author and fantastic events' chair.

Also, all the wonderful readers and reviewers who champion my books through social media and come to events and signings. It's so humbling to know you love reading my stories.

A special mention to those who have helped me research the rarefied world we enter in *The Screenwriter*. To Connie Nielsen, who starred in the television adaptation of my debut, *Close To Me*, for her insight into being a young actress in Hollywood, and to those I've met when writing for the screen myself, and those who helped me fill in the gaps, much gratitude for welcoming me and showing me the ropes. Particularly Alice Kuipers who answered all my questions about being a ghostwriter, totally fascinating! And to Nigel Hatton, who always keeps me on the straight and narrow in terms of police procedure. My main question always being, 'But is this possible, Nigel?'

And last but not least, my family. Especially Chris, Beth, Dan and George. Mum and Dad, Val, and special mention to my niece, Hannah Churchill, who narrated the audio book so brilliantly.

And last but not least, Scout, to whom *The Screenwriter* is dedicated. Because every writer needs a dog. Couldn't have done it without you, baby girl! X

ABOUT THE AUTHOR

Amanda Reynolds is the bestselling psychological suspense author whose debut novel, *Close To Me*, was adapted as a major six-part TV series for Channel 4 in 2021. Her books have been translated into multiple languages. Amanda lives near Cheltenham.

Sign up to Amanda Reynolds' mailing list here for news, competitions and updates on future books.

Visit Amanda's website: https://www.amandareynoldsauthor.com

Follow Amanda on social media

x.com/amandareynoldsj

instagram.com/ajreynolds2

facebook.com/amandareynoldsauthor

ALSO BY AMANDA REYNOLDS

The Assistant

The Screenwriter

Milton Keynes UK
Ingram Content Group UK Ltd.
UKHW041508070124
435562UK00004B/177

9 781837 513680